I0710255

List of Authors

Christy Aldridge
Simon Bleaken
Bridget D. Brave
Brooklyn Ann Butler
Lexx Christian
Rebecca Cuthbert
Blaine Daigle
Heather Daughrity
Jason Daughrity
Joe DeRouen
John Durgin
Stephanie Ellis
Joshua Loyd Fox
Jennifer Anne Gordon
Gage Greenwood
Caleb Jones
Marie Lanza
Stephen Mark Rainey
Jeani Rector
S.H. Roddey
Cat Scully
Westley Smith
Mer Whinery

HOSPITAL

OF

HAUNTS

EDITED BY
HEATHER DAUGHRITY

Parlor Ghost Press

Parlor Ghost Press

Published by Parlor Ghost Press, an imprint of
Watertower Hill Publishing, LLC
Copyright © 2023 by Parlor Ghost Press
www.watertowerhill.com
www.parlorghostpress.com

Cover design by Christy Aldridge at Grim Poppy Design
Cover creation by Susan Roddey
at The Snark Shop by Phoenix & Fae Creations
Cover copyright © 2024, Parlor Ghost Press
Interior format by Joshua Daughrity at Watertower Hill Publishing, LLC

Library of Congress Control Number: 2024945254
Hardback ISBN: 978-1-965546-03-1
Paperback ISBN: 978-1-965546-04-8
eBook ASIN: B0DF8H3RRH

Printed in the United States of America
First Edition
10 9 8 7 6 5 4 3 2 1

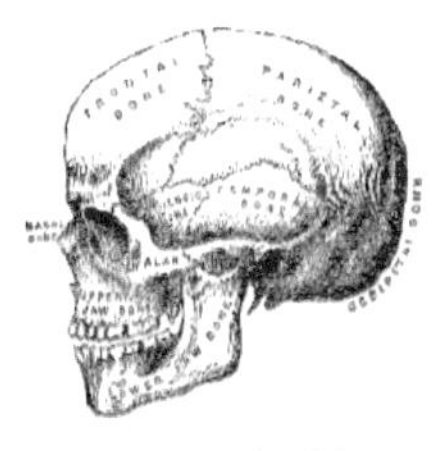

On Corpse Hill

Lychhurst stands, unloved, alone—
An edifice of hulking stone
Upon a hill of blood and bone.

Lychhurst crumbles 'neath the strain
Of years of grief and fear and pain;
Its purpose twisted, now its bane.

Lychhurst sighs and settles low,
Its dying breath labored and slow,
Yet in its windows pale lights glow...

Lychhurst thrums with restless dead;
Along its halls the sickness spreads—
A roiling fog of creeping dread.

Lychhurst beckons and assails you,
Makes your courage falter, pales you.
Your pounding heart flutters and fails you...

But never fear.
The doctor's in.
We'll cure what ails you.

{Heather Daughrity}

Table of Contents

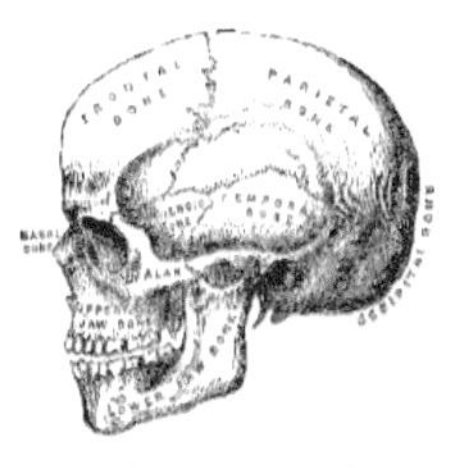

Foreword

Clay McLeod Chapman

I'm not insane.

I know how insane that sounds. I wouldn't believe it myself, but you need to believe me… Please. I'm not like the other stories in here. I'm not *crazy*.

I've been trying to tell everyone—someone, anyone—here, but nobody is willing to listen. They all nod and smile and pretend like they are, but they are not. Nobody will listen to me.

Why would I lie? Why would I make a story like this up? You—*you*, reader—need to believe me. Please, for the love of God, just get me out of this book. Get me out of Lychhurst.

I was asked to write a foreword for this anthology. Simple enough. I could read a few of the stories inhabiting the anthology you yourself hold in your hands at this very moment. Chalk it up to research. Get a vibe for this place. I could breeze in and breeze out in a matter of an afternoon. *Easy-peasy*.

So I dove in. I wandered the halls of this once hallowed institution. I drifted through its various rooms, tasting its legacy. Decades—over a century—worth of lost souls. Their stories.

The medical profession is an evolving entity, yes? It continues to grow. Procedures from years ago seem barbaric today—and yet, their aftereffects still linger within the halls of this hospital.

So I kept reading. Room after room. Patient after patient. I witnessed a bewildering myriad of mental health methodologies. Some cruel, some kind. Hydrotherapy. Lobotomies.

But I couldn't stop reading now. I'd come this far, yes? I had to keep going.

It reached a point where I felt as if I was dunked under dosage after dosage of medicated tales, until I could barely break through the surface of my own drowning mind.

The deeper I read, I don't know… Something odd started to happen. To me. Reality itself began to blur. I came to this hospital as a surveyor, someone to bear witness to the horrors of the Lychhurst Hospital.

Now I am one of its patients.

This is where I'm told that I am tired. That I need to rest. Perhaps there is a pill that will help calm my nerves. I could lie down, even for just a moment. A cot in one of the rooms here has been reserved just for me. All done with dulcet tones. With a gentle grip.

The editors lied to me. Heather Daughrity lied. She invited me to do this under false pretenses. My whole goal was to report back to you, dear reader, and preface the experience you yourself are about to undergo in some witty, pithy way… but that's a trap.

What the publishers don't want you to know is that this hospital is still in operation. Lychhurst continues to house those poor wretched souls that society has abandoned. Hysterical wives. Soldiers suffering from combat shock. Even a few physicians who have lost their way… It never stopped.

Every story contained within this collection is a padded cell. The writing itself, lavish as it is, achingly beautiful in its gasps, its lyrical screams, is nothing but a straight-jacket for the very author who penned their entry. They are cries for help… and nobody is listening.

Nobody… but you. You're listening, aren't you? You're here. That means you care. Or you're at least curious. You're willing to listen to us. All of us, yes? To the stories we have to share?

Just listen to me first, okay? I am the foreword. The introduction. Your first warning.

Please. Help me. Get me out of here.

You really don't believe me, do you? Fine. Suit yourself. I was just like you. Once. All the hubris. The confidence that I could read this collection and come out unscathed.

You'll see. You'll see for yourself soon enough. They all do.

There's a room waiting for you at the very end of this anthology, trust me.

Lychhurst still has so many more stories to tell…

Clay McLeod Chapman

New York

2024

LYCHHURST HOSPITAL

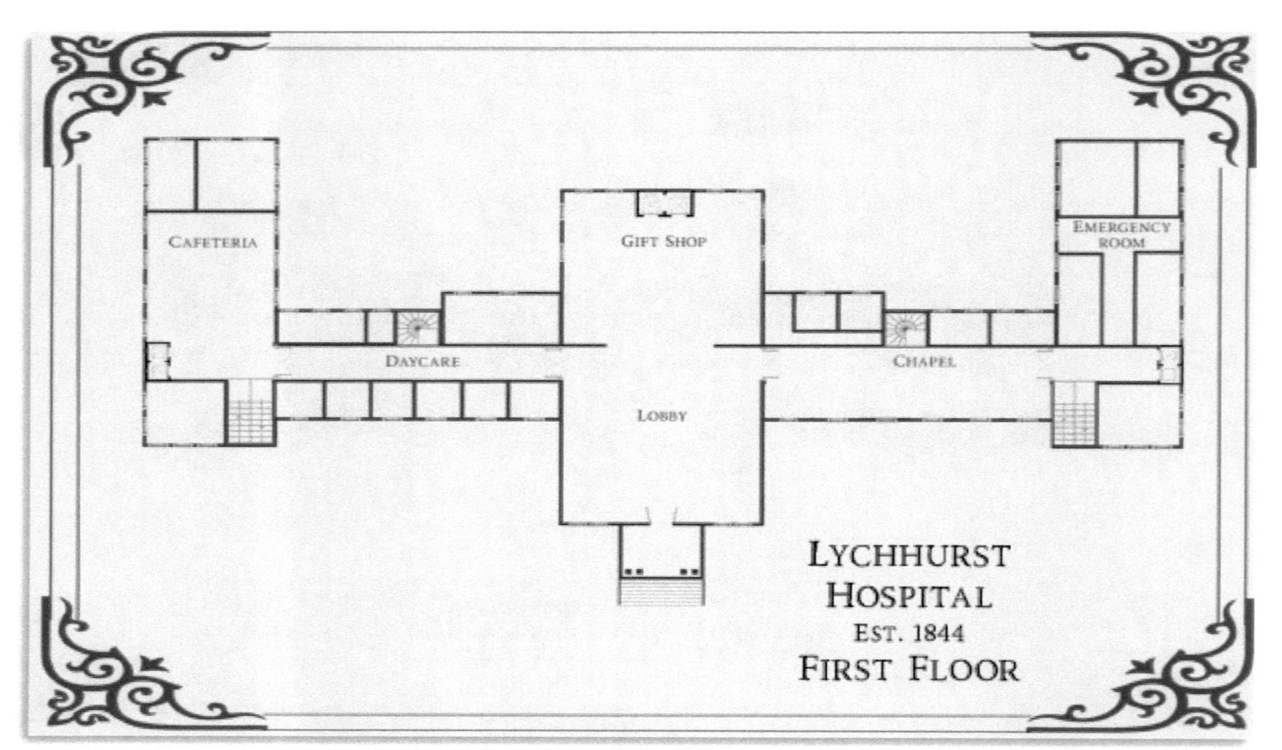

CAFETERIA
GIFT SHOP
EMERGENCY ROOM
DAYCARE
CHAPEL
LOBBY
LYCHHURST HOSPITAL
EST. 1844
FIRST FLOOR

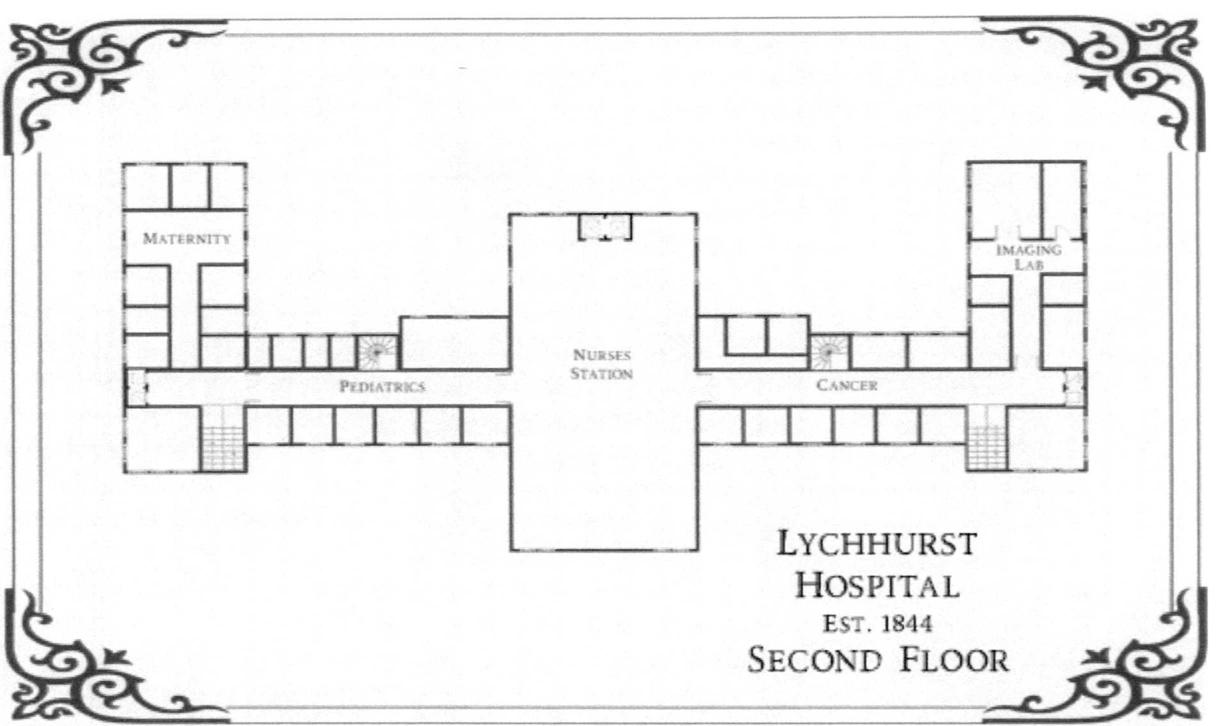

MATERNITY
IMAGING LAB
NURSES STATION
PEDIATRICS
CANCER
LYCHHURST HOSPITAL
EST. 1844
SECOND FLOOR

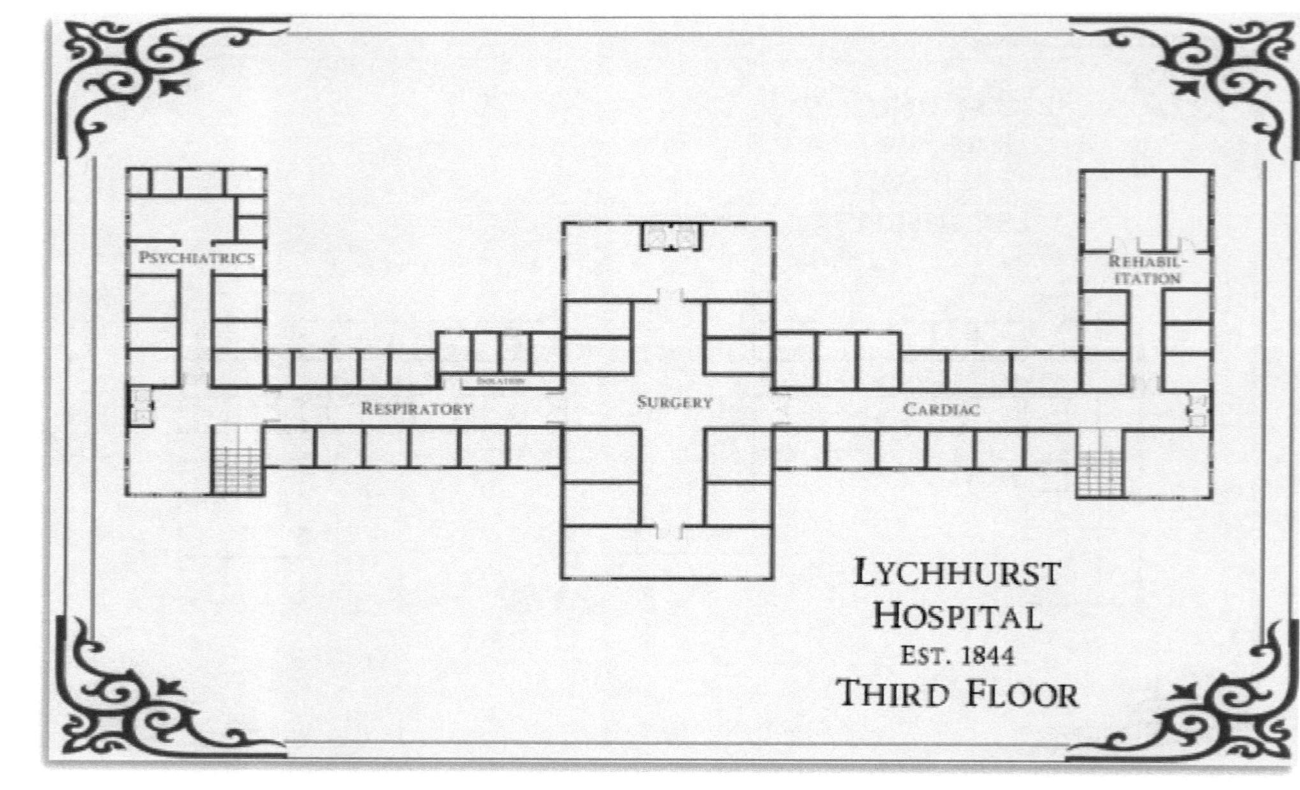

PSYCHIATRICS
REHABIL-
ITATION
SURGERY
ISOLATION
RESPIRATORY
CARDIAC
LYCHHURST
HOSPITAL
EST. 1844
THIRD FLOOR

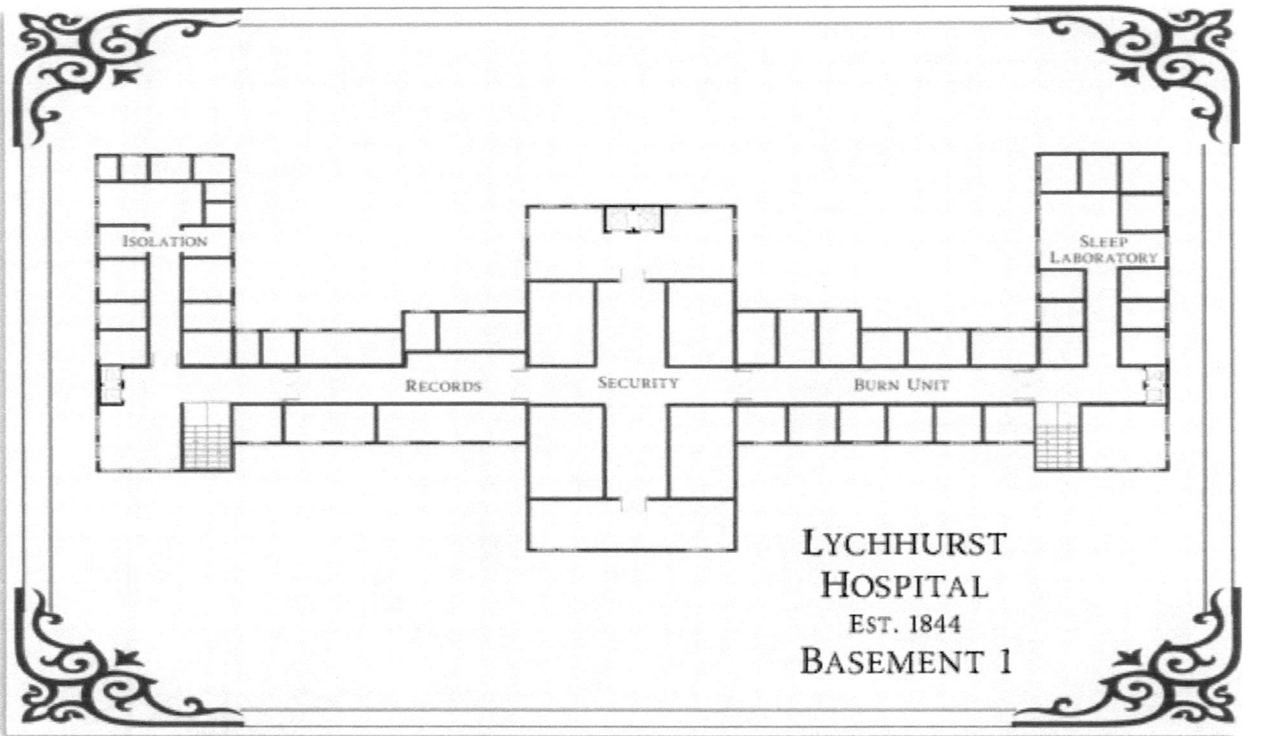

ISOLATION
SLEEP LABORATORY
RECORDS
SECURITY
BURN UNIT
LYCHHURST HOSPITAL
EST. 1844
BASEMENT 1

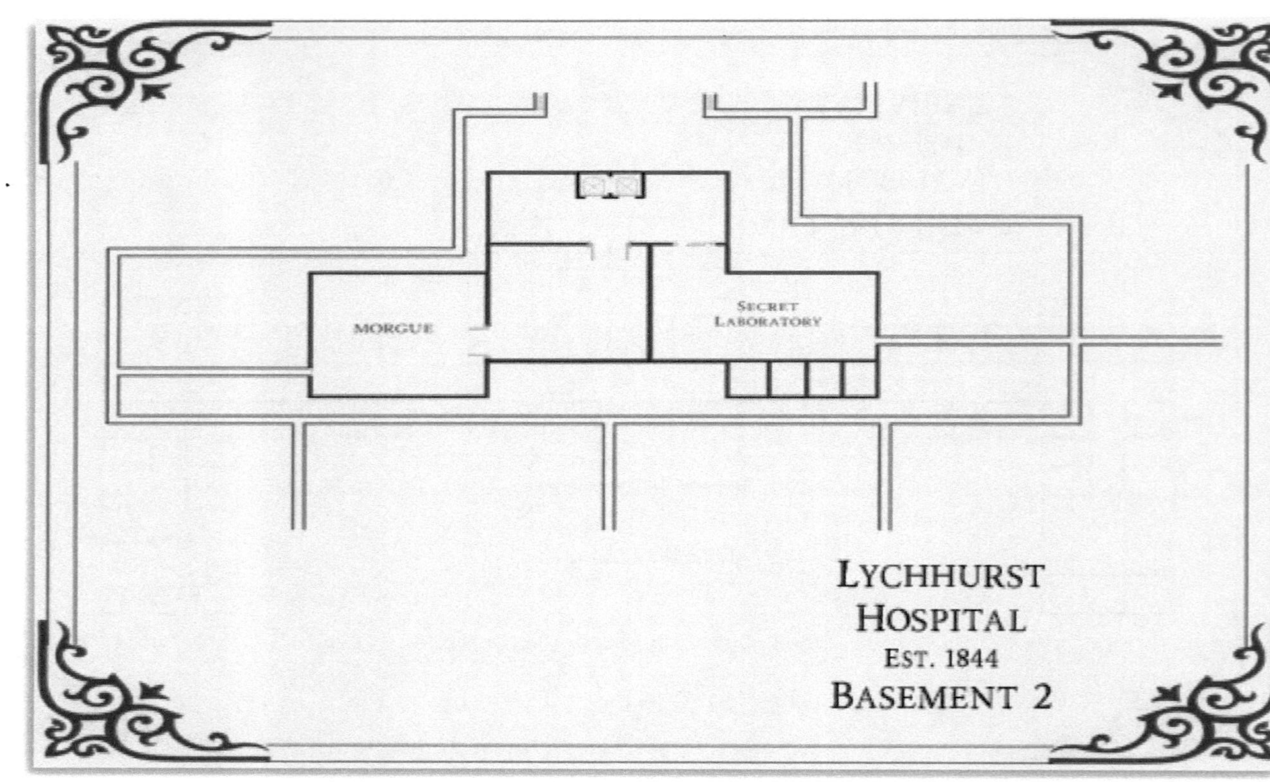

MORGUE
SECRET LABORATORY
LYCHHURST HOSPITAL
EST. 1844
BASEMENT 2

History of
Lychhurst Hospital

1844 – 1862
Lychhurst functions as an elite medical retreat for the wealthy.

1862 – 1865
Lychhurst is commandeered as an army hospital during the Civil War.

1865 – 1900
Lychhurst, still under control of the US government, is repurposed as a "soldiers and sailors asylum" (providing medical care and long-term housing for wounded veterans).

1900 – 1922
Lychhurst returns to private ownership as a sanatorium treating patients of tuberculosis.

1923 – 1950
Lychhurst changes hands once again, and functions for thirty years as a psychiatric hospital.

1950 – 1994
Lychhurst becomes a "normal" hospital, treating a variety of diseases and injuries, until it closes its doors to the public for the last time.

1994 – 2024
Lychhurst sits, abandoned, doors chained, windows boarded over. Local kids sneak in; all manner of dark deeds may occur within its empty corridors.

Welcome

A bright winter sunset is bleeding from the sky, brilliant tongues of vermillion flame flinging dying embers against the encroaching darkness. The skeletal arms of naked oaks and the ghostly white of tall birches intersperse with feathery pines, their conical tops like colossal witches' hats reaching into the night.

The trees press in along the path, a rutted road through a dark forest. They scrape the roof of your car as you drive slowly along, tapping against your windows, long fingers of bark and sap begging to be let in.

A fallen oak stops you in your tracks. You climb from your car and approach the tree. It has clearly been here a long time, its bark rough and dry, flaking at the lightest touch, but still it is far too solid and heavy to be moved.

With a hesitant backward glance, you leave your car behind and scramble over the massive trunk.

Even if the fallen giant had not blocked your way, you wouldn't have made it much farther in the car. Branches close in overhead, pushing closer until the path is barely a person-shaped tunnel through the darkness.

You press on, called here by some compulsion you cannot explain, cannot understand. You simply know that you must continue, must reach the end of this road and whatever heaven or hell lies beyond it.

The trees thin suddenly, a night sky the color of inky-black feathers opening above you, the sudden expansiveness that surrounds you prickling against your skin like the plunge into a black-market bathtub filled with ice.

The road curves into a circular drive before a hulking monstrosity of crumbling brick and broken glass, three stories high—four in the central column that bears down on you as you approach it.

You climb the steps toward the massive front doors, doors that hang open just a crack—both ominous and inviting.

A feeling of faintness, of vertigo, of nausea, washes over you, your knees buckling beneath the onslaught. You reach out to keep yourself from collapsing, hands grasping at something, anything solid enough to support you.

Your fingertips brush the heavy door.

It inches forward with a torturous groan. Above you, the eave that overhangs this darkened doorway comes alive, a startling swirl of oil-spill feathers and beady eyes as a hundred grackles take flight, screaming their displeasure as they go.

Your eyes follow the birds until they disappear within the trees, then you turn once more to the door before you.

The door creaks, opening farther, and you stumble against it, the lobby coming to eerie life before your eyes as you cross the threshold.

Your gaze lifts to the arched stonework above the entrance as you pass beneath it. There, chiseled into moss-riddled gray rock, your eyes scan the words as your mouth forms the name:

Lychhurst Hospital.

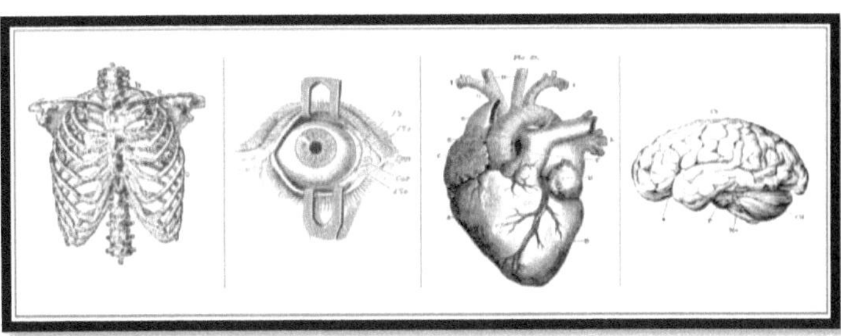

Triage Level: Green

Welcome to Lychhurst! You must be the new intern. We've been waiting for you.

Oh, the lights? They are dim, it's true. We're working on limited resources these days. But we do what we can with what we have. That's all you *can* do, right?

Me? My name is Ellie. I'll show you around.

Which part of the hospital did you want to work in?

What's that? I can't quite hear you. You're mumbling. You look a bit pale as well. Are you feeling alright?

Here, let me get you a seat. Tour by wheelchair—isn't that fun? We have to enjoy our bits of merriment where we can, you know.

Well, if you haven't decided on your area of study yet, that's okay. I'll show you the whole place, shall I?

Hmm. Let me think. I don't want to overwhelm you. Let's start with the fun parts.

Oh, of course a hospital can be fun!

Especially the places I'm about to show you.

No, no, sit back. Relax.

Would you like a snack? A drink? The Gift Shop has all kinds of goodies.

A bit mouthy, some of them, but Bert keeps them in line.

Hmm? Oh, never mind. Don't mind me! I say strange things sometimes.

If you're in the mood for a heartier meal, we can stop by the Cafeteria. Not a lot on offer this late at night, but they usually have a few selections ready to warm up. The baked ham and potatoes is particularly…thrilling.

No? Not hungry? Well, we can just make a quick circle around those rooms, then, and carry on.

What's that? Oh! This area? Isn't it sweet? The Daycare provides a place for the staff's children to be kept safe and loved while their parents work. We care *so much* about making sure children are safe and happy here at Lychhurst. I just love children, don't you? They make life… and death…so interesting.

Hmm? Oh, nothing. Just me being silly again.

What? Is it safe for children here? Of course it is! Let me show you our Security Office. Don't mind the mess in there. We've had a horrible time keeping guards employed, especially at night. They just up and leave right in the middle of their shifts. And they leave such messes behind.

Tsk tsk.

But, if you'd like to start somewhere a little cleaner and calmer, let's head to the Chapel first. Such a beautiful space, and so peaceful.

Tranquil.

Silent.

Secluded.

Insane.

Oops.

Gracious, look at me. Talking your ear off instead of just letting your see the places for yourself.

Why are you struggling, dear?

Oh, you want to stand up? Of course! I'll just follow along behind you, wheelchair at the ready, while you explore a bit.

Chapel
1949

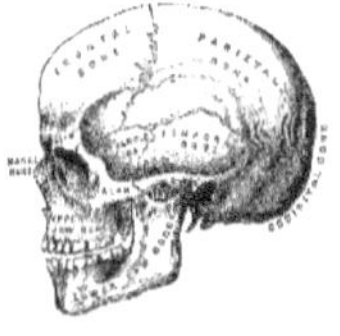

No Glory, No Closure
Blaine Daigle

Robert Callahan sat beneath the man on the cross, begging the carved idol of wood to make it all stop.

His hands shook, fingers clasped together in a prayer. Quick, staccato breaths left his lips, the silence of the chapel filled now only with the expulsion of air from his lungs.

Even the low sound of breathing seemed to echo, somehow holding on to just enough of its sound to reverberate off the white walls trimmed with the occasional golden swath of paint.

He sat in the front pew on the right-hand side of the chapel, the first of eight wooden benches lined in rows leading all the way to the door in the back of the room. Small windows of stained glass lined the walls on either side of the nave, and the images of Christ's final walk hung painted in all detail upon framed canvas between them.

Had Robert not been whispering a prayer in a desperate hope to make his torment end, he might have felt strange to be surrounded by white drywall instead of the carefully crafted stone of his childhood church. Or that the crucifix he faced was not perched atop its usual altar.

But these small differences barely registered to Robert. In fact, they were so far from his focus that he might have reasonably assumed the walls themselves *were* made of stone, or that the crucifix before him was not a carving of wood, but Jesus Christ himself.

Because that's where his mind was. That was how close he was to breaking in two.

From behind him, he heard the familiar sound of footsteps moving down the nave unaccompanied by the opening of the chapel door.

For a moment, he didn't look. He knew what would be there when he turned, knew what would be waiting for him when his gaze left the focal point of the crucifix and moved to the back door.

Even still, his skin shivered as a hollow chill worked its way across his nerves, nestling deep into his bones. Stabbing deeper with the soft fall of each footstep.

The footsteps continued, quieter than they should be. They barely registered above his own shallow breaths, soft sounds lingering in the cold, still air of the chapel. Less than the weighted and concrete sound they should have made, and more like wisps of smoke slowly dissipating even as they were created.

Every hair on Robert's arms stood at attention, every pore on his skin tightened closed at the cold approach behind him. *Don't look,* he told himself. *You know what's there.*

But even as he repeated his own advice to himself, he knew he couldn't follow it. He turned his head, his eyes glimpsing the macabre paintings as they travelled from the crucifix over the pews and toward his back.

Nothing was there. Only the cold, empty space. He was alone.

Robert's gaze returned to his hands as he slouched back into the pew. He'd come to Lychhurst Hospital shortly before the war had ended. After Hitler had put a bullet in his own head but before the US dropped the bomb.

He'd been sitting in his room when he'd heard about that. Most of his own deployment had been on the European front, but he often thought about how those men in the Pacific must have felt, to fight and kill and die for every scrap and inch of those godforsaken islands, only to have it all come to an end in a flash. No glory, no closure. Just a burst of bright light, the supernova of a thousand suns, and then nothing more.

He hoped those men at least got to leave their nightmares behind.

God knew he hadn't.

Nobody at Lychhurst was able to figure out what the hell was wrong with him. He'd come home from the war, but somehow the war had come with him. He'd never seen things that weren't there, never heard the phantom shots of guns long fired before. But now, the war was *everywhere* he looked.

Men on the streets suddenly lost half their faces to mortar shells that hadn't really fired. His nights were filled with the screaming, both from himself and from beyond the grave. The dead eyes from soldiers no longer glared at him from across smoky battlefields, but rather from across the bank teller's desk. He'd become a man haunted, and now the haunted man had become trapped inside an equally haunted house.

Lychhurst had been a hospital for soldiers and sailors back in the 1800s, and they'd told him it still was when he'd been admitted. But now he knew the truth. This was a psychiatric hospital. A place for the crazies. The loons. The lost causes.

The haunted.

He'd come to this place for peace, for tranquility. He'd come to the chapel because the quiet of this holy place was the only thing that could drown out the screaming everywhere else. Because, somehow, this place was separate. Different.

Every time the other patients would whisper about the people in the walls, or the figures that walked the halls, they never talked about the chapel. The first time he'd walked inside, he'd felt an instant lightness to the room, a feel so diametrically opposed to the rest of Lychhurst that he'd felt as though he might float away at any second.

But that feeling was long gone now. He had no idea how long he'd been in this room. It had been a bad day that drove him here the last time. Visiting hours from his buddies who he'd seen blown into bloody ribbons had finally broken him. He'd run through the hospital halls like a madman, making a beeline for this one sacred spot. This one untouchable place.

And now he couldn't leave. Every time he tried, he found himself right back in the exact same spot. He'd walk to that door in the back of the room, stand at its threshold. He'd press his ears to the door and listen, hearing the same creak and squeak of a gurney being pushed down the hallway, thinking that it was proof that the hallway waited beyond the door. But it never did. Somehow, this room of holy escape had become a nightmarish prison. It didn't matter how many times he walked out that back door, he always ended up right back in the same place. Alone in the chapel.

The quiet soon became deafening waves of dread, and the echoes of people not really there rang as loud as the hospital hallways themselves. He felt them more than he saw them. Presences moving throughout the space, and disembodied voices whispering in his ears as his mind slowly broke apart.

Another creaking along the floor, and Robert stiffened. He closed his eyes, tried to push it out. *There's nothing there,* he told himself. *Nothing but your mind.*

The footsteps moved closer now, growing in volume as his own blood rushed hot and fast beneath his skin. Horror formed in his stomach as he reminded himself that just because you couldn't see something didn't mean it couldn't hurt you.

How many of his friends had been killed by Axis soldiers hiding beneath thick vegetation with only the business end of their rifles sticking from the camouflaged cover? How many times had he watched pieces of his fellow soldiers separate from their body as bullets ripped through their fragile forms?

But then, the footsteps stopped and were replaced with a different kind of creaking. Not the sound of feet carefully moving across tiled floor, but the sound of a wooden bench slightly giving beneath the weight of someone atop it. Someone sitting on it.

He turned.

A man sat in the pew to his left, his head turned up to the crucifix. A dark-gray, twill jacket steeped over frail shoulders. He was older, Robert assumed into his sixties. His wrinkled hands sat atop his knees. Wisps of white hair ran down the back and sides of his head.

Someone was here. Someone was actually here.

"Hello?" asked Robert.

The man's mouth opened slightly and the faint registers of "Our Father, who art in Heaven" slowly leaked from his lips.

"Sir. I need help. I need to get out of here."

The man continued to pray, and Robert noticed something strangely familiar about the man. Not anything to do with his features, but rather the clothes he wore. Those old rags, pieced together with twill. So similar to….

No, he thought. *No, please.*

"H… he… hello?" he said again, his voice breaking apart as the words left him.

The man turned his head, his mouth still in prayer, and Robert gasped. The entire left side of the man's head was gone, blasted apart in a way Robert knew all too well. The remnants of a single shot from a service rifle. Ragged edges of skull and gore sat cracked and broken around the edge of the wound.

"Hello," said the old man, his eyes milky and hazed over. "Is someone there?"

Robert tried to rise to his feet, but felt his legs go soft.

Something changed in the old man's eyes. Something heavy filled the hazy space, and it looked like he might cry.

"Pauline?" he said. "Pauline, is that you? Can you hear me?"

The old man stood, the blood from his missing skull running in small rivers down the side of his face. Robert fell again.

"Get away!" he screamed. "I said get away!"

But the old man pushed forward, and Robert knew now beyond a doubt that the old twill jacket reminded him of so many famers overseas along the European front. Civilians used as cannon fodder for the Axis.

"Pauline! Oh, I know it's you!" said the old man again, pushing one feeble leg in front of the other. "I'm so sorry they couldn't help you! I'm so sorry, my dear!"

Robert stumbled again, falling out of the pew and into the right aisle. His back hit the wall, and the painting above him shuddered in its place. The old man pushed onward.

"What did they do to you? I'm so sorry, my love. Tell me what they did to you, and I'll turn them in! I'll hold them responsible!"

Robert struggled to his feet and then ran as fast as he could toward the back door.

"Please just tell me!" called the old man after him.

Robert reached the back doors and pushed, praying that this time would be different. That this time he would emerge into Lychhurst's hallway and see that gurney rolling down the corridor.

But all he saw was the chapel.

"No, damn it. No!"

The old man was gone, but the chapel remained.

Only, it looked somehow different. The walls were no longer the fresh coat of white he remembered, but a duller shade of gray. The wood of the crucifix also no longer held the tell-tale sharpness of fresh paint, but rather the chipped and worn signs of age. It was as though the room itself had grown somehow, lost some of its baby fat.

It felt less holy, now.

But Robert was *still* there.

A new sensation had arrived as well. A dull ache that radiated from the center of his head, burning behind his eyes. He rubbed them. For a moment, his vision blurred the space into a kaleidoscope of dull colors before the pieces all pushed their way back together into an unchanged portrait.

On weary legs, Robert walked down the nave toward the crucifix. He felt a heaviness overtake him, a weight untethered by any restraint falling atop his shoulders. He was so tired, so exhausted from this game, this unending circle.

His mind momentarily drifted away from the infinite room he found himself stuck in, away from the ghosts the populated his slowly breaking psyche, and away from the remnants of war that had somehow followed him home.

For a moment, just a moment, he thought of his family. His wife, Rebecca, whose picture he'd kept close to his heart as he'd trudged through the frozen European battlefields. Her face, the slender and softly falling features that fit so perfectly into his cupped hands. Her wide eyes that he'd stared into before shipping off.

He'd promised her he'd come home, and he'd kept that promise.

But what had he brought home with him?

He stared at the man on the cross again, and silently offered up something. A prayer, partially, but one mixed with a defiant challenge.

Had this been the answer to all those silent conversations freezing in foxholes overseas? Had this been the price he'd pay for what he'd asked? For pleading that bullets would find someone, anyone, else? Because somehow their families waiting back home were less important than his? Because it didn't matter if they made widows and orphans of those praying for their return, as long as he got to go home to Rebecca. Hold her face in his hands again. Gaze into her green eyes and know that the worst was all behind him.

But now the worst was both behind him and in front of him. It was never ending. He'd gotten his prayer, but at the cost of his sanity. He'd come home, but war had hitched a ride on that prayer. He'd seen her again, but the unending weight of the war had pulled him away again.

Away from her and into this place.

Into Lychhurst.

Into this damned chapel, this unending space with no exit.

The door behind him opened. This time, he didn't fight the temptation to look. He turned quickly to see a middle-aged woman moving down the nave. Her greying hair was tucked into a shawl and her eyes, pale-green, focused forward, unchanging with each step. As she walked, she moved past Robert as though he weren't there, before coming to a stop at the first pew. She stood there for a moment, staring up at the crucifix, before sliding slowly into the right pew.

Robert stood frozen. The ghost had behaved differently than the previous one, and for the first time he noticed the escalation in what he was seeing, if he were seeing anything at all. She sat, and he swore she looked almost real, as though she were really sitting in that pew.

Cautiously, he stepped forward. For a moment, he entertained the notion that perhaps his communication with these spirits was the way out of this endless cycle. That if he listened to them, maybe he'd be able to leave. *Something* was keeping him here, after all.

The woman began to cry. Softly at first, but then a flood.

He reached her, and saw the rosary clutched in her hands. A sudden sense of melancholia fell over him. The sheer madness of this place momentarily lifted, and Robert remembered, even if only in bits and shattered pieces, the gloom of tragedy.

He remembered his own father, sitting in a hospital bed as tuberculosis ripped through his lungs. He remembered himself, a young boy then, walking into a place like this and offering up his first prayer, the first of many. A prayer that his dad would be okay, and that this sickness would dissipate into nothing. A prayer that the world would retain some of its mercy and allow him that one little request.

He'd sat in a pew just like that. Cried, just like that, for a prayer that ultimately went unanswered.

"Are…" he started to say, shocked at how quiet his own voice sounded. "Are you okay?"

The woman picked her head up, and there was something intimately familiar about her. Something in her features, something in her eyes that touched something deep inside Robert. Her eyes widened and she looked all around, but never quite at him.

"Hello?" she asked.

Suddenly, Robert was acutely aware that they were not the only two people in the chapel. Each pew was occupied by someone, each ranging in age and appearance. One of them wore a leather jacket and jeans, his hair slicked back. Another wore a bright shirt of every color possible in some surreal pattern, along with an unshaven face and unkempt hair tied behind his head where it fell down his back. A woman wore black business wear in a style Robert had never seen, pants instead of a dress and her makeup not dolled on but rather subtly balanced across her face.

Others filled in as well, each somewhat different than the other. All of them looking forward. All of them seemingly oblivious to each other's presence. All their faces sorrowful and heavy. Their lips all barely moving in some whispered prayer.

He turned back to the woman who now stood from the pew, facing his direction but not looking at him. Slowly, he began to not only recognize some semblance of familiarity, but actually put a name to it.

He knew those green eyes.

He knew those soft features.

Everything inside him slowly churned, his nerves twisted among themselves, and the room suddenly felt smaller, slowly constricting inward, tightening around him. His hands began to tremble, and his lips quivered.

"Rebecca," he stammered.

"Why, Robert?" she said. "Why did you do it?"

"Why did I do what? I…I don't understand."

She reached her hand forward and gripped the edge of the pew tightly.

"I'm so sorry," she said.

"Baby, please talk to me. I'm right here. Sorry for what?"

Slowly, he reached out his hand and cupped the side of her face.

She screamed.

Falling backward, her voice erupted from her as her eyes went black. Strands of dark veins ran in jagged movements down her cheeks and neck. Within seconds, she looked less the woman he loved and more a corpse, decades of decay spreading across her in mere seconds.

Robert was suddenly surrounded by a cacophony of screams. He turned to see the other occupants of the chapel all going through the same horrific metamorphosis, their eyes going black and hollow as streaks of decay cracked across their skin like spiderwebs.

As death surrounded him, Robert's mind collapsed beneath the weight and the chapel seemed to shake.

Rebecca's withered figure looked up at him, a broken piece of a woman barely held together by rapidly fraying rope.

"Why?" she asked again, her voice a choked rasp. "Why did we send you here?"

She twitched, and reached a long, rotted arm forward. Fingers stretched out toward him.

"Why didn't they help you?"

Robert stumbled away, before climbing to his feet. The thing in front of him was not the woman he loved, but a sick amalgamation of all her parts. What horror had made this? What sickness had spawned this?

There was a flicker. A momentary disappearance of light. In its absence, for only a second, Robert saw a place consumed by darkness.

He ran. Ran to the back to the chapel. Ran back to the door. Past the slowly decaying forms reaching out for something, for someone. Anyone.

He pushed the door open.

He emerged on the other side, and the momentary darkness he'd seen during the flicker had now enfolded the chapel. The walls were peeling, old paint falling in destitute waves of connective tissue from blackened walls. Cracks ran up from the floor, and the wooden crucifix stood worn and weary amidst the black decay of the place.

Robert stood in the middle of it all, looking around hopelessly. Nothing made sense, and the world he found himself in now looked less like anything recognizable and more of something from some dark imagination.

He took a step forward and heard the crack of old, broken floor tiles beneath his feet. He looked down to see torn, molded carpet above the shattered tile beneath. The lights above were long destroyed, and no light shone through the stained-glass windows. Robert looked through them to see only the night outside. A starless sky blanketing a faded Earth below.

As his mind tried to comprehend the new location, his eyes found each and every sign of age and decay. He'd seen buildings like this in the war. Old farmhouses long abandoned, left to the elements and the battles. Their bones broken and blackened and battered into forced oblivion by the elements.

He was standing in a relic. A tomb.

From somewhere in the distance, he heard the chattering of voices. Youthful, male voices. He turned toward the sound and saw that one thing had seemingly avoided the wrath of whatever had set its sights upon the chapel.

The back door.

Still, it stood.

Then, it slowly opened.

Three young men walked through the door. For a moment, Robert struggled to figure out just what they were wearing. Two of them wore what looked like baseball caps, but they were turned around so that the bill was above the back of their heads. They wore baggy t-shirts and denim jeans that seemed far too loose for their figure. They each had facial hair seemingly styled with a patch of hair just below their lower lips and a scruff of hair at their chin. Robert wondered what in the world it was he was looking at.

"This is where it happened, huh?" asked one of the men as he walked forward to the front pew on the right side of the nave.

"Yeah," said another one. "First pew, right side. 1949."

Robert watched them curiously. Where what happened? Why was the pew important? Or the year?

"Wait," said the third man. "Which one is this?"

"Chapel ghost," said the first. "Soldier who was suffering from PTSD. Got sent here after the war."

"Guess he brought the war home with him," said the second man. "Like that other guy, the civil war soldier in the Sleep Lab. What was his name again?"

"Thomas Harlow," the first man answered. He ran his hand across the dusty, broken pew. "They didn't know what PTSD was then. God only knows what was happening to people like this guy…"

Why didn't they help you?

"…Anyway, I guess he couldn't take it anymore. So, he freaked out one day and stole a weapon off one of the guards. Went into the chapel and shot himself."

The man tapped the pew with his hand.

"Shot himself right here."

Robert felt his insides turn to liquid as a defiance crept into his mind.

No, he thought. *No, they don't know what they're talking about.*

"First person that saw him was a few weeks later. Old guy visiting his wife. She died while he was here, so he went to the chapel to pray. Said he thought he was talking to her."

"That's depressing," said the third man.

"Gets worse. Over the years, tons of people claim to have experienced the ghost. But get this, one day, the guy's own wife came up here. I don't know why, guess she needed closure. But she comes into the chapel and sits right here, and she gets *touched*."

"No shit."

The man nodded. "Yep. Can you imagine? Go to get closure and end up with anything but."

"Fits though, doesn't it. This place is beyond fucked up."

"Yeah. Let's go we've got more rooms to hit."

The three men moved down the nave. As they did, Robert reached out his hand, placed it atop the first man's shoulder. In horror, he watched as his hand moved right through.

The man stopped and jerked as if shocked by some electrical charge.

"Everything okay?"

The man looked around, then settled his gaze right on Robert's. For a moment, a single, lonely moment, Robert wondered if the man could see him. If anybody could see him.

"Yeah," said the man. "Thought I felt something."

As the men left, Robert felt his body go numb. As if all at once, decades of memories stuck in this place flashed before him. He no longer felt the ground beneath his feet, no longer felt the chill in the cold air. He stood alone and dead in the withered remains of the room he now understood he'd spent decades haunting.

He started to cry. Felt it all wash over him in a black flood of emotion bottled over years and years of futile and desperate attempts to reach out to anyone willing to reach back. He wanted to rage, wanted to scream, to throw things across this room now every bit as dead as he was.

But he knew it would be a useless gesture. All the raging in the world, all the screaming his withered lungs could muster were little more than tears in an ocean. It would be mixed and diluted down into the history of this place, even more so than he already had. His rage would become another ghost story. Another haunting.

So, he cried. He let himself feel it all. Let himself pass through the decades of memory and into the present. He thought for a moment he could cry until the end of time. Cry as long as he could imagine Rebecca's face in his cupped hands. As long as he could remember his father's last breaths and his desperate prayers. As long as he could remember…

As long as he could remember…

Remember what?

In time, those memories would fade as well. In time, they would dissipate into that ocean, and they would become no more than he was now. Ghosts, chasing everything forgotten and left behind. Desperately wanting and endlessly reaching even as they drift away.

All gone in a flash. No glory. No closure.

He turned and saw that something else had changed in the chapel. The back door was open.

He stood there for a moment longer, staring at the door which had so long been closed. He tried to remember…

Remember what?

In his last moments of clarity, he understood that he was already almost gone, almost part of that ocean.

So he went to the door again.

He reached out and grabbed the handle, and pushed. It opened, and he stepped through.

Nothing came out the door. The chapel was empty. All that remained were the echoes of those who'd once walked its nave and sat in its pews. Echoes that would eventually subside, just as all things eventually did in time.

Gift Shop
1921

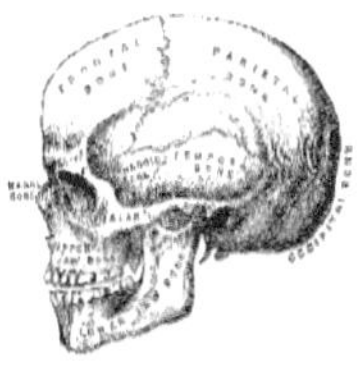

Bertram's Fine Gifts and Sundries
Cat Scully

The hospital was the last place Vinnie wanted to step foot inside of, yet here she was, standing outside the front double doors with flowers in hand, terrified to go in.

It wasn't her fault that the hospital gave her the heebie-jeebies. After her grandmother had been admitted here battling a strong case of tuberculosis when Vinnie was six, ultimately biting the big one after weeks of horrendous coughing, that horrible moment had left a deep scar in her mind.

She thought she'd never have to return to this godforsaken hospital until a few weeks ago when her little sister Sunny had suddenly produced the most horrible coughing fits and Vinnie knew where she had heard such a terrible sound before.

Over the past month, Vinnie had tried not to panic as their mother sent her out to find her sister some relief while she stayed home and tended Sunny. No matter how many bottles, Cushman's menthol inhalers, Parker's ginger tonics, Ayer's sarsaparillas, or magic cure-alls Vinnie brought home, nothing seemed to quell Sunny's cough.

Her sister appeared to be beyond any home remedy, virtuous tonic, or local drugstore offering, and their mother feared the worst. After Sunny's cough turned to bouts of spitting up blood that led to an urgent doctor visit in the middle of the night, their mother determined it was time to send Sunny to the hospital before her lungs gave out altogether. As their mother spent what little money they had on a taxi, Vinnie burned with wishing her father were still here and not lost to them in the great war.

This was 1921—modern times. They were supposed to be past the diseases of the past, Victorian ailments like tuberculosis weren't supposed to plague them anymore. Or they should have been. Maybe the remedies in their community were simply not modern enough and Vinnie would need to make the trek to a larger city with more access to current medicines.

For the first week Sunny was in the hospital, Vinnie had refused to visit her sister. Something about seeing her seven-year-old sister stuck in bed sent Vinnie rolling with grief, but her mother had delivered her ultimatum. So Vinnie had taken her money and spent a nickel on flowers, hoping they might brighten not just Sunny's day, but her own.

If only she could find the courage to walk inside.

Vinnie took a deep breath. Everything was jake. She would go in and visit her kid sister and deliver her flowers and be out. The worst of seeing her sister in whatever helpless conditions the doctors had her in would be over. All she had to do was take that first step.

Vinnie took the stairs two at a time to avoid hesitating. If she paused, she might not go in, and if she didn't go in, her mother would paint her back porch red.

Subsequently, Vinnie burst through the entrance with all the strength of a charging bull and sent both doors flying open with a clang.

Behind the counter, a rather sour-looking nurse glanced up from whatever she was scribbling away on a clipboard.

"Quiet in the hospital!"

"Sorry," Vinnie said, but she didn't entirely mean it. She kept her momentum all the way to the nurse's desk.

The peppery doll's nametag read Annie Hedgerow.

"Lavinia Fisher here to see my sister, Susanna Fisher," Vinnie said. She always felt so formal giving her full name.

The nurse took in Vinnie, looking her up and down over the bridge of her spectacles.

"You're too early." She pointed at the clock behind her. "Visiting hours are not for another hour. You can wait in the lobby."

"Better to be the early bird," Vinnie said, but the joke did not bring a smile to Nurse Hedgerow's face. "Can't you let a gal slip in to visit her dear little sister?"

Nurse Hedgerow set her pen down a little too decidedly. "No. You may wait in the lobby like everyone else."

Vinnie glanced around. There was only one other cat in the whole place, a rather dour-looking man sporting a fedora hat with a shabby suit. He cradled a small bunch of white flowers like they were his last bottle of hooch.

"How have you been able to keep up with all of these hospital patrons? This joint seems hopping!"

Again, the nurse did not like the joke.

"Take a seat or I must ask you to leave," she said with all the patience of a nun witnessing a sacrilegious act. "This is a hospital, not a vaudeville theater."

Vinnie hated that the nurse was trying to be a buzzkill. Humor was how she got through life, especially the uncomfortable things like witnessing your grandmother dying or visiting your sister in the hospital.

"It's fine," Vinnie said with all the ice she could muster. "I needed to go iron my shoelaces anyway."

Vinnie turned on her heel with a decided huff. She didn't want to sit next to the cat by the window with his sad face and even sadder flowers. There must be some other place she could go.

She wandered back toward the entrance, half a mind to return outside to light a cigarette while she waited, when a sign pointing to a gift shop caught her eye.

Vinnie checked what pocket money she had brought with her. In her little purse there was just some dollars and change. All the money she had in the world, but maybe there would be something inside to make her kid sister smile. That alone would be worth all the money she carried.

Vinnie practically skipped down the hall to the gift shop, change rattling in her pocketbook the whole way.

Having not frequented many hospitals, Vinnie had never been in a gift shop for one before. She half-expected the place to be just as dour as the rest of the hospital, but boy, was she wrong.

The gift shop was every bit as glittering as the ones Vinnie had visited in hotel lobbies, and stocked with just as much opulence. There was a sign by the entrance for the establishing listing its name as *Bertram Fine Gifts and Sundries.*

The store boasted a kaleidoscopic display of goods to choose from that might delight any fancy. There were advertisements for tonics, elixirs, the latest toys, fashionable accessories like scarfs or fine jewelry, lotions and perfumes, hats and gloves, and the most delicious candies and sweets that Vinnie had ever laid her eyes on. But what to choose?

She had enough dough to get her kid sister something really nice, but would a gift of a remedy meant to heal be more useful and thoughtful? Or should she choose a bright and shiny new toy that would perk Sunny up enough to fight the tuberculosis back into submission?

Vinnie wandered the many aisles of the expansive gift shop, her eyes never resting for long on any one item.

There was a familiar selection of typical drugstore fare and menthol inhalers, rows and rows of tonics and sarsaparillas, various shawls and scarves with matching gloves in all variety of colors, jewelry that glittered behind glass cases, soaps and cleaning supplies, and in the back, there was a toy selection to rival any downtown toy store.

Vinnie's mouth fell open as she entered the toy section stocked with every manner of doll and car, pop guns, Ferris wheels, Felix the Cat dolls, jacks, marbles, and toy horses. Many of these toys were things that might dazzle Sunny, but so far none of them seemed to be quite right for her either. Vinnie left the toys and searched deeper into the gift shop for the perfect item.

She eventually found the checkout counter located at the center of the store where a neat little card sat, reading *back in five minutes.* Vinnie had an hour to kill. She supposed whatever Charlie worked here would be back well before then so she had the pick of the litter when it came to selecting the best gift to give her sister.

Turning away from the center counter, Vinnie found herself back in the medical aisle, staring down at the familiar Cushman's menthol inhalers. The face of a Victorian child with big doll's eyes stared back at Vinnie from the box holding all of the inhalers. The girl appeared to be holding up the inhaler, which was wafting what appeared to be healing fumes, when her eyes moved and locked eyes with Vinnie.

"Choose me."

Vinnie blinked and could have sworn the image blinked back at her. She dropped her flowers in surprise. The voice was coming from somewhere inside the gift shop, but certainly not from the wrapper.

"Hello?" Vinnie called out into the gift shop, but there was no movement or sense that anyone else was there with her.

"Choose me, Vinnie."

Vinnie turned back to the advertisement. The girl's mouth in the picture had moved that time, she was sure of it.

Vinnie opened her mouth to answer back and stopped to laugh at herself. How wonderfully silly that sounded. Advertisements did not talk back to you, and they certainly didn't know your name.

"Nice try." Vinnie crossed her arms over her blue day dress. "I'm not seeing things. Not today. You can come out, wherever you are."

But Vinnie did have a moment of doubt flash through her mind when no one answered.

She had taken to sneaking bits of hooch when no one was looking, but she hadn't told anyone. The pressure of almost losing her sister had been too great. She had been telling herself just a sip here and there to cool her nerves, but those sips had turned to guzzles a little too quickly to help her fall asleep at night.

Thanks to the Johnny with a crush on Vinnie at the local club, she had become well-stocked in the local speakeasy's spare liquor, always for the price of a quick kiss. It may have been bathtub gin at best, but it was something to dull the pain. A fair trade in Vinnie's mind.

Besides, the doorman was never looking for a petting party, never asked for more than a few moments on Vinnie's lips, and in the end she got all the nightly alcohol the club wouldn't notice had gone missing.

To be honest, she hadn't been drinking *that* much. She was no flapper. Still, Vinnie didn't like to entertain the thought she had mentally descended to the level of the screaming meemies withdrawal after a nightly bender.

"Choose me, Vinnie. I'll stop those rotten coughs. With just a swift inhale of Cushman's menthol inhaler, I guarantee to stop Sunny's coughs for good. What do you say? Act now and your sister won't have to suffer anymore, starting today!"

"You're not talking to me," Vinnie said to the display, feeling a bit silly. "Advertisements don't talk back. I'm imagining things."

She turned on her heel and marched away, not wanting to hear anything else the girl had to say.

"Choose me, Vinnie."

Vinnie stopped walking. She craned her neck, unsure of where the second, very masculine voice was coming from.

"Come on down and take a swig of Ayer's sarsaparillas, the only choice when your throat needs a good, old-fashioned clearing. I'll whoop your little sister's coughs into submission, and ride that cold right on out of town. You hear that? That's the sound of your sisters lungs clearing right on up. Act now and you'll be the hero of the west. Choose me, Vinnie."

Vinnie's eyes went wide when she found the brawny cowboy staring back at her from the sarsaparilla stand. He winked at her. She gasped and stumbled back, hand over her heart.

"You're not real!" she cried.

Vinnie raced for the double doors of the gift shop. She found them closed and tried pushing on the handle and leaned into the door real hard, but neither of the doors would give. No matter how hard she rattled, the big oak-and-glass doors wouldn't budge. Vinnie peered through the glass.

The dour man was still sitting by his lonesome in the lobby. Through her position in the gift shop, she could see him sitting there with his head still down, staring into his flowers.

She banged hard on the glass. "Hey! Johnny! Look over here!"

He didn't look up.

Vinnie tried banging harder and harder, so hard the heel of her hand hurt. "Help me! Please! Let me out!"

The man did look up, but not in her direction. He glanced up over toward the nurse's station as if his name had been called, all the hope in his eyes. He left his seat and headed toward Nurse Hedgerow and out of sight. If he was leaving, did that mean the visiting hours had already started? Had an hour passed while she had been wandering the shop?

Tears welled in Vinnie's eyes. How was she supposed to get out of here now?

The shopkeep. His card read he was going to be back in five minutes. She could just wait for him to come back and unlock the door. Problem solved.

Again, that knife of doubt twisted in her stomach. The card reading back in five had been up there when she came in, and if visiting hours had started, that meant an hour of time had passed.

Vinnie turned around and let her back slump against the doors. She came all the way to sitting on the ground and tucked her dress underneath her for modesty. She couldn't stay locked in here forever.

Besides, she was just imagining things. The signs weren't talking to her. This was all because she had been drinking too much before bed, and now her habit had finally caught up with her. If she got out of here, she promised anyone listening that she would be a good girl and not partake in the sinful drink any more.

Well, she wouldn't imbibe *too* much anymore. She would be measured. She would be disciplined. No more hooch for her, no sir. Vinnie vowed she would be clean and never over-indulge again.

A tapping sound caught Vinnie's attention. She sprang up, hoping it was someone knocking on the glass, likely telling her to stop blocking the door so they could come in. There was no one outside the window.

In fact, there wasn't anything outside the window. It was total darkness out in the hallway, with only a few lights lit at the distant nurses' station around the corner.

Had hours passed?

Was it night now?

Smart footsteps clacked down the hall. A dark-haired nurse rounded the corner coming from the direction of the Entrance. She was carrying a clipboard and walking a brisk clip, but she dressed primly in a nurse's uniform that did not match anyone else at the hospital. She wore a nurse bandage on her arm and a dark bow at her collar in a style that seemed to be from more than a decade ago. It seemed strange to Vinnie that she would cling to so passé a fashion in so modern a time, especially when the nurse didn't seem much older than Vinnie herself.

Vinnie pounded her fists on the glass.

"Please, Nurse. I need some help."

The nurse paused and locked eyes with Vinnie with a cold detachment that made Vinnie's hairs stand on the backs of her arms. The nurse raised a long fingernail to her lips as if to silence Vinnie's unbecoming behavior. She held her finger there, held Vinnie's gaze a little too long, and never blinked. Not once.

"Let me out!" Vinnie tried again.

The nurse threw her head back and laughed long and loud as the lights in the hall went out, cloaking her in darkness. Vinnie squinted as hard as she could, but she couldn't make out the nurse anymore. She waited for a breath or two, but there was no sound, no movement, out in the hall. The nurse was gone.

"What is happening?" Vinnie asked herself, the room, and no one.

At least the lights were still on in the gift shop. Vinnie wondered for how long.

She wandered back out into the shop, hesitant to wander down any aisle for fear of having another advertisement yell at her.

If she were going to be stuck here for the night, she may as well make the best of it and get comfortable. The place had plenty of food and supplies at least. She shouldn't go hungry or thirsty. Needing to find a restroom, however… Vinnie very much doubted there would be a bathroom in the gift shop.

She turned down an aisle filled with blankets and decorative pillows. Bedding, check.

Now to find something to eat that didn't have a wrapper or case that yelled at her. Around the cash register, she found plenty of Baby Ruth bars, Oh Henry! bars, Charleston Chews, Chuckles, Goobers, Peanut Chews, and Crunchie bars. Vinnie always had had a terrible sweet tooth, and there seemed to be more options that ever in terms of candy.

She had a bit of money, but if she ate her fill and ending up spending more than she could afford, Vinnie could claim starvation due to wrongful imprisonment. How else was a girl supposed to eat?

Vinnie reached for a Baby Ruth bar.

"Choose me! All you can want for a nickel!" The girl on the box boomed at Vinnie. *"Slice and savor for all occasions! Rich in dextrose—the sugar your body uses directly for energy!"*

Vinnie recoiled as if she had just stuck her hand in a viper's pit. "Who was that? Where are you?"

"Why choose him when you can pick us, the Charleston Chew?" the dancing couple on the box asked Vinnie while keeping perfect time. *"You won't just be doing the Charleston all the way back to your kid sister's room if you choose us. You'll be doing every kind of modern dance there is when you put one of us in your mouth!"*

"What is happening?"

"Why, you got to pick one of us, kid," the old man snapped from the Parker's Tonic sign. He was sitting in a great red chair with a nightcap on and facing another, younger man sporting a blue suit and holding a dark tonic bottle he was pouring into a martini glass.

"That's right," the younger fellow in the Parker's ad said. *"You must pick one of us to leave. I was miserable until Parker's tonic cured me. An occasional dose before eating keeps me well. Choose us, and we can cure whatever ails your sister not just now, but for the rest of her days!"*

Vinnie bit her trembling lower lip in an effort to stop it. She took a deep breath and gathered herself before choosing her next question carefully.

"If I choose one of you, will you open the door and let me leave?"

There was silence for a moment, and then the roar of voices competing with each other to be heard was so loud, it forced Vinnie to cover her ears. She could barely make out what any of the voices around her were saying, they were so varied and numerous.

"We'll help you get out…"

"If you go with me, I swear I'll…"

"Don't worry, little lady. I got just the ticket…"

"If you don't chose me, I swear to Christ I will kill…"

"Why won't you pick me? Are you just a mean old…"

"Pick me up or I will murder you and everyone you love…"

Vinnie couldn't take it anymore. She kept her ears covered as she raced back to the front double doors. She banged against the doors, against the darkness, over and over again until her fists went numb and her eyes were so blurry with tears she could only see shapes.

There were too many of them, too many voices begging to be set free, threatening, bartering, yelling. She clasped her hands over her ears and slumped back against the door again. Vinnie rocked back and forth until the cacophony faded away and she retreated inside herself.

It's all a dream. It's all a dream. It's all a dream.

She repeated it so many times Vinnie didn't notice the voices had stopped talking to her until she decided to open her eyes again. Now the gift shop was dark too, and Vinnie sat there whimpering in the darkness unsure what to think or do next.

When Sunny was little, Vinnie and Sunny loved to play too-dark-cave. Each of them would dare the other to go deeper and deeper into the cave until they couldn't handle it anymore and cried to be led back out again with a lantern.

Vinnie had ten years on Sunny, and at five years old, Sunny was more daring to run farther and farther into the darkness only to shriek she had gone too deep and needed to be let out again. Vinnie always came running to save her, and she learned to live with her fear of the dark.

Plunged into darkness now in the unfamiliar terrain of the massive gift shop, Vinnie couldn't help but feel she was playing too-dark-cave all over again.

She'd have to gather her courage and try to find another exit out of here. If she could make it over to one of the windows, Vinnie could take the myriad of things and smash her way out of here. The whole plan was duck soup.

Vinnie covered her ears as she crossed the gift shop, careful not to look at any product and keep her eyes on the floor and the light glinting off the tile. She shuffled past the cash register and all of its candy, avoiding the eyes of the girl in the Babe Ruth ad. She glanced at the toy section and stopped herself before she could make eye contact with any one toy.

The light streaming from the windows was getting brighter. She must be close!

Vinnie shimmied her way through racks of clothes to the nearest window and released her hold on her ears. Still, there was silence, but she didn't trust the quiet to hold. Not for long, anyway.

Vinnie turned and found the closest blunt object she could find—a sitting chair near the rack of women's Patou coats. It must have been placed there for beaus waiting on their gals to finish trying on attire.

She grabbed the chair firmly from the back and the legs and did something she had always wanted to do since she saw it done in the pictures—launch a chair through a glass window.

With a deep breath, Vinnie threw the wooden chair. It was heavier to throw than she had anticipated and it took more force to lift the furniture that she meant to give. The chair went hard at the window, colliding and bouncing off with a reverberation that sounded like shattering, but there was no glass to be found. The window was still intact, as was the chair. It came to land in a neighboring clothing stand, which toppled over in a pile of dresses.

Vinnie stomped her heel.

"This whole place is screwy if you ask me," she announced to the entire gift shop. "I know someone is out there listening. What do you really want, huh? You say I can pick one of you and walk free? I'm no rube."

A nearby McCall Quarterly sign of several women wearing the latest fashion and boasting brand new patterns moved. One of the girls in a sheik, brown day dress shifted her eyes to glance down at Vinnie.

"Make your choice," she cooed in a sultry voice. *"You can't leave until you choose."*

She turned her attention away from Vinnie.

"Fine." Vinnie stormed through the department store as the lights began to turn on again. "I'll make my choice."

She made a decided turn into the toy section, far away from the squabbling tonics and their argument of who would be best suited. Vinnie wrapped her hand around a clown from the Humpty Dumpty circus. She threw the clown up above her head as if all the store could see her.

"There! You happy?" Vinnie practically shrieked. "I chose my item. Now let me leave the store."

There was a distant clicking sound and the doors to the front of the shop swung open on the opposite side of the store.

Vinnie got choked up as she clutched the clown doll and raced her way to the exit. Just a few more steps and she was out of here and this all would be a distant terrible memory she would never think about again.

She skidded to a halt at the sight of a man standing in the doorway with a bowler hat and cane.

"What?" Vinnie said. "Let me by. Please, sir."

"Aren't you going to pay for that?" the man in the bowler hat said. He did not look up from the brim of his hat, which kept most of his face obscured. His name tag read "Bertram."

"Oh." Vinnie clasped her dress over her heart. "You about made me croak. Are you the shop owner?"

Bertram held out one gloved hand, as if waiting her to put money in his palm.

"One moment," Vinnie said and rummaged around her bag until she produced the thirty-five cents the clown's label read. She placed the change decidedly in Bertram's hand.

"Now let me by," Vinnie said, but the bowler man was growing taller and taller.

She cried out as his form grew big as a building, towering above her. Vinnie reached for him and found her hand was a glove with ruffles at her wrist.

Clown ruffles.

She looked down. Her heels were gone, replaced by two giant red shoes. Vinnie reached up to her face, her head, but she had no more hair. She was completely bald, and she had a ruffle around her collar and a white hat with three red pom-poms on top.

"What did you do to me?" Vinnie cried at the giant form of the shopkeep, but he wasn't the only thing that was giant. The entire gift shop was enormous now, and she was the size of a doll—a clown-faced doll.

Bertram reached down and picked her up, a satisfied smile on his face. Behind him, there was another figure, a man with a fedora on his head and clown makeup on his face.

"Is it my turn?" the clown man asked. "Can I really go home?"

"Of course," Bertram replied with the sweetest voice Vinnie had ever heard. "You found your replacement. I'll add her to the collection until one day someone chooses her. Then she will be free to go."

Vinnie cried out. She thrashed and wailed, but neither gentleman paid her any mind.

That morning, there was a new display in the window of Bertram's gifts and sundries. It was an advertisement for a female Vinnie the Clown, boasting to be the favorite clown of Barnum and Bailey's circus, but no one could hear her tiny screams.

Cafeteria
1978

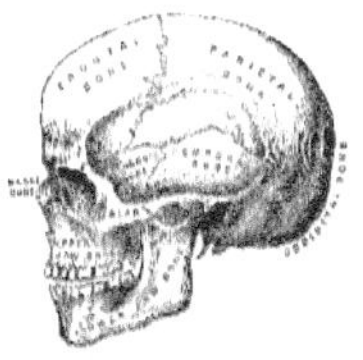

The Bitter Taste
John Durgin

November 16, 1978

Danny Nola entered the Lychhurst Hospital cafeteria, prepared for a normal day's work.

He kept to himself most days but was friendly to other staff members and patients every time they tried to start up conversations with him.

Raised alone by his abusive mother after his dad was killed in Vietnam while Danny was just a toddler, one would think Danny found solace the day his mother, Linda, was admitted to Lychhurst.

It felt as though everything had come full circle; after years of depending on her to raise him and care for him, she was now stuck in his place of work and dependent on his co-workers to live.

Sadly, he felt anything *but* solace. Because regardless of how terribly his mother treated him, she was still his mother. He still cared about her. Having her isolated in quarantine, deathly sick with smallpox, brought a gut-wrenching fear into the pit of Danny's stomach.

His mother's symptoms started minor—a low fever, vomiting, sore throat—but quickly intensified to scare the stubborn woman enough to have Danny bring her in to get checked a few weeks prior. Her condition escalated quickly, with sores forming around her mouth, followed by pus-filled blisters that spread across her body in rapid succession. She was in so much pain that it was a struggle to even move for days at a time.

After a few weeks of care, the nurses told Danny she was improving, that typically these cases lasted a few weeks before the patient rebounded. They also told him that he still wasn't allowed in to see her due to the quarantine restrictions, which applied even for close family.

While something didn't seem quite right, he took them for their word and just prayed the doctors did their job.

Over the past week, the doctors had gone radio silent on providing him any sort of updates, all while he continued to come into work a mere couple floors from where they held her prisoner.

Most days, he cooked breakfast, lunch, and dinner for the hospital, happy to work through the misery of his everyday life. At least when he was at work, he didn't have time to sit and wallow in self-pity, loathing himself for having nobody in his life that cared about him besides his mom, who he'd argue *depended* on him more than cared for him.

He'd often wonder what it would be like to leave the town behind, start somewhere fresh. Danny became borderline obsessed with communities that accepted outcasts with open arms. Someday, he would have the guts to leave and never look back.

This morning started out like any other day. Danny whistled "Black Betty" while scooping a large pan of scrambled eggs into the serving tray. He was alone in the kitchen, which he preferred in the morning as it allowed him to wake up before having to force interactions with others.

With the cafeteria empty, every passing sound was amplified by the echoes of the open space. He heard footsteps approaching and looked up from the food. A few nurses and a doctor approached him, their faces full of sympathetic smiles.

"Breakfast will be ready in ten minutes if y'all don't mind waiting," Danny said.

The doctor, a tall skeleton of a man, took the lead. He had thin glasses that sat on the edge of his nose, as if that somehow made him look more intelligent. He was bald on top with a white horseshoe haircut surrounding it, with liver-spotted marks decorating his shiny dome.

"Mr. Nola?"

"Yeah, that's me."

"I'm sorry to bother you at work and all, but it's about your mother… I'm afraid I have bad news," the doctor said.

"You guys told me she was getting better. Is her fever back?"

"I'm afraid it's worse than that, Mr. Nola."

"Cut to the chase, Doc."

"She passed away this morning. I'm sorry…"

Danny felt as if he'd been struck by an imaginary fist, grabbing hold of the counter to stop himself from falling. It had only been a few days since they told him there was a strong likelihood she would be ready to go home sometime this week, and now she was dead.

"I-I don't understand. You said she was getting better. You said I couldn't see her yet but that I could soon. What the hell happened?" The friendly tone he'd spoken with before was gone, and co-workers or not, Danny was ready to get answers by any means necessary.

"Well, it wasn't the smallpox, Mr. Nola. Due to her struggling immune system, she came down with pneumonia and we did everything we could. We would have let you in to see her, but with the recommended quarantine, we couldn't risk that. I wish I came bearing better news, really, I do," the doctor said.

"I didn't even get to say goodbye…"

He said it to himself more than to anyone else, but the crew continued staring at him with their half-assed smiles, as if that were supposed to ease the news they had given him. Danny stared straight ahead, ignoring the team of medical professionals until they felt uncomfortable enough to retreat.

"If you need anything, please know we are here to answer your questions," the skeleton doctor said.

When Danny didn't speak, they slowly turned and left the cafeteria, leaving him alone once more.

It wasn't until his right hand started tingling that he realized he was squeezing the large metal spoon he'd been scooping the eggs with so tight that it was digging into his palm. He slammed the spoon into the tray of eggs, biting down on his lip to prevent the scream trying to force its way out of him from escaping.

Part of him wanted to take the day off and go home, be with his mother's stuff. Smell her blankets, lay in her bed one last time, just like he always did as a kid when he was scared of something in his closet.

Another part of him, the part currently winning out, wanted to stay at work and keep his mind occupied. As much of a bitch as his mother often was, she was the last person to have any sort of love in her heart for him, even if she didn't always like to show it.

He decided to tough it out and finish his day, then worry about requesting time off to get her funeral arrangements and all the other stuff nobody likes to talk about in order.

So, that's what he did. Danny went through the monotonous motions of his workday, feeding both staff and patients alike, with a smile on his face. If anyone took a second to consider how his day was going, they would have been able to see the pain behind that smile. But nobody cared enough to even ask if something was wrong.

After dinner was served, Danny was the last cook in the building and went around cleaning up the kitchen—washing dishes, mopping the floor, scrubbing the stovetop. It was only then that he allowed himself to sit down and really think about the news he'd been delivered earlier.

His mom was dead. He was going home to an empty house, one where most of her belongings still resided.

Danny turned off the kitchen lights and sat in the cafeteria office, letting the tears flow. It was quiet enough for him to hear himself crying, and he despised himself for allowing the weakness to show, even if there was nobody else around. His mother would've chastised him for allowing others to bring him to this point.

He aggressively wiped the tears away, continuing to sit in the dark room. His focus shifted to the wall, where a large photo of Otto Klug stared down at him, and Danny couldn't help but feel the revered former employee was judging him.

He shook his head and went to grab his keys, but they dropped to the floor. He bent over to pick them up and noticed a message scratched into the bottom of the desk. "Until the fire…" He sat there for a minute, rereading it, remembering rumors of the cannibalistic cult a few decades prior. While he couldn't ever bring himself to eat a person, he was fascinated by the thought of a leader strong enough to get so many to buy into their beliefs. Danny craved that sort of respect.

Danny was about to get up and head home when he heard a sound coming from the kitchen. Like someone was dragging a knife along the metal counter. *What the fuck is that*? He poked his head out of the office, still unable to see the kitchen in detail.

One of the janitors had turned off all the lights in the cafeteria, not just the back-office area. Danny paused, trying to hear if the noise repeated. When nothing happened, he shook his head and headed back toward the kitchen to do one last lap and make sure his workspace was tidy for the next day.

His eyes still hadn't adjusted to the darkness as he rounded the corner into the kitchen. He scanned the area, searching for the culprit of the scraping, but the room was empty.

When he was sure he was alone, he proceeded forward, deeper into the darkness. He wasn't sure if it was his mind snapping after the horrible news of his mother, or maybe there had been a rat getting into the kitchen, skittering about as it searched for food. It wouldn't be the first time a rodent found its way into the kitchen.

As he prepared to exit the kitchen, he noticed three long scratch marks across the metal countertop, proving that he wasn't hearing things. He sensed something watching him from the darkest corner of the room. He whipped around, knowing there would be someone there before he even saw them.

A silhouette stood motionless in the corner; only the contours of their obsidian mass were visible. Danny swallowed down the fear and cleared his throat.

"Who's there? Kitchen's closed for the night."

The figure didn't move, and he had a fleeting thought that maybe it was just something hanging that resembled the shape of a person. A jacket? Maybe a chef's apron? But no, Danny knew nothing like that could be in that corner. He beelined for the lights, ready to see what the hell was scaring him like a damn child.

"D-d-dannn-yyy…"

Danny froze in place. He'd recognize that raspy smoker's voice anywhere.

John Durgin

"Mom?"

"*Son... They... they l-l-ied to you...*" she said, her voice now escaping in a low rumble.

He didn't know what to do. Was his mother really standing there, hiding in the shadows? And why did her voice sound like she'd swallowed a bag of rocks?

"Is it really you? Wha-what are you talking about? Who lied?"

"*You... damn fool! The doctors... They tried to cover up... my d-death.*"

It was hard to concentrate on what she was saying; her voice sent chills down his spine. He both wanted her to come forward to know for sure it was her, and also wanted her to stay right the fuck where she was, terrified of the possibilities he'd see if even a sliver of light hit her.

"What did they do to you?"

There was no response, and for a second he thought the shape vanished as well, that it was all in his head. Then the figure *did* step forward. It was far worse than anything he could have imagined. It was his mom, but she was... *different.*

Her once beautiful eyes were milky white, as if a cloud of smoke now filled each orb resting in her sockets. Her skin was covered in quarter-sized sores, all scabbing around the perimeter as a white fluid swam against the transparent skin, which was expanding from the pressure, close to popping.

Her white hair clung to her skull like it was lathered in grease, thinning to the point that Danny saw even more sores traveling along her scalp.

"*This... Dannny. They did thisss. They didn't want my case to become public knowledge, so they... turned a blind eye and let me die.*"

A blind eye. It seemed fitting. Danny realized her eyes were cloudy because she'd gone blind, one of the severe symptoms of smallpox. The staff never once told him that her eyesight was going. If what she was saying was true, she could have lived. They could have saved her and chose not to. Just so her case, or even the *news* of her case, wouldn't spread.

Danny wiped another tear away, embarrassed his mother might see him crying. Now that his eyes had adjusted to the darkness, her features were more pronounced. The sores spread across not only her face, but her entire body. She wore her johnny, wrinkled and stained from what was likely an accident she could no longer hold in.

The veins in her legs bulged out, creating a trail through the scabs and wrinkled skin that journeyed up beneath her dress where he couldn't see.

Her fingernails had something caked beneath them, and he realized it was chunks of dead skin from clawing at the sores. Bile rose up in his throat as he found himself unable to look at her for another second.

"I'll go to the state. Have them look into your case. They can make Lychhurst pay for what they did to you…"

"*No… That'll do no good, I'm afraid. They need to pay, son. They need to… suffer. Make Mother proud, Dannny…*"

The tears were now coming full force. He didn't recall the last time she ever claimed to be proud of him.

He was a grown man, pushing forty years of age, yet a complement from his mother—dead or alive—meant the world.

"What should I do? How can I make them pay?"

His mother's mouth widened with an insidious smile. Pus slid down her lip onto her tongue. "*You will know… There will be a sign, very soon. Now, stop crying like a baby and go, boy.*"

Danny turned away from her to hide the tears that she already knew were there, wiping them on his shirt. The day had hit him like a hammer to the skull, it was all so hard to take in. He turned back to face her once more.

"I can't—"

His mother was gone.

Not just back in the shadows, but he sensed that her spirit was no longer present. And just like that, he was left on his own, with nothing but a dead woman's riddle to solve.

What did she mean there would be a sign? Danny considered that he might be losing his damn mind, that he'd need to check himself into the rehab wing of the hospital and get proper help.

As he went to leave the kitchen, his eyes were again drawn to the countertop.

To the scratch marks that he knew weren't there before tonight.

November 18, 1978

After the incident with his dead mother, Danny went the next few days working like nothing was wrong. Everywhere he went, he looked for the sign his mother talked about. And every time he doubted himself, he stared at those scratch marks as a way to remind him it wasn't all one big nightmare.

He met with the funeral home to prepare the services for his mother. He cleaned the house from top to bottom—except for his mother's room, which he left untouched, the door locked shut and never to be opened again.

Doubt started to creep in. Maybe those scratches were always there, and he just noticed them. But that didn't make sense, because Danny cleaned the kitchen meticulously every single night.

Still, he was ready to give up and accept that his mom's death would not be avenged. Nobody would listen to him if he went to the state and complained. It would get swept under the rug to avoid the bad publicity.

That night, when Danny got home from work, he grabbed a beer from the fridge and sat down in his recliner. He turned on the television and flipped through the channels, until he came to the evening news. The anchorman solemnly talked to the camera about hundreds of deaths at the compound of Jim Jones. Danny sat upright, leaning closer to the television to hear every single word.

"Reports are coming in that over nine hundred members of the Peoples Temple, led by the controversial figure Reverend Jim Jones, are dead in what appears to be a mass suicide. The details are still emerging, but it seems that the members, including many children, were tricked or even forced into drinking a lethal mixture of cyanide-laced fruit punch.

"Earlier today, Congressman Leo Ryan and several journalists, who had traveled to Jonestown to investigate allegations of abuse within the community, were attacked and killed by members of the Peoples Temple as they attempted to leave the area. In the wake of this violence, it seems that Jim Jones ordered or persuaded his followers to participate in this 'revolutionary suicide.'"

Danny's heart was slamming into his chest. This was the sign. This was what his mother had been talking about. He thought back to the message carved into the office desk. "Until the fire..." It was a sign. He would earn the respect he craved so greatly.

"Eyewitnesses describe scenes of chaos and heartbreak, with bodies strewn across the compound, parents and children lying together in their final moments. The exact motivations behind this horrific act remain unclear, but what is certain is that this is one of the largest mass suicides in modern history."

Danny turned off the television with goosebumps spreading across his arms. His mind immediately went to ways he could obtain something like cyanide. He needed to be careful, especially with the news of the Jonestown massacre so fresh on everyone's mind.

For the first time in weeks, Danny felt something besides sadness or hate. He felt excited. He went to bed, planning out the steps he would take to get the payback his mother rightfully deserved.

December 25, 1978

After weeks of thorough preparation, Danny was ready to proceed with his plan. Christmas dinner seemed as fitting a night as any to jump to action.

In the days leading up to Christmas, Danny spent countless hours in the town library on his time off, researching what ingredients were needed to concoct cyanide, how to obtain those ingredients, and more.

He also followed the Jonestown case religiously, getting sucked into the story, almost looking to Jim Jones as a hero of sorts. A man that believed in his cause so much that he was willing to sacrifice everything. That was what Danny needed to do.

He knew it would fall back on him, that his life beyond this evening would be changed forever. He was okay with that.

Danny made a few trips to an industrial supply store, posing as an owner of a pest control service and buying quantities he thought safe enough to not garner any attention. While that set his plan in motion, he needed more. And what better place to look than the place responsible for his mother dying an unnecessary death?

When he volunteered to work so much overtime and cover hours nobody else wanted to work, his colleagues assumed he was just trying to keep busy and take his mind off his mother passing away. What they didn't realize was not only was he saving up money to buy supplies, but he was taking advantage of what the hospital could provide him in way of those supplies, and working at odd hours gave him a better chance of sneaking stuff from the building without being caught.

Once he discovered the hospital stored certain amounts of cyanide for pathology labs and other tests, he found a way to get access to that area of the hospital and take what he needed.

Weeks of planning all led to this day. As he stared at the Christmas dinner he'd prepped for the staff and patients, he knew he was ready. He was committed to recreating the "revolutionary suicide," even if these people had no idea they were about to die.

Mother would be proud.

The menu consisted of baked ham, mashed potatoes, a vegetable mix, and many other traditional Christmas side dishes. He wanted to make sure there were plenty of options for the evil people responsible.

While the patients had nothing to do with his mother's death, they were getting far better care than she did, and that needed to be accounted for as well.

People slowly trickled into the cafeteria, forming a line to be served what would be their last meal. Danny fought to contain his excitement—there was no doubt in his mind this was the right decision. The first face he recognized was the skeleton-looking doctor, who grabbed a tray and moved down the counter to be served.

"Good evening. Merry Christmas, Doc. What will it be?"

Skeleton-doctor forced a smile and scanned the food options. If he remembered breaking the news to Danny about his mother, he showed no sign of it. It was just another day on the job to him.

"I'll get a bit of everything, thanks."

That's it. No "I'm sorry about your mom. Hope you are doing well," Danny thought.

He gave the doctor an extra scoop of mashed potatoes and tipped his chef hat in salute as the doctor moved down the line to grab silverware. Danny would be busy the next hour or so serving people, but he really wanted to watch the doctor take those first bites. Wondering if the doctor would enjoy the bitter taste of death. Nothing would be more satisfying.

Over the next few minutes, the dinner rush picked up, and Danny lost count of how many people he served. It had to be at least a hundred. Nothing compared to what the great Jim Jones sacrificed, but Danny wasn't trying to outdo his new idol. He was trying to honor his mom.

Just as he wondered when his meal would start taking effect, he heard the first scream.

What followed was absolute chaos.

A nurse stood from her table, clutching her throat. Danny watched as her eyes bulged. A bloody foam pumped from behind her clenched teeth, and then she vomited across her table, splashing two other nurses sitting with her.

One of the sitting nurses jumped to her feet, staring down at the mess staining her white slacks. The third nurse ran to her vomiting coworker to check on her, only to clutch her own stomach, keeling over in pain.

Danny scanned the cafeteria, looking for skeleton man, feeling a bit of momentary disappointment when he didn't find him in the terrified crowd. But then, in the back corner of the cafeteria, he saw something else that made him smile.

His mother.

She remained in the shadows, hiding her disfigured face, but her milky white eyes burned through the darkness, watching the scene unfold.

Danny felt tears come at the sight of her, and he couldn't help but think he had made her proud. He didn't want to stop looking at her, but he couldn't miss the scene unfolding.

Another scream echoed through the dining hall, vying for Danny's attention. Through the cries, through the swarm of people running and falling to the floor, he spotted the tall doctor, Dr. Skeleton.

The skinny man had fallen across the top of a table, convulsing so aggressively that the table began to slide across the tile floor, reminding Danny of nails on a chalkboard. The doctor's arms stiffened, clutching at the table edge. Another doctor ran to his side, attempting to grab Dr. Skeleton's shoulder, but then the second doctor began to cough, softly at first, and then it escalated to a violent bark as blood splashed across Dr. Skeleton's back.

The smell of vomit and shit overpowered the wonderful Christmas dinner scent that had permeated the kitchen just moments ago. Sick children dropped to the floor, shitting themselves and going into shock as the seizures taking hold of their bodies were too much for them to handle.

Eventually, there were only a few surviving people scattered through the warzone. The screams and sounds of victims violently puking faded.

Danny walked back to the kitchen, grabbed his car keys, and exited the cafeteria. As he walked down the hallway, he came across a few scattered bodies that had fought a bit longer than others, but still met their demise in the end. Danny whistled "Black Betty" while weaving in and out of sprawled figures, smiling as the blaring sirens came into earshot from the distance.

As he made it to the parking lot, multiple police cars and ambulances sped into the ER section, followed by a fire truck with its siren blaring. Grackles dispersed from the surrounding trees, flying off in every direction at the loud noises. Danny started his car with a smile on his face and pulled out of the hospital parking lot for the last time.

Later that night, Danny sat in the living room of his mother's home, his grin illuminated by the Christmas lights wrapped around the tree. He was in the middle of watching *How The Grinch Stole Christmas*, when a rapid pounding at the front door came.

He didn't bother answering, instead deciding to continue watching the movie through the commotion. Because he knew who was coming, and he knew this would be the last time he sat in this house. He was okay with that.

If this event put the spotlight on the hospital, leading to an investigation into their unethical handling of his mother's death, it would all be worth it. And he planned to expose them for the evil scum they were.

He double-checked to make sure the letter he wrote was sitting on the coffee table, ready for them to discover.

Eventually, the door splintered down the middle as the police broke it down with a battering ram. He counted at least seven armed officers before sticking the end of his pistol into his mouth. The officers screamed for him to stop. Aiming their own weapons, as if that would prevent him from pulling the trigger himself.

"Put the weapon down! Put your hands in the air," the lead officer said.

Danny tasted the metallic flavor of the barrel, then closed his eyes and pulled the trigger, just like Jim Jones did. Brain and skull fragments exited the back of his head in a shower of viscera.

In the following weeks, an investigation was initiated on Lychhurst. The media was in a frenzy, comparing the event to the Jonestown massacre. The public feared more copycat incidents, but authorities reiterated it was a one-off event.

The letter Danny left, while a confession to the poisoning and deaths of over one hundred people, also laid out the timeline and step-by-step incidents leading up to his mother dying. It was determined that Danny's mental health led to his decisions, and not the hospital mishandling her case.

Instead of the hospital coming under fire for hiding a case of smallpox, they instead got heat for their management of security and chemical-handling protocols. A strict mental health test was also required to be included in all future employee applications.

In the letter, Danny mentioned the scratch marks on the countertop in the kitchen. While authorities said anything could have caused those marks, it did lead to many of the kitchen staff quitting their job. They stated they would often hear sounds coming from the darkness, and one employee insisted he saw an old lady with white eyes, covered in sores, sitting in the kitchen staring straight ahead at nothing in particular.

To this day, many say the ghost of Linda Nola haunts the cafeteria of Lychhurst Hospital.

Daycare
1988

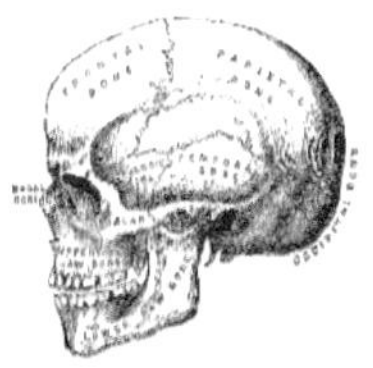

The Boy from Limbo
Brooklyn Ann Butler

Bree Thorne trudged behind her mother up the walkway to Lychhurst Hospital, fists clenched at her sides in resentment. She was ten years old. Too old to go to Lychhurst Little Folks, the daycare her mom started running last year.

Why couldn't she go to Grandma's house instead? Or even stay home alone while Mom was working? She could take care of herself. She even knew how to use the stove to make Top Ramen.

"Come on, Bree," Mom called. "I don't want to be late."

The worried look in Mom's green eyes gave Bree a pang of guilt and she quickened her pace.

The old hospital was a mishmash of different styles as it had been remodeled and expanded over the ages. The gray slate roofs were conical over some towers, gabled in others, and had those *Addams Family* roofs in others.

Big smokestacks protruded behind a wing on the left and the center was dominated by a clock tower like in *Back to The Future*. The chipped, faded, reddish brick walls were covered with crawling ivy on some of the wide wings, and dingy with moss in others.

Bree tried to think of something nice to say.

"This place looks spooky."

Mom gave her a small smile, knowing how much her daughter admired all things creepy.

"It does, doesn't it? Lychhurst was built back in 1844 and has a long history. Some of it *is* kinda scary. If you're good today, maybe we can learn more about it."

"Is it haunted?" Bree asked eagerly.

"Without a doubt. All hospitals have ghosts," Mom said cheerfully, then suddenly went serious.

"The daycare *definitely* doesn't have any, though."

To Bree's disappointment, the inside of the hospital didn't match the creepy outside. Instead, the hallway they entered resembled the ones in the boring soap operas Mom taped on the VCR to watch when she got off work. White walls, light blue wainscotting, yellowish linoleum floors, and boring paintings of flowers on the walls.

The stupid daycare was worse. The walls were covered with cheery murals of fairytale figures gamboling through flowery fields and forests; some looked like they'd been painted by her mom.

The main room had a mini playhouse in one corner, craft tables in another, shelves full of blue padded mats for naptime, and a wall of cubbies just like in her fourth-grade classroom. Another shelf held various toys, dolls, and stuffed animals.

One clown doll, with giant red shoes and a ruffled collar, looked ancient and somehow malevolent. Bree couldn't help shuddering in revulsion at the sight of it.

"Miss Kayla!" a mass of little kids cried out with exuberance before they flocked around Bree's mom.

Bree's shoulders slumped in dejection. This summer was going to suck.

A boy her age met her eyes and gave her a sideways smirk, like he understood how lame this babyish place was. Bree gave him a matching cynical smile as she wove through the mass of kids laying claim to her mother and made her way to his side.

"I'm Bree Thorne." She held out her hand. "Miss Kayla is my mom."

"Jeff Tanner." Jeff high-fived her.

"My mom works in the records room. I'm glad to see you. I thought it was just going to be me and Rani Sharma stuck here for the summer."

"Rani?" Bree asked.

"Yeah. Her mom's a doctor. She's in the playhouse. Come on." He tugged her arm.

The brown playhouse was wonderfully dim inside, a welcome change from the glaring brightness of the playroom. Rani sat inside with a sketchbook on her lap. She had umber brown skin and long legs with dinosaur Band-Aids on her knees. She grinned at Jeff and peered at Bree curiously.

"I love your drawing!" Bree beamed down at the sketch of a crow perched on a tombstone. If Rani also liked spooky stuff, they could become great friends.

"Thank you." Rani shifted her straight, shiny black hair behind her ear and lifted her sketchbook to give Bree a better look.

"It's hard to get the feathers right."

Right after introducing themselves, Mom called them for outside playtime. They were instructed to line up single file and led out a door into a rectangular area surrounded by brick walls that had bits of moss growing between the grout. Instead of grass, the majority of the playground was sand framed by a boardwalk.

There was a swing set and slide on one end and two more playhouses under the eaves opposite the daycare's wall. Plastic buckets and shovels were scattered everywhere in the sand and a bin full of chalk sat on one corner of the boardwalk.

One of the daycare "teachers" —as Mom told her they were to be called—settled herself in a chair outside like a lifeguard. She even wore a whistle around her neck.

The littler kids charged out into the giant sandbox, shrieking obnoxiously. Bree, Jeff, and Rani exchanged annoyed looks. Bree felt a flare of kinship. Maybe this summer wouldn't suck so bad.

They walked around the boardwalk, weaving around running kids and the daycare teacher, whose nose was buried in a copy of *Newsweek* full of articles about the latest stuff going on in the USSR, talking about their lives outside of the daycare.

All three were ten and going to be in the fifth grade when school started, but Rani and Jeff went to another elementary school. They were fascinated at the fact that the Bree was the daughter of the daycare's boss.

"Does that mean you can do anything you want and not get punished?" Jeff asked.

Bree shook her head. "No. I'll probably be punished *worse* if I do something wrong. So no one thinks she's picking favorites."

Rani nodded. "My mom thinks the same way." She pointed up to a smokestack on the hospital roof.

"What do you think they're burning in there?"

Bree's imagination immediately flitted to the macabre. "Maybe dead bodies."

Jeff shook his head. "People get cremated at the funeral home. But I bet when stuff gets amputated it gets burned."

"And tumors that get cut out during surgery," Rani added.

The rest of the playtime was spent coming up with the grossest things they could think of burning in the hospital's incinerator.

When they were called inside, Bree was pleased to see that there were separate activities for the older kids. While the little ones were given coloring pages and Play-Doh, the big kids got clay that they could shape into anything they wanted and Mom would then bake it in the oven to harden and tomorrow they could paint their creations.

Jeff made a dragon, Rani a cat, and Bree a raven like her new friend's drawing. There were four other "big kids," but they were all younger and either scared of Bree's and her friends' talk about the incinerator or too babyish and dumb to bother talking with.

Then came lunchtime. Some kids took lunchboxes from cubbies, others had bag lunches that one of the daycare teachers handed out from the daycare kitchen. Bree got one of those. A tuna sandwich and a little bag of Lay's potato chips.

Jeff had a *Thundercats* lunchbox and Rani had a *Jem* one. Bree was envious of both. Maybe Mom would let her bring her *Real Ghostbusters* lunchbox tomorrow.

After lunch, the tables were pushed up against the walls and the stack of padded blue mats laid out for naptime. At first, Bree felt a tremor of horror at the idea of taking a nap, but then Mom escorted the big kids out into the hall. Jeff, Rani, and a couple other kids grabbed their jackets from their cubbies on the way out. Bree frowned in confusion.

A voice from a speaker in the ceiling called out, "Doctor Slaughter, Two-one-seven… Doctor Slaughter, Two-one-seven…"

"There's a Doctor Slaughter?" Bree giggled even as she was fascinated that the daycare was still plugged into the hospital's communication system.

Mom laughed. "And a Doctor Cutteroff, Doctor Butcher, and Doctor Cutting. You'll hear a lot of interesting things."

She opened a door and gestured for the kids to go in.

"This is the TV room. You can pick out movies from that cupboard, or read books. I'll come get you when naptime is over and there will be a snack."

Immediately Bree understood why the other kids brought jackets. The TV room was cold!

Bree looked for a vent that would explain the cold, but the only one she found wasn't running. She then noticed the worn linoleum floor, the hard metal chairs, and couches covered in orange fake leather and realized the TV room used to be a hospital room.

Along with the cold, an air of despair hung heavy in the room, pressing on her shoulders, and for a moment, Bree swore she could hear the sluggish beeps of heart monitors and pained moans of the patients who used to be here.

A little panel with a call button and an intercom in the wall right by where a bed would be captured her attention, though Bree couldn't say why.

While the other kids rifled through the VHS tapes and argued about which movie they'd watch, Bree approached the call button. The amber and green lights were dead. She flipped the metal switch, but it didn't light up.

"I tried that too," Jeff said.

"Only the main intercom system is still plugged into the daycare. The room call buttons are disconnected."

"There's another one in the bathroom too." Rani pointed at a door that Bree hadn't noticed. "I thought it would be funny if I told the nurse station I was pooping, but it doesn't work."

They all laughed. The other kids had put on *Return to Oz*, a movie Bree absolutely loved. She, Jeff, and Rani sat on a long chaise-like seat that had probably originally been for visitors to sleep on if they were staying overnight with a patient.

Just when they got to the part where Dorothy was being sent to the scary insane asylum, Bree noticed a light from the corner of her eye. The call button was on. She got up on her knees, turning her ear toward it.

The little speaker crackled and she heard the voice of a young boy.

"Help me."

Bree jumped as Rani tapped her shoulder. "Did you hear that too?"

"Hear what?" Jeff whispered.

The voice spoke again. "Help me."

Bree pushed the button to speak. "What's your name? I can ask my mom to call a nurse."

"Help me," the boy repeated. "I'm so cold."

"Where are you?" Bree asked.

"In this room. Please…"

Rani gasped. "Maybe you should get your mom. Or another teacher."

Bree nodded and slipped out of the TV room. But when she opened the door of the playroom, Mom looked up from the magazine she was reading and made a stern gesture for her to go away. She didn't want Bree to wake up the napping little kids.

With a sigh, Bree headed to the front desk. She didn't want to talk to a strange grownup, but the front desk lady *would* know how to get in touch with a nurse in the hospital.

The lady at the desk frowned at her as she approached. Her hair was dyed black in a beehive and she had big horn-rimmed glasses just like Bree's grandma wore in the old black and white Senior photo. Her name tag read *Miss Sue*.

"What do you want?"

"The call button is on in the TV room and a little boy is calling for help. Can you call a nurse?"

Miss Sue's eyes narrowed.

"I don't have time for pranks, young lady. Those buttons were disabled when this ward was converted to a daycare."

"I'm *not* pranking," Bree insisted, frustrated with grownups' reluctance to believe anything a kid said. "The button *is* working and that boy needs help! I'll show you!"

Miss Sue scowled. "Fine. Miss Kayla says we need to report any wiring issues."

But when they got to the TV room, the call button lights were dead and no amount of fiddling from either Bree or Miss Sue would make it work.

Miss Sue glared down at Bree. "I don't appreciate fibs. Your mother will hear about this stunt."

"I wasn't fibbing!" Bree argued. Rani and Jeff backed her up.

But Miss Sue was good on her word. When Mom came in after naptime, she scolded Bree until the other kids swore she wasn't lying.

"Maybe there's a gremlin in the wiring." Whenever Mom had a problem that only showed up sometimes, she blamed gremlins. "I'll call Pediatrics and tell them we heard a boy asking for help. Now, who wants a snack before outside time?"

Later, on the drive home, Mom turned down Rick Astley's "Never Gonna Give You Up" and glanced at Bree. "A nurse called back. None of their patients called for help. Are you sure you weren't making it up?"

"I wouldn't lie about something like that."

Then something the boy said crept into Bree's memory. "He said he was in 'this room.' I thought he was talking about his own hospital room, but what if he meant he was in the TV room?"

"You mean another kid was making it seem like he was speaking through the button?"

Bree shook her head. "No, the buttons wouldn't have lit up if it was that. I mean, maybe it was a ghost."

For the longest time, Mom was quiet. Bree *knew* Mom believed in ghosts. She'd grown up in a haunted house and had all sorts of stories about it.

"Bree," Mom spoke in a stern voice that made her fear the worst, "I don't want you to say *anything* about ghosts at the daycare. Not to anyone. I *need* this job. Your father left me with nothing but the house and if I can't pay the lawyer fees, we'll lose that."

"Okay." Bree relented, then changed her strategy. "You said if I was good, we could learn more about the history of the hospital."

Mom gave her a knowing look. "If you're trying to track down your ghost, it won't be easy. A *lot* of people die in normal hospitals, sweetie. But this hospital is older. It was around all the way back in the Civil War."

"*Wow*." Bree was daunted at sorting through so many prospective hauntings. "I still want to try, though."

"Okay, honey. I'll call Salena when we get home."

Bree gave Mom a grateful smile. Aunt Salena was a member of the Historical Society, so she would definitely know about the hospital's history.

The next day at Lychhurst Little Folks, Bree told Jeff and Rani about her mom's planned visit to the historical society that evening.

"That's awesome!" Jeff high-fived her.

Rani raised her hand for Bree's high-five, then returned to business. "We'll have to try to get more information from that boy when the little kids are napping."

"And I'm going to remember to bring my jacket this time," Bree said with an exaggerated shiver.

But when naptime came and the big kids were herded into the TV room, they didn't learn as much as they wanted.

For the first several minutes, listening to the intercom and attempting to speak to the boy only got a repetition of yesterday.

"Help me, I'm cold," the boy would say, over and over.

Questions about where he was were always answered with, "Here in this room."

"What's your name?" Bree asked.

Silence and light crackles through the little speaker went on forever before the boy finally responded.

"I can't remember."

"Is there anyone else with you?" Rani asked.

"No. I'm the last one. It's so lonely here. And I can't move."

Jeff frowned. "Why can't you move?"

"Stuck in here." Sobbing sounds came from the intercom. "Help me. I'm cold and lonely."

By the time Mom came to tell them it was snack time, Bree and her friends turned to see half of the other big kids ignoring the TV and staring at them and the call button with wide, frightened eyes.

Jeff gave them a stern look and Rani gestured at them to stay quiet. They all breathed sighs of relief when the kids obeyed for now, but Bree worried there'd be some tattletales.

After the day was done, Mom took Bree to the Historical Society. The place was rad! The building was an old Victorian house with tons of rooms full of cool stuff, like glass-covered displays of clothes and tools and other things from the olden days, and *so many* books.

After the tour, Aunt Salena led them to a parlor with fancy velvet-covered chairs. A book was tucked under her arm.

"I don't know if this is a good idea, Kayla." Aunt Salena's gaze flicked to Bree, then back to Mom. "The history of Lychhurst is so ugly. I don't know if it's fit for a ten-year old girl to hear about."

"It's okay," Bree said defensively. "I've been watching scary movies since I was four."

Aunt Salena gave her a patient smile. "I know, sweetie. You're very brave. But still, some things are just so bad that…" She looked back at Mom. "There was a Jonestown incident in the cafeteria."

"What's Jonestown?" Bree asked.

Mom's face paled. "I'll tell you when you're older. *Jesus.* That's why I *hate* eating lunch in there. But all Bree really wants to know is what ward the daycare used to be."

Aunt Salena opened the book to a page with a map. "Point out the daycare again?"

Mom leaned over and pointed to the spot. "There."

Bree's aunt flipped through the book, found a section, and read quietly for a few minutes. "*Ohh.* That's so sad."

"What?" Bree and Mom asked.

Salena looked up. "D Ward originally started as the Negro ward back in the Jim Crow Era—I see that look, Bree. I'll tell you about that later—anyway, after desegregation, it became the poor ward, then, eventually, a sort of catch-all for the long-term patients who didn't have much money or family, or were lost causes, like the last few iron lung patients. In those days, the nickname for that ward was 'Limbo.'"

"Oh, that *is* sad." Mom's green eyes were shiny with tears.

Salena bowed her head a moment as if in silent prayer, then patted Mom's hand. "I'm glad you're making much happier use of the place."

"What's an iron lung?" Bree asked.

"They were used for severe polio patients who couldn't breathe on their own. Do you know what polio was?"

"Doctor Bell told me about it when I last got my shots." Bree shuddered in memory of his description. "I knew it made some kids have to wear leg braces and made others unable to walk at all, like President Roosevelt, but I didn't know it could make them not able to breathe!"

Mom put her hand on Bree's shoulder. "The polio epidemic was a very bad time. Your Grandma told me she cried in relief when there was a vaccine. She was pregnant with Salena when she heard the news."

"Is there a picture of an iron lung in there?" Bree asked.

Salena flipped through the book. "Here."

Bree gasped in horror at the black and white photo of a man enclosed in a metal tube with only his head sticking out. "Those poor people!"

"I know. Many of them recovered, though." Salena closed the book. "Did you learn what you needed?"

"Uh-huh." At least, all the information the Historical Society would have. She'd promised Mom not to say anything about ghosts to Aunt Salena, who didn't believe in them. "But I want to read that book!"

"I'll make you a deal." Salena's voice was stern, but her smile reached her eyes. "You can read it when you're thirteen. Maybe I'll even be able to find a copy for your birthday."

On the drive home, Mom remarked, "It's spooky that the ward was called 'Limbo,' and your ghost is a little boy."

"Why?" Bree thought it was a silly name. "Is it because kids are better at bending down to walk under the stick?"

Mom laughed. "No, honey. It's not named after the game. Limbo is a place that Catholics believe babies and children go when they die to if they're not baptized."

Bree shuddered in horror at the idea of kids being stuck in a lonely place for reasons that weren't their fault. "Do you think that's where the boy is?"

"No, otherwise he wouldn't be able to talk to you and your friends." Mom sounded confident. "Did he tell you his name? Maybe there's an old newspaper article or obituary at the library that says what happened to him."

"He said he can't remember his name. And that he was cold and lonely and couldn't move."

"That's awful!" Mom looked like she was about to cry again. "Can we talk about happier things for now? I don't want to have bad dreams."

"Okay."

Mom turned on the stereo and they sang along to the Bangles' "Walk Like an Egyptian" before pulling into the McDonald's drive-thru as a surprise treat.

The next day, Bree told Jeff and Rani everything she'd learned about the former ward turned daycare.

"I think he might have been one of those people in those iron lung things."

"Me too," Rani said. "That's why he said he couldn't move."

Jeff shook his head. "If he couldn't move, how could he press the call buttons?"

"Telekinesis," Bree suggested. "Like in the movie, *Carrie*." At her friends' blank looks, she sighed. "He used his mind. Ghosts don't have real bodies so they *have* to use telekinesis."

When it was time to go to the TV room, they again tried to get the ghost boy to tell them his name.

"Can't remember," the boy repeated. "Please, help me."

"How old are you?" Rani asked.

"I don't know. I've been here so long and they stopped telling me what day it is."

"What happened to your mommy and daddy?" a younger girl behind them asked.

"They stopped visiting me." The boy started crying.

Throughout the rest of the TV room time, they said nice things to the boy to cheer him up.

Afterward, Mom pulled Bree aside while the others went out to play. "Some parents came to me worried about their kids talking about a ghost in the TV room. You need to stop this."

"I can't, Mom!" Bree protested, overcome with determination. "He needs help. I'll tell the other kids to quit talking about him."

Mom shook her head. "You know how kids are. Someone *always* tattles."

That was true. Then, Bree had an idea. "I'll tell them he's an imaginary friend. Lots of kids have those."

"Okay, but if I hear any more complaints, you'll have to spend naptime in the playroom with the little kids."

Bree, Jeff, and Rani spent the rest of the outside time talking to the other kids and convincing them that the boy was just an imaginary friend.

When they believed they'd accomplished that mission, Jeff pulled Bree and Rani aside. "I have an idea. My mom works in the records department and sometimes takes me with her when she has an evening or Sunday shift when the daycare's closed. Next time that happens, I'll see if she can find the 'imaginary friend's' name and what happened to him."

They spent the next few days talking with the ghost and pretending to the other kids that he was imaginary. Mom said the parents were satisfied with the explanation for now.

The boy was curious about all sorts of things, like what the daycare was like and what games and toys the kids liked to play with. Rani asked what he looked like and tried to sketch him from his description.

He remembered that he had brown hair and brown eyes, but not much else.

Then, after a seemingly endless weekend that Bree normally would have enjoyed, Jeff was waiting anxiously for her by the little inside playhouse. Rani was already inside.

"I talked to Mom about this ward and how we're pretty sure there was a little boy in Room 237… I lied and said there was an old drawing on the wall. She said she didn't think there were kids in this ward before it was a daycare, but she looked it up and there was. Back in 1976—which was also when the call buttons were installed—there was a boy named Boone Robertson in an iron lung, just like you guessed, Bree.

"He was one of the last polio cases in this area. He'd been there since 1970, and his parents stopped visiting in 1973. After that, he was alone all the time. After he died that year, the nurses working in Limbo were fired for neglect. He was only nine years old."

Jeff sighed heavily, suddenly looking older than ten.

"I wrote down the parents' names. Maybe one of us can go to the library and check out the old newspapers to see if something happened to the parents in 1973."

"I live by the library!" Rani took the slip of names—Buella and Hutch Robertson—and put it in her pocket. "I can ride my bike over there today since Mom's picking me up at three."

Bree wished she could go to the library too. But today, they had something even more important to do. "We need to help Boone get free."

Jeff's head tilted in confusion. "You mean cross over? Or just get out of the call button?"

"Get out of the call button." Bree peeked out of the playhouse window to make sure no kids were playing close enough to hear them. "We don't know what the other side is like, and what if the Catholics are right and there is a real Limbo that kids get stuck in? I think if we can get him out, then he can play with us and not be lonely anymore."

Rani nodded. "That's a wonderful idea!"

During the little kids' naptime, Bree, Jeff, and Rani told Boone his name while the others watched.

"How is he imaginary when we can hear him talk?" one of the girls asked.

"Because imagination is sometimes that powerful," Rani whispered. "So if you talk to your Mom and Dad about this, tell them we named him and are playing a pretend game."

Unfortunately, Boone had a hard time when Bree told him he'd died twelve years ago. "I'm not dead! I'm stuck in this thing and I'm cold and lonely and the nurse won't come!"

For the remaining TV room time, the only response they could get from the call button was piteous sobs.

"I don't like this game," another girl complained. "It's sad and scary."

"Sometimes stories have sad parts before they get happy. Like in this movie." Bree pointed at the TV, where the *My Little Pony* movie was playing. "The whole kingdom gets covered in that gray goop before the ponies save it."

"Ohh." The girl nodded sagely. "I'm going to go watch the movie. Tell me when Boone gets to the happy part of his story."

"Great idea," Jeff said, then whispered to Bree and Rani, "If we could get them all to ignore us while we talk to Boone, this will get a whole lot easier."

Bree nodded. She had no clue how the others would react to them getting a whole ghost out of the wall. "I have an idea, but I need to talk to my mom about it first."

Rani's eyes widened. "Miss Kayla believes us?"

"She's not allowed to say she believes us, or it could make her lose her job."

"Ah." Jeff's blue eyes shined with comprehension. "I get what you mean."

On the ride home with Mom, Bree told her about Jeff accessing the old records to Limbo and finding out about Boone, the poor little boy who'd spent years in an iron lung and died of neglect.

"But he doesn't believe he's dead, so he thinks he's still trapped in the iron lung. We can convince him, so he can get out of wherever he is, but we don't want to scare the other kids after we finally got them to believe Boone's our imaginary friend. So, I was wondering if tomorrow, we can get an extra hour in the TV room. Just the three of us."

Mom tapped on the steering wheel as she pondered the idea. "I'll have to come up with a way to do that without making it look like favoritism. Also, I hope the other kids don't know about how you found out about the little boy's history. Mrs. Tanner could get in big trouble for accessing those records, much less letting Jeff see them."

"Don't worry, he made sure we were alone in the playhouse, and even then, he whispered. And Rani's riding her bike to the library to find out if anything happened to Boone's parents around the time they stopped visiting him."

Mom was quiet for a while before reaching over and patting Bree's hand.

"You're a special kid, Bree. Jeff and Rani too. Not because you three can talk to a ghost, but because you care enough to try to help those who need it."

The next morning, it was Rani who waited for Bree outside the playhouse. Once they were safely ensconced with Jeff, she told them what she'd learned about Boone's parents.

"They died in a car accident. But that's not the saddest part." Rani peeked out the playhouse window, then lowered her voice.

"Did you ever wonder *why* a kid got polio in 1970? Apparently, Boone's parents were part of this church that didn't believe in any medical care. They just believed in prayer and God's will."

Bree gasped. "That's awful!"

Jeff's horrified eyes blinked as he absorbed that heartbreaking fact. He shook his head slowly. "But they must have changed their minds if they brought him to the hospital instead of letting him die at home."

"I *hop*e they changed their minds." Rani looked doubtful. "But some states have laws against that stuff, so maybe they had no choice. I couldn't ask Mom much about it. She was getting suspicious. She doesn't believe in ghosts, so she can't know about Boone."

"Yeah, I had to be careful with my mom too." Jeff turned to Bree. "Hey, did you tell your mom about your idea to get us some alone time in the TV room?"

"Yeah, and she came up with a good plan. After naptime, when we go outside to play, we need to pretend to play-wrestle with some of the other big kids and get the blame for roughhousing or being a bad example. Then we'll be put in time-out in the TV room, but she's going to take away the VCR so it looks like a real punishment."

"That's genius!" Rani grinned.

"Yeah, but we gotta be careful and make sure the kids are having fun so we don't actually hurt them and they don't get in trouble."

During TV time, they talked to Boone, but didn't say any more about him being dead. They only promised to help him. The other kids promised they'd play with him when he got out.

"Is the story going to get to the happy part?" Sarah Odom, the girl they'd upset yesterday, asked.

"Soon," Jeff promised.

Then, during outside time, they convinced Sarah and two other big kids to play *Ninja Turtles* with them.

"I'll be Shredder." Bree tried her best to sound excited. "So you can kick me, just not in the face."

They wrestled and karate-chopped each other, making the other kids laugh in wild abandon. Then Mom came marching across the giant sand pit and delivered a scolding so believable that Bree's knees shook before she ordered them inside.

Once she escorted Bree, Rani, and Jeff to the TV room and unplugged the VCR, she smiled.

"Good luck, kids. I hope you free that poor little boy."

Getting Boone to understand that he was dead took a long time. Then, when he finally grasped the truth, it took almost longer to soothe his crying.

"It's not all bad." Bree imitated her mother's soothing tone.

"Now you can get out of the iron lung and come through the button and play with us."

Rani's voice was imbued with sincerity. "You have lots of friends here waiting for you."

"What about my mom and dad?" Boone asked.

"They're dead too," Rani answered gently. "Car wreck. Three years before you died."

Boone started crying again, so Jeff spoke quickly. "That means they didn't abandon you on purpose, and they probably still love you. Maybe when you're done playing with us, we can help you cross over and find them."

"And," Bree added, "no matter what happens, you won't be stuck anymore and you won't be lonely again. Just float out of the iron lung, imagine your favorite clothes, and come through the call speaker you're listening to us through."

"Okay," Boone sniffled. "But I'm scared. What if it doesn't work?"

"You can do it." Rani's voice sang with hope and encouragement. "If you can push the call button, that means you're already getting out of the iron lung without realizing it."

Bree, Rani, and Jeff joined hands then because it felt right. "Come on, Boone," they chanted, over and over.

The speaker holes in the call button glowed light blue, then a pale fog flowed through the speaker, taking the form of a transparent head. Then came the shoulders, then came the rest of him.

"I did it!" Boone exclaimed.

"Whoa," Bree gasped.

Before them stood a boy who looked a little younger than nine. He wore blue denim bell-bottoms, and a white and blue ringer tee with a rocket on the front. His brown hair was tousled and his brown eyes glittered with playfulness.

Two dimples appeared in his round cheeks as he grinned at them.

Without warning, he ran into Bree's arms and hugged her. Though he was still see-through, he felt like a real kid. Rani and Jeff's faces reflected her surprise when Boone hugged them.

"Thank you," Boone said, "for getting me out of there and for being my friends. I always wanted friends."

"You'll have a lot more friends," Bree told him, wiping away a tear before her friends saw. "Do you want to meet them?"

Three months later

Kayla Thorne watched the ghostly boy playing "the sand is lava" in the outside playground with the other children. None of the other daycare workers could see him, and she wasn't certain all of the kids could, either.

The ghost was a little sweetheart, and she made sure to give him a place at the table during lunch and craft times and to include him in other activities.

But it took a couple days to keep him from causing trouble. She didn't mind when he moved toys around at night when the daycare was closed, but when he moved things in broad daylight in front of other adults, they were unsettled.

And then something else happened.

Another ghost of a little boy around Boone's age appeared in the daycare a few weeks after that. He looked scarier than Boone, with his bloody ancient hospital gown and missing arm.

He had a yellow ball that Kayla often saw Boone rolling back to him. The other kids aside from Bree, Jeff, and Rani didn't seem to see that boy, and Kayla prayed that would remain the case. She needed this job.

Mrs. Harris, mother of Jessica, one of the preschoolers, stood beside Kayla, watching her daughter play a bit before calling her in.

"Come on, Boone!" Jessica shouted, gesturing at the sand even though to most eyes, nobody was on it.

"Who, or what, is Boone?" Mrs. Harris asked.

"The children's imaginary friend," Kayla answered with her most professional smile.

"Imaginary friends are part of healthy child development. And since we believe in sharing here at Lychhurst Little Folks, Boone is everyone's friend."

She breathed a silent prayer of thanks that the other boy wasn't here today.

"Oh." Mrs. Harris smiled and looked back at her daughter and the other children, playing with the ghost. "That is so cute."

Kayla nodded, meeting Boone's smiling eyes. Her daughter, along with the rest of the big kids, were back to school and wouldn't return until Christmas break. But thanks to Bree, Jeff, and Rani, Boone wouldn't be lonely again.

At least as long as Lychhurst Little Folks stayed open.

Security Office
1992

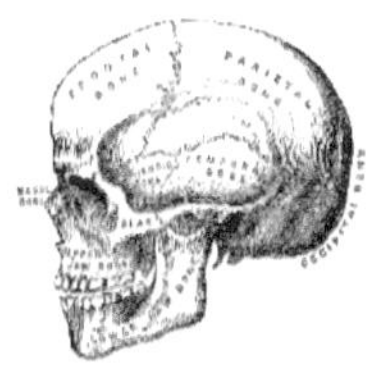

The Security Guard
Westley Smith

"So you're the new guy working the graveyard shift, huh?" the old security guard asks as I enter the security office in Sub-Basement A for my overnight shift at the infamous Lychhurst Hospital.

"Sure am."

"Henry Grady."

He extends a hand to me. I take it, feeling the rough callous across his palm. Besides guarding the hospital before the witching hour, I wonder what he does in his free time.

Carpentry? Mechanic? It doesn't matter. I won't be here long enough to get to know him.

"John Thompson."

"Nice to meet ya, John."

He studies me with the wary eyes of a man who has seen a thing or two while working evenings at the hospital.

"How'd Clayburn con you into taking the graveyard shift?"

"I requested it."

"You…" His mouth snaps shut, considering what I said with a troubled gaze that works its way under my skin.

"No one requests the graveyard shift. Not here. Not at Lychhurst. Those unlucky few Clayburn does manage to wrangle to take the job only last a night—two at most."

The tone in his voice raises my earlier suspicion that he's seen things—unspeakable things—while working at the hospital in the evenings.

"I work better at night. Less people to deal with."

This is true. I've never been much of a people person; it's easier to survive not being close to anyone.

He cocks a bushy white eyebrow as if he's skeptical of my reasoning.

"Did Clayburn fill you in on what your duties are?"

Grady's referring to Mason Clayburn, Head of Human Resources. I didn't think I'd land the job since I'd never worked in security.

Hell, after my mother's tragic passing, I could barely function, let alone work, lost in a sea of confusion, sadness, and crippling depression.

So, I was surprised when Clayburn offered me the position. But maybe that was why—because no one else would take it.

"I'm supposed to watch over the place, walk the grounds, and check the wards."

Grady nods and rubs his hand across his chin. I hear the crinkling of his whiskers against his rough hand.

Looking around the room, I realize how utilitarian it is: a desk, a rotary phone, and a small radio with a tape deck. In the far corner is a gray filing cabinet with a coffee pot. The glass carafe is stained brown from lack of washing. The pea-soup green lead-painted walls are peeling and curling away as if they're slowly dying, like everything else inside and out of Lychhurst.

"You have a torch?"

"A what?"

"A flashlight?" Grady's hand shoots to his side. He pulls a long-barrel flashlight from a round sling on his belt and flicks it on like a lightsaber.

The beam hits me in the eyes. I flinch.

"You'll need one of these to get through the shadows."

He pauses, thinking. "Didn't Clayburn tell you?"

I shake my head. *Tell me what?*

"Since the funding cutbacks, electricity has been turned off to unused areas to help keep costs down. With only Level Two still in operation, twenty-five patients of varying ailments, and three nurses of varying quality of care per shift remaining, the powers-that-be felt there was no sense in wasting money and resources on unused sections."

That explained the lack of upkeep in the old hospital. I'm also sure some of the hospital's recent scandals have added to the cutbacks.

Grady looks at the flashlight in his hand.

"Though I'm not sure even the brightest light could penetrate the darkest parts of this place."

His gaze drifts outside the room to the hallway as if he believes someone is listening to our conversation. His pale blue eyes dance not exactly with fright but with something else—recognition?

Turning, I follow his gaze. I don't see anything in the hallway. But from the standing hairs on the back of my neck, I get the strange feeling we aren't the only ones down here.

When I turn back, Grady's eyes are on me again. I'm struck by their seriousness, a little frightened even.

"Word to the wise, young man. Stick to the places you're supposed to check. Don't go into areas you're not."

"Aren't I supposed to check everything?"

"No."

He turns around, pulls a clipboard off the wall, and hands it to me. It is an itinerary list of the areas I'm supposed to check on my rounds—the lobby, gift shop, the patient ward on Level Two, and the grounds around the building, including the rear parking lot.

Also on the list are Level Three, a few rooms on Level One, and Subbasement B—all are marked OFF-LIMITS.

Why would the hospital not want security to check everything, even the closed-off areas? An intruder could get in, and no one would know.

Given the hospital's seedy history, I find this odd but not out of character.

"We ain't got no fancy CCTV here at Lychhurst, so you'll want to do your rounds about every hour to an hour and a half. Here." Grady thrusts his flashlight into my hand.

Westley Smith

"You can use mine for the night. Pick one up from the hardware store tomorrow after your shift—make sure it's a good one. And make sure you always have extra batteries on you. Batteries tend to die fast in his place."

He reaches into his pocket, pulls out two D batteries, and lays them in my palm.

"Oh. You'll also need these."

Grady undoes a button clasp holding a ring of keys on his belt.

"There are five keys on here." He picks one out and holds it up for me to see.

"This key is to the Security Office. Make sure it's locked every time you leave. I don't know why this is a rule; there's nothing in here to steal, but it's the rule nonetheless."

He picks out another one.

"Main entrance. It stays locked until six a.m. when visiting hours begin." Grady finds a third key and holds it up. "You'll need this key to check the rear entrance and the parking lot behind the hospital."

He finds the fourth key.

"This one will get you into Level Two, the patient ward."

Grady holds up the fifth key, which is different from the rest—a skeleton key.

"This is a master key. It opens all the interior doors. You won't need this key, understand?"

I nod.

"Understand?"

"Yes, sir."

He studies me for a long moment with a probing gaze. I wonder if he's trying to decide if he can trust me to stay away from areas of the hospital I'm not supposed to venture into. Finally, he passes me the keys.

"Well, that about does it."

He picks his lunch pail and coat off the chair and moves to the doorway, but he stops and turns back before stepping into the hall.

"Remember what I said: Stick to the places you're supposed to check. Don't go into areas you're not."

With that said, Grady crosses the hall to the steel cage lift, which had to have been installed in the latter part of the nineteenth century. He steps in, closes the cage door behind himself, and presses the button on the operating panel. The motor clicks and the lift rises with a *chinging* sound.

I'm left alone in Lychhurst Hospital's bowels.

You have a job to do, so get to it.

After placing the batteries, keys, and flashlight on the desk, I pick up the phone and dial the number Lynn gave me before leaving her office yesterday.

The line connects. It begins to ring.

"John?" Lynn's voice cracks with flecks of worry.

"I'm in."

"Great! Have you gotten what we need?"

"Not yet."

I look over my shoulder into the hall. I wonder what Grady was so focused on out there. Still, I see nothing, but the sense of being watched hasn't abated.

"Find your mother's file so we can prove your theory, and I'll expose Lychhurst for the hellhole it is."

During my interview for the position, I hadn't told Clayburn I was working with Lynn Croft, a local journalist who's been trying for years to prove the rumored atrocities surrounding the hospital.

So far, she's been unsuccessful. I'm hoping I can help change that tonight. I also hadn't told Clayburn that my mother, Elisa, had been a patient here in 1989—that I believed malpractice was the reason for her death.

The hospital has existed since 1844 and has faced a mountain of scrutiny, from patient abuse and neglect to staff mistreatment to the questionable ethics of its rotating doctor staff and administration.

But something inside tells me Lychhurst isn't going to give up its ghosts easily.

"The records room is just down the hall. Everything we need should be in there," I say, studying the skeleton key standing out amidst the others on the ring.

"Be careful, John. If someone finds out why you're there..."

"I know."

My stomach turns at the thought. I shudder to think what would happen if I got caught with my hand in the proverbial cookie jar.

Westley Smith

Claims had seeped through the cracks over the years that barbaric acts, far beyond the abuse of staff and patients, were taking place behind these walls. I don't know if there is any merit to these ghastly stories or if they're just urban legends. Still, I would have to proceed with extreme caution.

"I'll call you back when I find something."

I end the call and pick up Grady's flashlight and keys. I slip the extra batteries into the breast pocket of my shirt and step out of the security office.

The hallway is cavernous, with an arched ceiling like a cathedral. The walls are painted the same pea-soup green color as the Security Office and are peeling just as severely. Six caged light fixtures dimly illuminate the length of the hall from above, casting a bell-shaped pattern onto the floor. However, the light only spreads so far, leaving chunks of the hall bathed in shadows.

At the end of the hallway to my right is what used to be the Sleep Lab. Directly across from it is the Burn Unit.

When I first stepped off the lift, the air smelled moldy and damp, like the basement of my grandparents' house. But now, I smell the slightest hint of rotting flesh and sulfur mixing with the dank air.

A creaking, squeaking noise, like someone is pushing an old cart, pulls my attention in the opposite direction, toward the Isolation Ward... and the Records Room. I search the hall and peer into the shadows, believing I'm not the only one down here. I don't see a soul. Living or dead. And the sound has vanished. I wonder if my mind is projecting things that aren't there. The stories of this place working their way into my psyche, tricking me.

Settle. It's just your imagination.

Lychhurst had its share of ghost stories as well.

Moving down the hallway to the Records Room, my boots clop on the stone floor, echoing through the silence like shotgun blasts.

Passing out of the glow of the overhead light and into the shadows, I feel something scrape my forearm in the darkness—like someone lightly running a scalpel across my flesh as they pass.

Ouch!

I jerk my arm into myself and hurry back into the light. A warm heat begins to rise on my skin, and I see a thin white line in the middle of the reddened area.

Looking into the darkness from which I emerged, I don't see anything in the middle of the hallway that could have scratched me.

So… what did?

Letting out a long, uneasy breath while rubbing the discomfort away, I start for the end of the hall.

I find the thick, wooden door into the Records Room beside a stairwell that leads down to the tunnels under Lychhurst. I don't want to imagine what lurks in that dark labyrinth.

I take the cold handle and turn it. It's locked as I suspected it would be.

No worries there.

Tucking the flashlight under my arm, I find the skeleton key on the ring and slide it into the lock.

It doesn't turn.

I try again.

The key won't budge. I wonder if there's a build-up of rust inside the lock from the dampness down here.

Wiggling the key back and forth in hopes of knocking free whatever is preventing the tumbler from turning, I hear the click of the lift's motor, and the carriage starts to descend.

Shit!

I turn the key back and forth.

C'mon!

Force the key up and down.

Come ON!

I hear the lift getting closer, the cage *chinging* as it drops through the shaft.

I twist the key until the tips of my fingers and wrist ache. Nothing.

Grady's words flood my panicking mind: *Stick to the places you're supposed to check. Don't go into areas you're not.*

I look back to the lift while my hand tries to manipulate the lock. Someone is standing inside.

Shit! Shit!

Suddenly, the lock turns with an *urnnnt.*

Westley Smith

Taking hold of the handle, I wrench the doorknob and push into the room as the lift settles to a stop. I close the door as someone steps off the lift and into the hall.

Holding my breath in the darkness, praying I haven't been seen, I hear footsteps moving toward the Burn Unit.

Another door opens.

Closes.

Silence once more.

I sigh and rest my hot forehead on the door's cool surface.

That was too close.

Flipping on the flashlight, the room is bathed in light.

It's filled with old, rusted metal filing cabinets lining all four walls, with eight more sitting back-to-back in the center. Black mold is growing up the walls and onto the ceiling. The air stinks with the smell of decaying paper and… wood.

Looking down, I see a wooden floor; the boards are gray and warped, moldy like the walls. Since we're in the basement, I find it strange that this room would have a wooden floor.

Add it to the list of strange things about Lychhurst.

A moment of fear grips me. Is there anything left to find? Or has the fustiness down here eaten all the records away?

There's only one way to know for sure.

To my right, I find personal administration and staff employment records. Nothing is useful there, so I move to the first filing cabinet in the center of the room.

The identifying label is faded and yellowed, and the typed script is unreadable.

The next cabinet contains files for **Media Project 8 – Summer 1978 – Class 6**. *What the hell is that?*

The following cabinet's identifying label is also faded and yellowed, part of it torn off. I can only make out half of what it says: **-ief Study Program.**

I'm positive there's something incriminating in these cabinets. But I came here to find my mother's file.

The patient records, listed alphabetically, including the years the patients were admitted to the hospital, are along the back wall.

Grabbing the metal handle to the drawer marked **88-89**, I try to pull it open, but the slides catch with an ear-piercing screech of rusted metal, and the entire cabinet pulls away from the wall. My breath hiccups into the back of my throat, and every muscle seizes taut. Had I been heard by whoever had come down earlier?

I listen, waiting to hear footsteps approaching, but I don't hear anything.

I work the drawer out carefully, wiggling it back and forth, trying to make as little noise as possible. Once I have it open, I begin shuffling through the files with my fingers. Names flash before my eyes: Tabert, Tenerowicz, Thilges, Throb, Thom, Thomason… Thompson.

Thompson, Allen.

Thompson, Cara,

Thompson, Elisa.

Yes!

I pull my mother's file from the others and stare at it, my eyes burning with tears.

My mother was thirty-seven years old when she entered Lychhurst that sweltering evening of July 25th, 1989, sick as a dog and doubled over in pain with what we would soon find out was appendicitis.

After her surgery to remove her inflamed appendix, I was assured by Dr. Gruber that she would be fine. But the following day, I got a call from the hospital informing me that my mother had suffered a heart attack overnight.

Since there was no DNR on file, she had been resuscitated, and a ventilator had been administered.

I didn't understand at the time why she'd been put on a ventilator. But I would soon find out.

When I got there, nearly out of my mind with worry and confusion at how a healthy woman of thirty-seven could have suffered a sudden heart attack, I was informed by Dr. Gruber that though they had got her heart started, there were no signs of cognitive response.

In frank layman's terms… she was just a vessel of meat and organs being kept alive by a machine.

Westley Smith

Dr. Gruber gave me two options: let her live on a machine—*which isn't living at all,* he assured me—or pull the plug and set her free.

Trust me; it is not an easy decision to make at eighteen years old to take your mother off a ventilator. It would have been my father's cross to bear had he been there, but he had run off with a lot lizard years ago.

So, the decision was left to me as my mother's only living heir.

It was the hardest decision I ever had to make, and it changed me on a microcosmic level. It simultaneously stole the innocence of my youth and scarred me for the rest of my life with doubts about whether I did the right thing or not, leaving me in a drifting state of depression, hurt, and anger—at the world, at myself, at God who put me in that position.

There's an old saying that goes *where there's smoke, there's fire.* And with Lychhurst's unscrupulous reputation, I have long believed that my mother's death wasn't because of a freak heart attack.

They did something to her—the doctors and nurses. The same doctors and nurses who took the Hippocratic oath to save lives, not take them.

I'm about to turn away when something catches my eye behind the filing cabinet. *What the...* Aiming the beam, I find a phrase has been hacked into the stone wall...

Until the fire...

What the hell does that mean?

I don't care to find out. Rushing to the door with my mother's file in hand, I crack it and peer into the hall.

It's empty.

I slip out, close the door softly behind me, and start toward the Security Office. I pass out of the dingy overhead light and back into the thick, black-as-ink shadows. I swear I can feel the darkness on my skin like I've slipped into a vat of oil, and the air is foul with rot...

What was that?

Something moved in the shadows.

Spinning on my heels, I see a silhouetted humanoid shape, somehow darker than the shadows, charging forward herky-jerky-like, as if all its joints are dislocated.

A raspy wheeze emanates from it like a man with the worst case of emphysema possible. Its large hands are curled into twisted, sharp talons that could easily open my flesh.

I feel the blood drain from my face and a shiver so deep in my core that it touches my soul. I want to move, want to flee, but I'm frozen stiff as this dark mass nears me, as I was while I watched my mother die in her hospital bed, unable to process the consequences of my actions, how my decision to end her life would change mine so drastically.

"Hey, you okay?"

Someone tugs on my shirt and pulls me from the shadows and into the light. I spin around, my heart in my throat, my chest heaving, to find a man in his late forties wearing a janitor uniform standing there.

"What?"

"You okay?" he asks with a quizzical yet concerned gaze etched on his face.

I look back into the shadows. There isn't anything there. I feel the fear of sweat on my forehead and back and the stickiness under my arms.

I could have sworn there was…

"I… I… what are you doing down here…" I say, turning and looking at the name patch sewn onto his shirt. "Clark?"

Clark holds up a tied trash bag.

"Collecting the trash, man," he says in a voice that reminds me of Tommy Chong.

"Oh." I quickly hide my mother's file behind me, hoping Clark hasn't noticed it.

"Are you sure you're okay, man?" Clark asks. "You don't look so good."

"I was…"

Think of something, quick.

"I was just looking for the can. Damn bean burritos, ya know."

"I've been there, brother. No shitter down here, though. In the lobby." He points an index finger at the ceiling.

"Right. I forgot. First night and all."

Clark studies me skeptically, much like Grady did earlier. I realize I need to shift the focus off me and onto something else so he doesn't ask more questions.

Westley Smith

"You work the overnight shift, too?" I asked.

He huffs.

"Are you kidding? I wouldn't spend the night in Lychhurst for a million dollars and a night with Cindy Crawford, man. No, my shift ends at one. Down here is the last place I clean before I head out, since it's only the Security Office."

Clark had come down the lift, and I heard him walking toward the Burn Unit. What was he really up to?

"Well, I better be getting back," I say, guiding Clark away so he can't see the file in my hand.

Together, we head toward the Security Office and the lift. There's a skunky smell coming off him that I know well—marijuana. I've smoked enough of the stuff to kill the pain, the memories of my decision.

Was that why he went to the Burn Unit, to burn one? I can't help but see the irony in him firing up a joint in that place.

Stepping into the office's threshold, I lean on the doorframe, keeping the file in my right hand hidden behind the wall.

"You have a nice night," Clark says, extending his right hand to me.

I swallow, studying his outstretched hand. My throat is dry as dust. He's expecting me to shake his hand. My first instinct is to offer him my left, but I realize how obvious it would look that I'm hiding something.

I let go of the file behind the wall, and it falls silently to the floor.

I take his hand.

"Nice to meet you, Clark."

He nods, smiles, and turns away to the lift. I look back into the security office and see the paperwork scattered across the floor.

"Oh, one more thing, man," Clark says, causing me to snap my head back to him. Though it feels awkward on my face, I force a friendly smile.

"Make sure you lock the office before stepping out, even if you're just going to the can. Clayburn discovers you left it unlocked while unattended, and he'll have you drawn and quartered."

"Thanks. It won't happen again."

Once Clark is out of sight, I hurry into the security office, gather the pages, and take them to the desk. Grabbing the phone, I tediously dial—*damn rotary phones*—Lynn's number. She picks up on the first ring.

"I found my mother's file, Lynn."

"Great. Tell me you have something juicy." She sounds downright giddy.

I begin to look through the pages. But it all looks routine—just a normal patient admitted to the hospital for appendicitis.

"This can't be…"

"What?"

I scan everything again. *No! No!*

"What is it, John? Talk to me."

But my eyes don't deceive me. And I feel that emptiness grow inside. An emptiness that has been there since the day I had to say goodbye to my mom.

I wanted to believe something nefarious was going on so I didn't have to admit to myself that my decision, as soul-crushing as it is, was an excuse to drink, get high, and hurt people I care about by pushing them away so I don't ever have to feel the pain of a loss ever again.

"John?"

"There's nothing here, Lynn," I croon out. "It all looks—"

Wait!

I spot another page, sticking out from under the desk. I had missed it in my rush to dive into the file while gathering everything.

Grabbing the paper off the floor, I raise it into the light.

It's an internal memo.

Lychhurst Hospital
Date: 7/25/89
TO: Dr. Udo Kieser
FROM: Dr. Jonas Gruber, PhD
SUBJECT: Grief Study Program

Dr. Kieser,

I recently treated a female patient for appendicitis, who I believe is a perfect subject for your Grief Study Program. According to Patient 55991, she has no living family besides her son. She's in good health, besides appendicitis (which we have treated with surgery), and is scheduled to be released in the morning – 7/26/89.

Please inform me and my team if (and how) you want to proceed. If Patient 55991 fits your research needs, we will get the ball rolling.

Sincerely,

Dr. Jonas Gruber, PhD
Lychhurst Hospital

What. The. Fuck?

I reread the memo, trying to put the pieces together. But as I do, I feel a sort of vindication coursing through my veins, warming me.

I was right!

"Lynn, I have something."

"What is it?"

"There's a memo in my mother's file. It's from the physician who treated her, Dr. Gruber, to a Dr. Kieser—Udo Kieser. The memo suggests that she was a candidate for something called the Grief Study Program."

"What the hell is that?"

"I have—"

A memory zings across my mind with such force that my temples begin to throb.

"Wait, wait, wait, wait…"

"What? John, what is it?"

"Can you find out who Udo Kieser is?" I ask.

"Let me reach out to a few contacts and see what I can do."

"I'll call you back."

I slam the phone down into the cradle. The bell dings hollowly.

I know what I saw…

Grabbing the flashlight off the desk, I rush back into the hallway, hurrying to the Records Room again. *It was there—right in front of my eyes.*

I can feel my adrenaline shooting through me like a bullet, knowing I'm on the cusp of bringing this god-forsaken place to the ground. I just need to prove…

I charge into the shadows, my mind solely focused on what I'm about to uncover when I immediately feel something grab ahold of my right ankle and rip it out from under me.

I come down hard on my stomach. The flashlight is knocked from my hand. My chin clips the concrete floor, and I bite a chunk out of my tongue. Stinging, intense pain, and the coppery taste of blood fill my mouth.

I glimpse the ominous shape I saw earlier, popping and unlocking against the dark, flanking me.

Whatever resided in the shadows of this hallway is still in here.

I rise to my knees and spit a bloody wad onto the floor while my hands search blindly for the flashlight. I feel only the cold concrete under my fingertips.

Son of a bit—

I freeze when I notice it standing before me, its silhouette highlighted against the light in the hall at its back. Its chest rises and falls, the wheezing so pronounced it echoes off the cold green walls.

Its claws *clink* and *shink* off each other like a chef sharpening his carving tools in preparation for a fine meal. The air is repugnant, thick with the smell of roadkill and rotten eggs.

Anger and rage waft off it—whatever *it* is—and fill the void around me like radiation, blistering my skin.

My hands continue to search for the flashlight.

It lunges forward at me just as my hand finds the flashlight. I bring it up, flicking on the beam in the process.

It's gone.

I shine the beam around, but it's nowhere to be found.

I remember something Grady told me earlier about needing the flashlight to get through the shadows. Was this what he meant? That whatever lurked in here feared the light?

I believe it does.

The flashlight dims. I knock my palm against the barrel, and it brightens.

Westley Smith

There's no time to doddle. I hurry out of the shadows and return to the Records Room.

Once inside, I go to the filing cabinet in the center of the room marked **--ief Study Program.**

Grief Study Program; my mind fills in the missing letters.

If I can prove that they did something to my mother so she could be admitted into the program, then Lynn would have the ammunition she needed.

The program's patient records are in the bottom drawer. Kneeling, I start going through the names, my fingers like spider legs picking through the files.

Finally, I see the name THOMPSON.

Yes! This is it.

My fingers cramp suddenly. I don't see my mother's name on the file.

I see…

My name.

THOMPSON, JOHN (18/M)

I try to swallow but can't; something at the back of my throat is clogging my esophagus.

Why is there a file on me?

I rip the file out and open it up, finding…

A *cassette tape?*

I can listen to it in the Security Office, using the radio on the desk, with the tape deck.

Just as I step out of the Records Room, the overhead light at the end of the hall, by the Isolation Ward, flickers out.

That's when I see it.

Its dark shape stands in the middle of the hallway, watching me with a hungry, eyeless gaze as if it's looking to feed on my soul. ***"TOOOOOOM!"*** it gurgles out before starting toward me with an unnatural, long gait.

I think it will stop—because it can't go into the light—but just as it is about to step into the light, the next overhead bulb flickers and then blinks out, and it keeps coming.

Oh, shit!

I turn and bolt up the hall. Behind me, I hear its thunderous footfalls on the concrete. Looking over my shoulder, I see it quickly gaining ground.

I look back and see the lights at the other end of the hall beginning to go out, one by one, starting by the Burn Ward.

It's trying to trap me in the dark.

The light from the security office spills out on the floor. If I can make it inside, the light will keep me safe.

I just need to make it…

Its massive hand hits me in the center of the back, and I'm lifted off my feet and thrown forward about five feet. I crash on my knees and faceplant into the unforgiving concrete floor.

Dazed, I climb to my feet and teeter into the wall, catching myself before I fall. The third and final light in the hall before me snaps off.

Only one light is left, the one bathing me overhead.

I lumber for the safety of the security office, my knees screaming with each step I take, my tongue swollen and thick. I feel it—whatever it is—right on my ass, its rancid stink filling the air around me like a noxious gas. I sense it's reaching for me, about to take hold and pull me into the forever darkness from which it dwells and thrives.

But I can't let that happen—not when I'm so close to exposing this wretched place and what they did to my mother, to me.

I stumble through the door into the security office just as the last overhead light goes out and slam the door shut.

The shadow figure crashes into the door, exploding into black wispy smoke tendrils like a vampire might if exposed to sunlight.

What the hell is that thing?

I rush to the desk, pull the cassette tape from the file, shove it into the tape deck with a shaking hand, and press PLAY.

A raspy voice with a thick German accent begins to speak.

Subject: Thompson, John. Age: Eighteen. Sex: Male. Case Number: 14,458

> *Phase One: Ignition*
>
> *This is Dr. Udo Keiser of Lychhurst Hospital. Dr. Jonas Gruber, PhD, is assisting me in this particular series of tests for the Grief Study Program.*

Westley Smith

> *On the twenty-fifth of July, in the year of our lord nineteen-hundred and eighty-nine, Dr. Gruber administered Patient 55991 into a medically-induced comatose state with a dose of anesthesia to lower her metabolic rate. She has been placed on a ventilator, and her vitals are being monitored by Gruber's staff. The subject will be contacted in the morning to inform him of his mother's condition.*
>
> *On to phase 2.*

There is a shuffling on the recording before it snaps off with a *click*, followed by the low hiss of static that fills the room eerily. I'm trying to understand what I've just heard when Dr. Keiser's voice comes back on.

Phase Two: The Subject

> *On the twenty-sixth of July, in the year of our lord nineteen-hundred and eighty-nine, Dr. Gruber broke the news to the subject that his mother had had a heart attack and that she was clinically brain dead. I find the subject's reaction rather fascinating. He's distraught over what he believes has happened to his beloved mother. But he's dealing with it rather favorably for someone of such a young age.*

Tears burn my cheeks.
My mother and I were unknowingly a part of some sinister study.

Phase Three: Decision

> *Dr. Gruber has informed the subject that the only humane thing to do is to take his mother off the ventilator. The subject has agreed. Still, he is holding up better than I expected, certainly better than other subjects I have observed in the past. And, what's even more striking is that he has no one to comfort him in this time of need, and yet, he's performing above and beyond what I would have suspected a boy of his age capable of. Truly remarkable...*

I want to scream. I want to tear this place apart. Set a fire and watch it burn until this entire building is a pile of ash.

The tape continues.

Phase Four: Completion

The subject performed remarkably under such pressure. He ordered Dr. Gruber and his team to remove the ventilator, and they did so as instructed. I observed the subject go through a litany of emotions—sadness, anger, frustration, and despair—all in the blink of an eye when his mother passed. And yet, when it was all over, he rose from his mother's bedside, kissed her on the forehead, and left without shedding a tear.

I wish to study him further and see what this day's long-term effects will be on him.

Alas, that is not my purpose with the program.

The results are positive but inconclusive. More studies will need to be conducted.

End of the study for Case Number 14,458.

With a trembling hand, I dial Lynn's number.

"I know what the Grief Study Program is!" I scream-mumble from my swollen tongue.

"Dr. Keiser was researching how the patients react when they're put in situations that cause extreme grief."

"John, listen to me…"

"They put her in a comatose state and then made me…"

The weight of the whole thing is too much.

"Made me… kill her."

I crumble to the floor—bawling and broken beyond repair.

"I spoke to some contacts I've made regarding Lychhurst," Lynn says.

I want to say something, but I don't have the energy now, not after what I learned.

"Dr. Keiser was a Nazi scientist. According to records, he escaped after Germany fell in forty-five. He fled first to Argentina for ten years, then to

Brazil for fifteen, and finally to the United States, ending up at Lychhurst, where he worked until he died in 1990.

"But this is where things get interesting. His studies on the effects of grief go back to the Second World War. Fearing losing support from both his military and the German people due to the massive amounts of casualties and the atrocities of the Nazis, Hitler ordered studies to be conducted on grief suppression.

"If they could find a way to disconnect those feelings, Hitler would have an entire nation standing behind him, ready to fight to the death to save the Reich.

"The first experiments, nasty ones, were done on the prisoners in concentration camps, then on the military, and finally the German citizens themselves, unknowingly, of course. Nothing worked."

"But you can't steal someone's pain, Lynn. You can't take that away from them no matter…"

The light overhead flickers.

"J-hn," the line crackles.

"Lynn?"

"—ohn?"

"Hello?"

The light snaps out, and the line goes dead.

I reach for the flashlight and flick it on. It can't get me, not in the safety of the light.

But the beam starts to shudder and dim, like the evil of this place is sucking the batteries dry.

It winks out.

The batteries!

I reach for them in the breast pocket of my shirt.

They're not there! They must have fallen out of my pocket when I was knocked to the floor.

The door creaks open.

Its nasty odor fills the room around me, gagging me.

I hear it approaching me in the dark; its wheezing like a needle inserted into my eardrums. I realize it can't let me leave, not with what I now know.

The Security Guard

This featureless black shape is the hospital's real security guard, ensuring the atrocities behind these walls are never exposed.

I'll be another victim—in a long line of victims—of Lychhurst Hospital.

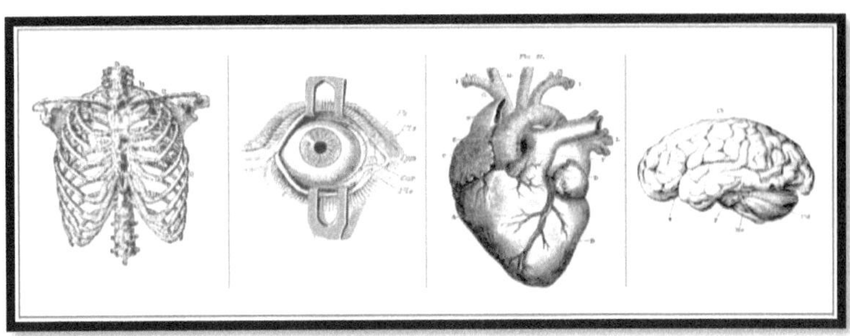

Triage Level: Yellow

Ah! I thought you might get tired again. Yes, yes, come, sit. No, I don't mind pushing.

I know! I told you the Security Office can be a mess. We're working on that.

But onward! And upward!

These next sections are still pretty fun.

You don't think *fun* is the right word?

How about *inspiring*?

Like the Maternity Ward! What's more inspiring than new life coming into the world? I just love all those sweet little babies cooing and gurgling and crying and screaming, all red-faced and demanding and always so needy all the damn time and…

Oh. I apologize. I get a little overexcited at times. As do the babies. But a lovely lullaby is always calming. To them. And their mothers. So sweet.

Pediatrics is right next door. A cheerful place, indeed. All those quiet, sleeping children up there right now, curled up in their beds. Alone. In the dark. So sweet. So innocent. Such easy prey.

Patients. Such easy patients.

And easily subdued, when needed.

But let's continue!

Yes, yes, the lift is perfectly safe, I assure you.

Let me show you some of the most fascinating places in the hospital.

The Sleep Lab does amazing work. I just love seeing all those big strong men in there, whimpering in their sleep like babies. Isn't that funny? Not so strong then, are they? And the less sleep they get, the more fascinating they become.

In a medical sense, of course. For research.

The Imaging Lab is full of all kinds of interesting machines. I just love technology, don't you? We can see so many things inside the human body…

Blood.

Organs.

Bones.

Souls.

Oh? Yes, of course, Just a bit of wishful thinking.

Maybe.

No, no. Ignore me! It's just all this roaming the halls at night—it makes my brain a bit addled at times. But nothing to worry about.

The Surgery Ward is the most beautiful part of the hospital, by far. Of course it's all broken up into individual spaces now, but can't you just picture how it was in the beginning, a doctor performing his art in the center of the room, students watching on the risers that surround him like some sort of gloriously macabre play?

And, oh, the screaming! When the ether wore off, the pitches those patients' voices could reach were nothing short of celestial.

Of course, not everyone made it off the operating table alive, but such is the cost of medical advancement. Progress is built on a hill of dead bodies.

Oh! That's what Lychhurst means, did you know? *Lych* means corpse, and *hurst* means hill. So you put them together and *voila!* Corpse Hill. A great name, don't you think?

Oh, no. I've upset you.

I apologize.

It's not all doom and gloom and death here!

I love seeing people make full recoveries in the Rehab Ward. Not everyone makes it out healed…or breathing. But we certainly do our best to make them happy, no matter what. Dr. Wade is particularly wonderful at making patients feel comfortable and relaxed. Perhaps you'll meet him if you just peek your head in for a moment.

Go on.

I'll be right here.

Rehab Ward
2018

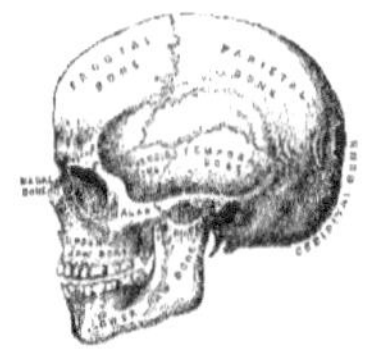

Insensate
Stephen Mark Rainey

May 2018, Lychhurst, West Virginia:

"How do you feel?"

The voice might not have been a voice. It didn't sound human. More the buzzing of a swarm of bees somehow modulated to form words. But the thing hovering in near-darkness before William Caswell's eyes was no massed congregation of bees.

It resembled a man—if a man could be molded from a column of roiling smoke that somehow held its shape. In the center of a billowing bulge atop the wavering "body," a pair of golden slits blazed with intelligence.

"How do you feel?" The buzzing voice sounded more insistent.

Caswell forced his eyes to lock onto those fiery slits.

"I feel nothing."

It was the truth.

November, 2017, Aiken Mill, Virginia:

He had killed his mother.

Yes, I killed my mom.

No, she hadn't been his mother anymore. The dementia had robbed that frail shell of every vestige of self, of soul, and the "life" he had escorted from this world had been nothing more than collection of neurons that had forgotten to stop firing. The organic vehicle might have remained animated—if just barely—but the pilot had long ago abandoned it.

He had loved his mom, loved her *so* much. But that goddamn disease had crowded her right out of her own body. So many years, so many doctors, so much heartbreak.

The toll it took on him, as her caregiver, had soared beyond any measurable cost. Destroyed his marriage. All but bankrupted him. Damn near caused him a stroke at age forty-eight.

And, finally, turned him fucking *numb*.

That was it. To preserve his mind and body, he'd exiled his emotions, sealed them in a dark, escape-proof prison where they couldn't undermine what remained of his health.

That prison, though, had not been entirely escape-proof.

His mother had become argumentative, even belligerent, and started swearing—which *Mom* never would have done. When he drove her to the doctor's office, she'd rail at traffic lights that stayed red too long for her liking.

Mom wouldn't do that.

She began wandering away from the house, usually late at night. Not *Mom*, she couldn't have dreamed of doing anything so foolhardy.

On that night, only few months ago, she'd gotten outside and begun ambling toward the woods. She'd made enough noise fiddling with the three locks that it awakened him.

Once he figured out what she'd done, he took off after her and glimpsed her pale, unsteady figure in the cloud-diffused moonlight—heading straight for a rocky drop-off above a stream.

When he'd reached her, she'd been babbling angry nonsense, and his emotions came roaring out of their prison just long enough for him to reach forward and, rather than pull her to safety, nudge that animated shell over the edge.

And that was it. Officially, a terrible accident. Despite his precautions to stop her wandering, she'd gotten out of the house and, in the dark, tumbled to her death.

Such a tragedy.

Afterward, his emotions had retreated into their dark prison, and that was where they seemed destined to remain. He could not even grieve for *Mom*, for his memory of her seemed to go only as far back as the dementia's onset.

Occasionally, he would look at himself in the mirror and say, "I feel horrified. I feel sorrow. I feel guilt. I feel remorse."

Every word of it was a lie.

May 11, 2018, Silver Ridge, West Virgnia:
Three mornings running, it happened.

As he had for a couple of months now, Caswell had started his day searching for a new teaching job—somewhere, anywhere.

During those final weeks of his mother's decline, due to his excessive time off, he'd lost his position as math teacher at Aiken Mill High School. After her passing, though, the high school in Silver Ridge, West Virginia, had accepted his application. This required him to move, but it didn't matter a whit, since he no longer felt any ties to his old hometown.

However, in only a matter of weeks, he'd lost that job as well because, according to the administration, "he established no connection with his students and failed to enforce any discipline whatsoever."

True enough, he supposed.

He more than half-suspected his days in the classroom now lay behind him, but he knew no other profession. So, he kept at it.

He'd inherited just enough from his mother's all-but-exhausted estate to keep from starving, but he could hardly go forever—even a few more months, for that matter—without any regular income.

As he'd sat at his aging desktop computer, his phone, resting on the desk beside him, sprang to life without warning.

"Turn right on Morgan Creek Road."

The voice of the lady navigator inside the phone, whom he seldom trusted when trying to get anywhere.

He picked up his phone and looked at the screen.

Indeed, as it had these past few mornings, the Google Maps app had opened itself and now displayed a route from his little rental house, a short distance out of town on Morgan Creek Road, to *somewhere* at least four backroads away, a distance of about twenty miles.

But at the location marked by the destination pin, there was nothing. Nothing labeled, anyway. When he switched from map view to aerial view, he saw only a blob of deep forest and what *might* be the contours of some structure the trees had long ago swallowed.

He rather disliked the lady in the phone.

When he'd first moved to Silver Ridge, he had directed her to navigate to a grocery store in town. On the way, he had detoured to get gas. While there, he'd studied the street map, and—without alerting the lady—found what appeared to be a quicker route to the store.

All the way there, until he was sitting in the store's parking lot, she'd nagged him to do a U-turn, return to the gas station, and follow *her* route.

He had refused, and the two of them had not been on speaking terms since.

He had no idea what kind of glitch could cause his phone to randomly attempt to lead him out to the middle of nowhere, and until now, he had ignored it.

Yet, this time, the lady seemed somehow more insistent, and for a brief second, he felt a twinge of both annoyance and curiosity. The moment passed, and that emerging hint of emotion fled back to its familiar dark place.

But he was done here. He'd applied to one school—in Point Pleasant, of all places—and that had been it for any suitable teaching opportunities.

His recollection of the grocery store experience reminded him he needed to pick up some food for the refrigerator as well as coffee for the machine.

He'd used the last of it this morning, and going without was not an option. Perhaps, while out running his necessary errand, he should follow the lady's navigation instructions and discover where they led him.

Escaping from the house's confines for a time might do some good for his damn near insensate mind.

In fact, better to drive there first, before he picked up a carload of perishable items.

His 2011 Nissan Rogue had over 100,000 miles on it, and he could only hope it would hold out for the foreseeable future. He sure as hell couldn't afford a new vehicle, and nowadays, even used cars—or "pre-owned," as they insisted on calling them—came with ungodly price tags.

If he intended to make this one last a few more years, it might be better not to embark on some unknown quest. And even in this relatively rural area, gas wasn't cheap.

As if to spite the numbness, the *deadness*, that had become his constant companion, a curious impulse to explore overwhelmed him.

Half-convinced he might be less sane now than at any other moment of his life, with his Google map still open and the lady navigator waiting with uncustomary patience, he set out in his Rogue, bound for someplace that, by all indications, looked like a whole lot of nothing in the middle of a whole lot of nowhere.

"Continue on Morgan Creek Road for five miles."

The lady's cheerier-than-usual delivery suggested his decision must have satisfied her.

May 11, 2018, Lychhurst, West Virginia

"Jesus. Where the hell am I?"

The navigator had led Caswell out these shadowy, secluded backroads until he finally arrived at a point perhaps a quarter-mile short of the location pin on the map. Here, he found a half-hidden opening in the dense trees, just wide enough for him to glimpse the cracked, weed-choked remains of an asphalt road that led up a long incline into the woods.

From the two stained, lichen-covered yellow posts to either side of the opening, he gathered it had once been chained off. Not anymore.

A little farther in, he made out a pair of stone columns that had almost certainly once borne a sign for whatever establishment lay up the road, still well out of view.

A hotel, maybe? Some long-closed resort? There sure as hell wasn't much of anything around here, civilization-wise.

He knew West Virginia boasted its share of ski lodges, but while the terrain was hardly flat out here, he didn't figure it was high or steep enough for ski slopes. Those mostly lay farther east, in the mountainous regions.

A sharp, female voice from his phone startled him. "GPS signal lost."

The lady seemed less happy now. Still, he'd come this far. Might as well see it through.

He turned the Rogue into the opening and, at little more than a creep, started up the incline.

To his surprise, he found the road wide and relatively straight, though in many places, nature had done a job on its surface. Weeds and tree roots had erupted through the cracked asphalt, and numerous tree limbs hung low on either side, which forced him to weave around them.

Then, as he rounded a long curve, he hit the brakes. A short distance ahead, a huge, rotting pine had fallen across the road, blocking any further ingress—at least by vehicle.

"Well, shit."

Still, he couldn't be far from his destination, whatever it might be.

He grabbed his phone, shoved the car door open, and slid out, minding that he didn't step into a pothole or fissure that might turn an ankle. Upon locking the vehicle's doors, he clambered over the fallen tree and trudged forward.

The service icon on his phone showed only a circle with a bar through it; hardly a surprise way out here. But even the location icon had disappeared. The phone's GPS didn't rely on available cell service to connect with the global positioning satellite system.

Curiouser and curiouser.

A couple of hundred feet farther on, amid the dense trees, he glimpsed a series of broad, angular contours that suggested some kind of sprawling structure.

Another hundred feet, and he drew to a sudden halt, awestruck by the brooding hulk that now rose out of the woods before him.

"Jesus."

He faced a gigantic, crumbling, Victorian monstrosity with a central, four-story block from which a pair of three-story wings extended in either direction. At each end, these adjoined another set of perpendicular three-story wings.

Tall, gnarled trees grew up to—and in some cases, *out of*—the building's myriad dark windows, most of which appeared either boarded up or shattered. Up a long, semicircular flight of stairs, a huge, gaping doorway, like a yawning mouth, revealed a well of impenetrable darkness.

If a truly haunted-looking structure ever existed on this planet, he had found it.

To his right, he noticed a large, fallen sign emblazoned with the word "EMERGENCY" and an arrow that pointed to the right.

A hospital? But way the hell out there?

For a few moments, he debated proceeding farther. But he had hardly come this far to discover something like this, turn around, and go home.

He kept a flashlight in his vehicle, but he felt no inclination to hike all the way back to fetch it. He'd charged his phone in the car, so it indicated almost one-hundred percent power. The phone's flashlight had a powerful beam, so he'd have to make do with it if he intended to set foot inside this incredible relic from God knew when.

Acute curiosity had crept from its prison to compel him forward.

In front of the building, a circular turnaround extended from the road toward the front door. The road itself veered to the right, presumably leading to the emergency room entrance and a parking area, which the trees had totally overtaken.

A disintegrating, bramble-choked concrete walkway led from the turnaround to the stairs. He took slow, careful steps toward them, eyes flicking in every direction to ascertain that no hidden hazards might trip, snag, or skewer him, and thus end this venture before it began.

A sudden, sharp sound from somewhere nearby froze him in mid-step. A shrill, squeaking sound, ending in a harsh creak, like the rusted hinges of an old gate swinging open.

As if in response, a second, similar sound rose in the distance, soon followed by more and more, until it sounded like a chorus of rusty iron gates swinging open and shut somewhere in the shadows.

He sighed. Birds. Just birds.

Grackles.

Shaking off his discomfiture, he mounted the stairs and ascended to the veranda. A length of chain lay on the moldy concrete before the gaping double doors; at one time, the place must have been sealed up.

Inside, he could see only a short distance before darkness swallowed the sparse daylight that filtered down through the branches. He turned on his phone flashlight, aimed the beam into the darkness, and followed it inside.

His foot had barely crossed the threshold when, with sudden *whoosh* and roaring of air, a cyclone of pure darkness descended on him and extinguished every vestige of light that had ever illuminated his world.

"How do you feel?"

The low voice drew Caswell back to the moment like a slap across his cheek. Stark white light dispelled the darkness before his eyes. He realized it came from a fluorescent fixture in the ceiling of the small room where he stood.

"I feel nothing," he said. And he meant it.

"What's that?" A low, hoarse voice, barely more than a groan.

It took several moments for him to realize the first voice had been his. *He* had asked the question.

He stood in what appeared to be a hospital room. A single window— tall, with ornate framework and panes that looked like thick, leaded glass— admitted a trickle of sunlight from outside.

In the narrow, railed bed before him, a withered figure, connected to an IV and an oxygen hose, lay partially covered by a dull white sheet. The skin covering the narrow skull looked thin, almost transparent, tinted pale gray. Feathery wisps of white hair hung from the temples like desiccated dove wings.

Murky, gray-blue eyes stared at him with obvious incomprehension. He couldn't tell whether this person was male or female.

"What did you say, Doctor Wade?" The voice creaked like an ancient door drawing shut.

Caswell glanced down and saw that he was dressed in a white lab coat, gray pants, and white rubber shoes. At his left breast, a small name plate adorned the coat.

Once he'd managed to decipher the small, upside-down print, he realized it read "DR. DAVID C. WADE, PHYSICAL MEDICINE AND REHABILITATION."

Pure emotion crashed into him with the force of a tsunami.

Confusion. Curiosity. Incomprehension.

Shock.

His memory, his thoughts, his perceptions, everything seemed scrambled. Was this right? What was he doing here? Where the hell was *here*?

His gaze fell on a whiteboard mounted to the faded, cream-colored plaster wall next to the bed. On it, printed in blue marker, he saw the name "Wilma Cotten."

Below the name, clearly the patient's, a barely legible scribble read, "Your 1st shift nurse today is Loretta Jackson, RN."

He barely heard the soft murmur. "I'm not hurting so much now, Doctor."

Nothing made sense here. Not this room, not this bedridden individual, not the strange, silent directives that seemed to flow from somewhere beyond his consciousness. The last thing he recalled was a female voice saying something about a GPS.

What the hell was a GPS?

He gazed down at the pathetic-looking creature before him. His heart ached at the sight of her. So much pain.

But he didn't even know who *he* was. Where he was. Or when.

"What year is this?" His voice sounded far, far away.

"Eh? Doctor?"

A voice that sounded like some weirdly modulated buzzing of bees: "Don't you remember?"

His eyes fell on a calendar next to the whiteboard.

December 1993.

That could *not* be right.

Could it?

The only certainty in his mind now was that *no one* should suffer like this woman. A little thread of memory wriggled from his inexplicable, internal darkness. Tuberculosis. Terminal. Wilma Cotten was in rehab.

Rehab?

She's going to fucking die!

Something moved at the corner of his eye, somewhere in the shadows beyond the door to the hallway.

A shadow within shadow, just distinct enough for him to recognize a woman's figure, with a hint of dark, billowing sleeves at her sides, a pale frock tied in the middle over her dress.

Bright eyes shining at him like jewels in the sun.

Somehow, he recognized her. He—whoever *he* was—had seen this figure before. Initially fearsome, yet now familiar, as if it were the half-corporeal manifestation of some dark, kindred spirit.

His body moved, not by any volition of his own, but by some kind of programming, it seemed. He was an automaton, witnessing what was happening from inside this body, whoever it belonged to, but not controlling it. He inhabited the physical envelope, but it was not *him*.

Yet it was.

"I'm glad you feel better." He touched the woman's skeletal arm with involuntary tenderness.

The unknown force guided his hand into his coat pocket. It withdrew an unlabeled vial of clear liquid. Then a sealed syringe, which he unwrapped.

"This is not me. I am not from his time." His voice again, now a hoarse whisper.

"Eh? Doctor Wade?"

He shook his head again, trying to clear the cobwebs. They didn't go anywhere.

"You're going to be fine." He inserted the needle into the rubber cap of the vial, drew almost a full syringe, and dropped the vial back into his pocket.

"Just a few moments, and everything will be lovely."

He inserted the needle into the saline lock in the IV tube. Pressed the plunger.

Potassium Chloride. Quick. Not likely to leave a trace.

He stepped back, replaced the plastic cap on the needle, and thrust the syringe back into his coat pocket.

She was gone in a few moments. A momentary look of confusion in those dull eyes. And that was all.

This was Rehab at Lychhurst. Quick. Efficient.

Merciful.

"How do you feel?"

The almost-familiar, buzzing voice. Near-darkness again surrounded him.

A smoky figure, roiling, shifting, wavering before his eyes.

A pair of gleaming slits watching him.

He shook his head. "I feel nothing."

Mostly true. Or at least partly.

"You're a doctor, aren't you?" The soft voice sounded confused.

"Yes," came the voice from his mouth. "I am Doctor Wade."

No. Not my name.

"You have a kind face."

An impulse that originated from somewhere else drew his lips into a smile.

"How do you feel?"

"I..." A little frown darkened the ancient woman's wrinkled face, and her gaze seemed to turn inward. "I don't think I need a doctor. I need to go home."

Mrs. Hastings, little more than a skeleton now, lay in her narrow bed with her back partially raised. Alzheimer's, late stage, mostly docile, occasionally argumentative, frequently delusional.

Three months ago, she'd wandered outside her home, fallen, and broken her left arm. Her husband had brought her to Lychhurst, left her here, and no one had come to visit her since. The bills were being paid, but by all indications, she had been otherwise abandoned.

At the moment, she seemed calm enough, but she'd been agitated all evening. When he'd come in and checked her blood pressure, it was through the roof. One-ninety over one-twenty.

How do I know all this?

"Do you remember your home?" His own voice sounded alien. *Wrong.*

"Of course, I—" She stopped, frowned again. "It feels like a long way away." Her wide brown eyes scanned the room. A shadow of fear crossed her features. "What is this place? Where am I?"

"You were injured, and you are in the hospital, in the rehabilitation center. You're getting much better. I expect you'll be leaving here soon." His hand lowered to his coat pocket and withdrew a soft rubber ball. He reached for her left hand, no longer in a cast, and gently placed the ball in her palm.

"Can you squeeze this for me?"

She appeared to think for a moment, glanced at the ball, and gave it a brief squeeze.

"Did that hurt?"

She shook her head, but now her eyes narrowed at him. "You hurt me!"

"No, I didn't hurt you. You had an accident. And you're getting much better. Would you squeeze the ball again, please?"

Mrs. Hastings shook her head. "No!" Then she hurled the ball toward the dark window. "I want to go home."

The ball had bounced off the wall and rolled back toward the bed. As he bent down to grab it, his eyes fell on the calendar on the wall beside her bed.

May 1977.

"What?" The voice that came out didn't sound like his. "This can't be right." His body straightened, but every muscle seemed to have a will of its own.

Not my body.

He must be as confused as this poor creature. Alzheimer's wasn't contagious, but his mind felt jumbled, somehow dissociated.

In the shadows beyond the door to the hallway, a familiar figure stood, watching, the pale frock and the bright eyes all he could make out in the darkness.

"You tried to hurt me." His patient's voice, raw and angry, drew his attention back to her.

"Not at all," he said, trying to sound soothing, but a twinge of anxiety buzzed at his temples. He hated when his mother got agitated. "You…" His voice trailed away.

Mrs. Hastings was *not* his mother!

"What did you say?" The woman's eyes glared at him. "And what is wrong with you? I want to go home!" Her voice became a near-hysterical shout. "I *need* to go home!"

A flash of memory reminded him why he had come here.

"I need to give you an injection," he said, barely above a whisper. "Just something to make you feel better."

He took the syringe, vial, and alcohol swab packet from his coat pocket.

"What the hell are you doing? You're not a doctor!"

"Yes, Mrs. Hastings, I am your doctor. I'm Doctor Wade."

No, no, I'm not!

"I know you're uncomfortable right now. I just want to make you feel better."

He realized his heart had begun to pound like a jackhammer.

At least she wasn't thrashing or acting violently, as she did on occasions. He filled the syringe, leaned close to her, and whispered a lulling, "You're going to feel better. You're going to feel better."

She didn't move or protest as he swabbed inside her elbow and located the median basilic vein, prominent beneath her thin, parchment-like skin. Thankfully, his fingers didn't tremble. Somehow, with his usual adept hand, he inserted the needle, pressed the syringe plunger, and drew the needle back out.

Her demeanor had returned to docile and pleasant as quickly it had risen to angry. "You have a kind face," she said with a little smile.

He smiled back at her, but now his chest hurt because he had been holding his breath during the injection. He released the lungful of air, recapped the syringe, and thrust it back into his pocket. The evidence would need to be destroyed.

It shouldn't take long for the methylamphetamine to do its work. With her blood pressure being so high, stroking out was inevitable.

She had recognized the kindness in his face, for he *was* showing her kindness. The agony of her existence would soon fade away.

Still, he found himself forcing back tears, for he felt no animosity toward her. Only a profound need to show her mercy. But it was hard. So damned hard.

It will get easier.

Wait. How did he know this would get easier?

HOW DID HE KNOW?

Caswell shook himself, unsure what had happened, where he'd been—or where he was standing, even at this moment. Darkness surrounded him, though it wasn't total. His phone flashlight was still on.

The beam fell on the dirty, cracked plaster walls of a small room, empty but for refuse strewn around the floor—old drink bottles and cans, what looked like some ragged old clothes, and clusters of sticks and leaves from outside.

Then the beam lit on a tall window with ornate framework. The stark white light reflected on a partially intact glass pane. Outside, it was dark.

He smelled something sharp, smoky, *heady*, and he recognized it from…some hidden moment from the past.

Corn whiskey.

Moonshine!

"What is going on here?"

He remembered driving out to the middle of nowhere and finding the ruins of a big, Victorian building. He'd stepped inside, and…

Oh, my God, was that where he was now? But it had been daylight then—late morning. What the hell had happened to him?

His phone battery showed only three percent power remaining.

"Really?"

Picking his steps carefully, he made his way across the uneven, trash-strewn floor to the window. Yes, it was nighttime out there.

A cool breeze wafted through the openings where the thick, leaded glass panes had broken out. Outside, highlighted by his flashlight beam, he saw clusters of leaves and gnarled tree branches pressing close to the exterior wall. He leaned outside and looked down.

Jesus, he was three floors up. How in Christ's name had he gotten here? He'd never lost time in his life, not even when he'd drunk himself damn near into oblivion, back when Mom was going through the worst of her struggle.

Mom. Oh, God, Mom.

A series of images flashed through his mind—of hospital rooms, medical equipment, old people.

The name "Wade" crept out from his fragmented memory.

Wade. A familiar name. But how so?

Yes, that was it. The owners of the house he'd rented in Silver Ridge. He remembered the middle-aged gentleman—Zack Wade, that was his name—mentioning that his father had died and left the house to him and his wife. They had decided to put it up for rent.

Zack's father. A doctor.

Doctor Wade.

"How do you feel?" The voice came from behind him. It sounded like the droning of bees, somehow modulated to form intelligible syllables.

He spun around, leading with his phone flashlight. The light abruptly vanished.

Power dead.

As his eyes adjusted, he found he could barely make out the room in the little moonlight that crept in through the window. Something was in the room with him.

He saw a pair of gleaming gold slits.

Eyes!

Eyes full of intelligence, of intent. They hovered near the top of some roiling, wavering column of what looked like smoke—almost in the shape of a human figure.

Caswell's mouth went as dry and rough as sandpaper.

He'd encountered this thing already. His memory felt cloudy, muddled, but he somehow recognized what he was seeing.

"Why am I here?" His voice came out like the rasp of a dull saw blade on hardwood.

The buzzing sound formed words again. "Because our beings touched. Because of where you settled to live."

"How is that possible?"

"You and I are of a kind. Once you came here, we joined, so that you might bear witness."

Those images in his mind. Little by little, they began to come together. Now, Caswell could barely draw a breath.

"That was you I saw? Like I was *inside* you? Those things you did…"

The buzzing came again. "You saw the first and the last acts."

"But there were more."

A long silence. "So many that needed help. That needed mercy. You yourself have committed such a merciful act."

"Merciful?" He felt tears beginning to burn in his eyes. "I killed my mom. It was horrible. It was wrong. *I* was wrong."

"You saved yourself. You would have died otherwise."

"Maybe I *should* have died. Don't you know what this has done to me?"

The smoke figure began to glide toward him, slowly. He took a step back, but he could only retreat as far as the window.

"Yes. We joined. I feel the agony inside you."

"It was because my mother—she wasn't *mine* anymore. She was gone. So far gone."

Now the thing hovered only a yard in front of him. He could feel waves of cold radiating from the figure.

His voice almost failed him. "What happens now?"

Another long silence before the droning voice began again.

"What *should* happen now?"

Only one thing came to his mind. "Penitence."

"Penitence." Another silence. "Yes. Penitence. But do you also believe in mercy?"

He didn't know how to answer that. But he nodded.

"Do you wish to receive mercy?"

Hot tears now streamed from Caswell's eyes. "I do."

A streamer of smoke, which almost resembled an arm, rose from the figure's side and extended toward him. The golden slits brightened.

As the leading edge of the arm made contact with his chest, ice swept over and through his entire body. Then, as if from a point above his head, he saw the shell that had been *him* drop onto the warped, littered floor. A heavy *thump* reverberated through the dark room.

The cold sensation gradually passed, to be replaced by an odd sense of tranquility. A feeling—a state of mind—he had not known in so long that he could not remember it.

He knew his body lay on the floor. Yet his *awareness* still hovered above it. With what he could only think of as an effort of will, he turned his *awareness* away from the figure until the window slid into his field of vision.

In one of the intact panes, he saw a new pair of glinting, yellow-gold eyes floating within a column of roiling smoke.

Then he felt himself drifting. Moving silently through the dark corridors of the vast, hulking structure. He became aware that other shadowy, smoky beings drifted in this darkness, yet on many different levels of existence. Some were not like him at all. Some might never have been human.

Was *this* mercy?

As he drifted, the drone of bees rose again from somewhere around him.

"How do you feel?"

The thing that had been William Caswell slid into the walls, so that only a pair of gleaming eyes stared out from the cracked, crumbling plaster.

"Fine," came his low, buzzing voice. "I feel fine."

Sleep Lab
1865

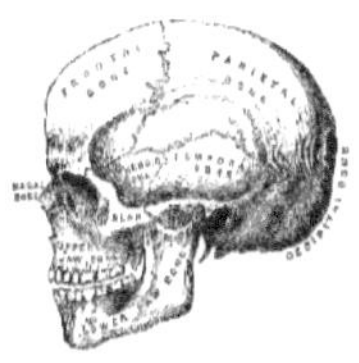

Dreams of the Damned
Marie Lanza

Private Thomas Harlow stood amidst the carnage; the stench of death and gunpowder filled his nostrils.

The battlefield stretched out around him, a grim picture of the twisted bodies of broken men under an orchard of peach trees. The once-green fields were now a wasteland of blood and mud.

Pink petals fluttered down around him, gently falling on his dirty uniform. His hands shook and his knuckles were white as he clutched his rifle. He listened to the distant cries of the wounded, their voices merging into a haunting symphony of agony.

He took a step forward, his boots sinking into the wet, spongy earth, and looked around. His eyes scanned over the faces of the fallen. He recognized them—men he had fought beside, men he had laughed and cried with.

The pink petals, some still pristine, others darkened with the blood of the young men who lay beneath them, covered the bodies like confetti.

As Thomas passed by the bodies, the dead soldiers' eyes began to open. One by one, they began to stir. Their limbs moved with a grotesque, jerky motion, as if pulled by invisible strings.

Thomas's breath caught in his throat and his heart pounded in his chest. He tried to move, to run, but his legs refused to obey.

The first soldier rose to his feet, his uniform stained crimson, his flesh burned. Muscle and tendon hung in place of his right arm. His eyes were a haze of gray. He turned to face Thomas, his gaze piercing and cold.

One by one, the others followed, rising from the ground like marionettes brought to life by a malevolent force.

Their lifeless expressions seemed to accuse him, as if blaming him for surviving.

Thomas's mouth went dry, and he could feel the icy tendrils of fear creeping up his spine.

The dead soldiers formed a circle around him, their mangled bodies swaying as they stood. They didn't speak, didn't make a sound, but their eyes—those haunting, accusing eyes—never left him.

Thomas wanted to scream, but no words came out. His voice was trapped in his throat, choked by terror. He could feel their silent judgment pressing down on him like a weight.

The dead soldiers surrounded him and began slowly closing in. They reached out for him as they moved closer.

Thomas's legs betrayed him, and he collapsed to the ground.

"I'm sorry! Pl-please, I'm sorry!" He begged for forgiveness.

As the dead were inches from reaching him, Thomas woke screaming and gasping for breath. Sweat drenched his body, and his heart was still racing. He was no longer on the battlefield, but in his bed. For a moment, his mind struggled to separate the nightmare from his reality. He could still see their faces, still feel their eyes on him.

He jumped out of bed screaming, trying to get away from the dead. His feet found a corner of the dark room and he collapsed against the wall. He closed his eyes, trying to calm his racing thoughts, but the dead rising flashed through his mind. Thomas ran his fingers over his head, clenched his hair, and began to cry.

When the bedroom door opened, his wife Lyla, holding a candle, entered the room. "Thomas?" she asked, staring at the empty bed.

Movement in the dark corner of the room caught her attention. "Thomas?"

As she approached, she found her husband sitting, holding his knees close to his chest.

"Are you alright?"

Thomas just held a blank stare.

"Sweetheart, please… please let me help you back to bed," Lyla whispered.

"No…" He met her gaze.

"Your mind isn't right, Thomas. Please. You need to sleep," she said.

"They find me there…" His eyes moved to the bed. "They find me in my dreams."

It was the spring of 1865. Lychhurst Hospital was a grim fortress of brick and mortar. It stood isolated in the hills of West Virginia and its silhouette was a dark stain against the blue sky.

Thomas, escorted by two nurses, walked down the sterile halls. His clothing hung from his thin frame and his eyes were hollow from months of sleepless nights. The walls were thick with the stench of carbolic and the low moans of men too broken to die. Beneath the murmur of voices and the shuffling of footsteps, he caught the faint sound of a gurney being pushed, its creaky, squeaky wheel just audible. The noise seemed to trail them, always just below the level of the conversation, a persistent whisper in the back of his mind.

The nurses took Thomas to a stairwell. A sign above the door read *Basement Level 1*. They walked down a dark set of stairs to another hall.

Thomas ran his eyes over a sign reading *Isolation, Records, Burn Unit, Sleep Lab*. There were arrows showing in which direction they would find their destination. They turned right for the Sleep Lab.

A tall man wearing a white coat approached. He welcomed Thomas with a firm handshake.

"Private Harlow, welcome. I am Doctor Cyril Cole. I will be working with you during your stay here. Please follow me." Doctor Cole turned and walked further down the hall.

The lab was a large open space. It had no windows, and the only light came from flickering oil lamps that cast long shadows across the damp walls. There were beds along each wall and dividers between them. A long table was in the center of the room, and thick leather-bound journals lay on every surface.

"Will there be others here?" Thomas asked as he scanned the empty beds.

"Not yet, but in due course," Doctor Cole said with a smile. "This endeavor, the exploration of sleep, is quite novel to this institution. I am grateful for your willingness to take part."

Thomas felt Doctor Cole studying him and knew that his eyes betrayed how much he was questioning this decision.

"You have been through so much, Private Harlow. Here, we look to understand the nightmares that plague our brave soldiers. Perhaps, even cure them."

Thomas gave a small nod.

"Please, take a walk with me," Doctor Cole said.

They left the confines of the hospital and stepped outside into a courtyard.

"Private, I hope there are no doubts of the purpose behind our sleep study here. We aim not just to treat, but to understand a soldier's heart."

Thomas glanced at the doctor and his brow furrowed. "Sir, if I may speak freely, I don't rightly see how watching a man sleep can help with the horrors he faces in his waking hours, much less the dreams that haunt him."

Doctor Cole nodded his head. "A fair point, Private, and plainly spoken. Consider, though, that the mind is a battlefield as complex and daunting as any you've encountered. In sleep, the defenses are down, and the mind parades its fears and memories like soldiers on review. What I hope to do, through observing these dreams, is to identify the enemy hiding… be it guilt, terror, or sorrow… and then to strategize our approach in helping you to face it."

They stopped beside a small pond. The surface was a perfect reflection, mirroring the men.

"Think of it as scouting, if you will," Doctor Cole continued. "In your dreams, we see the shape and form of the adversary. With this knowledge, we can better prepare you for the skirmishes you face when awake, ensuring you do not fight them alone."

Thomas looked out over the water, considering the doctor's words. He stared at his own reflection and didn't even recognize himself. "And what of those dreams that seem as real as you standing before me now? What of the dreams that follow me into the day?"

"That, Private Harlow, is precisely why we must venture into this realm of sleep. These phantoms that pursue you into the light of day are the very foes I aim to disarm," Doctor Cole replied.

Thomas nodded slowly and his expression softened. "I reckon that's a cause I can stand to fight for, Doctor."

"Excellent," Doctor Cole smiled, clapping Thomas on the shoulder. "Then let us begin our work together, with hope as our ally. And remember, Private, in this fight, you are never alone."

Doctor Cole and Private Thomas Harlow made their way back toward the hospital.

Ahead of them, in the courtyard walking in their direction, Thomas noticed a young nurse carrying a tray of glass bottles and metal instruments, carefully navigating the loose cobblestones. Suddenly, a little boy ran by. As he passed Thomas, he turned and flashed a mischievous smile. He looked about seven years old, with blond hair, light eyes, and his left arm missing.

Could he be a patient here? A nurse's son?

"Watch out!" Thomas shouted.

The boy darted past the nurse's feet, unseen by her. The tray flew from her grasp, crashing to the ground with a harsh mixture of clinks and clatters that shattered the quiet afternoon.

Instantaneously, Thomas's body tensed and his face blanched; the sudden noise sent him back to the battlefields, where the air was alive with bullets and the blasts of artillery. Without conscious thought, his muscles coiled and propelled him to the ground, his arms shielding his head as he dove for cover.

Doctor Cole was startled by Thomas's sudden movement but quickly realized the cause. The courtyard, for a moment, became a field of war in

Thomas's mind. Doctor Cole rushed to his side and placed a firm, calm hand on Thomas's shoulder.

"Private Harlow, it's alright. You're safe," he said in a soothing tone, attempting to anchor the young soldier back to reality.

Thomas slowly lifted his eyes to Doctor Cole as the echoes of the crash died away.

The nurse, her cheeks flushed with embarrassment and concern, hurried over to help Doctor Cole and Thomas.

"I'm so sorry, Private Harlow. I didn't mean to startle you," she said.

Doctor Cole waved her away as he helped Thomas to his feet, keeping a steady grip on his arm.

"Are you alright? Is the boy alright?" Thomas asked.

"A boy?" Doctor Cole asked. "There are no children here, Thomas."

Thomas's eyes darted around the grounds, scanning every corner.

"Take a deep breath, Thomas. You're at Lychhurst Hospital, remember? There are no bullets here, only friends."

Thomas's chest heaved as he drew in a deep, shuddering breath. The imagined dangers receded, leaving behind only the reality of his surroundings.

"I—I'm sorry, Doctor," Thomas muttered, his voice hoarse with the residue of fear. "It's just..."

"There's no need for apologies, Private. What you experienced is a vivid reminder of why you're here. Let's use this moment to learn and strengthen your defenses against these intrusions," Doctor Cole reassured him, guiding him gently to a nearby bench.

"Where did you go in that moment?" he asked.

"Back on the battlefield," Thomas simply said. "Noises, they… they seem to be ten times louder than they were before the war. Like cannon fire."

They sat down on the bench, and for a few minutes soaked in the quiet. The doctor's presence calmed Thomas as he regained his composure.

"Seems I've got a lot more fighting to do," Thomas whispered.

Doctor Cole nodded and said, "And fight you shall, but not alone, Thomas. We'll battle these ghosts together, and we'll win. Now, let's get you back to the lab, so you can get some rest."

"Rest…" Thomas whispered. He couldn't remember the last time he had rested.

Doctor Cole and Thomas stood.

"Nurse!" Doctor Cole called the young nurse back over. "The nurse will escort you back to the lab. You should get washed up and comfortable. For this first night, I want you to go to sleep like you normally would. I'll return to the lab in a few hours, and monitor you," Doctor Cole said.

Thomas nodded and watched the doctor cross the courtyard.

"This way, sir," the young nurse said with her hand out to guide his way.

Thomas was escorted to his small space in the lab that had a plain cot and a washbasin. He sat on the cot as if to test its comfort. The coarse fabric of the blankets scratched at his skin.

Thomas lay in bed with the covers pulled to his chest. He stared at the ceiling, feeling the pull of sleep but not wanting to let it take him. From the hallway outside his room, he heard the familiar faint sound of a gurney being pushed, its creaky, squeaky wheels echoing through the quiet. The noise seemed to grow louder, then fade, only to return again, creating an uneasy rhythm that kept his mind from settling.

His eyelids grew heavy, closing for moments that stretched longer with each blink. Just as his eyes would seal shut, he'd startle himself awake, jerking them open again. It was a desperate battle as he fought to remain alert.

They find me in my dreams, he thought to himself.

Flashes of gunfire, the stench of smoke and blood, and the screams of dying men replayed in his mind.

Bodies of the dead, broken, and burned began standing back up, their eyes a gray haze.

Then, *him*, a familiar face…

Thomas startled awake, sucking in deep breaths.

"Breathe, Thomas… breathe…" Doctor Cole was by his side holding his notebook. "What did you dream?" he asked.

"Them… it's always them," Thomas cried out. "I don't want to sleep. They find me in my sleep."

"Who, Thomas?" Doctor Cole asked.

"Men I knew. Men I fought beside," Thomas said.

"Will you tell me about them?" Doctor Cole asked.

"I'm not ready to face them. I…" Thomas put his face in his hands.

"But you are ready to face them, Thomas. That's why you are here. You are a fighter."

Thomas took a deep breath and met Doctor Cole's eyes. He nodded.

"Who did you just see before I woke you?" Doctor Cole asked again.

"Marcus…" Thomas paused. "I had known him since before the war. We were in school together as boys."

"Why him? Where were you?" Doctor Cole pressed.

"He meets me on the battlefield," Thomas whispered. "We had been roused early the morning it happened. But I was late… I was late waking up. We hadn't slept in days; I almost forgot where I was."

Marcus standing over him, smiling, flashed across his vision. Get up, he said. You're going to miss the battle!

"It was earlier than scheduled. I was scrambling to join my unit. Normally I was positioned at the front, but my tardiness relegated me to the rear… I was so tired… I…" Thomas cried. "We formed our lines, barely able to see through the fog. It was so quiet at first. He was in the line ahead of me. I should have been there, I… I should have been on that front line. We sat hidden in the fog. The orders came swift for us to move out."

Doctor Cole jotted down notes as Thomas talked about Marcus, but it quickly became clear to the doctor that this was all too much for him.

"It's okay, Thomas. We can go slow."

Thomas sat with Doctor Cole every evening confronting his nightmares. Each session took place before it was time to sleep. They had long discussions about his family, his experiences in the Army, the battles he fought before his last. Doctor Cole was determined to untangle the nightmares from reality.

Doctor Cole monitored him while he slept, scribbling his observations by the flickering candlelight. He noted every time Thomas's face contorted and every murmur he whispered.

It had been days and Thomas still found himself unable to sleep. Doctor Cole hadn't made it back to the lab yet.

He swung his legs over the side of the bed and noticed the door to the lab was slightly ajar.

A figure limped past the door—once, twice, as if pacing.

Thomas approached the door and opened it just as the figure passed by.

"Hello?"

It was a man—a soldier—and he kept walking down the hall.

Thomas followed.

As Thomas got closer, he could see the uniform was tattered and burned.

"Sir?"

The man stopped and turned slowly.

In the flickering light of the oil lamps, Thomas could see half his face was missing, torn away by shrapnel, yet his one good eye laid on Thomas.

Thomas stopped and his breath caught in his throat. He recognized this soldier, despite his disfigurement.

"Jennings?" he whispered.

The figure stared, his one good eye glaring back.

"Why, Thomas?"

Thomas stepped backward.

"Jennings, I…"

As Jennings stepped closer, Thomas could smell his burned flesh.

"Why, Thomas?"

Thomas turned and fled back to the lab.

As he ran through the doors, he slammed into Doctor Cole.

"Thomas!" Doctor Cole grabbed him by both arms. "I was looking for you, Thomas."

Thomas looked back down the hallway, then back to Doctor Cole.

He *thought* it was Doctor Cole, but it wasn't—he knew this face—another face from his dreams.

"We are all looking for you, Thomas!" The Doctor's face contorted into anger.

Thomas screamed, "I'm sorry!" He tried to pull away from the grip of the doctor. "No!"

"Thomas!" Doctor Cole's voice pulled him back. "Breathe, Thomas… Breathe!"

Thomas was standing in the doorway of the lab.

Doctor Cole was holding onto him along with the nurse.

"You're alright…" Doctor Cole sighed.

Doctor Cole escorted Thomas back to his bed and helped him settle down. He retrieved his notebook from the table and pulled up a chair next to him. "Who was it tonight, Thomas? Who were you running from?"

"Jennings…" Thomas whispered.

Hey Thomas, he remembered Jennings shouting from the front line with a big grin. Don't shoot me in the back!

Thomas rubbed his eyes. "When the fog cleared, the gunfire came… then cannons… then the screams of men. The ground beneath my feet became slick with blood and mud… But the command was to press forward." Thomas took a deep breath and held it for a moment before exhaling slowly.

"Did you press forward, Thomas?" Doctor Cole asked.

"Yes… there was so much blood, so much death I could taste it in the back of my throat." Thomas gently brushed his neck as he thought about the memory. "Next thing I knew, Tillmans shoved a grenade in my hands. He had a whole box."

Light and throw! Tillmans shouted.

"He gave them to anyone he could. My hands were trembling. We hadn't slept in days. My mind couldn't understand what I was holding at first. *Light the fuse and throw*, I told myself. I had performed this task many times before. But my mind was… tired… clouded…"

Thomas began to pull at his hair.

Doctor Cole wrote down his notes and closed his book. "That's enough for tonight, Thomas. You indeed need to sleep. Try and get some rest."

Darkness finally claimed Thomas after a few more restless moments.

Then, suddenly, his eyes snapped open.

He sat up abruptly, his breath shallow, as he rubbed his eyes. Thomas froze. His stare was fixed on the bed just across the lab from his.

It was no longer empty. A figure lay there under the standard-issue wool blanket, a silhouette that hadn't been there moments before.

Thomas's throat tightened, his pulse quickening again as he watched, unblinking, while the figure began to stir.

The blankets shifted, and slowly, the figure sat up. In the flickering light of the oil lamps, Thomas could discern the outline of a military uniform, the brass buttons glinting dimly. The shadows cast by the lamps veiled the man's face in darkness.

The soldier swung his legs off the bed, standing unsteadily.

Thomas's eyes fell to the soldier's feet, or rather, where both feet should have been. One was missing, replaced by a ragged stump. The soldier began to hobble toward Thomas, each step an awkward, lurching motion between the foot and the stump, the sound unnaturally loud in the quiet room.

Thomas recognized him. Another face from his dreams—from the battlefield. Panic surged through Thomas as the figure drew nearer. His voice, strangled with fear, finally erupted in a desperate scream. "No! I'm sorry! No, please!"

Just before the soldier could reach him, Thomas threw himself out of bed and slammed his head hard against the wall.

He jolted awake to find Doctor Cole and a nurse standing over him.

"Private, it's just a nightmare," Doctor Cole said soothingly.

Thomas's breaths came in heaves as he looked wildly around the room. The bed across from him was empty, just as it had been when he'd first lay down. No soldier, no bloody stump, just the quiet shadows of the Sleep Lab.

"What do they want from me?" Thomas stammered, his eyes still scanning the room for any sign of the apparition. "They always find me."

"Let's get you back to bed."

Doctor Cole and the young nurse guided Thomas back to the bed and helped him sit.

Thomas's eyes lingered on the empty bed across from him. The oil lamps cast trembling shadows on the walls. "They always find me..." he whispered.

"I'm going to be sitting at the table observing." Doctor Cole pointed to the table in the center of the room. "No one will bother you. I want you to tell yourself that. No one will bother you while I'm here. Try to relax." He patted Thomas on the shoulder.

Thomas watched Doctor Cole take a seat at the table. He lay back down and watched the doctor sit quietly until he fell asleep.

When Thomas woke the next morning the Sleep Lab was empty.

As he got dressed, he stared hard at the bed across from his.

Thomas slowly walked over to the bed and noticed the blankets weren't pressed but crinkled like someone had been under them. *Someone…* Thomas thought. His nightmare flashed across his vision, and he took a step back from the bed.

"Private Harlow?" The young nurse's voice pulled him from his thoughts. "Good morning, Sir."

"Good morning," Thomas said.

"Did you sleep okay, sir?" she asked.

"As expected."

"Do you need help to the cafeteria?" she asked.

Thomas looked at the young woman curiously. "What's your name, if I may ask?"

"Irene," she said.

"Irene," Thomas repeated. "No, I can find it on my own. Thank you."

"Very well, sir." Irene nodded and left the lab.

Thomas made his way to the hospital's cafeteria. The clattering of trays and the murmur of voices was a welcomed distraction from his internal battles. Just enough noise to keep him from thinking about other things—from thinking about *them.*

Suddenly, the relative peace was shattered. A man several feet ahead in the line, his face pale and eyes wide with some unseen horror, began to scream. "They're coming! We're all going to die!" His cries pierced the morning bustle like a siren.

Thomas winced, each shout echoing the screams from his nightmares, the sounds of battlefields and dying men.

Despite the tumult, Thomas forced himself to breathe deeply, closing his eyes briefly to steady his racing heart. Around him, other patients and staff paused, some startled, others with expressions of weary resignation that spoke of too many similar outbursts in this place.

As Thomas slowly opened his eyes, he saw two nurses rush toward the screaming man. They approached him with practiced calm, one gently speaking to him while the other helped. "Get him to Isolation," one of the nurses said.

Breathe…

Thomas felt a sudden need for fresh air, picked up a biscuit from the line, and headed outside.

Outside, Thomas found a secluded bench under a blooming peach tree. He set his biscuit down on his lap, no longer feeling an appetite. He breathed in the crisp air, letting the tranquility of the garden seep into him, soothing the raw edges left by the night's terrors and the morning's chaos.

As he sat, the sun broke through the thinning clouds, casting a warm glow over the courtyard. Thomas tilted his face toward the light, closing his eyes to let the warmth wash over him, grounding him. He felt he could almost sleep here—peacefully.

Breathe…

Thomas felt the soft brush of petals against his skin and blinked his eyes open, startled by the unexpected touch. He picked up the pink petal from his leg, holding it delicately between his fingers as he gazed up at the peach tree above him, its branches swaying gently in the breeze.

A flash from the battlefield crossed his vision. The bodies of men lying in mud and pink petals stained in their blood.

As petals continued to drift down, a quiet movement caught his attention from the corner of his eye.

Thomas didn't want to look. He knew there was a man standing just across from him. The man's presence was as still as a statue, but the damage wrought upon him was unmistakable—a single gunshot wound to his head, a dark, gaping hole above his temple. Blood matted his hair, trailing down his face in thick, dried streaks. The skin around the wound was torn and jagged, and his vacant eyes stared ahead.

Thomas began to cry. They seemed to find him even as he sat awake.

"I'm sorry if I frightened you," the man spoke.

Thomas, overwhelmed by the man's voice, decided to look—he was… just a man—a soldier in a uniform that was unfamiliar to Thomas. The uniform was a dark olive-green, made of thick wool. The jacket was neatly buttoned up with shiny brass buttons and had two large pockets on the chest. A belt cinched the waist, giving the jacket a sharp, structured appearance, while the pants were tucked into tall, sturdy leather boots.

Thomas could only nod in response, his eyes brimming with tears.

The man limped slightly as he approached, asking in a low tone, "May I sit?" Without waiting for an answer, he carefully positioned himself on the bench next to Thomas.

Thomas watched him for a moment.

"Are you real?" Thomas finally managed to whisper, his voice cracking under the strain of his emotions.

The man looked down at his body, then to Thomas. "What's left of me," he said with a slight smile.

Thomas released a sigh of relief. "I'm sorry, I… What happened to you?" he asked, his gaze fixed on the man, hoping he didn't seem rude.

"I don't remember much," the man replied slowly, as if piecing together fragments of a distant memory. "There was a moment of darkness, and then… nothing. I just remember feeling so alone, so lost. I think… maybe I did this to myself, but it's all so foggy now." He touched his head where a dark wound marred his temple.

"How long have you been here?" Thomas asked.

"A long time, I think. My name's Robert," he said.

"Thomas."

"Nice to meet you, Thomas. What are you here for?" Robert asked.

"I can't sleep. I don't actually remember the last time I rested," Thomas's gaze looked up at the peach tree.

"Ah, the Sleep Lab. Doctor Cole trying to understand the soldier's heart by understanding what haunts them in their dreams."

"You don't believe it?" Thomas asked.

"Oh, I definitely believe it. But what we've seen… I'm not sure there's a way of fixing it," Robert said. "I've learned to live with my scars, those you can see and those you cannot."

Thomas nodded. "It's difficult, isn't it? To keep living when parts of you still linger in those moments?"

"Very difficult," Robert agreed.

"Doctor Cole… he says talking about my dreams will help with the things… the things haunting my mind. I guess I don't know what's real anymore and what's part of my delusions." Thomas paused. "That's why I thought you were…" he trailed off.

"Do you ever wonder, Thomas, if the people we meet, the conversations we have, are just what our minds conjure to help us cope? Sometimes I think I'm just a reflection, not really here, but exactly what someone needs to see, to hear. One might say I put things in perspective…" Robert smiled gently.

The men sat, quietly admiring the blossoming peach tree.

Thomas wiped the tears from his cheeks. He looked at the peach tree, then back at the man beside him. "How do you do it? How do you keep the past from swallowing you whole?"

Robert shrugged slightly. "One day at a time, Thomas."

He held out his hand to catch a falling petal. "And sometimes, one petal at a time."

Robert stood and looked down at Thomas, who remained seated.

"Thank you for the conversation," Thomas said.

"I'll see you around, Private." Robert walked across the courtyard and disappeared into the hospital.

Thomas thought for a moment. He hadn't told Robert his rank. He stood up quickly, his heart racing as he tried to get a grip on what was his reality. Thomas ran toward the hospital doors that Robert had entered.

The doors were locked.

"No… no no no no…" Thomas ran for another entrance and the doors opened.

Thomas rushed through the corridors of the hospital, his eyes darting frantically around as he searched for any sign of the man. His heart raced as he spotted him slipping into a doorway at the end of the hall. Without a second thought, Thomas followed, pushing past nurses and doctors, his urgency palpable. Breathless and determined, he dodged a cart of medical supplies and offered hasty apologies to a group of hospital staff he nearly collided with. He had to know if Robert was real or if he'd imagined him.

Thomas made it to the door he saw him enter—the Chapel. He pushed the heavy wooden door open and stepped inside. The chapel was dimly lit, the only light coming from a few flickering candles scattered across the altar.

Rows of wooden pews stretched before him, some empty, others occupied by patients and staff seeking solace. The air was thick with the scent of wax and incense.

Thomas moved slowly down the aisle, his eyes scanning each row, searching for a glimpse of Robert. He had been so sure he saw him heading this way.

A nurse noticed him and stepped forward. "Sir, can I help you?"

Thomas felt a tightness in his throat. "Umm…" His eyes wandered around the Chapel, trying to catch any sign of Robert. He must be here—*where else could he have gone?* His thoughts swirled, desperate for answers.

"Are you alright, sir?" the nurse asked again with concern in her voice.

Thomas nodded, unable to speak, his eyes lingering on the rows of praying figures. The quiet, the solemnity of the chapel—all of it pressed down on him, a stark contrast to the chaos in his mind.

Just then, the people in the chapel began to turn toward Thomas, their movements slow and deliberate. One by one, they stood up, their eyes fixed on him.

Thomas took a step back, retreating toward the door until he found himself back in the hallway.

"Private?" Doctor Cole's voice broke through the silence, pulling Thomas's attention away from the chapel. "Thomas, are you alright?"

"I… I was looking for someone…" Thomas whispered, still catching his breath.

Doctor Cole approached Thomas at the chapel doors. "In there?"

"Yes," Thomas said, his voice wavering.

"Private, it's time for our session. Will you join me?" Doctor Cole gently placed a hand on Thomas's shoulder, guiding him away from the chapel.

Thomas glanced back at the chapel door, then reluctantly followed Doctor Cole back to the sleep lab.

The door shut behind them with a thud, sealing off the sounds of the hospital corridors.

"Sit down, Thomas," Doctor Cole instructed. He pointed to the same old, iron-framed bed where Thomas had endured countless nights of monitored sleep. "Let us start by talking about who you saw in there."

Thomas sat on the edge of the bed. His body was tense; his eyes darted around the room.

"Take some deep breaths. Remember you're safe." Doctor Cole pulled up a chair and positioned it close to Thomas, his eyes never leaving the young soldier's face. "Tell me about the man you were looking for, Thomas. The one you were looking for in the chapel."

Doctor Cole opened his journal.

Thomas's hands clenched into fists. "I met him in the courtyard. He was real. I mean, I didn't think so at first, but I saw him, talked to him. But his uniform was... different..." His voice faltered as he struggled to articulate the surreal nature of the encounter. "He was there, then he wasn't. Like he vanished into thin air."

Doctor Cole nodded, scribbling notes in his ledger. "And could it be, perhaps, that this man is a representation of something else? Maybe a part of you? A memory or a feeling? Had you seen him before, maybe on the battlefield?"

Thomas shook his head, frustrated. "No, he was real. I'm not making this up!"

"Thomas," Doctor Cole said; his tone was firmer than it had been. "It's not uncommon for patients suffering from your kind of trauma, and on top of that no sleep, to see things that aren't there. To create figures that embody aspects of their fears or guilt."

"Why is this happening to me?" Thomas's voice rose. His breathing became erratic, his eyes wide and searching.

Doctor Cole leaned forward. "Because sometimes the mind tries to resolve its trauma in ways we can't fully understand. It creates scenarios where we can face what haunts us, or it manifests our guilt and pain into something tangible, something we think we can converse with, or confront, or escape from."

The room seemed to close in around Thomas, the shadows twisting into shapes that looked almost human. "But... he wasn't one of them. He..." Thomas glanced around wildly, half expecting to see Robert standing in a dark corner. "I really don't know what's real anymore do I...?" he admitted. "I don't trust my own mind."

"That's why you're here, Thomas," Doctor Cole said gently, reaching out and placing a reassuring hand on his shoulder.

But as Doctor Cole's hand touched him, Thomas flinched, the contact feeling too real and yet not real enough.

The room spun slightly, and for a moment, he was unsure if he was still in the hospital or back on a battlefield, surrounded by the chaos of war rather than the quiet of a doctor's lab.

Doctor Cole carefully observed Thomas's weary demeanor. He set aside his notepad.

"Thomas, I believe your suffering is only getting worse because you're not sleeping. You're fighting two fronts and it's clear that the strain you're under is immense. Proper rest is vital for both body and mind, especially for someone recovering from your experiences," Doctor Cole explained.

Thomas, feeling the weight of his exhaustion, nodded slowly.

Doctor Cole stood and walked to a small cabinet in the corner of the room. He returned with a small glass bottle and a cup. "This is laudanum, a common remedy for easing pain and encouraging sleep. It's quite effective in providing relief from ailments of the mind and body. A small dose should help you find the peace you need to rest properly," he said as he carefully measured a few drops into the cup and filled it with water.

Thomas watched warily but understood the necessity. "I just want to sleep without the nightmares, without them... without them finding me," he said, his voice tinged with desperation.

"That's precisely what we're aiming for," Doctor Cole reassured him, handing him the cup. "Drink this and try to relax your mind. The laudanum will help."

Doctor Cole watched Thomas with a careful eye as he took the cup. The liquid inside was bitter. Thomas drank slowly, feeling the warmth spread through him.

"Rest now, Thomas. I'll be right here throughout the night, and we can talk more in the morning, after you've slept," Doctor Cole said.

Thomas settled back against the pillow. His eyes were heavy as the laudanum began to take effect. His surroundings seemed to soften.

"Thank you, Doctor," Thomas murmured, his words slurring slightly as sleep beckoned.

Doctor Cole gave a small nod and watched Thomas drift away.

Thomas woke and the Sleep Lab was empty. His head felt clouded, and his body was heavy, like the medicine Doctor Cole gave him was still wearing off.

He got himself washed up and dressed. Thomas didn't have an appetite, so he skipped going to the cafeteria and found himself in the courtyard under the peach tree by the pond.

Thomas leaned over the water and stared at his reflection. He didn't recognize himself—gaunt, almost ghostly. He watched as pink petals floated on the surface.

As he stood there, the water began to ripple, and then it began to roil and bubble. One by one, the soldiers—the men from the battlefield, those who haunted his dreams—the very men he'd been seeing throughout the hospital—rose from the water.

Their lifeless eyes stared hard back at Thomas. Their hands reached for him and pulled him under the water, but Thomas found himself back on the battlefield.

He was holding a grenade. His hands were trembling from sleep deprivation…

Light and throw! Tillmans shouted. Light and throw now, Harlow!

Thomas fumbled a lucifer match from his jacket. He struggled to light it, then suddenly the match's head flared but it was too close, too fast, and ignited the fuse too soon.

Panicked, Thomas threw the grenade, but not far enough. He barely had any time to understand his mistake—no time to warn those near it.

The blast was deafening, knocking Thomas off his feet. The explosion tore through the entire unit, setting off other grenades carried by the soldiers and claiming the lives of everyone around him—men who trusted him, relied on him. It was a catastrophic chain reaction.

Marie Lanza

Thomas looked down at his hands. He was holding another grenade, and the fuse was lit. Thomas looked at all the bodies around him, then back at the grenade. He watched the spark travel down the fuse until...

Thomas jolted awake.

He gasped. He was in his bed in the Sleep Lab. As he lay there, he somehow felt... rested.

Thomas looked around in astonishment—the lab was now filled with other men.

Standing slowly, Thomas walked over to the nearest bed. The man was—sleeping.

Thomas stumbled back and over to the next bed. The man was sleeping.

Thomas's mind circled around as the dream and reality collided. He couldn't untangle any of it.

"Private Harlow, are you alright, sir?" Irene, the young nurse, was standing in the doorway.

Thomas was relieved to see her. "Is this real?" he asked. "Are they real?" Thomas looked around the room at the men sleeping in their beds.

Irene looked confused as her eyes wandered around the lab. Her gaze then landed on him hard.

"What's left of them... sir."

Then, the bodies of the soldiers began to rise.

Imaging Lab
1979

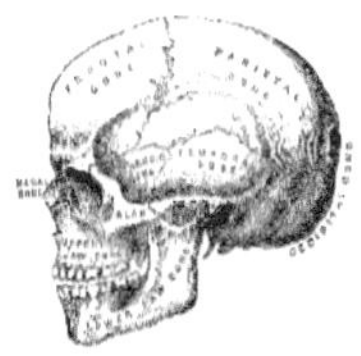

Unknown Artifact
Bridget D. Brave

Roger Davis threw his glasses onto the desk and rubbed at his eyes hard enough to produce stars. His fingers trailed down his face, running over the two-day stubble he'd once again forgotten to shave. This near-beard would be an issue if he worked a daytime shift, but on overnights the administrators cared fuck-all about appearance.

The administrators cared fuck-all about most things these days.

Roger lit a cigarette and tapped nervously at the desk with his smoking hand. With the other he lifted his glasses back onto his face.

The artifact was still there.

Noise, they called it: something wrong with the scan through no fault of the machine. Just something unexplainable that causes a strange phantom image on the film. Regardless of explanation, the artifacts usually followed some simple rules: they tended to be uniform in shape, indicating an error, and they tended to not be repeatable.

But not this one. This fucking artifact was shaped oddly. And, worse yet, it was in four separate images.

Roger put the lit cigarette between his lips and lifted the top film out in front of him, allowing the dim desk light to illuminate the unexplained smudge.

It was oval in shape, small, with milky trails that nearly looked like smoke radiating out. Not the stark white of the pelvic bones outlined in the image itself, so not the result of some dense material floating to some other place it didn't belong.

No, this was something outside the body, something that seemed to be almost beside the body. If this were a photo, you'd think the something was in the background, sneaking up on the patient being x-rayed. But that was impossible. The patient was laying supine in this scan, the metal table beneath him. The only thing in the background would be the table, then the floor.

Nothing that would explain this.

He'd arrived at work at half past eleven, the hospital staff parking lot down to essential personnel: emergency room and janitorial. After clocking in and shrugging into his blue overshirt that read "RADIOLOGY, DAVIS," Roger had found the stack of films waiting for him, a handwritten note paper-clipped to the top.

"Artifact image disrupting imagery. Run diagnostic."

So he ran the diagnostic, placing the sample tray down and taking three different images. Nothing came through, no weird smudge in the corners, no odd trailing wisps of milky white indicating a problem with the lens.

He pondered this as he pulled open his desk drawer, finding one of the coconut-and-caramel chocolate bars that seemed only to be sold in the hospital's gift shop. He'd often wondered if it was a regional brand, something so small and obscure that you couldn't find it at the gas station, or grocery store. Not surprising, the snack was wrapped in what had to be the most off-putting packaging he'd ever seen: an infant dressed as a cowboy, with a smirk that was almost menacing.

Sometimes he could swear the thing *winked* at him.

At 12:15, Andrea Phillips poked her head into the dimly lit office. "You can disregard the images from the Normann patient."

Roger glanced up at Andrea, a freshly-lit cigarette dangling from his lips. "They finally get a clear image?"

She shook her head. "Nope. He died. Came in for a bruised hip and bam!" She clapped her hands together loudly. "Coronary right in the ER while they were waiting. Crazy. Guess you never know."

"Guess not," he mumbled as he shuffled the three images marked "Normann, M" off to the side.

"Did you figure out what caused the weird blurs?" Andrea leaned in the doorway, her arms folded across her chest.

"Whatever it was, it's gone now." Roger lifted the two blank films, the only visible object the metal tags indicating this was a "test."

It was a blissfully quiet forty-five minutes of quiet until he got the call.

Car accident. Possible arm fracture in one patient, back and shoulder pain in the other. Roger plucked a ballpoint from his pocket and clicked it into action, jotting down the ordered image sequence.

Andrea rolled in the first patient in a wheelchair, the teen girl sullenly cradling one arm against her waist. Roger gingerly positioned the arm into a stretched posture, cringing internally when he heard the tell-tale sign of bone grinding on bone as he turned her wrist. Andrea made soothing noises before they both backed behind the shielded wall.

"Bit late for her to be out driving alone," he said quietly as he clicked the shutter.

Andrea chuckled and inclined her head in a conspiratorial manner. "Oh, she wasn't alone. She had her boyfriend with her. Daddy is on his way to the hospital now and he is none too happy."

"Oof," he breathed in response. "Might want to alert security, lest we end up with more broken arms."

Andrea didn't seem to hear him, leaning in close to look at the imaging screen. "I thought you said you fixed it."

Roger followed her gaze.

"Nothing to fix."

Then he saw it, in the corner.. The faint oval-shaped outline. The wispy tendrils. A bit more pronounced than on the Normann films.

"What the fuck?" he whispered.

"Print them anyway." Andrea sighed. "It's not obscuring the image and a five-year-old could see that wrist is broken. But you'd better check that machine. You know Dr. Peters will be up here to pitch a shitfit once he sees that."

Dr. Peters did appear, shitfit at the ready, just as Roger was examining the shoulder films of the previously-mentioned boyfriend.

Peters was barely 5'5", even when he wore his lifts. What he lacked in stature he made up for in vocal volume and self-importance.

"I *explicitly* asked that you run a diagnostic after Mr. Normann's films were nearly incomprehensible." The smaller man tapped his foot against the sickly green floor tiles.

"I ran them," Roger responded calmly, pushing the test images across the desk. He didn't mention that the x-ray images from Normann were hardly *incomprehensible*. There was nothing technically wrong with the imagery, the pelvic bone and hip clearly visible. The artifact made the image weird, but in a comprehensible way.

"Run. Them. Again." Dr. Peters hiked his pants up by the belt before spinning to leave the room.

Roger was comparing two recent test images, a frown deepening across his face, when Andrea reappeared. She hopped onto her toes to stare over his shoulder. "Huh. Still clear on the tests?"

"Yeah, it's like it's only there when…" He trailed off, contemplating. "Mind helping me with something?"

Andrea splayed her hand across the x-ray table as Roger disappeared behind the shield. "I'll just do two quick shots, let's see what comes up."

They both frowned at the test images this time, the artifact larger and more prominent beside Andrea's bony fingers.

"You know," she said thoughtfully, her fingertips drumming on her lower lip. "It almost looks like…."

"A face?"

"Yeah." She stepped closer. "Look, those are the eyes and you can see a nose and…" She trailed off again.

The lower part of the oval, where the mouth would be, showed the faint outline of lips yawning open in a silent scream.

That was when the code alarm sounded. Andrea quickly shivered before straightening her shoulders and snapping into action. She left Roger alone to stare at the strange almost-face.

He later learned the code was the teen girl with the broken wrist. She'd experienced some sort of seizure that they were unable to stabilize her from.

Suspecting a drug overdose, Dr. Peters had called the local authorities. As a result, Roger had to x-ray the boyfriend while the poor kid was partially handcuffed, a police escort waiting just outside the room.

At least his shoulder was going to be okay. No sign of structural damage. Just that artifact again, looking like a ghostly painting. Wide eyes staring out, warning against some unseen danger. Mouth frozen in shrieking horror.

Christ, it even looked like there were faint hands beneath the face, reaching out.

Roger startled at the sudden touch on his shoulder. Nurse Jennifer Sutton smiled a closed-lip apology. Sitting down heavily in his chair, Roger fumbled for a cigarette and lit it with shaky hands. "I didn't hear you come in."

"Sorry about that," Jennifer said gently. "I came to collect the films for the Collier boy."

"Where's Andrea?" Roger asked.

"On break."

The code alarm sounded again, Jennifer checking her watch before excusing herself. Roger could hear the distant sound of shouting and hurried footsteps.

The Collier boy had gone into a seizure similar to his girlfriend. Dr. Peters returned to give Roger the news, shaking his head disapprovingly as he spoke of "dopers" and "listless hippies," his frequent appraisals of Roger's hair indicating he considered the radiology tech one of them. Peters finished his lecture with a pointed request to "fix that damned machine."

"It's been happening since yesterday morning."

Roger blinked. "I'm sorry?"

"The blur. I noticed it in some of the post-mortems from the day."

"Post-mortems," Roger said faintly, an impossible idea beginning to form in his head. "There have been other deaths after x-ray?"

Peters let out a derisive snort. "I hope you're not saying the machine is killing patients, Davis. You of all people should know that the risks of x-ray are minimal at best. Safe as churches, isn't that what they say?"

Davis nodded silently, the gears in his head still turning.

Once Peters had blustered his way back toward the ER, Roger pulled open the second drawer on the filing cabinet third from the left. The one with the scans from the past week.

The x-rays from four days prior showed no sign of blemish or shadow, all clear as expected. Then, without warning, the faintest trace of ethereal strands began to come into view, starting with a sprained ankle the morning prior.

Roger picked up the desk phone and dialed down to reception.

"Hi, Katie. I needed you to quick check on a patient status for me. A Jennifer Cunningham."

Roger nodded as he listened, making a notation on the file.

"And then could you please check on an Amelia Nevis?"

He made another note.

"And Betty Monroe-Sweeney?"

Another notation.

"Mmm-hmm. Michael Crossmoore?"

The phone returned to the cradle and Roger leaned back in his chair. There was an unpleasant cold sweat gathering at the base of his spine. He had spread the films from the prior day across the surface of his desk. Directly in front of him, a pad of paper had the last names corresponding to each scan, with a word beside each one.

That word, in block letters, was "DECEASED."

Roger reached for another cigarette, surprised when he found a lit smoke already in his mouth. He lit the new cig with the butt of the old one, taking in a shaky breath and exhaling smoke. Then he returned to the filing cabinet and pulled the stack of films from two days ago.

Katie seemed surprised when he called back so quickly, but she read off the disposition of each patient as he requested. This time, when he hung up, the pad of paper was full of a different word, "DISCHARGED."

All except for the last entry. This film had no unexpected artifact, but the patient, a girl barely aged fourteen, had died prior to discharge. As far as he could tell, it was a standard chest x-ray to rule out pneumonia. No pneumonia was found.

Roger hurriedly walked through the empty halls, heading for the records room. With his pad beside him, he pulled the files for every person who had received an x-ray over the past seventy-two hours, stacking them into piles of deceased and discharged.

He clicked on the orange desk lamp in the back of the room and began poring over the files from the deceased pile, murmuring under his breath as he read.

"Crossmore - reported to ER complaining of knee pain. Cause of death: suspected aneurysm. Autopsy ordered.

"Monroe-Sweeney - brought to ER by daughter after fall on sidewalk. Suspected fracture of left wrist. Cause of death: heart attack. Autopsy ordered.

"Nevis - brought by ambulance following car accident. Cause of death: internal bleeding. Autopsy ordered.

"Cunningham - follow-up ordered by GP for suspected metatarsal fracture. Cause of death: unknown. Suspected heart attack. Autopsy ordered."

Roger had reached the last file, the death that did not have an artifact in her scans. The last clear x-ray before the artifact started appearing. The first of this strange string of deaths.

Robinson, Catherine.

Her file was three times as thick as the others, with a series of handwritten notes clipped to various imaging, blood test results, and medication orders. Roger began to leaf through the notes.

"Ms. Robinson once again reports to ER with vague complaints of stomach pain. Given ibuprofen and discharged.

"Ms. Robinson presents this evening with complaints of hip discomfort. Suspected constipation. Given magnesium citrate and discharged.

"Ms. Robinson is frequently paranoid and difficult to speak with.

"Ms. Robinson's mother reports she exaggerates.

"Ms. Robinson reports with pelvic pain. Confirmed date of last period twenty-two days ago. Given ibuprofen and discharged.

"Hysterical.

"Hypochondriac.

"Possible attention-seeking behavior."

The last page detailed her final visit.

"Ms. Robinson reports to ER with complaints of difficulty breathing. X-ray ordered to rule out pneumonia or lung obstruction. No abnormalities reported. Ms. Robinson a frequent visitor, has issues with hypochondria. Ms. Robinson sent home at 2:45 a.m. with a mild sedative.

"3:50 a.m. Ms. Robinson returns to ER via ambulance. Unconscious. Patient did not regain consciousness. Distended abdomen and discoloration indicate possible bowel obstruction. Patient time of death declared 4:14 a.m., suspected bowel perforation and sepsis. Autopsy ordered."

Roger flipped back to the first page, the first intake form. There was a tiny black and white photo of the patient affixed to the upper right corner. He stared in silent horror at the wispy strands of long blonde hair, the wide, seeking eyes, the upturned nose.

Familiar features, all.

As he searched each of her features, wanting himself to be wrong, the image shifted, the mouth widening into a black hole of pain and terror.

He slammed the file shut and ran from the room, his thoughts only on Andrea. *She'd had a fucking x-ray.*

Roger pushed through the double doors into the emergency room proper, finding it largely vacant save for Katie at the desk. "Where is Andrea?" he roared.

Katie's eyebrows pinched together as she took a moment to think. "She went on break a while ago. I saw her head down to the basement—" she stopped, watching in shock as Roger threw himself through the door to the stairwell.

The stairs were dark, the cost-cutting measures resulting in only a single dim overhead fluorescent at the top of the staircase. Dim and, judging by the steady flickering, on its way to burning out completely. The nauseating buzz of the yellow light faded as he shuffled down a flight of stairs, rounding the corner with one hand anchoring him to the railing. The moment he started his next descent, the dark concrete step grew slippery and he felt his feet fly out from under him.

Roger only had a moment to register that he was falling before he landed, hard. The hand he had shoved out to brace himself folded as he landed, the wrist making a sickly crunching noise shortly before the back of his head collided with a stair's metal edge. He managed a strangled cry as he fell.

Above him, he could hear someone shouting in the stairwell, yelling his name. The voice he barely recognized as Katie's was now yelling for help as Roger lifted his maimed arm into view, grimacing at the bent angle of his wrist in the half-light.

It also appeared coated in blood, too much blood to be from his fall. His head woozy and spinning, Roger tried to sit up slightly, feeling his good hand slip beneath him in a cooling sticky-wet something.

There were footsteps ringing toward him. The lights began to blink on. Below him, on the landing, he could see the crumpled body of a woman in a nurse's uniform, her arms and legs stuck out at odd angles.

"No," he managed before the shouts reached him. A strangled woman's scream as they saw the body below him. He was vaguely aware of being lifted, then of the flash of lights overhead as he was carted down a hall. The ceiling tile stains began to look familiar.

"No," he said again, his voice sluggish. "No x-ray."

"What did he say?" he heard Jennifer ask.

"He's hit his head," Dr. Peters snapped back. "He isn't making any sense."

"No x-ray!" Roger tried again, struggling to roll to one side. Rough hands held him against the thin mattress of the gurney.

"We don't have time for this. We already have a nurse dead and the police on the way," Peters' voice was full of irritation. "Sedate him if you have to."

"No... no x-ray." Roger felt the tears burn at the edge of his vision. "No x-ray."

He felt the sharp prick of a needle in his uninjured arm. Then everything faded to black.

Maternity Ward
1975

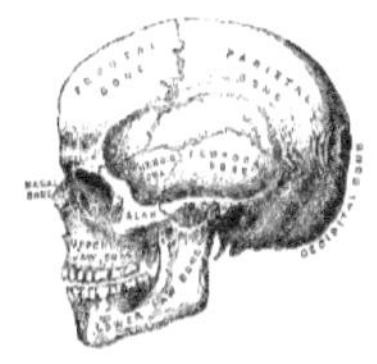

Hush, Little Baby
Christy Aldridge

Laura clutched her overnight bag tightly, her knuckles white with anticipation. As she stepped through the entrance of Lychhurst Hospital, the reality of what lay ahead finally began to sink in. Her heart was racing, both with excitement and fear.

She was about to become a mother—a single mother to a little girl she already loved more than anything in the world. The fear of being pregnant had disappeared, and now she was filled with the joy of knowing her baby girl would be here soon. Despite all of the fear of what their lives might look like after, Laura was mostly filled with excitement at knowing she'd hold her precious baby soon.

The hospital's maternity ward was a bustling place, filled with the comforting sounds of newborns and the hurried footsteps of nurses and doctors. Laura's heart pounded with a mix of excitement and nervousness. She had prepared for this moment for months, but now that it was here, she couldn't help but feel a flutter of anxiety.

"Welcome, Laura. We're ready for you," said a cheerful nurse named Becky, who had a warm smile and a reassuring demeanor. They had met before, during her appointments with the doctor. Laura liked her.

She guided Laura down the corridor, chatting amiably about the induction process and how everything was going to be just fine, trying her best to reassure the first-time mom.

They stopped outside Room 213. Becky opened the door and ushered Laura inside, helping her settle into the bed. The room was small but cozy, with a large window that overlooked the hospital's overgrown garden. Laura could see the remnants of an old fountain, now cracked and covered in ivy.

"Is there anything you need right now?" Becky asked, fluffing Laura's pillows.

"No, I think I'm good," Laura replied, smiling nervously. "Just... a little anxious, I guess."

"That's perfectly normal. You're going to do great," Becky assured her. "I'll be back in a bit to check on you."

As Becky left the room, Laura tried to relax, taking deep breaths and rubbing her swollen belly. Her baby girl gave a little kick, as if to remind her that she wasn't alone. Those little kicks had been her lifeline for months now, because besides the baby inside, Laura was alone. The little one's dad ignored her phone calls from the moment she told him she was pregnant.

Her own parents had kept their distance since she revealed the news as well. Having an unwed pregnant daughter that was just eighteen years old didn't fit with the image they wanted to convey to the world. Their interactions were limited, and they were too busy with their lives to come to the hospital now. After she gave birth, they might come by.

Her friends were more supportive, but they were in college or enjoying the freedom that came with becoming an adult. None of them were as excited about Laura having a baby when they realized she wasn't going to go out as often as they were.

Life felt a bit isolating, but every little kick from her baby made her feel less alone in this big old world.

Just then, she overheard voices from the hallway.

"Are you sure about putting her in there?" an older nurse's voice said, tinged with concern.

"Oh, come on, Ruth. Don't start with that again," Becky responded with a light laugh. "You've been here too long."

"But Room 213... you know the stories," Ruth insisted, her voice dropping to a hushed whisper. "It's not just rumors. I've seen things."

"Ghost stories and old wives' tales," Becky replied dismissively. "Besides, we're short on rooms. She'll be fine. And she's a first-time mother. We don't want to freak her out with ghost stories."

Laura's curiosity was piqued, but before she could process what she'd heard, Becky reappeared with a clipboard. She smiled brightly, but Laura couldn't shake the uneasy feeling that Ruth's words had planted in her mind.

"Ready to get started?" Becky asked, her tone cheerful.

"Yeah, I guess so," Laura replied, forcing a smile. "But... what was that about Room 213?"

Becky's smile faltered for a split second before she recovered. "Oh, nothing. Just some silly old superstitions. This hospital has been around a long time, longer than you can imagine, and every old building has its ghost stories. But that's all it is."

"So, no ghost in a white sheet is going to try to crawl into bed with me?" Laura asked, cracking a smile.

Becky laughed. "No, but I can always wear one if you need a laugh!"

Laura nodded, trying to brush off the lingering doubt by smiling.

But as Becky began the induction process, Laura couldn't help but feel a chill in the room, as if she were being watched. She shook her head, telling herself it was just nerves. Her mind was incredibly overwhelmed and was clinging to every anxious thought she could find.

She was going to be a single mother. That was scary enough. But she was also eighteen. She was scared of what her future looked like. And what her little one's future held.

"So, Dr. Michaels is planning to induce you, right? Looks like you're two weeks past your due date," Becky said, looking at Laura's belly.

Laura smiled, running her hand over the baby bump. "Yeah, I don't think she's ready to join the world yet," Laura said.

"Can't say I blame her. At least it looks like the war over in Vietnam is over. So maybe there's some hope yet," Becky said with a slight shrug. "I'm going to get your vitals and Dr. Michaels should be in any moment now."

Becky tested her blood pressure and put in an IV. As she was finishing up, Dr. Michaels came into the room, smiling big.

"You ready to meet your little girl?" he asked.

Laura smiled. "Absolutely."

"Good. I'm going to get Becky to start the IV drip to get your induction started. This being your first child, it could still be hours, days even, but keeping both you and baby safe is my main priority. Your preference is a natural birth, right?" he asked.

Laura nodded.

"Then that's the goal. I'm hoping she just needs a little push to come on out."

They started the medication and talked her through what to look out for. They listed out all of the possibilities with her, but Laura had been reading as many pregnancy and labor books as she could find at the library. She knew most of it and she was prepared. When they left, she knew that now, all she could really do was wait.

Later that night, as the hospital settled into a quiet lull, Laura lay in bed, trying to sleep. The dim light from the hallway cast eerie shadows on the walls. Just as she was about to drift off, a soft, lilting melody reached her ears, so faint she thought she might be imagining it.

A lullaby, sad and haunting, floated through the air. Laura's heart raced as she strained to hear the source of the music. The melody grew louder, wrapping around her like a cold embrace. Her baby stirred uneasily, mirroring her discomfort.

She sat up, looking around the room, but there was no one there. The music seemed to come from the walls themselves, filling the space with an eerie presence. Her breath quickened, and she felt a chill run down her spine.

"Nurse Becky?" Laura called out, her voice trembling. But the hallway outside her door was empty, and the only answer was the continuing melody, growing more insistent and mournful.

As she lay back down, trying to calm her racing heart, Laura couldn't shake the feeling that she wasn't alone in Room 213. The lullaby seemed to be a prelude, a warning of something sinister lurking in the shadows, waiting for the right moment to reveal itself.

When the door opened, Laura jumped. Nurse Becky gave her a surprised look and smiled. "I'm sorry. I didn't mean to scare you. I was told to check your progress," she told her.

Laura nodded. The sound was gone, and she didn't think about it much as Becky checked to see how far dilated she was. When the nurse gave a slight frown, Laura's heart began to race.

"Is everything okay?"

Becky smiled reassuringly. "Oh, of course. You're just not dilated enough, or where we'd hoped you'd be yet. I'm going to let Dr. Michaels know," she told her, leaving the room.

Dr. Michaels entered Room 213 with a reassuring smile that did little to ease Laura's anxiety. She sat upright in bed, clutching the thin hospital blanket tightly around her, her eyes wide with fear.

"Good evening, Laura," Dr. Michaels greeted her gently, setting aside his clipboard. "How are you feeling?"

Laura managed a weak smile. "Nervous, Doctor. Is everything okay? Becky said I'm not dilated enough... is that bad?"

Dr. Michaels pulled a stool closer to the bed and sat down, his expression serious yet empathetic. "It's not uncommon, especially for first-time mothers. These things take time, Laura. Your body needs to adjust."

Laura nodded, trying to hold back tears. "I just... I'm so scared. This baby... she's everything to me. I can't lose her. I don't have anyone else."

Dr. Michaels reached out and gently placed a reassuring hand on Laura's shoulder. "You're in good hands, Laura. We're monitoring you closely. Sometimes, it just takes a bit longer. Try to rest and let your body do its work."

Laura nodded again, her mind racing with worries and what-ifs. She glanced at the window, where the moon cast a soft glow into the room. The song from earlier still lingered in her mind, adding to her unease.

"I know it's hard, but try not to stress too much," Dr. Michaels continued. "Stress can delay things even more. You're doing great, Laura."

As Dr. Michaels prepared to leave, Laura hesitated, a nagging thought gnawing at her. "Doctor, what Becky said earlier... about Room 213. Is there something I should know?"

Dr. Michaels paused, his expression thoughtful. "There are stories, Laura. Old stories from years ago. But they're just stories. This hospital has a long history, and with that comes tales passed down through generations of nurses and staff."

Laura frowned, feeling a chill run down her spine despite Dr. Michaels' attempt to reassure her. "But... the lullaby I heard earlier. It felt... real."

"Lullaby?"

"Yeah, I heard it just before Becky came back in."

Dr. Michaels' gaze softened, and he chose his words carefully. "Sometimes, in places like this, our minds play tricks on us. It's a stressful time, and your senses can be heightened. Rest assured, Laura, we're here for you and your baby. Everything will be okay."

With that, Dr. Michaels left Laura alone in the room, the silence closing in around her.

She lay back on the bed, her thoughts racing. Outside, the hospital continued its nocturnal rhythm—the occasional footsteps, the distant hum of machinery—but inside Room 213, Laura felt an unsettling presence, as if something unseen watched over her and her unborn child.

She closed her eyes, trying to push away the fear and uncertainty. But as she drifted into an uneasy sleep, the tune returned, faint yet persistent, echoing in the corners of her mind like a plea from beyond.

The night pressed on in Room 213. Nurses came to check on her and how she was progressing. The air was thick with tension as Laura drifted in and out of restless sleep. Each time she closed her eyes, the melody crept closer, its notes woven with an unsettling darkness that seemed to seep through the walls.

Laura woke with a start as a sharp pain shot through her abdomen. She clutched her belly, feeling her baby's frantic movements. The room was shrouded in shadows, the moonlight casting eerie shapes across the floor. And there it was again—the lullaby, now clearer and more sinister than before.

Tears welled in Laura's eyes as she reached for the nurse call button, pressing it urgently. The lullaby continued, wrapping around her like a suffocating blanket. Her heart raced with fear for her unborn child.

Within moments, Nurse Becky burst into the room followed closely by Nurse Ruth, the older woman who had voiced her concerns earlier. They found Laura gripping the bed sheets, her face contorted with pain and fear.

"What's happening?" Becky asked, her voice tinged with worry.

Laura's breath came in ragged gasps as she struggled to speak. "The lullaby... it's back. And my baby... she's moving so much, and I feel... pain."

Ruth moved swiftly to Laura's side, her experienced hands gently palpating Laura's abdomen. "Let's get you hooked up to the monitor, dear," she said soothingly, guiding Laura's hands away from her belly.

As they adjusted the monitors, Laura's heart pounded in her chest. The lullaby, haunting and desolate, seemed to echo through the room, filling the space with an oppressive presence. She glanced anxiously at the monitor screen, searching for any sign that her baby was okay.

Suddenly, as if sensing the nurses' presence, the lullaby ceased abruptly, leaving an eerie silence in its wake. Becky exchanged a worried look with Ruth, who continued to monitor the fetal heartbeat and Laura's vitals.

"Is... is she okay?" Laura asked, her voice trembling.

Ruth smiled reassuringly, though her eyes betrayed a hint of concern. "The baby's heartbeat is strong, Laura. And you're doing fine. Sometimes these pains are just part of the process. Contractions can be awful. It just means she's getting ready to join the world."

Laura nodded, trying to steady her breathing. But the memory of the sinister lullaby lingered, leaving her shaken and vulnerable. She couldn't ignore the feeling that something was terribly wrong—that the lullaby was a warning she couldn't afford to ignore.

Becky stayed by Laura's side, offering words of comfort as Ruth continued to monitor her closely. The hospital around them hummed with activity, oblivious to the supernatural turmoil unfolding in Room 213.

As the night stretched on, Laura clung to the hope that her baby would be born healthy and safe. But deep down, a nagging doubt gnawed at her— the fear that the lullaby, with its dark and inexplicable presence, harbored secrets that threatened to unravel her fragile world.

As the sun rose, casting a warm glow through the window, Nurse Ruth came into her room to give her ice and check her vitals. She seemed really quiet, nervous even.

Laura decided to ask her, since it had been her that was weary of this room.

"Ruth, please," Laura implored, her voice quivering with a mix of fear and curiosity. "You mentioned something about Room 213 when I got here.

Is there something wrong here? I've been hearing this… lullaby. My baby seemed to get frantic when it was happening."

Ruth hesitated, her gaze flickering between Laura's anxious face and the hallway beyond. Finally, she pulled up a chair and sat down beside the bed, her expression grave.

"I've been a nurse here for over thirty years," Ruth began slowly, her voice tinged with solemnity. "And in that time, I've seen things… things that don't have easy explanations."

Laura listened intently, her heart racing as Ruth recounted the tale that had become part of the hospital's lore.

"Years ago," Ruth continued, her voice dropping to a whisper, "there was a nurse named Evelyn. She was kind and dedicated, loved by patients and staff alike. But she carried a sadness within her—a grief that few understood."

Ruth paused, her eyes distant as she recalled the past. "Evelyn had a child of her own, a baby girl who was born prematurely and didn't survive. The loss broke Evelyn's heart. She blamed herself, convinced that she hadn't done enough to save her baby."

Laura's breath caught in her throat, her own fears mirrored in Evelyn's tragic story.

"After her baby's death," Ruth went on, her voice trembling slightly, "Evelyn would sing a lullaby to soothe the newborns in her care. It was a song full of longing, filled with sorrow. But as time passed, something changed in Evelyn. Her grief consumed her, twisted her lullaby into something… darker. The mortality rate for newborns began to jump. Healthy newborns, preemies, no difference, they would just die without any clear explanation.

"I still remember the day it happened. January 8th, 1965. I can't believe it's been ten years now," she said, taking a moment to take in that realization before continuing. "One of the staff watched Evelyn smothering a baby. They immediately told, but Evelyn had seen them. By the time they came back, she had come into this room and hung herself."

Laura's skin prickled with unease, the pieces of the puzzle slowly coming together in her mind.

"Patients and nurses began to hear the lullaby at night soon after," Ruth continued, her voice barely above a whisper. "It wasn't comforting anymore. It was menacing, filled with a restless spirit that refused to find peace."

Laura's eyes widened, her grip on the bed sheets tightening. "But why? Why would Evelyn's spirit haunt this place?"

Ruth shook her head sadly. "No one knows for certain. Some say she couldn't bear to leave the hospital where she had lost her child. Some say she wants to continue whatever twisted mission she had been on while alive. Either way, I prefer to keep women out of this room. It's just… safer."

As Ruth finished her tale, a chill settled over the room, a reminder of the spectral presence that lingered unseen yet palpable. Laura swallowed hard, her mind swirling with questions and a growing sense of dread.

"What do we do?" Laura asked, her voice barely a whisper.

Ruth's eyes met Laura's, filled with compassion and a hint of resignation. "We do what we can to protect ourselves and the babies in our care. We listen for the signs, and we trust our instincts."

Laura nodded, her thoughts racing as she processed the sad truth behind the lullaby. She couldn't shake the feeling that her own connection to Room 213 and its tragic history ran deeper than she dared to imagine.

The rest of the day did nothing to calm her uneasiness. It felt like her baby was unwilling to come, despite the contractions intensifying. Everyone continued to assure her that everything was okay. It was all normal, but Laura didn't think anything about this was normal.

The sun had set once more, casting Room 213 into a dim twilight. Laura lay in bed, her anxiety simmering beneath a thin veil of exhaustion. The events of the previous night haunted her thoughts, the spectral lullaby echoing in her mind like a sinister refrain.

As Laura closed her eyes, hoping for a moment of respite, the melody returned—louder, more insistent, and laced with an unmistakable menace. She jolted awake, clutching her belly as a sharp pain shot through her abdomen.

"Not again," Laura whispered through clenched teeth, her heart racing with fear. This was worse than a contraction. The pain was unimaginable, piercing through her entire body as the lullaby rang through the air, causing her heart to race even faster. Between her legs felt wet and when she looked toward them, blood seemed to be coming through the sheet.

She fumbled for the nurse call button, pressing it frantically. Within seconds, Becky and Ruth burst into the room, their faces etched with concern.

"Laura, what's wrong?" Becky asked urgently, rushing to Laura's side.

"The lullaby... I heard it again," Laura gasped, tears welling in her eyes. "Something's wrong. I think I'm bleeding. Am I bleeding?"

Ruth's eyes widened with alarm as she saw the blood seeping through the sheets. "We need to get her to the delivery room, now," she said firmly, her voice betraying a hint of fear.

With practiced efficiency, Becky and Ruth unlocked her bed, guiding her through the corridors of the hospital. The lullaby continued to echo in Laura's ears, a chilling soundtrack to the urgency of their movements.

Laura's hands clutched her stomach, clinging to the life inside her as they wheeled her through. In the midst of her fear, a strange sight gave her a moment of comfort. A young boy, missing an arm, was standing in the corridor as they passed. A sweet smile crossed his face as they passed him in a rush. Laura turned her head, staring at him as the nurses pushing her bed didn't even give him a passing glance.

He held out a yellow ball in his hand, as if offering it to her, but she was too far away to reach for it. He was becoming smaller and smaller as they went further down the hall.

"Who was. . ."

A sharp burst of pain spread through her abdomen and she clutched it, crying out. As they entered the sterile confines of the delivery room, Laura's pain intensified, each contraction a cruel reminder of the fragile life she carried. She glanced around the room, her eyes darting nervously as she searched for any sign of the ghostly figure she had glimpsed earlier.

"Stay with me," Laura pleaded, her voice trembling as Becky and Ruth prepared her for the delivery. "Don't let anything happen to my baby."

Becky squeezed Laura's hand reassuringly. "We're right here with you, Laura. You're doing great."

Ruth monitored the fetal heartbeat, her brow furrowed with concern. "The baby's heartbeat is strong, Laura."

Laura closed her eyes, willing herself to find strength amidst the fear and uncertainty. The room seemed to pulse with an otherworldly energy, the air heavy with the weight of Evelyn's sorrow and longing.

Suddenly, a shadow moved in the corner of Laura's vision—a fleeting glimpse of a figure, ethereal and translucent. Panic surged within her as she struggled to sit up, her instincts screaming that the ghostly presence meant harm.

"Becky, Ruth, please," Laura pleaded, her voice rising to a desperate cry. "I saw her. The ghost... she's here."

Becky exchanged a worried glance with Ruth, their expressions mirroring Laura's fear. But before they could respond, the room filled with the melody once more—a woeful lament that seemed to emanate from the very walls.

Dr. Michaels came rushing into the room. Laura watched through tensed eyes as the nurses helped get him ready for the birth. Her mind felt so fuzzy, between the lullaby echoing throughout her ears and the pain spreading through her entire body, it was hard to focus on anything.

Laura screamed, the sound reverberating through the room as she clutched her belly, consumed by pain and terror. The nurses exchanged a look of grim determination. Whatever was in the room had now set its sights on Laura and her unborn child.

"Okay, Laura, stay with me," she heard, but everything else felt like an out-of-body experience. She pushed, but she wasn't sure if Dr. Michaels was telling her too.

The lullaby seemed louder than any of the other voices in the room. She saw Becky and Ruth trying to speak to her. Dr. Michaels' mouth was moving. There were a few other nurses in the room as well, each with their own worried expressions.

With a final push, Laura brought her daughter into the world, her cries mingling with the melody that filled the room.

The delivery room fell into an eerie silence as Laura's consciousness ebbed away, the lullaby fading into distant echoes. The nurses exchanged somber glances; their hearts heavy with the weight of what had transpired.

Amidst the solemn stillness, a nurse approached Laura—a figure she didn't recognize, her presence strangely comforting yet tinged with an otherworldly aura. Without a word, the nurse gently placed a swaddled bundle in Laura's arms.

Laura's eyes filled with tears of joy as she cradled her baby girl, her heart overflowing with love and relief. The room seemed to brighten as she gazed at her daughter's peaceful face, cherishing the precious moments they shared together.

The mysterious nurse hummed a soft lullaby, a melody that calmed Laura's shattered nerves and soothed her soul. She watched as the nurse moved gracefully across the room, a guardian angel in the quiet storm that enveloped them.

But as quickly as she had come, the nurse disappeared from sight, leaving Laura with the bittersweet comfort of her daughter's presence.

Hours passed in a blur, and when Laura finally stirred from her fragile slumber, the reality of her situation crashed down upon her like a tidal wave. The nurses who had been by her side all night gathered around her, their expressions filled with sorrow and sympathy.

"Laura, we're so sorry," Becky began gently, her voice trembling with emotion. "Your baby... she was born stillborn."

Laura's heart skipped a beat, her mind reeling with confusion and disbelief. "No... that's not possible," she whispered hoarsely, clutching at the memory of holding her daughter in her arms.

"We understand this is difficult," Ruth added softly, her eyes brimming with tears. "But your baby... she didn't make it."

Tears streamed down Laura's cheeks as she recounted the nurse who had handed her the baby, the lullaby that had filled the room with fleeting hope.

"I held her," Laura insisted, her voice cracking with anguish. "The nurse took her away."

Becky and Ruth exchanged a solemn glance, their hearts breaking for Laura's shattered reality. "Laura, sometimes... in moments of grief... our minds can play tricks on us," Becky said gently, her voice filled with compassion.

Laura's shoulders shook with sobs as she struggled to accept the heartbreaking truth. The room around her seemed to blur, the walls closing in as she grappled with the devastating loss of her daughter—the only light in her world extinguished before it had a chance to fully shine.

And as the nurses gathered around her, offering words of comfort that felt like empty echoes in the vast emptiness of her grief, Laura heard the soft hum of a lullaby.

Pediatrics Ward
1993

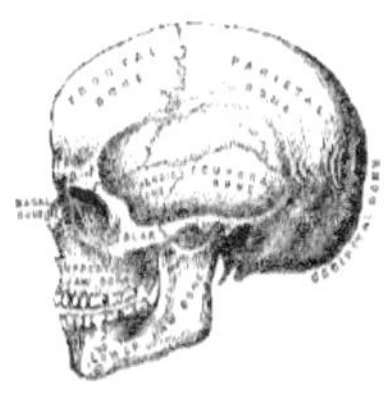

Hide
Stephanie Ellis

The warmth inside contrasted strongly with the scene beyond the window. Snow blanketed the manicured lawns of Lychhurst Hospital, the pond frozen over, the fountain spewing icicles.

The stillness of nature, the feeling of magic, when confronted with winter's scenery, was something Elspeth Carter usually adored; a feeling shared by her seven-year-old daughter, Josie.

On any other day, the two would be making for the local park, where Josie loved to pretend they had found Narnia, but not now, not today. A grackle flew close to the window, its beady eye piercing the glass, accusatory, unnerving.

More were gathered beyond it, silent statues in the trees, around the pond. She had not seen such numbers for a long time. The spell was broken as the bird flew away and a nurse's voice pulled her back to the hospital.

"Mrs. Carter? If you'll come with me. I need to go over a few things with you—"

"My daughter, Josie. Can I see her?"

There was sympathy in the nurse's eyes, but the face mask hid her smile—if there was any. Ever since the doctor had seen Josie at the clinic, masks had been insisted on, as had been her daughter's immediate admittance.

Elspeth followed the nurse further down a corridor which wound its way through the pediatric ward. Large windows to their left displayed small bays decorated in pastel colors, sunshine paint and cheerful prints. Anything to lessen the idea that the hospital was a frightening place—and failing miserably.

The children she glimpsed, where curtains had been pulled back, lay mute and listless. One child was weeping in a nurse's arms. Elspeth returned her focus to the walk ahead, not wanting to think that Josie might be sobbing alone in her bed, wondering where her mother was.

Above her, she spotted a brick archway; it seemed out of place in this modernised interior. Etched into it in capital letters was the word *Isolation.*

"I'd have thought they would've removed that when the place was refurbished," said Elspeth.

"Huh?" The nurse looked up to where she was pointing.

The archway had vanished.

"Oh, nothing, nothing," mumbled Elspeth, looking again at the smooth ceiling, empty now of any sign of old brickwork.

The nurse opened a door and led her into a tiny consulting room.

"If you're thinking it, you're right," she said, gesturing to a chair, while she took her own seat behind a desk.

Now it was Elspeth's turn to raise her eyebrows.

"Used to be a broom cupboard. The architects did their best with this old building, but if I'm honest, I'd have much preferred they pulled it down and rebuilt it from scratch. It's never felt quite right…"

The nurse—Bridget, according to her name tag—seemed distracted for a moment, gazing at something beyond Elspeth's shoulder. Then she shook herself.

"Oh, I'm sorry, Mrs. Carter. Please ignore me. The wards are lovely for the children—and it's their care that's important, isn't it? Now, to Josie. The doctor confirmed with you that we suspect your daughter has contracted TB?"

Elspeth nodded. Yes, the doctor had, and he had given her a look which had piled on the guilt at Josie's predicament.

"From what I understand, she wasn't vaccinated?"

"No... I..."

The crushing guilt returned. It was the memory of her own TB jab which had caused her to baulk at seeing Josie go through the same. Her daughter had heard the horror stories about the number of needles that went into your arm.

"I... well, I thought TB wasn't a thing anymore. It wasn't mentioned during her routine checkups until..."

The irritation in Nurse Bridget's voice was evident. "It's only *not* been a thing because of our vaccination program, but rates are climbing again *and* we've seen the emergence of new strains, some of which are unfortunately proving resistant to treatment. And unfortunately, in your area, there was a marked increase. It's why we targeted the children."

Elspeth felt sick. The doctor's earlier words, repeated by the nurse, condemned her for her neglect. She *had* been told, had received a letter, but...

"When will you know what strain she has?"

"When we get the results of her blood tests back." The nurse had been filling in a form as she spoke and now put down her pen. "But we also need to test you. Bump test *and* bloods."

Nurse Bridget stood up and went over to a small cabinet, taking out some sealed packets. The needle of the syringe emerging from its wrapper made Elspeth feel woozy, and she could feel her heart rate speed up. She pushed her chair back, the scrape of its legs on the tiled floor causing the nurse to turn.

"You don't like needles? Okay, but we really need to test you. You need to do this for Josie. Just look the other way."

Josie. Her daughter's feverish face swam into focus. Elspeth needed to be okay for both of them. They had no one else, only each other. With her thoughts dwelling on recent events, she barely noticed the sting in her arm.

"There we go. All done." A test tube half-filled with her blood sat labelled in a rack.

Elspeth pictured her daughter scared and frightened amongst strange children. "Can I see Josie now?"

The nurse's earlier brusqueness had vanished, and an air of sympathy had returned. "Of course you can. She's been put in a room of her own as a precaution. You'll be able to stay with her if you wish."

Elspeth had brought an overnight bag just in case this was allowed, although initially it had seemed unlikely. "Thank you, I didn't think I'd be able to."

For the first time, the nurse looked uncomfortable. "Well, actually, considering the nature of your daughter's illness we don't usually allow it, but the room—"

Whatever she was going to say, however, Elspeth never discovered, as there was a knock at the door and another nurse appeared. "Josie would like to see her mother."

Elspeth jumped to her feet, barely noticing the look that passed between the two women. Then she was back into the hospital corridor, passing a small nurse's station and another bay of children, before heading for a room at the end of the passage.

Another nurse's station was positioned opposite these remote rooms, and seeing a nurse working quietly at the desk reassured Elspeth. As did seeing that each room also had observation windows next to the door so that both patient and nurse could see each other. Except for one. One room had both curtains and door shut, and it was to this that Elspeth was guided.

"Is there someone in there with her?" she asked. It could be the only reason for the room to be closed off.

Her comment prompted the station nurse to shoot round the desk and rush to the door. "No, no," he said. "We left them open…"

Josie's room was shrouded in gloom. The blinds on the external wall window were closed and the curtains around the bed were also drawn. Behind the bed curtains, Elspeth found her daughter sobbing and shaking beneath her bedclothes. Exactly as she had been imagining.

"Hey, sweetie. Mommy's here. It's okay now. Hush."

As she rocked her daughter, the nurses moved to let the light back in.

"She's only seven! How could you leave her like this?"

"We didn't," said the station nurse, his eyes avoiding hers.

"Then who?"

The nurses all looked at Josie.

"You've got to be kidding," said Elspeth. "She's hooked up to a drip, she barely has any strength. There is no way!"

The nurses refused to give ground, however, and in the end, Elspeth had to let it drop.

"Well, it doesn't matter now. I'll be staying with her."

This time, Elspeth caught the shared look. It was one of apparent relief. There was no argument from them considering the contagious nature of the disease. Another bed had been made ready and the room also had its own toilet and shower.

"Promise you won't leave, Mommy?" Josie had calmed but exhaustion seeped out of her.

"I'm not going anywhere, sweetie."

"I'll be back in an hour to give Josie her meds but we'll leave you be for now," said Nurse Bridget.

The nurses left mother and daughter alone, deliberately closing the door behind them this time.

"Come on," said Elspeth, "snuggle up." She stretched herself out on the bed alongside Josie, allowing her daughter to curl up into her.

"The man closed the curtains," said Josie.

"Oh, you mean the nurse who just came in?"

The one who had vehemently denied being responsible.

"No. Another one. A soldier."

"A soldier?"

Her daughter's imagination had obviously been working overtime. Perhaps a side-effect of whatever the doctor had given her.

"Yes. He said he didn't want anyone to see him. That he was playing hide-and-seek. He said it was best if I hid too." Josie started to cry again.

Elspeth felt a spark of fear. "Did he… did he… do anything?"

"No, no. He… he just pulled the blanket up over my head. Then you all came in."

The flicker of anger she had felt on seeing her daughter alone and in the dark grew into a flame. Where the hell was security in this place?

"Ssh, honey. It must've been a bad dream."

As Elspeth continued to hug her daughter, whose regular breathing told her she had finally succumbed to sleep, she watched the snow falling once again outside. Beyond the glass, the world was white, but inside the hospital she felt nothing but darkness.

They were interrupted briefly by Nurse Bridget who had returned with the promised meds, the injections administered barely disturbing Josie. Her daughter continued to sleep.

Elspeth maneuvered herself off the bed and stretched out her aching limbs.

"Josie told me who closed the curtains," she said. "She said it was a soldier."

Nurse Bridget stared at her. Her eyes were blank, giving nothing away. "A dream, that's all."

"That's what I said, but are you sure no one else could've got in here?"

The nurse waved in the direction of the corridor. "We have cameras, CCTV. We'd have seen."

"Then you can check for me?"

"We can, and we will. But I promise you, there'll be nothing there."

Movement from Josie's bed drew Elspeth back to her daughter's side, holding her hand, the shared touch enough to soothe the little girl. When she looked back, Nurse Bridget had gone.

Josie slept for the remainder of the day. A deep slumber vastly different from the feverish thrashings at home. The coughing fits with their bloody phlegm had also subsided.

For the first time, Elspeth was able to relax a little, allow her mind to wander away from her daughter's condition and her own role in its appearance. Unfortunately, her thoughts meandered back to the soldier. How had nobody seen him? She hoped Josie would be able to tell her more when she woke.

She hoped it was a dream.

Although night had fallen and exhaustion ate at her, Elspeth's mind would not rest. Rising from her bed, she looked out at a sky tinged with orange, the snow-laden clouds making it almost look like daytime. At first glance, all appeared peaceful, but when she took in the heavy sky, it felt as if a storm threatened, something was coming. Even the grackles, roosting along rooftops and branches, seemed to be on alert. And with that thought, all sense of feeling warm and safe vanished. The temperature in the room plunged so that when she breathed out, her breath misted before her.

"Hide," came the whisper.

A man's voice murmuring the word into her ear.

Elspeth didn't want to turn from the window, but an intruder was behind her. Between her and Josie. She swallowed and then spun round fast, hoping her movement might unbalance him.

There was no one there.

"Hide," came the whisper. The voice again murmuring into her ear.

Elspeth looked to her daughter's bed. The curtains were once more pulled around it, the corridor window curtains also closed. And as the gloom grew, she knew the blinds of the window behind her had also been closed. It was so cold. White vapor spilled over her, solidified into ice preventing her from getting to Josie.

Should she call to her daughter? If she woke her, wouldn't she frighten her further? But what if she were already awake and wanted her mother? The thoughts tumbled through Elspeth's mind, but just as she went to speak, the door opened and a nurse entered.

The cold, the numbness, the whispering voice, all disappeared.

Ignoring the nurse, Elspeth dashed over to Josie's bed and pulled the curtains back. To her relief, the little girl continued to sleep.

"Why did you close all the curtains?" she asked the nurse; Vernon, according to his name badge.

He gave her a look. "I've only just come in with Josie's meds. This is nothing to do with me."

Part of her had known that, even before she had accused him. And he was gentle with her daughter, taking her readings, administering the injection without disturbing her. That she was sleeping so deeply had been reassuring; now it began to ring alarm bells. She followed Vernon out of the room.

"Should she sleep so much?"

"It's all perfectly natural. Her signs are all good. Rest is always the best medicine."

Beyond Vernon, the rooms which had formed part of this remote corner appeared empty.

"The children have been moved? Is there something you're not telling me? Aren't we isolated now?"

He shook his head, placatingly. "No, no. Nothing to worry about. One was well enough to go home, the other two were found beds on the ward. We're a bit short on staff tonight and had to reshuffle.

"It means we don't have to man the desk here. Josie has you with her and you have the call button if we're needed. I'm sure you can understand."

Elspeth watched him walk back down the corridor, the lights flickering on and then turning off as he passed, until he disappeared into the light at the end of the tunnel, and their little corner of the hospital suddenly felt a million miles away from the rest of the world. She felt abandoned.

With no one at the desk, Elspeth closed the door behind her, shutting out the dark which fell with the absence of movement in the hallway. Yet still it spilled in, through the observation window, from the corners of the room.

She closed the blinds, turned on the light in the bathroom, and left the door open so that combined with the room's lights, it banished the gloom.

Unable to sit still, however, she opened the door again. She'd noticed a stack of magazines beside the nurse's desk, no doubt meant to occupy the minds of any person waiting in one of the chairs beside it.

Elspeth dashed across, grabbed the pile, and ran back in. She moved quickly, terrified that for some reason the door would shut behind her, keep her from her daughter. An irrational fear but one she couldn't shake off.

Once back in their room, she settled herself on her bed, raising its head behind her so she could sit comfortably, and started to flick through the magazines. Most were trashy celebrity style mags, or those with "real life" stories which she never believed.

She had almost given up on finding anything to distract her when she came to the last magazine in the pile. Somewhat old and battered, it was dated 1944 and purported to be a *Centenary Celebration of Lychhurst Hospital.*

Not quite the real thing however, as a small label declaring it a facsimile was stamped on the corner of the page.

"You're a bit older than that, now, aren't you?" she murmured to herself. One hundred and forty-nine years old. It made her feel insignificant and suddenly alone again, despite her daughter's presence, the knowledge that others were only a short distance away.

She rooted around in her overnight bag and pulled out the small portable radio she had thrown in at the last minute. Fiddling with the dial, she managed to find a station playing the hits of the year.

Depeche Mode started to play and she hummed along quietly. It was one of her favourite songs and helped soothe her nerves.

She returned to the magazine. The pictures caught her attention, old sepia prints of a time long gone: Civil War soldiers lying in their beds, bewhiskered Victorians, tuberculosis patients in beds placed outside to enjoy the fresh air…

Tuberculosis. Her thoughts went straight back to Josie and the awareness that she could have, *should have* prevented her illness.

Elspeth turned the page. "Ghostly Goings On," ran the headline. Wondering if anyone had ever reported a similar experience to her own, she began to read. It wasn't long before she found a reference to the presence of a soldier, an officer seemingly from the time of World War I.

In 1917, Sergeant Andrew McCornall had entered the hospital in search of conscription dodgers. He had entered but never left. And nobody had ever found his body, not even during renovations, although not every stone had been turned in those days.

Who on earth would hide in a TB sanatorium? wondered Elspeth. She'd already dismissed the idea of the sergeant being the ghost referred to by Josie and the magazine. He'd probably just left and no one noticed, maybe even decided that fighting was not for him either.

No. The soldier was a figment of Josie's imagination and she had caught it, one of those shared psychosis things people talked about, brought on by stress. That was all. She turned the page.

As she did so, she suddenly noticed the silence. Her radio had stopped playing. But the batteries were relatively new! She picked it up, took the batteries out and put them back in again. Flipped the switch on and off.

Nothing. It was dead.

Then the light in the bathroom went out, and with only the soft overbed lights illuminating them, the dark crept in once more. Elspeth shivered.

It wasn't just the dark returning but also the cold. A mist spilling toward her. She jumped up and went to turn the bathroom light back on. Nothing. She headed to the door, pausing as she opened it.

Peering down the corridor, she could see the glimmer of light, of life, in the pediatric ward, only a short distance but already feeling a world away.

The call button. She would get someone to come to *them*, bring normality back. Turning to Josie's bed, she realised the mist was getting thicker. Cloaking everything.

Heart pounding, Elspeth stumbled back to her daughter's side, noticing as she approached how still she was. Only the steady beat of the monitor which she was hooked up to gave Elspeth the reassurance her child was okay.

"Hide," whispered the voice.

She didn't look. Couldn't look.

"Hide," he repeated. "They're coming. They won't let you go."

This time she turned. A soldier stood before her, one in the uniform of World War I. *Sergeant McCornall? Hallucinatio*n, she thought. She'd been reading about the man and now here he was in front of her.

Her mind was playing tricks on her, that was all. A good night's rest was all that was needed, but it was so cold.

Shivering, she reached out to touch him, her hand passing right through where his body stood, the temperature dropping even lower as she did so. She jerked her hand back.

"Hide," he said again, and pointed to Josie's bed, then began walking toward it.

Elspeth backed away in front of him, until she bumped up against the edge of the mattress. To her surprise, he didn't come any closer; instead he tugged the curtains around them, closing out the swirling vapor. He remained on the other side.

Elspeth pressed the call button above the bed; then, terrible curiosity getting the better of her, she found a gap in the curtain and peered out.

The hospital she saw beyond the curtains was not the one she had walked into. She barely had time to take in the beds in the wide ward, before a figure appeared, a young man. He was walking straight toward them, his eyes bright, a hacking cough erupting from his mouth, accompanied by a trickle of blood. A trickle which became a stream, pouring down his chest. Elspeth wanted to turn away, close the curtains on the terrible vision, but she found herself frozen on the spot.

Nor was it one man; there were others behind him. Two, three, four. All coughing, blood spewing from their mouths. A nightmare vision, and they were heading toward their cubicle.

Sergeant McCornall—she had decided it was definitely him—continued to stand guard in front of her.

"Hide," he murmured again. "Don't let them see you."

The four bloodied men were closer now. This time, Elspeth shrank back, let the curtain close the gap through which she'd been peering, climbed onto the bed with Josie, and pulled the blankets over both of them. She lay there, shaking in the darkness, as she held onto her daughter. How could any of this be happening?

Beyond them, she could hear the coughing and spluttering come ever nearer. The darkness of her hiding place began to take on a crimson tinge, and for a brief moment, she felt she was swimming in a sea of blood. Tides of it swelling up and over and into her.

She wanted to push the blanket off, away from her, but still that voice commanded her to stay, to hide. The feeling of drowning grew; she started to cough and choke as the phantoms she had seen had done. She was suffocating. Elspeth reached out an arm, feeling for the call button, only for icy fingers to grab hold, begin to pull her out.

No. This is a dream, a nightmare. This is not happening, she told herself. *You'll wake Josie if you keep this up. Get a grip.* With renewed determination, she pushed the blanket from her and rose to face whatever lay beyond.

There was nothing, except a trail of blood disappearing with the mist. The light in the bathroom suddenly came on, as did her radio. This time, Whitney Houston.

Creeping cautiously to the door, she peered out. Everything was as it had been. Heart thumping, Elspeth returned to her daughter's side, holding her hand as she tried to make sense of what had happened.

"Is everything alright?" Vernon stood in the doorway.

"I… um… yes. I… the lights went and… it got cold…"

Vernon looked around the room. "Well, it all seems to be working now. Lovely and toasty. Definitely much better than being outside at the minute. Blowing a proper gale out there."

Elspeth rung her hands, uncertain what to do, what to say.

"Look, I'll get you a nice cup of tea," said Vernon. "Make you feel better. It's always tough for parents, isn't it? That feeling that you should be the one to protect your children and then finding you can't—well, not always. Sometimes, some things are beyond us. We're only human after all."

As he left her alone to fetch her drink, she pondered his words. What had he been getting at?

When he returned, she took the offered drink and sipped it gratefully, allowing its warmth to dissipate the chill which had remained inside.

"I… I saw something," she blurted out, just as he was about to leave.

He stopped but didn't turn around.

"A soldier, just like Josie said. But I don't think he was here to harm anyone. I think he was actually here to… to protect us, her."

Vernon merely nodded, still with his back to her, and left.

Elspeth took her drink over to the window and peered through the blinds to see the snow swirling beyond, flakes coming down thick and heavy. A blizzard which continued well into the next day.

She pushed the events of the night to the back of her mind as Josie woke at regular intervals, appeared much stronger, even able to eat small meals.

The drip was also removed, allowing Elspeth to relax further. Neither of them mentioned the soldier. Josie seemed to have forgotten him and Elspeth didn't want to upset her on top of everything else that had gone on.

Well into the evening, everything continued as normal. Elspeth had been told her daughter had responded well to the medication and she could continue to take the antibiotics at home. Neither of them appeared to be contagious. Tomorrow they could leave.

That evening, Elspeth settled herself on the bed and this time allowed herself to indulge in the trashy stories penned in the magazines she had discarded the previous night. After she had exhausted their pages, she felt the urge to stretch her limbs; she'd been cooped up too long. But she couldn't go far from Josie, now sleeping peacefully once more, a healthy glow returned to her cheeks.

Elspeth stepped out into the corridor. It was dark, but as she walked, the lights came on around her, turning off again once she had moved on. It was a short walk to the ward where the nurses were now stationed, the staff shortage of the previous night continuing today as some had been unable to get into work due to the weather.

"Stretching my legs," she said to one with a smile.

Then she turned around and saw the long dark tunnel and felt a sudden pang. Josie was down there, all alone. She walked quickly, the lights continuing to turn reassuringly on—until they didn't.

Elspeth had passed the empty rooms before Josie's, she was sure of it, but could not make out the door to their room. She moved to the wall, allowing her hand to trail along and guide her, looking back at the distant light to try and use that to gauge the distance. All to no avail.

Her heart rate stepped up, began to beat loudly in her chest.

"Josie," she whispered, "Mommy's coming."

She continued to walk along a never-ending corridor, unable to see her daughter's room, feeling the temperature dropping all the time. When her hand felt the frame of an observation window and moved on to find a door, she let out a sigh of relief.

Elspeth went inside, but it wasn't her daughter's room. Instead, she found herself in an empty ward, beds either side of the wide space with its high ceilings and old whitewashed brickwork.

At the far end, a figure emerged, hacking coughs erupting from him, blood dribbling down his front. Behind him emerged his three companions, their white nightshirts stained crimson.

Elspeth started to back away, her hand feeling for the reassurance of the wall, only to find that had vanished, whimpering as she moved. "No, no, no."

They were coming closer, slowly, steadily. Elspeth turned and ran, back into the dark tunnel, briefly noticing the Isolation sign carved into the archway through which she sped.

Heart pounding, terror-stricken, she ran on. Stopping only when she collided into someone, some *thing*—fear drove her to fight whatever held her, subsiding when a familiar voice said her name.

"Mrs. Carter. Mrs. Carter. It's me, Vernon."

She stopped struggling then, was able to make out his face in the gloom.

"Oh, thank God. I'm going mad. I'm seeing things. Josie…"

Then Vernon spoke, his voice coming out as a whisper, drifting in the growing mist.

"Hide."

Icy fingers gripped her hand, dragged her through the pitch, pushed her into a room. *Their* room, she realised, rushing once more to her daughter's bedside.

"Vernon! Nurse!"

He didn't hear her. He had remained beyond their room, and through the gap in the curtain, she watched as the four bloodied spirits swarmed over him.

Elspeth pressed the call button, again and again, but no one came. There was nothing she could do except climb beneath the blankets like a child and hide from the dark.

When morning came, she opened her eyes to find the doctor smiling down at her.

"Lovely day outside," she said. "Snowplows have cleared the roads, so it looks like you'll be able to get home."

"I thought we'd have to stay here much longer," said Elspeth.

"Oh, there's no need for that. It seems our results were wrong. A virus, that was all, but we will give her the vaccination with your permission."

She thought back to the visions of the men, their blood enveloping all as they chased her and Vernon down the corridor.

"Nurse Vernon not here?" she asked. "I'd like to say goodbye, and thank you."

The doctor and nurse looked at each other; they beckoned her away from Josie's bed.

"I'm sorry," said the doctor, voice low. "But it seems Nurse Vernon has contracted an illness of some sort, quite nasty. He's been placed in isolation."

Elspeth swallowed. "What about Josie, me? Are we at risk?"

"No, no. I shouldn't think so. And we really think it's best you went home. Josie'll get better much quicker in a familiar environment. Wouldn't want to *hide* away here any longer than you have to, would you?"

Elspeth stared at the doctor, at the nurse. Both returned her gaze, unflinching. They were right. She would not stay in this hospital a moment longer.

Taking her daughter's hand, she led her to the lift which would take them to the ground floor and to the world beyond.

The normal world, the safe world, a place where no one told you to run and *hide*.

Surgery Ward
1938, 1957, & 1960

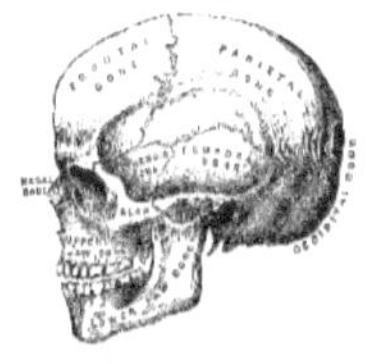

The Night Nurse
Jennifer Anne Gordon

1938

The dew was still wet on Clarinda's sixth year of life the first time she spent the whole night at Lychhurst Hospital, but she was only four the first time she laid eyes on the building. And maybe that was all it took, that moment of seeing. Of being seen.

Maybe at just four years old, Clarinda was already destined to be one of the hospital's ghosts.

When she was four, her father was still alive. They would walk up to the hill in the mornings to meet her mother when she finished her nightly shift— eyes weary, shoulders heavy.

A night's work at Lychhurst, a night's work on Corpse Hill was different. It was different than a night spent at home. A night spent safely tucked in.

A night spent loved.

Clarinda didn't know anything about the big building on the hill, she did not know if a night spent inside its walls was a night where *anyone* could feel loved. She certainly didn't think her mother *looked* loved when they saw her again in the mornings.

Clarinda did not know what Corpse Hill meant; she understood *hill*… but *corpse*… that was a word that made the air in their kitchen feel heavy and stale. The word felt like a storm that would never break.

Corpse.

Clarinda did not know what a night nurse at a sanitarium did, how her mother spent her hours. She only knew that in the mornings her mother's emerald eyes would had dulled to swampy green… transformed not by magic but instead by madness, winding its way into her like the climbing bittersweet that snaked up the wall outside Clarinda's bedroom window.

But what did that mean?

Madness?

It was a joke she didn't understand. It was a thing her father would say, his voice a coarse whisper. His words were more like wheezes every day. His eyes did *not* change colors, but he would look sad when he said it.

Her mother would slap his arm; her laugh was dry. It sounded the same way that walking through autumn leaves did. She would rest her head on Daddy's shoulder and wind her arm through his. Holding onto him as if she already knew he was fading away. She was already packing him in boxes.

She understood Corpse Hill in her way.

Clarinda knew to stay behind them when they walked like that. She knew how to let the grownups have their time. She didn't mind. She didn't feel left out. It gave her time to stare up at that building.

She loved to see the windows just as lights were starting to go on. She imagined that seeing through the bars was a way to see into the very soul of that place. If a place could have a soul…

She didn't know what went on in there, but she did know that when she looked at it she felt it looking back at her. She knew that when she looked at it, she felt alive—awake. She knew when she looked at Lychhurst that she felt loved in a way that she didn't feel when she looked at her mother's eyes, whether they were emerald- or madness-green.

Clarinda's Daddy became a memory only a few short weeks before her days and her nights were forced to switch places.

Was this magic? Was this madness? She and her mother now had to sleep during the day. They would lay in the big bed; it still smelled like her Daddy. They had pinned up bed sheets and blankets over the windows. Her mother called it "fool's midnight." They wrapped their arms around each other. Clarinda's skin was clammy. She felt her mother's arms around her, but she didn't feel anything else.

When they woke up her mother would make them pancakes. One to eat right away, and the other to fold into a hanky to have later. Then they would leave the house and make their way up and up. All the back to the top of Corpse Hill.

Like ghosts. Like climbing bittersweet. Mother's eyes didn't change colors anymore. There was no emerald left.

Clarinda had to walk twice as fast as she was used to. There was no walking behind her mother anymore, there was no Daddy wheezing his *madness* jokes into her mother's ears. She had to be a big girl. She had to keep up. Big girls got to go to the hospital at night.

"This place isn't supposed to be for little girls like you. We are going to need to keep you secret."

Big girls like Clarinda didn't just keep secrets. They were the secret.

"But I'm a big girl." Clarinda's voice was breathy and tired, she was not used to being out in the night air so long after dark. Was this fool's dawn? She wanted to ask her mother but thought better of it. She knew who she would ask. She knew what she would ask.

In the weeks since Daddy became a memory, they had developed a routine. Clarinda would wait outside, her bony shoulders pressing tight to the shadows. Her skinny body was almost invisible in the little nook that was tucked in by the back doors to the kitchen.

Clarinda hated this part of the night, being so close to the building but unable to really look at it, and worse, the building was unable to look at her. While she waited for her mother, she would press her lips against the gray stone walls and whisper, "Soon I will be inside of you. You will swallow me up, and I will be your baby."

Her words didn't make sense to her, but it felt right for her to say them. She liked the way the words felt in her mouth, like a prayer. She loved the way the stone wall felt against her lips, like shaved ice during the weeks before August gave up and finally stopped being so hot. She wanted to belong to Lychhurst. She wanted to somehow be this building's beautiful favorite daughter.

She counted time in mosquito bites, and usually between four and six of them her mother would open the door. They would sneak through the empty kitchen. The floor was still sticky with potatoes and gravy. The air: thick with the musk of rodents, body odor, and burned bread.

Before they left the kitchen, Mother would give Clarinda the same warning she did every night. Clarinda was to be quiet, and no matter what she heard, no matter how unearthly the noises, she could not let out so much as a peep.

Her mother would take her favorite gardenia scarf out of her pocket and wrap it tightly around Clarinda's eyes so she could not see anything.

"Remember, baby girl, no matter what, you don't make a sound, no matter what you hear or think you hear. You will be safe when we get to your special room, nothing bad will happen to you there."

But Clarinda was never scared. Clarinda loved the blindfold; she knew even without seeing what was around her. She had this feeling that every part of Lychhurst was there to take care of her. Love her. On some nights she knew she was not alone, she felt a little hand in hers, knew there was another child with her, she could hear a ball bouncing down the hallway as he took her hand—yes, *he*—she wasn't the only secret here. Clarinda considered herself one of the children of Corpse Hill, its favorite daughter. Though, she didn't know what any of that meant.

Clarinda was not allowed to remove the scarf until she heard the heavy metal door click closed behind them. When the scarf was removed, she was no longer swaddled in the scent of dead flowers and dried grass. There was nothing left of her home. Her Daddy. Her fool's midnight.

There was no more of the smell that would follow her mother like a cloud, especially when Clarinda was told to stay away from her parents' bedroom… on the nights her mother would put that same scarf over the lamp and turn their room into a dream not meant for children.

But now, in Clarinda's special room, she knew that this dream was made for her. This waking dream. Without the scarf covering her eyes, the lights were too bright. It made the backs of her eyes ache at first, but still, that ache was welcome. Clarinda didn't see the sun as much as she used to, now that her days and nights had switched places.

Clarinda's special room had high ceilings and a balcony with rows of seats. Her special room was a theatre. Clarinda was the star of the stage. Her special room had trays of the most beautiful shiny objects that Clarinda had ever seen.

"Are they diamonds?" she asked on one of her first nights there.

"No, not diamonds but just as sharp, so you never touch them. It's important that they stay sharp and clean."

There were small mirrors on sticks, and diamond knives in all sorts of shapes; they did not look like the knives they had in the drawers in their kitchen, these looked—beautiful. *These…* felt like home.

Clarinda knew that her mother would leave her there, locking the door behind her. She knew that Clarinda's special room was not used at night. And Clarinda knew that this room was meant for her. There was a skinny bed in the center of the room. It had wheels that locked in place and thin bed sheets that smelled like a clean floor. Sheets that smelled sharp with just a hint of lemonade, as if it had spilled and been cleaned up.

Not by her. No, Clarinda would never spill lemonade in her special room. Her mother brought over a special step stool and put it close enough to the bed with wheels that Clarinda could climb up in there to sleep.

To wait.

Sometimes she would lay there, listening to the beetles' scuttle in the murky corners of the room—shadows that were alive. Shadows that loved the smell of cleaned-up lemonade.

Sometimes she would hang her head over the side of bed with wheels and stare into the drain on the floor below.

Tonight, there was the beginnings of a vine climbing out of the drain, reaching its tendrils toward the bottom of the bed with wheels. Silverfish danced in the drain, and on occasion a house centipede would stroll through, leaving a trail of a million pink footprints. Small kisses of rust or blood. Around and around like a carousel.

Clarinda had been on one of those painted horses once, back when day was still day, and her father was not yet a memory.

This special room, it was better than a carousel.

When her body would become restless, she would climb down and press her face against the drain, she wanted what was in there to see her, to know that she was home. The drain smelled like pennies and her mother's monthly ladies' belts that Clarinda would wash in their kitchen sink.

"Is this fool's dawn?"

Then she would press her lips against the cool metal grate. She could feel that drain kiss her back. The way her father would before—a little light summer kiss on her cheek.

This was love.

This was her real home.

She knew she was not supposed to touch the tray of sharp diamonds, but she wanted to. Boy, did she want to. She wanted to know them; she knew that they were somehow a part of her—part of her home.

So, with a centipede-kissed cheek, she would drag the step stool close to the tray, she would climb up and whisper to them. "Soon you will be my babies. You will be inside of me. I will be your mommy, and we will all be home."

The Ones Who Were Here Once

If I were able to
I would make her out of clay
I would keep her away from drain kisses
They are both beautiful
And empty
Baby pink pennies
My fingers would say
I love you
I never walked ahead
My fingers would say
I am glad night and day have switched
My fingers would say
I am cold walls
I am a blindfold
I am not fingers

I am

I am

I am Corpse hill

Lychhurst

I saw that you loved me

I loved you

too

Maybe you will know me

Maybe you will understand

Not now

Not this

I am Corpse Hill

So much more and

So much less

than diamonds on a tray

untouched

we are

your children

Your mother switched day to night—

not for her, not really.

For you.

You are my daughter

home

My daughter with diamonds who have not been born.

And never able to.

But fear not

This is a love story on

Corpse Hill.

The Night Nurse
1957

Madness green had been replaced with calming green. Green like algae on the duck pond. Mossy green on the corners of the stone stairs that lead into this building's mouth. Moldy green, like the fuzzy ends of bread, scraped off and toasted.

Eyes still changed color for the staffers here at Lychhurst—especially after a shift as a night nurse—it happened for most of them.

Not for nurse Clarinda Meyer.

Her eyes have not changed… not for years. Whatever green hues that bloomed there when she was a child were replaced years ago. Now her eyes were gray like stone walls. Gray eyes with a shimmer like silverfish. Gray eyes like the fog on the meandering path up Corpse Hill during fool's dawn.

As a perioperative night nurse at Lychhurst Hospital, Clarinda cannot remember the last time she thought of her own eye color. *Had she ever?*

She did not perfume herself; she did not look in a mirror. In fact Clarinda Meyer had no memory of looking at herself. No mirrors, no school dances… no fumbled sweaty groping while parked in the shadows of the winding drive up to Lychhurst's front door.

Many of the nurses chose this profession for just those reasons. Promises of doctors working long hours, promises of attractive men with hero complexes… Clarinda was not looking for a hero. She had already been saved. This building, her special room—there could be no greater love story.

Sometimes at night, she would put her fingers inside of her and remember the centipede's million little legs across her cheek. She would remember her mouth on a drain—she would remember the blindfold and two different kinds of lemon scents.

She *was* happy.

Maybe that was not the right word—but she was content. She knew that sometimes… and maybe more than sometimes… she longed to be invisible. To be asleep, and awake. To finally be alive—she did not need to see things, only to feel. She wanted. She wanted. She wanted.

Fool's midnight.

Fool's dawn.

She wanted her diamonds on a tray. Until then, she was… content. She was a ghost—just not of the dead—but a six-year-old with centipede kisses…

She was a ghost—not a real thing at all—just a reflection on a tray of shiny tools under bright lights—she was a ghost haunting herself.

The night nurse.

This is not a love story. She was wrong. It's a ghost story.

The perioperative night nurse was not the position that the post-Florence Nightingale acolytes hoped to be. Surgery at Lychhurst was not performed at night unless there was an emergency.

Clarinda hated emergencies.

She hated the emergency symphony. The cacophony of saving a life. But… she could do it. She did do it. When necessary.

Mainly her job was one of preparation. While technically a nurse—in title and in training—Clarinda was more of a caretaker.

Not for people, but… this special room, and these shining-like-diamond tools were hers. They were her children.

The Doctor

Doctor Jared Sayre found her in her special room… She was whispering to her cold, shiny children… her sharp untouchable diamonds. Her back was hunched. Her uniform was spotless. He saw her. Clarinda's lips were pressed against the shiniest set of dissecting forceps, her lips moving against them as if she were reciting poetry.

"Is this fool's dawn?" Her mouth pressed against the tool, waiting for herself to let it open her.

"I'm sorry, I'm not trying to interrupt. I… I am… just trying to check the instruments, I have my first… I am supposed to be here…"

He looked down at his feet. Silverfish and centipedes seemed to dance around the soles of his shoes before they turned into nothing.

Clarinda was finally seen. She was a living ghost stepping from the shadows. She thought to apologize, but instead a silverfish crawled from her mouth.

It tasted like lemon. The silverfish… yes… but more so… the moment. A different kind of lemon.

It was not until they turned to each other that Clarinda's eyes changed. They matched his… both hues of madness green.

"You're the new surgeon? Doctor…?" Clarinda didn't remember his name, though she had been told that Doctor… Doctor… So-and-so… was very particular about his surgical instruments—*her children.*

"Doctor Sayre, Jared Sayre."

"Yes, of course. Our names rhyme a bit. I should have remembered. Forgive me. I am not used to conversations this late at night. Fool's dawn…"

"Or fool's midnight."

He said this, and neither of them laughed, though Clarinda wanted to do something…

"When I heard you were coming, I thought that was strange, or… not strange, but… *right*. Nice. Yes…I thought it was *nice*." Clarinda realized as she was stammering that she was still holding her favorite child, her first born, her shiniest set of forceps.

"I have my first surgery in the morning, I just wanted to make sure— and I'm sure your *ways* are fine—but I wanted to make sure that the instruments were… I wanted them, needed them really, to be perfect. No mistakes."

"Of course." Clarinda walked to the surgical tray and placed the forceps down, crooked and coated with her breath's condensation still lingering like a kiss.

"I can be very particular, I have my ways, things I like to have done."

"I understand, Doctor, I can do my best… But, just so you know… the surgeons that came before you have never asked for… something particular. I'm not usually here during the procedures themselves unless it's an emergency."

"So, you won't be here tomorrow? I'm performing an endometrial ablation, using electrocoagulation, it's not a new procedure but I was told this was the first time it would be performed at Lychhurst." He wasn't looking at her, but instead focused on Clarinda's surgical tray—her children.

He held her favorite forceps in his right hand and moved her shiniest scalpel next. He was both delicate but confident when he moved the forceps to the first position, like the lead role in this theatre. He still held the scalpel in his hand as reorganized her work.

"Normally the forceps would not be here, but tomorrow they will be very important, but this…" His movements were gentle as he took her hand

and placed the scalpel in it. "This is normally the most important. *She* is my favorite. Please disinfect her and place her here." Doctor Sayre air tapped above the blank space on the tray.

"You should watch tomorrow, from the cheap seats." He gestured to the balcony, the already-starting-to-rot wooden seats that had not been used in years. "I do love my work to be appreciated."

Clarinda did not leave Corpse Hill that night; instead she spent the rest of her shift disinfecting doctor Sayre's favorite—now her favorite. She placed it on the tray, admired it. Admired her. Admired all of them, her beautiful sharp daughters.

She wiped down every surface of the operating theatre, her special elixir of bleach, white vinegar, lemon juice, and just a hint of her mother's smell, her Daddy's favorite gardenias, chewed up and spit into the atomizer.

This surgery is their song.

Her children, her shining sharp babies did not feel this kind of love. They had jobs to do. They were not flowers and lemons. They were precise, they were perfect. They would never need to be watched. They were the heart of this special room. They taught her… Without them, would Clarinda be a nurse…?

Would Clarinda be anything?

The next morning Clarinda made her way to the balcony, and found an empty seat in the top row, next to a dark-haired woman, another nurse, wearing stiff puffed sleeves. Clarinda's fidgeting arms rubbing against the woman's old-fashioned sleeve as if she were trying to keep warm.

The woman never looked at her, but Clarinda could feel her, like lightning during a winter storm. She felt her, the same way she felt the air in the operating theatre change as Doctor Sayre entered. Without a thought Clarinda reached out to take the dark-haired woman's hand, the same way the little boy took her hand so many years ago—but her hand grasped at nothing.

The nurse was no longer there.

Lychhurst

Early morning was never reality
Just a place that

wounds bleed through.

Fools this.

Fools that.

Stippled blood like memories kept

Safekeeping—pressed in books

Molding in boxes

It is only when it stops that you know

you are…

You know you are.

Home

Healed.

But still bleeding

You will always be bleeding until—

You are not.

1960

A Ghost Story

"Doctor Sayre?"

"Yes, Clarinda?" The doctor stood up; there was an eagerness that washed over his face the moment he realized it was her.

Clarinda thought perhaps he had known she was coming, maybe he heard her kitten heels walking down the hall. But she didn't think so. Her first thought was that somehow Lychhurst had whispered it in his ear. She hoped that he had been sitting there waiting for her.

Clarinda's palms rested against the door jamb. Her fingers and arms felt like invasive vines growing up and out of this hill, this Corpse Hill. She had so many questions. Her arms, her wrists, her fingers. She could not explain it, but she wanted them to be vines, hoped for it. Hoped that they would reach out, leafy fingers and toes growing over Doctor Sayre's body.

Lush. Awful. Green.

The opposite of red, the opposite of blood, the opposite of…

"I have been bleeding for two years, it's my—"

178

"—For two years?" The doctor did not look shocked, if anything he looked giddy, like a child opening a gift.

"I'm not lying, I am bleeding, a lot. I don't know how much longer it's safe to go on like this. Something needs to happen. I've heard of procedures…"

The air in the room changes, she feels it pressing against her, as if this very building were holding her close, keeping her safe. She can feel something inside of her let go. This air is a blood clot.

Everything inside her is this. She is bleeding to death, she fears.

No. She hopes.

No. She fears.

She looks at Doctor Sayre. She feels the imaginary vines growing from the earth and though her, touching him. Touching Doctor Sayre, guiding his hands, her hands. Not so much in an embrace, but something more intimate, more personal.

A scalpel. Clarinda on the bed with wheels. The bed isn't moving. It's held in place. Holding her in her special room.

Climbing bittersweet.

Clarinda was still too polite to come right out and ask Doctor Jared Sayre to save her life. Too polite to ask if her beautiful shiny children could be inside her. Too polite to ask if instead of ether she could have her mother's gardenia scarf tied around her eyes. Yes. That would be enough for her.

She was too polite; instead, she leaned in the hallway.

Yes, her body was letting go. She looked down. Blood around her feet. Memories of silverfish and centipedes finding their home.

Her body had been bleeding for two years. The other doctors, the ones who came before, told her this was because she did not have children… but she *had* children. She *has* children.

Forceps and diamonds. A bed with wheels where she is safe, scalpels she can never touch, and never control because she is not allowed to… she is a little girl, she is a big girl. She is the night nurse and she needed help— she needed her children, now, before it was too late for her.

Clarinda felt the pull of her special room… the operating theatre…

She wants to feel safe. She wants to listen to the room's shadows scurrying. So many silverfish.

Her vines are in his office.

Creeping. Creeping. Climbing bittersweet.

Her roots are deep; her life winds all the way from the base of Corpse Hill up here to this office, with this doctor all the way to her special room.

"I have been bleeding to death for two years."

"Yes. I can see… I know, I know—I can help you. I can help you the way you want me to. Tell me how to help you. This place. It wants me to help you, it wants me to give you everything you have always wanted."

Nervous now, Clarinda asks, "How do I know you will help me the way I want it to be?"

"I have heard a whispering, from the walls, the shadows. I have heard a voice from inside the drain in your special room…it wants to help you; it wants *me* to help you… its wants me to make sure to tie your mother's scarf nice and tight. It wants me to tell you not to make a noise, no matter what you hear, what you feel. No matter what happens. And if you get scared, it wants you to remember the second pancake… *in a hanky,* it wants you to know that it's not fool's dawn. It's dawn, just dawn."

"You can hear it too? The way this place can know a person… I want you to help me. I want my children to help me…"

"Yes, Clarinda, I know."

He was standing close to her now; she could feel his breath against her skin. Lemons and disinfectant. He held her hands now; she closed her eyes and let him guide her to the larger room next door. She heard the echo of their steps as if it were Lychhurst's heartbeat.

He walked her to the bed with wheels and helped her up. She kept her eyes closed while she reached into her pocket and wrapped her fingers around the gardenia scarf.

She breathed in the faded smell of her mother as Doctor Sayre secured the scarf around her eyes.

She whispered a quiet thank you to her mother for bringing her here so many years ago. She thanked the silverfish, and the bittersweet.

She thanked Lychhurst.

Her voice started to fade as she lowered onto the bed. There was not much time left. She knew that. She knew that soon she would meet her children, and they would welcome her to Lychhurst in a way that she always knew was meant to be.

She felt the night air on her bare skin. She heard the tray of her children being brought to her. She felt Doctor Sayre's hand on hers as it placed the diamond scalpel into her hand. She felt him guiding her, a line like a sunrise, like fool's dawn across her lower abdomen.

She felt herself open. She felt her children inside her at last. She was a daughter. She was a mother. A little girl. A big girl.

The ending of a love story. The beginning of a ghost story.

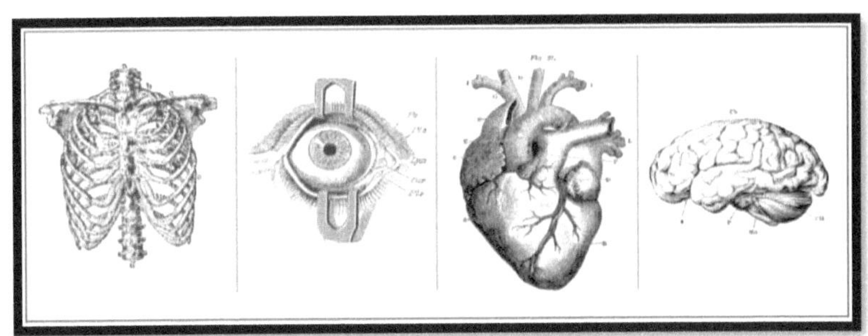

Triage Level: Red

Yes! Scalpels and forceps and oh, isn't that gardenia smell lovely?

But it's getting late—seems like it's always late around here, actually…

No! No, don't scurry off. Sit down.

I said *sit.*

Dear, I must insist that you follow all instructions I give you. Hospitals are dangerous places you know.

Scalpels and forceps and syringes, oh, yes!

Sit.

Don't make me strap you in.

Or sedate you.

Thank you.

Let's continue.

We're getting into the less fun parts of the hospital now, I will admit.

Many people consider these the sadder parts, but I just think they are fascinating and full of the most interesting people.

Who? Oh! Yes, let me introduce you.

Dr. Danforth in the Respiratory Ward is excellent. A bit handsy, it's true, but extremely handsome—he'll literally take your breath away!

Old Frankie in the Burn Unit is one of my favorite people, ever. He's a bit forgetful, though, and…well, just don't mention Bed 5 to him. It gets him all hot under the collar. Tends to set off a whole series of screams and commotion. Highly unprofessional.

You'll find Dr. Albright in the Emergency Room. Lovely man. He has brought more worthy people back from the brink of death—and beyond—than anyone else in the whole hospital. Of course, it's up to him to decide who is worthy. But I'm sure he'll like you. You look like you come from good money.

The Cardiac Ward is a happening place, though I suspect the staff in that section have been getting a bit lax of late—here, let me lean down and whisper in your ear, this is just our little secret, you see—I think they're all imbibing on the job. Ah, well. Sometimes you need a little something to take the edge off, in a place like this.

Careful when you visit the Psych Ward. All kinds of fascinating types in there, but best to stick to the well-lit hallways and away from the doors.

And if you run into dear Abby while you're there, please tell her I said hello. And that she can't keep me out forever.

Ahem.

Yes, yes, alright.

You can stand up again.

No need to get upset. I'm just trying to make sure you're feeling tip-top, bright eyed and bushy tailed. We wouldn't want anything bad to happen to you while you're here, would we?

Yes, you seem strong enough for a few more rooms.

Go on.

We're right here at the Cancer Ward, anyway, so may as well start there. Jeb is always happy to see a new face. Fine man, old Jeb. Just keep a close eye on him…he's always got a trick up his sleeve.

Cancer Ward
1866

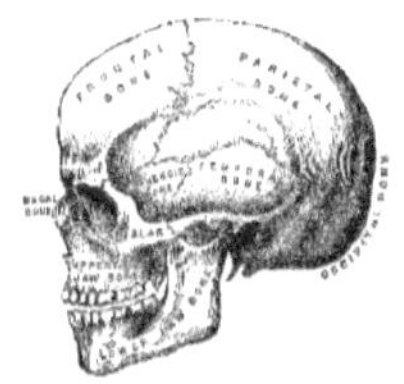

The Highest Stakes Game
Joshua Loyd Fox

Jeb Watson was a mean ol' sonofabitch.

A cantankerous, ornery sot, and would as soon shoot you as converse nicely with you.

He was built like a grey-weathered barbed-wire fence post, with gristle for skin, wrinkles from wear, and sunburned patches on his body more than not.

He was made out of piss and vinegar, wild-caught cougar, a half patch of Injun' blood, and the dust and dirt that covered him from head to toe.

And Jeb Watson was dying.

The orderlies wheeled him into the tuberculosis wing of Lychhurst Hospital, the Soldiers and Sailors Asylum in eastern West Virginia, because they didn't know what was wrong with him.

Jeb was spitting up blood, his skin, eyes, and under his fingernails was urine yellow, and he could barely breathe. He would just scream obscenities at the orderlies and nurses when he could draw breath.

The TB ward was the best place for him until they could figure out just what was killing the old, wiry coot.

Soon enough, however, a wet-behind-the-ears young doctor, medically trained at the new King's and Columbia Schools of Medicine up in New York, ran a few tests, listened to old Jeb's lungs, tapped on the old man's chest here and there, and declared that the man had cancer of the lungs.

And about two months of living left, if the young doc had anything to say about it.

They had found out Jeb had fought out of the rebel Kentucky Regulars during the Civil War, and he was none too quiet about still believing the South had had the right of it.

Him dying, and dying real soon, didn't seem to bother the old man none. To Jeb's way of thinking, he should have been pushing up daisies long since, and this protracted, painful way to die just didn't sit right with the man.

In the darkness of the night, him lying awake, coughing his lungs literally out of his body, he told the good old Lord, or anyone listening up there, that he wasn't going no-where's and that was that.

Jeb Watson died the next morning.

But true to his word, and the man upstairs listening, Jeb didn't go no-where's, that was fact.

He stayed right there in that Cancer Ward, watching the other sorry sods around him come and go with as regular timing as the old black and white clock that would eventually live on the northward wall of the ward.

But that clock would come years later.

At that exact moment, Jeb's ghost was left right where his body had laid, and it couldn't leave the ward neither, or else the darkness outside the walls of the hospital would claim him.

He looked down at his spectral form, wispy tendrils of foggy mist following him and all.

Well, old Jeb though, *that was as fine as fine to him*. He could just live out his eternity right where he was, watching the living and dying, coming and going.

He got downright bored with it all within a few months of haunting and hollerin' and trying to scare the invalids of the ward though. Bored as bejesus, that was for sure.

He didn't stay alone long, however. And he knew he wouldn't. He couldn't understand how most, if not all, of the dying chose the light above or the darkness outside the hospital.

Surely, he thought to himself, *someone would eventually do what he had done, and choose to stay right there, damn the gods and devils each.*

And then, one day, as he watched the cancer patients around him in the living… slowly dying… one man chose just the way old Jeb had done, and Jeb wasn't alone no more.

John Taylor had been near as old as old Jeb when he kicked the bucket. Only thing, John Taylor died on the operating table, and as he left his living body, his ghost stayed right there, lord willing, staring over at old Jeb, guts and organs damn near falling from the hole opened up by the surgeon's scalpel, nipples to navel.

"Your innards are showin'," Jeb told John, his ghostly voice as scratchy and mean as when he was living.

John Taylor looked down at his spectral form and mumbled, "Well, shit. They are."

"Fancy a game of poker?" was all old Jeb asked his new Ward mate, and when John Taylor nodded, the Game began.

The Game would last for the next hundred and fifty years, with players coming and going, but the stakes, and the pot, all being the same.

Ghosts abounded in Lychhurst Hospital, that was true. Some were as evil as sin while others were just lost and looking for the light.

But in the Cancer Ward, the Game had the highest stakes of all.

For all a ghost had to bet was its very existence. Its choice to stay in Purgatory, playing along to the whims of Jeb and John, Tin Cup Debbie, a little Asian fella they could never quite figure out the pronouncing of his name, so they just called him Dim Sum, and a small boy named Tom, one armed, and quiet.

That boy was never quite right, and just came and went when it was time to pony up your losings, or your winnings.

Those were the main players. But some other ghosts came and went, winning and losing, appearing and disappearing as the time went on.

Winning though, winning meant more than just staying in the Game. It meant feeling alive.

Winning the existence of a losing ghost gave the winner a few precious seconds of feeling alive again.

It was like a drug for a ghost, sucking in the soul of a newly dearly-departed specter.

And it was a drug that old Jeb soon found a hankering for, that was for damned sure.

So, mostly he cheated. Mostly he stole.

But he ended the purgatorial stay of more ghosts than he knew what to do with, and the only one who could calm him down, who could keep him playing the Game, was Goodman John Taylor.

"Alright, I got the kid in Bed 4," Jeb said, holding tight his five cards in front of him, away from prying eyes.

Ornery Tin Cup Debbie liked to cheat by rolling her left eyeball across the table to rest where she could gander up at a fella's card hand.

Cheating old minx, Jeb thought, looking over at the skin-and-bones woman with barely a wisp of hair left on her bald pate.

She grinned back at him, holding her own five-card hand, couple of teeth missing and one emaciated breast hanging out of her hospital gown.

"And put yer tit back in your dress, Debbie!" he told her. "We done all seen it!"

Little Tom let out a snicker behind his five cards, and Goodman John looked away, ashamed.

"Pony up folks, we ain't got all day," Jeb said, the joke as old as the smell coming off a new man, his body still encased in the metal lung device he died in.

The seven players at the table in the middle of the Cancer Ward glanced around at the living souls clinging to dear life and tried to find their own pony.

And some of the living souls looked back at the players in the middle of the large open room, seeing beyond the veil, and what awaited some of them there.

Goodman John, as usual, was the second to bet.

"I've got the coot in Bed 7," he said, as he placed his glowing yellow chip in the middle of the table. (His soul chip was yellow as the sun, where Jeb's was blackest night.)

The soul chips, as the group came to call them, were all a mix of colors, never the same for any one ghost, but when a ghost lost, theirs turned a shiny dull gray and wasn't good for nothing, no more.

Tin Cup Debbie pointed at a woman surrounded by family in Bed 2. It was a newer bed, the area around it full of machinery that none of the poker players recognized.

And that was another queer thing about the hereafter.

None of the beds were quite in the same time zone.

Old Jeb come out of the Civil War, and Goodman John not long after. But Tin Cup Debbie explained that she was from something called the Roarin' 20s, which should have been damn right impossible, but she knew things the other two old hound dogs ain't never heard of.

Like *auto-mo-bills*. That's how Jeb pronounced the contraptions, and spit to the side every time the two spoke on 'alive-times.'

And Dim Sum wore a gown made from a gauzy fabric that none of the other ghosts had ever laid eyes on, alive or dead, and while they couldn't understand his garbled speak, he knew what the others said well enough to play the Game.

In his mind, Dim Sum wished he could tell the others at the table that he had been born in Hong Kong, China, at the apex of the city's bustling infrastructure. He had found himself, full of bone cancer, as the English doctors had called it, in West Virginia through a series of unfortunate work events wrapped around a bad heroin addiction.

Dim Sum, whose real name was Zhang Lee, had died in 1972.

"Alright, alright, you bas-turds," Jeb was saying. "Let's see how this here round shakes out."

They had made their bets. The soul chips were in the middle of the round table that sat in the middle of the ever-changing Cancer Ward, which sat close to dead center of the second floor of the large Lychhurst Hospital.

(The squeaks and squeals of the dying around them made even ghost hairs stand on end. The bumps and grumps heard in the hallways every night were the same for the ghosts watching the dying by candlelight, no attesting for where the sounds were coming from, as if they weren't the only dead'n's around, as Jeb Watson was keen of saying. No one right listened to the ornery old goat anyways.)

Now it was time to just turn and watch, and see who would be dying of the Cancer illness next. Every ghost at the card table just kept their eyes on their own bet-on pony, urging death to come rapidly.

The man in Bed 12, bet on by Dim Sum was the first of the bet ponies to die. And when he did, instead of going into the light, or the black ink shadows out the hospital's windows and doors, he chose to stay and join the game.

Too bad the losing fell to another fella who hadn't been at the table long. His name had been Harold Something-or-nother, but never no care. He was a good as gone when old Jeb picked out his emerald green soul chip, flipped it to Dim Sum, and watched as the old Chinaman absorbed it into his own countenance, reveling in the sensations only felt once before in the long years since he had died.

Harold Something-or-other blinked out of existence in the Cancer Ward, a wayward scream dying on his lips.

And old Jeb looked at Dim Sum with hate and spit in his eyes... waiting to take everyone's soul chips that sat around this here table he had built shortly after arriving in their Purgatorial hell.

"Better pony up again, you bas-turds," Jeb told the table, years later. "Times a' runnin' out for all y'alls!"

Eyes around the table rolled, and more than one ghost's thoughts went to finding a way to end the terrible reign of the monster they all knew as Jeb Watson.

But every ghost at the table, in every form of look and guise, were afraid of the old coot, and so no one would do anything about the bad-mouthin' old soldier. They all wanted to, however.

Jeb looked around the room, trying to figure out his next show pony. And that's when he noticed a peculiar thing.

All of the patients, in all of the beds around the large ward, were looking right at him. Even the fella with no legs and arms, and a machine making his chest rise and fall.

All of their alive-yet-almost-dead eyes, yellow and reds matching blues and browns… were gazing deeply at him, and it made his ghost spine bristle up, wondering what was happening.

Feeling those ghost-bumps run roughshod up and down his spine, it pissed Jeb off something serious. So, he pushed back. He pushed back with everything he had within him, and like the table and cards, and everything else old Jeb Watson had created there in that cancer ward since day one, he pushed out at the eyes on him in the ward.

And every single one of those alive eyes, which had been on the cusp of dying, closed, dead to the world.

Jeb had killed every single man, woman, and child in that particular version of the Cancer Ward, down through the years and years, and it made him feel bigger and brighter than he had since he, himself, had kicked the bucket.

If all of the ghosts and ghouls around him had been scared before, now they were downright terrified of Jeb Watson.

Jeb Watson became the cancer of the Cancer Ward of Lychhurst Hospital.

Darkness grew out from behind where the old man sat. And not just darkness. Spiderwebs of grays and white wisps scattered around the dusty old ghost.

The ceiling cracked, the walls crumbled, and the darkness that had looked solid and deep as darkest night outside the walls began to splinter, breaking apart.

Black wings flapping, falling.

Beaks, bloody and black, cawed their displeasure at the ghost world trying to take over the living one.

Jeb Watson's dead eyes turned milky white, and interspaced in the darkness around him, greenish lightning flashed, showing the other spectral beings at the table what terribleness spawned from within the powers Jeb was messin' with.

The shadowy folks in various sickbeds around the hospital ward, alive one minute, convalescing or dying the next, began to shake apart.

Ghosts were made in the blink of an eye, wherever old Jeb looked. And a terrible pale rider rode asunder the sickness within Lychhurst Hospital, all centering around the man who had begun the Game.

The Game which now seemed to everyone else had the greatest stakes of all.

Even Goodman John, whose countenance remained the only deathly light in the maelstrom of evil that was the Cancer Ward, looked down, admitting defeat at the hands of the evil Jeb Watson.

Goodman John didn't even have the apparitional energy to reach for his cards, to see if a winning hand could calm the cancerous nature of cantankerous Jeb Watson, who now appeared more like the biblical caricature of Death incarnate.

Deep, evil words came from the mouth of what was once the ghost of a hillbilly soldier from deepest Kentucky roots, and the Game was forever changed.

"Pony up your bets, ladies and gents. Death's ridin' in, and your souls are what's in the pot!"

Some time later, seeming seconds, but spanning decades, the Game quieted down, and more souls were added to it.

Some stayed, some left easily and lightly, disappearing into the scattering darkness of grackles outside the walls, or up into a bright light that stung old Jeb Watson's new eyes.

Bets were given, pots were taken, and more and more hands of Soul Poker went round and round, never settling on any one given time or number of folks dying of cancer.

Jeb, now floating above the table, streamers of sickness moving to an invisible wind around him, taking lives amongst the living at will, won a pot or two, here or there.

But what he really did was keep the Game going. He kept the specters at the table, dancing to his whims, playing his Game, winning and losing at will.

Until the day came that Jeb looked around at the Ward that had become his, and his alone, and there were no more bodies in the beds. No more beds in the Ward, and almost no more Ward in the Hospital.

Old Jeb Watson looked at the walls of the Ward he had been sustained in as a ghost for the last 150-odd years, and saw a striking sight.

Graffiti decorated decaying walls, crumbled stone rubble lining the floor where nurses' and doctors' feet had trod.

The outside light all but extinguished by the darkness of which he was both a part of, and subservient to.

And old Jeb, now formed of the Cancerous Illness himself, saw the ruin and destruction he had helped usher in, as Lychhurst Hospital crumbled around him.

Jeb looked down at the table in the middle of the forsaken Ward, and saw not a living or dead soul anywhere. All he saw was the overflowing pile of gray Soul Chips on the tabletop before him, shining in the darkness all around, and he knew but one thing.

Old Jeb Watson, Cancer-incarnate, had won the Great Game itself.

As he pulled the pile of half-glowing Soul Chips toward himself, cackling and whining with glee that he had championed all the souls who had come since him, he felt the lightest touch on his blackest of forms.

Looking up, he saw the deep red eyes of a tall, winged bird, peering deeply into his greenish-white ones, and he grinned a toothless smile at the grackle alit on his shoulder.

Jeb Watson turned toward the light spilling in from the broken and forlorn hallway outside the Ward and smiled.

He had won the Game.

And would forever stay right there in his home he had created. A Cancer on any and all who happened to mistakenly come exploring the ruins of what had become of Lychhurst Hospital's Cancer Ward.

A final smile lined his ragged, motley face, and he uttered the last words he would ever say, as the darkness settled in around him.

"All those old damn bas-turd's couldn't play worth a crap against Jebediah Watson… the greatest Poker player who had ever lived, or died!"

Psych Ward
1942

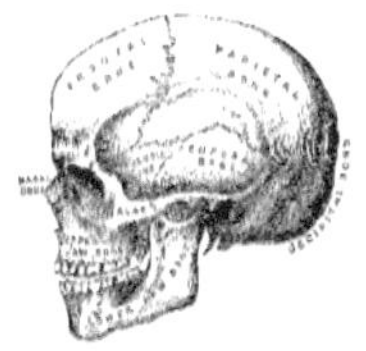

Queen of the Burning Castle
S.H. Roddey

Thunder cracked and the lights went out. The loose wheel on the gurney continued on. It was driving her mad. Up and down the hall… up and down, up and down.

Up.

And.

Down.

Every time a *creak-creak-scritch-creee–*

One.

Two.

Three

Four.

Five.

The lights flickered back on, but illuminated little.

The woman in the dark room at the end of the hall could not remember her name. It had been so long since someone said it out loud and even longer since she acknowledged its ownership over her. She was, in a word, *forgotten.*

Lightning flashed through the tiny window, and despite the thickness of the walls, thunder followed close behind. Wind whistled, catching on the crack in the glass with a shrill, soul-shattering shriek. The chilly November air leaked into her room, seizing her muscles all the way to the bone. The thin blanket covering her did little to stave off that chill.

Meals arrived on time. Fresh linens and gowns appeared on what she vaguely remembered to be Fridays. Sometime late in the night when the rest of the world was silent around her, the hinges of her door would creak and the smell of rye whiskey would fill her senses just before the unspeakable would happen.

But otherwise?

Nothing.

Nothing but the goddamned creaking.

And a voice. Low and distant, the echo of a familiar, beloved memory in her mind yet foreign in its sound. A whisper of a scream, perhaps. There, but never close enough to understand.

It came and went, tidal in its movements, sometimes close enough to make out the sibilant susurrus of words, other times not. Yet it remained constant like nothing else in her tiny, padded world except the squeaking of that gurney wheel and the dimming of the light fixture overhead when someone new received a treatment.

Even the dim, watery, thunderstorm-cloaked light filtering through the tiny, dirty window wasn't enough to adequately mark the passage of time. Only the same dull, yellow light overhead kept her company, coupled with the metallic rattle of the shackle and chain binding her to the bed.

So the mad one cannot escape, someone had said of her after a particularly brutal "therapy" session that had left her twitching and burbling, foam spilling from the cracked corners of her mouth.

And still, that voice remained.

You ain't gon' ignore me forever, little one.

She wanted to. Gosh, did she want to. That deep, echoing rumble instilled more fear in her than the forced solitude ever could. Even though she was alone, she was never truly *alone.*

You sure?

No. She was certain of *nothing.*

Laughter echoed in her head, reminiscent of the blue bottles hanging in that tree in her garden back in the Lowcountry. A combination of clinking glass and howling wind.

Good girl.

Praise? So far he—because the voice was definitely male—had done nothing but torment her. Despite his voice, she still felt she'd stumbled on some absolute truth when thinking about that tree, her family, and the strange direction her life had taken.

But why?

You got two options, girlie: you can admit you hear me, or you can admit that you is crazy.

"I'mnotcrazyI'mnotcrazyI'mnotcrazy…"

Hands clasped over her ears while rocking back and forth.

The metal legs of the narrow hospital bed squeaked against the old screws with each movement.

"I AM NOT CRAZY!"

Oh, but you are, *my little one.*

She froze mid-rock, rivulets of tears and snot rolling down her face, dripping onto the front of her dirty gown. That voice… so clear. So *close.* She was alone, locked in a corner cell in an oubliette inside a place no one *out there* dared speak of. Yet the voice remained.

"Am not," she said aloud, ignoring the lie in her own words. At least, it *felt* like she said something. Her words came out rusty, her voice thin and crumbled, so long had it been disused for more than screaming. Her heart thumped hard against her ribs, its erratic pace increasing as the sound of her breathing echoed off the grimy walls and back to her.

Oh? You got some kind of proof on that? Why else would your beloved lock you away three states over? Certainly not only because he been fuckin' that little maid girl, yes?

The one she shooed back into the house when she caught the girl hanging those blue bottles in the old crepe myrtle near the road? That girl couldn't have been more than fourteen when…

Follow that thought, little one. Couldn't have been more than fourteen when what happened?

"When I woke up here."

And when was that?

"I don't… remember."

Her brain buzzed from the touch of some long-erased memory. The remembered pain of electrical current zipped through that soft tissue and she flinched away. The pain followed, persistent.

Effective as a wet cloth on a dirty table, the shredded fingers of memory receded, leaving a charred, black hole in her mind. She dared not reach for it again. If the doctors wanted that memory erased, perhaps it was better left forgotten.

Except…

Except forgetting felt like a mistake.

It is.

"But I *can't* remember."

Try.

"I did. I am."

Try harder.

The rumble of thunder made her jump. The storm was close now. The lights flickered. Dimmed again. Her pulse sped up again.

One.

Two.

Three.

Four.

Light returned.

Remember what happened.

She closed her eyes and counted her fluttering heartbeats. She picked at the edges of that memory again, but nothing.

"I don't remember."

No answer came for a long time. She'd just reached the point where she'd convinced herself the entire thing was a hallucination when he spoke again.

What do you remember? Your name?

No.

Wait…

Maybe?

"H—" She paused. "Ha… Harrison. Harrison… A-Ab…"

Yes.

"Abi… Abigail?"

Abigail what?

"Abigail Harrison."

And before that?

Abigail—because that was her name—squeezed her eyes shut again and forced herself to think.

"I don't know."

You do know, little girl. You do.

It was no use. No matter how she tried to remember, the thoughts wouldn't come. She just knew she was Abigail Harrison, and she was from another state. And if her invisible companion was to be believed, her husband put her in this hospital to get rid of her.

Yes, little one, yes! That good for nothin' man of yours be livin' it up in your house with your daddy's money and that little girl who ain't old enough to know that what he be doin' to her ain't love.

The thought turned her stomach. That voice seemed to be part of her own memory rising to the surface. Maybe that was what it had been all along? She needed to start listening to it if she wanted to learn anything… even if a voice couldn't get her out of that coffin-like box.

For all that she knew, Abigail's husband could have all of Charleston society thinking she was dead. So young, so tragic… and he once again eligible and even more desirable now that he had control of her father's estate and fortune.

What would it do to his reputation if she somehow managed to get out?

She hated this room and everything it stood for.

Afraid of small spaces, are you? Shall I open the door? Perhaps you would like to stretch your legs.

How quaint. Now she was telling herself she'd let herself out of the room! If only she had such an ability, this hospital wouldn't be necessary at all, now would it?

Whatever you gotta tell yourself, girlie.

The loud *click-clunk-shink-clunk* of the tumblers echoed through the room. The last time she heard that sound, it was when the door closed behind her following her last treatment. Yesterday? A week ago? She had no idea.

The sound was followed by another creak. Those damned hinges, this time. Then, a slow, tooth-jarring sound that, despite hands pressed painfully to her ears, echoed in the hollows of her brain long after the noise itself ended and brought with it the remembered physical pain of—

Don't go there anymore. Or if you do, go there and come back angry, little girl.

Abigail chose not to go there, but she did look over at the door, which stood open now. The fact that it wasn't a hallucination, that she could feel the cold draft from the hallway whispering across her skin, told her it was real.

"H-how…?"

Go ahead. Office is down the hall on the left.

Abigail stared through the open door, her eyes watering from the sterile brightness of the fluorescent bar lamp overhead. Somewhere in the distance, the tinny vibrato of a radio warbled. The squeaking gurney wheel had stopped, thankfully, because she couldn't even begin to imagine how horrid the sound would be without the insulation of the door between her ears and that noise.

She placed her bare feet on the cold floor. The bed creaked beneath her. Thunder rumbled. She swallowed a nervous squeak and pushed her weight into her shaking legs.

Eight steps to the door.

Seven.

Six.

She raised her hand to shield her eyes from the light.

Five.

Four.

Squeak-squeak.

She froze. Someone coughed. A bed frame shifted.

Three.

Two.

Abigail lifted her foot but hesitated to let it cross the threshold.

You ain't gon' get another chance.

She knew that.

Taking a deep breath, she placed her toes on the cold tiles of the hallway. There were no ground-shaking consequences. Poking her head out of the door, Abigail expected to see the doctors and nurses come running, arms waving, to force her back into her room, but it did not happen.

Out in the hallway, she discovered a row of closed doors marching down either wall. Hers was the corner room, nothing but cinder block wall at her left hand and a loosely-hanging chandelier overhead.

Chandeliers seemed an odd choice for a place like this. Empty, oppressive, with still, heavy air… and sparkling chandeliers. The dichotomy would have confused her even without the fissures in her brain.

Abigail turned to her right and took her first step into the cold. Gooseflesh rose along her arms, legs, and neck, chasing its way down her spine.

Near the end of the hall, she noticed the way another corridor angled back, thirty feet or so before the large, wooden double-doors marking the end of the ward. The warbling radio chatter was louder out here, no doubt coming from that other corridor.

Thunder boomed again as she reached for the knob of the door marked *office*, and the lights flickered off.

One.

Two.

Three.

They came back on. A single, excited whimper wafted up the hallway from that corridor.

Abigail turned the knob and pushed. The office door swung open on silent hinges, revealing a small, utilitarian space lit by a single lamp atop a single, metal desk. A row of four-drawer filing cabinets lined the back wall.

You done found a treasure trove.

Yes, it appeared she had. She pushed the door closed and went immediately to the cabinets, organized by last name, and thumbed to her own file.

HARRISON, ABIGAIL - DOB 06/09/18 - COOPER, DANIEL, MD

The records were hastily scrawled in a doctor's messy writing, interspersed with the perfect cursive of a secretary. They told a horrifying story of lies and medical abuse, but a story she would have no recourse to refute, should she be given the opportunity.

Her husband had indeed locked her away.

"Out of state, for her own safety," the file said.

It spoke of all the things that spectral voice had whispered for far too long. It hurt, but the truth liberated her heart from the chains weighing it down. A sinister smile formed in her mind, though whether it was a projection of the spirit or a product of her own fractured psyche, she could not be certain.

Yes, little one. You ain't so dumb anymore.

"Leave me alone."

Can't do that. Ain't in my nature.

Abigail turned her gaze back to the files in her hands, taking in the words and letting them show her the truth of the men around her.

Displays signs of mania. Screams and cries followed by long periods of catatonic silence. Hydrotherapy treatments ineffective. Recommend lithium therapy.

"They… they drugged me."

Naturally. Look where you are.

Social therapies unadvised. Symptoms of psychosis evident in pyromania activities.

"But I didn't start that fire! I tried to put it out!"

Not what the man of the house said.

She turned the page to find more of the same in reverse chronological order, back to the bottom of the stack. With each new page flip, her heart rate increased. Her fingers trembled from the force of her hammering pulse.

Your fear tastes of strawberries.

"Hush," she growled. The word came out more fearful than forceful and the spirit laughed.

So sweet, little one.

The first page of the file was her admittance application, dated November 1, 1937.

"Five years," she breathed.

Told you.

Not that she thought he'd lied at this point.

Fury—slivered, disjointed, and every way *wrong*—boiled to the surface. Red haze clouded her vision. The edges of the world dimmed while she fought to put the pieces of her anger together. So focused was she on the files in her shaking hands that Abigail didn't hear the door open behind her.

Might want to consider turnin' round now, little one.

Before she could, the scent of rye whiskey touched her senses, turning her stomach over in her belly.

"How'd you get out?" he asked. It was the first time she'd ever heard real words from that oily voice. Until now, the most she'd ever heard was a grunt or a strangled groan as he came all over her gown.

"No matter."

Abigail didn't turn. She gripped the files tighter as the sharp *snap* of the lock echoed through the quiet.

"But bad girls need to be punished."

You gon' just take it?

"No!" she shouted, her voice straining with the force of her rising anger. The crisp folder crumpled in her grip, the crinkling of cardstock and paper louder than the shocked gasp of her would-be assailant. "I am *not* going to take it!"

Abigail turned, her hand sweeping over the desk and landing on a pair of scissors, taking them up as she did so.

"I. Did. Nothing. Wrong!"

Her voice grew in volume and intensity with each word. She turned then, looking into the face of her abuser. He was so close now. Taller than she, though not by much, balding and sweaty with the splotchy, mottled red-and-pink of rosacea and booze webbing his cheeks.

Yellowed teeth peeked out beneath pale, cracked lips. Each hard exhale carried with it the noxious odor of whiskey. The way he leered at her made her feel dirty in so many wrong ways.

"Don't fight me now," he said, hands raised more in anticipation than surrender. She took a step back and he followed. "Go on, now—" Another step. Another answer. "—and be a good girl."

He lunged.

A scream tore from Abigail's throat. Her arm rose, scissors gripped tightly in her fist, and drove them into the soft meat of his neck. He stopped immediately, eyes blown wide, and his outstretched hands curled back toward the puncture.

Her stomach flopped again, sickly this time, as he gripped the makeshift weapon and yanked it free.

Blood followed closely behind; thick, dark, angry spurts from a deathly fountain.

Her heart thumped. Then again. A third time.

He slumped to the ground.

You done gone and done it now, girlie.

"Shut up."

Yes, ma'am.

The rage faded to numbness. She looked down at her shaking hand—one coated in blood and the other gripped tight around the crumpled papers from her file; the very same papers which had only moments before proven her sanity.

Then.

But now?

I just killed a man, she thought, looking down at the heap of quivering skin and bone bleeding out at her feet. If that wasn't the hallmark of a crazy person…

When the doctors found out, they'd lobotomize her. Or maybe worse.

Abigail stepped over the dying man and let go the handful of paper. It fluttered to the ground, sticking and soaking up the pooling blood, blossoms of vibrant red indelibly staining the once-brilliant white.

One page in particular caught her attention—one she hadn't noticed at first glance.

It was little more than a tattered strip, no doubt ripped from the bottom of a ledger of some kind. Aside from the blood soaking into its edges, it contained only three words, written in black ink in a neat, clean hand: Until the Fire.

That was ominous. Oddly out of place as it was neither medical nor psychological. No reference. No explanation. No other documentation she could see. Just the words.

The dying man's blood was nearly to her bare feet. It was time to go. But where… she had no idea.

It's cute you think you got a way outta this.

Abigail paused. There was a truth to his words. A locked room at the end of a closed ward? He was right.

"They think I'm crazy," she said aloud. "I'll show them I'm crazy."

Good girl.

She circled back to retrieve the discarded scissors, now sticky with congealing blood, then closed her hand around the doorknob and turned.

The hall was exactly the same as it had been the first time—empty and sterile with the harsh hum of bright overhead lights interspersed with the delicate fanciness of chandeliers. No airflow at all.

And those large double-doors blocked the far end of the hall, menacing as a set of snarling jaws.

And that one, lonely corridor expelled the coughs and moans of the infirm. The doctors *had* to know what that beast of a man was doing to patients, including *those*. She couldn't be the only one.

That thought infuriated her.

"Bastards," she muttered under her breath. The word felt hard and foreign on her tongue, but not unpleasant. Cathartic, almost.

Abigail crept down the hallway, her footsteps loud with the sticky creak of drying blood where it fought to hold on to the cold tiles. A scream ripped through the silence, causing her to jump as she turned toward the door from behind which it came.

"No!" The muffled, feminine shout was quickly followed by messy sobs. "No, no, no, no, no…"

The whimpering pleas grew clearer with each step Abigail took. She reached for the doorknob, surprised when it turned and the door swung inward on silent hinges.

A chair, anchored to the center of the tiled floor, yawned like a wrenched-open bear trap, a slender, thrashing woman positioned in its maw. A tray of shining, silver tools sat to one side, and a pair of men in white coats stood laughing near the far wall, an unlit cigarette dangling impotently from the lips of the taller one.

They'd not yet noticed Abigail peering in. But the woman in the chair had.

"Nonononono… please… please no… help… help me…" Her eyes went wide, pleading with Abigail for help.

Fury—her now-familiar companion—boiled forth, and with it, a euphoric sense of calm.

"We are helping, darling," the tall one said, still not yet aware of Abigail's presence. "It will all be over soon." The expression on his face was odd and indescribable: a manic sort of glee mixed with malice, with a hint of something far more sinister lurking beneath.

That man ain't right.

For once, she agreed with the voice.

She raised a finger to her lips, catching the trapped woman's gaze, and bid her be quiet. The patient ceased her screaming, but could not seem to control the frightened whimpers.

No matter. The doctor was right about one thing: it *would* all be over soon.

Abigail tightened her grip on the bloody scissors and stepped fully into the room. So focused were the doctors on their experiment that she remained unnoticed long enough to creep close and view the tools lying on the shiny, silver tray: a long, slender needle with a t-shaped head and its matching hammer, two scalpels, a suture needle and thread, and a pair of unfamiliar tools that vaguely resembled tongs and a paddle.

They ain't up to no good at all. You gon' take care of it?

Abigail nodded.

Good.

She reached for a scalpel. It wasn't until the scrape of metal on metal echoed through the quiet room that the doctor and his assistant turned.

Thunder rumbled. The lights went out.

One.

Two.

The lights came back. The storm was overhead now. She tightened her grip on the blade.

"Missus Harrison—" the doctor gasped, taking in her bloody, shambling form and the anger etched into her once-soft features. "Why are you not in bed?"

He tried to sound stern and disapproving, bless his heart, but there was a distinct tremble to his voice. She'd startled him.

Abigail tilted her head just slightly and allowed him to truly accept the full sight of her—disheveled, bloody, and wielding a murder weapon plus one. He swallowed, Adam's apple bobbing in his long throat. The assistant backed away.

"Missus Harrison. Abigail." His eyes narrowed and he forced authority into his voice. "Put down your weapons and return to your room this instant."

Abigail turned her attention to the crying woman in the chair.

"And her?" she asked. "What will you do to her?"

"It is not your concern."

You gon' let him talk to you like that?

She was calm. Strangely so. Shock, perhaps? Or maybe it was the sense of liberation that came with knowing she had the upper hand.

The fact that this doctor knew her name spoke volumes, particularly to the gaps in her memory. The menacing downturn of his lips, both foreign and familiar, tickled those frayed and smoldering edges of thought. The dead man on the office floor had used her for his own brand of disgusting pleasure, but this man?

He was far, far worse.

"That was an order from your doctor, Abigail."

"No," she answered.

The doctor—Cooper, she realized; the very same man who had spent the last five years torturing her—blinked in surprise and motioned for his assistant. "Isaiah, if you would."

"Yes, sir," the assistant muttered. He inched forward, hands raised as if he were soothing an angry animal. "M-miss H-H-Harrison," he stammered, "p-please allow m-me t-t-to t-take you b-back to your r-room."

At least that one is polite. Shame you gotta kill the kid.

Not a shame at all, she thought, since he was complicit in these atrocities.

"No," she said again. "I'm fine right here."

The kid's shaking hand drooped, heading toward the pocket that no doubt held some sort of chemical to make her sleep.

Do it now.

Abigail struck fast as a viper. The shiny, silver blade split the boy's skin like warm butter and after a pair of heartbeats, a curtain of red fell from his throat, cascading downward to dye the pristine white of his coat. He slumped to his knees with a gurgle.

When she turned her attention to the doctor—

Yeah, he scared now.

—the tall man took a step back, unconsciously if she had to guess, and swallowed again. She could see in his eyes that he knew he was going to die.

"Stay there," she ordered, then turned her attention to the girl in the chair. One by one, she released the buckles and straps holding her captive. As soon as the final strap slid free, the girl scrambled from the chair, tripping and stumbling into the hallway.

"Now… your turn."

"Missus Harrison—"

"You are going to let me out of this ward. Then I might consider letting you live."

"I can't do that."

"You can."

"You won't escape."

"That is not for you to decide."

My, how you've grown.

The doctor's bravado faltered. He obeyed, leading her out and toward the locked ward doors. With each step, the catatonic moaning grew louder, until it eclipsed the tinny screech of the radio. Thunder rumbled overhead again. The lights flickered, but did not dim.

Her skin rippled in combined fear and anger, and when they passed the corridor on the left, she froze.

It wasn't a hallway. It was a room. Rows and rows of beds lined the large space, each one containing a body of some kind. Most *looked* alive from what she could see, but some… some stared blankly at the ceiling. Unwilling to move? Unable? Alive at all?

This is where they send you to die after they scramble up your brains like eggs.

"What have you done?" she asked, her voice a reedy hiss as she tore her eyes away and fixed her attention on the doctor. Her gaze caught momentarily on a familiar phrase, hastily scribbled on the wall above the nearest bed in… what? Blood? Excrement? She was unsure which.

Until the Fire. The sight of it, repeated in a jagged, drooping line sent a shiver down her spine.

The doctor's voice pulled her back. "We have relieved them of their suffering."

A lie.

"You've trapped them!"

"We are *helping* them."

"No! Shut up!" Abigail lunged with a shriek.

The doctor deflected, the blade slicing through the fabric and skin at his forearm. Red bloomed from the fissure, but he took no notice, reaching toward her with his other hand.

Abigail caught herself on the door frame just as his fingers closed around her upper arm.

Panic flooded her senses and all reason left her. She swung the scalpel again, unsure whether she connected with anything or not. Then pain exploded behind her ribs, radiating up and out as she doubled over with a gasp.

What you doin', girl?

Some sense returned. Abigail inhaled as deeply as she could, given her aching gut. The doctor yanked hard on her hair, pulling her toward him, and that was when she turned and struck.

Her hand came away from his body, wet and sticky, but empty. His hold loosened and she twisted away, still coughing from the impact of his fist. Abigail slipped and stumbled farther down the hall.

You better hurry. He still comin'.

Abigail drew in a sharp, painful breath and ran, bursting through the now-unlocked wooden doors and into the hallway on the other side. It was empty, dimly lit, and much more pleasant than her lodgings. Rather than the harsh sterility of the ward, this hallway was painted a soft blue. More of those pretty chandeliers hung from the ceiling, placed at regular intervals so the light diffused rather than pooled. This, she realized, was the part that families got to see.

The doors flapped open behind her.

Uh oh.

She turned and found the doctor there, panting and bloody, his features twisted into an angry scowl. He barely seemed to notice the scalpel protruding from his belly. He stalked toward her.

There. End of the hall.

Abigail spotted the fire axe hanging on the wall and scrambled toward it. The doctor outpaced her two steps to one, but his injuries slowed him. She reached for the metal-studded wooden handle. It was heavier than she expected, tipping her head-first toward the wall when it finally came free from its cradle.

Now, girl! Now!

With a shout, she swung in the direction of the doctor. She missed, the blade bouncing harmlessly off the wall with arm-jarring force. The doctor paused and laughed.

Abigail huffed, adjusted her grip, took a step back, and swung again. The blade glinted under the flickering light, but this time it connected, tearing open a deep gash in the man's side. He screamed, and having been thrown against the wall, shoved at the handle. It came loose with a sickening *squish,* and again, Abigail stumbled under the weight of it.

This time she was quicker to regain her footing. She swung again and the blade flew wide, embedding itself in the wall and severing the conduit running up to the overhead chandelier. The broken wires inside sparked and spit, and the zip of current running up her arms made Abigail's body tense and spring back.

The doctor, once again steady on his feet but holding his bleeding side, laughed. It was little more than a thin, gasping chuckle, but the sound itself carried so much contempt that she could feel it. He reached for her, fingers closing around her wrist, and tugged.

You out of options, girl.

Either way, she was going to die. Abigail pulled against his grip, still strong despite his injuries, and finding it impossible to break, grabbed for the axe one last time.

Fingers connected not with wood, but with metal. Pain, unlike any she'd ever known, raced up her arm. Froze her in place. Bent her backward like a bow. Locked down muscle and bone. To her right, something popped and sizzled, and raw heat tickled at her cooking fingers.

Oh, my tainted angel, you are magnificent.

And then… she died.

The first thing she saw were eyes the color of a moonless night. Deep, endless black surrounded by stark white and a fringe of long, curled lashes. A broad, slightly flat nose. And a bright white smile set in the darkest skin she'd ever seen in person.

"Welcome to the other side, girlie."

"Am I… dead?" she asked, even though she knew the answer. The look he gave her was as full of disdain as his voice when she couldn't see him. "Are we ghosts?"

"You is."

"And you?"

"Can't be a ghost. Was never human." He looked down at her, a small grin lifting one side of his mouth. "Yo' people know my people as somethin' different. Call us *haints*."

"You're a trickster!" She did not mean her words to sound so accusatory. He seemed to take no real offense.

"Guardian," he corrected. "That maid girl set me on you when she figured out you was in trouble by yo' man. To protect you."

"But I'm dead."

"And free." He nodded to the right with a small grin. Her gaze followed. "You might'a been innocent in life, but you did start *that* fire." She watched the flames climb the line of the conduit, melting and twisting, blackening the wall behind it while the hospital staff fought to put it out.

Stepping over her body and the body of the doctor to do it.

At least the doctor was dead. Something good came of her death. He'd never hurt anyone else again and, if she were lucky, word of his atrocities would get out and the rest would be saved.

"Come wit' me, little one."

"No," she replied, "I'm sure you'll take me somewhere lovely, but I can't let what happened to me happen to another woman."

"What you gon' do?"

"I'm going to protect them."

The slender man smiled, bright teeth beneath dark lips. "Then you don't need me no more."

He turned and walked away, leaving Abigail to watch two orderlies lift her sheet-covered body to the gurney while the rest worked on the flames.

"No, I don't."

Respiratory Ward
1920

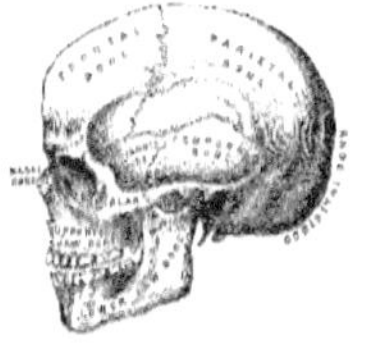

Past Lies Latent
Rebecca Cuthbert

Find Dell's letters, Meg heard, and became conscious of the hospital buzzing around her, half-dream fading to full reality under the glow of fluorescent lights.

"Wha' was that?" she asked, her words slurred and sleepy.

She'd nodded off again at her grandma's bedside—Grandma Leeanne, who looked to be asleep herself, oxygen mask in place. The *whoosh* and *hiss* of air flowing through the tubes, the *shushing* sound of the little bellows that helped her grandma breathe, had come together like a lullaby.

Meg worked late nights at a bar and cleaned offices three mornings a week. So often, when she sat down to visit her grandma, her eyes drooped before she'd even been there an hour.

"Who's Dell?" she whispered, remembering what she'd heard—in case Grandma was still awake. In case it was important.

But her grandma, dying of COPD in the Respiratory Unit of the rundown old Lychhurst Hospital, did not answer and did not stir, so Meg got up, kissed her on her papery cheek, and snuck out, promising silently to be back the next day.

In the morning, Meg's mother was able to call her at her grandma's house and talk for a few minutes.

For now, her mom was stuck in Bangladesh, helping the engineering firm she worked for figure out how to un-poison the drinking water. The cyclone that hit there had torn up cities and killed tens of thousands of people, and Meg had to remind herself her mom was living in a muddy tent, not vacationing in Cabo.

Still, it bothered Meg that she had to do this alone. Even at twenty-eight, she felt young and helpless. She wanted her mom.

"Maybe a —k?" her mom was saying through the static and gaps of the bad connection. "But that's if th— room for —e on a trans—rt. I'm so sorry, —ney. I want to b— there."

Meg felt bad. Of course her mother wanted to be with her own mom, and a week wasn't so long to wait. She opened her mouth to reply but a burst of static interrupted her and the line went dead.

Meg put the phone back in its cradle on the wall and went to feed Cornflake, her grandma's mean cat.

Visiting hours didn't start until noon. Meg didn't have to work that morning. Her grandma didn't get cable.

She stood in the kitchen, eating a cold Pop-Tart, when the words from the day before came back to her: *Find Dell's letters.*

She couldn't be sure she'd heard it—or that if she did, it had been her grandma talking. It could have floated in from the hallway, or been part of a dream.

But she had nothing better to do, so she searched, and she snooped, and after an hour and a half, she found them.

Dell's letters.

They were in a box, on a low shelf in the garage, covered with dust.

It was marked *COUSIN DELL* in block letters, and on the side, in pen: *Sent by Libby*—or did that say *Lizzy*? The writing was faded and hard to read.

Meg had never heard those names—not Cousin Dell or Lizzy or Libby. Grandma had gotten a divorce well before it was fashionable, and didn't talk much about her family. Meg's dad had left when she was a baby, so all her life, it had just been Meg and her mom and Grandma Leeanne. And they were enough for each other. Though she guessed that would change when her grandma's lungs filled with more fluid than air—when the machines couldn't breathe for her anymore. And the tired doctor who'd spoken to her a few days before had told Meg that would be soon.

But she didn't want to think about it, so she took the box from the shelf, then pulled over a rusted stool to sit on. The mysterious package was taped shut, like her grandma had never opened it. But Grandma Leeanne's health had been bad for months. Maybe, like so much else, she just hadn't gotten around to it.

Meg tore off the tape and pulled on the cardboard flaps, sending up a cloud of dust. After she wiped her watering eyes, she took inventory of the box's skimpy contents: faded silk flowers tied to dry-rotted elastic that might've been a corsage. A thin lock of dark hair, tied tight with a ribbon. And a fat bundle of letters, held together with twine.

Meg left the other things, because when she held the lock of hair she felt something like vertigo. But the bundle of papers she took inside the house.

She grabbed another Pop-Tart, not bothering to toast it this time, and found a pair of scissors to cut the twine. And knowing he wouldn't leave her alone if she didn't, she filled Cornflake's food bowl to the brim, then headed into the living room for some reading.

The first letter was marked August 3, 1919.

Dear Cousin Dell,

Essie and I start at Lychhurst Hospital in just a few days. I'm near bursting with excitement, though these are somber times and I try to keep the smile from my face, at least in public. While Lychhurst mostly treats tuberculosis, a few beds have been put aside to treat cases of the Spanish Flu and scarlet fever. So many of the patients are soldiers—coming home by the shipload, sickened and dying. It's enough to break your heart ten times over. That's why I chose Lychhurst. It's where I felt I could do the most good. Of course, at Lychhurst, the respiratory ward is always full to bursting. It's where they house the sickest of the patients.

Essie followed me here, as she so often followed me in childhood, but this time, I can tell she regrets it. She is nervous and homesick, though we've just arrived at our boardinghouse. It's about William. They had such plans—a farm and six children, as soon as he came home. I know she needs to grieve, but I hope hard work will prove to be both distraction and balm. We can honor William's memory—his and the other soldiers who gave their lives—by comforting and tending to our sick and injured countrymen. Essie says that's idealistic. It's hard seeing my little sister become so bitter. We all need our ideals.

With love,
Lorna

Lychhurst Hospital? The same place Grandma Leeanne was stuck in now… It was even the same ward. Meg shuddered—the coincidence gave her the creeps, though she guessed it wasn't too strange. Lychhurst was nearby, and used to be primarily a TB hospital.

What about the name *Lorna*? Another one Meg hadn't heard. Essie, though, short for Esther, that was Grandma Leeanne's mother, if Meg remembered right, so that would make Lorna her aunt? And… She counted on her fingers. Her own great-great aunt. Someone she'd never met, but Lorna's voice, on the page, sounded familiar. Kind of homey.

Meg wanted to read more of it, but it was getting late and she couldn't miss visiting hours. She changed into clean clothes, and on a whim, grabbed a few of the letters before she left the house. Maybe Grandma Leeanne would get a kick out of them—especially if it was one of her bad days, when she couldn't talk much, when every breath seemed like a fight she was losing.

Those days, Meg just held her hand and babbled until she ran out of things to say.

Meg hated the hospital. She hated its weird vibe—like the past and the present got mashed together, or one was laid over the other, like a double-exposed photo.

The building itself was an antique, with green marble floors showing through broken linoleum tiles, ornate doorway arches, and a lobby where voices and footsteps echoed.

The medical equipment was modern enough, though not new—1970s stuff, if she had to guess, which made her a little worried about their reliability. If they failed, so did her grandma.

She walked down the hallway to her grandma's ward, trying to ignore the framed photographs of staff and patients from long ago hung on the walls—in sepia, in black and white, in grainy color. Meg didn't like looking at their faces—they were all dead now, or probably.

When she reached Grandma Leeanne's bedside, Meg saw that it wasn't one of her bad days. She was awake, and though she had an oxygen mask on her face, she smiled when she saw Meg come into the room.

"Hi honey," her grandma wheezed. "How are you? Tell me everything."

That was always the way Grandma Leeanne greeted her, and Meg did her best to stay cheerful, pretending her own life was wonderful, pretending her mom would be there any day. And Grandma always smiled through her monologues.

But today was different, because she had the letters.

"I brought a surprise," Meg told her. Then she explained the letters, and where she'd found them. Her grandma seemed confused, like she hadn't been the one to ask Meg to get them. But she was forgetting more and more these days, so Meg just smiled and asked if she should read a few, and her grandma nodded her head and closed her eyes.

Meg set the little pile of letters on the bed, unfolded the one on top, and started reading. It was marked January 2, 1920.

Dearest Dell,

Doctor Danforth has Essie and I on separate shifts now. We barely see each other—she falls into bed as I'm preparing for work, and it's the same after my shifts. I sleep and dream only of the ward, of rattling breath, the clipped steps of nurses' heels, the grackles' chirps and whistles, pencils scratching on charts, and coughing. Endless coughing...

The letter went on but Meg drifted, slipping under Lorna's words, falling asleep or something else, no longer there at her grandma's bedside...

She opened her eyes and looked down. Green marble beneath her feet, and those in low white heels, the laces double knotted. She was walking, steps quick, in a hurry. What was she hurrying to?

Then the sound broke in—coughing, murmurs, and above it, a male voice, booming down the hallway: "Nurse! Nurse Schaffer!"

Schaffer. Her great-grandmother's maiden name. Essie Schaffer. So Lorna's, too.

"Here!" her own mouth said. "Coming!" And then she was jogging, hard-sole shoes striking the marble, her own breath coming faster, a little pocket watch fastened above her breast bouncing up and down.

She turned left, into a room, looping a cotton mask over her ears. The voice belonged to a doctor, tall with neatly combed hair and dark-framed glasses, cheeks shadowed with black stubble.

"Yes, Doctor?" Meg's voice said, though that wasn't quite right—it was her voice but not. Then she saw the problem.

Dr. Danforth—the tag on his white coat said—was holding a young woman upright in a hospital bed while she coughed and coughed. Blood droplets spattered the front of her light blue gown and white blanket.

"Oxygen tent, now," the doctor said, and Meg—but it wasn't Meg, not really, the way things are and aren't in dreams—hurried to the side of the room and pulled over what looked like a clear shower curtain hanging from a long arm, attached to a cart with a tank and dials and tubes.

Her hands—long-fingered with clean, buffed nails—fitted the tent over the woman's upper body with practiced, deft movements, then hooked up a tube and turned a dial. After a moment, the woman's coughing stopped, and Meg heard the hiss of oxygen filling the tent.

The doctor had stepped back, out of the way. Meg looked at him, feeling an anxiety in her chest—for what? And hope, too, that twisted her stomach. Why?

The doctor reached out a hand and squeezed Meg's arm. "Well done, Nurse," he said, and his fingers lingered on her skin.

"Thank you," she said, and her cheeks lifted with her smile, but she looked at him too long, so she turned on her heel, face hot, glad for the mask, and lifted a hand to her hair, her cap, which were perfectly arranged, perfectly neat, as always (as always? why did she think that? Meg's hair was a mess), and she said, "I'd better finish my rounds," without glancing back at the doctor, who was still looking at her—she could feel his eyes on her back, on her waist, then lower—and she put her hands at her sides and squared her shoulders and focused on the doorway.

Meg sat up in her uncomfortable visitor's chair, her back cramped and her neck sore. She looked down; her grandma was asleep too, oxygen mask hissing away. The room had sunk into late afternoon shadows, and someone cleared their throat pointedly. Meg's head whipped toward the door; a woman stood there, scowling. She wore a weird blouse with puffy sleeves, a floor-length skirt, and an apron.

"I'm sorry," Meg stammered. She checked her watch: 3:42. Visiting hours ended at four. She looked back at the woman to say she was leaving, but the doorway was empty.

She leaned forward to smooth her grandmother's hair and something crinkled. The last letter she had been reading lay in her lap. Meg put it and the rest of the letters into her purse and stood.

She stretched, kissed her grandma on the cheek, and left, her mind on which fast-food restaurant she'd stop at for dinner on the way home.

***

She went to bed early—it was her night off from the bar, and she had to be up at five a.m. to clean offices the next morning.

Usually she had trouble sleeping, tossing and turning in the spare bed at her grandma's long into the night, taking turns worrying about Grandma Leeanne and then her mother and then herself.

But not that night.

Seconds after her head hitting the pillow, it seemed, the waking world faded away.

She was back on the ward. She sat on the edge of a man's bed, holding a cold compress to his bare chest. He was missing an ear, and his left eye was melted mostly shut.

"Is that better, Captain?" she asked him, and he wheezed, then smiled and said, "Marry me, Lorna," and she laughed—she who was Lorna and no longer Meg.

"You're a rascal," she said to him, "and I bet you propose to all the nurses."

"Can't blame a guy for trying," the man said, and he tried to laugh too, but it turned into a cough.

Meg/Lorna smiled, but then someone was behind her, huffing out an irritated sigh. She turned. The doctor, frowning.

"Nurse Schaffer must attend her other patients, Captain Fitzpatrick," he said. "I'm sure you understand."

Then he was lifting her by the elbow, mumbling, "Do try to act professional, Lorna," in her ear as he gave her a little push across the long aisle, toward the bed of an old man with gray skin.

Her eyes burned with tears she wouldn't let fall. What harm did it do to cheer up her patients? She'd just been talking. Dr. Danforth had been so short with her, ever since—

"Help," said the poor old man, his voice strangled. "Can't…" he wheezed, "breathe…"

Lorna pulled down his bed sheet and loosened the neck of his gown. She tried to pull his hands away when he clutched at his throat, and she turned her head to yell a name, "Nurse Wilcox!" and when she turned back the man's eyes were already glassing over, and whatever she'd been wanting Nurse Wilcox to do, it was already too late.

She passed a hand over his face to close his eyes, said a little prayer, like she did every time, and went to find Dr. Danforth to report the death.

"How's Cornflake?" her grandma was saying, and Meg blinked out of her daydream.

"He's great," said Meg. "Sweet as ever."

Her grandma tried to laugh. "He's a rascal."

Rascal. That's what she'd called the man in her dream. It hadn't felt like a dream, though. She'd been at Lychhurst, but it wasn't *this* Lychhurst. She closed her eyes. *Nurses' shoes on green marble. The doctor's hands on her, rough. The man in the bed...*

Fitzpatrick. Why was that name familiar?

A tapping sound made her open her eyes and turn toward the window. On the sill perched a black bird. No—not quite black. A rainbow shimmer on its feathers, like spilled oil. It tapped again with its beak, then chirped and whistled and flew away.

Unsettled, she cut the visit short, telling her grandma she didn't feel well. It wasn't a lie. Leaving the room, she almost ran into the angry woman she'd seen the day before—still scowling, still in her weird outfit. A nurse here? Meg thought she must be part of one of those religions that made women cover up neck to toes, lest a bare wrist send a man into a frenzy.

The thought made her smirk as she said, "Excuse me."

The woman scowled harder, and Meg hurried down the hallway. She was almost to the staircase when a crash to her right froze her steps.

A picture frame had fallen off the wall, its glass shattered. Meg looked around, hoping to see a custodian or other staff member who would clean it up, but she found herself alone.

She knelt, thinking she could at least gather the larger glass shards, maybe push the whole mess closer to the wall and out of the way. But when her eyes settled on the photograph, she dropped the pieces she'd been holding and picked it up to get a better look.

In it, twelve young nurses smiled in two rows, hair pinned beneath white caps, starched dresses to their knees, white heels. A large building loomed behind them, and Meg recognized the front steps of Lychhurst. Turning the photo over, she saw a label and corresponding names, written in spidery, faded ink:

Orientation, Lychhurst Hospital, Autumn 1919

Top Row, L-R, Heather, Bridget, Lorna, Cat, Jeani, Alexandra

Bottom Row, L-R, Jennifer, Essie, Stephanie, Susan, Marie, Christy
Essie. Lorna.

Meg's relatives.

It was hard to tell in black and white, but Lorna's hair looked dark, and Essie's blonde. Meg spent a moment being jealous; she didn't get that blonde hair. Hers was dark as molasses, and so was her mom's, and Grandma Leeanne's, too, before it faded to white.

The photo was a little grainy, but Meg could see that Lorna was smiling ear to ear, head thrown back, her arms looped around the shoulders of the women next to her. Essie's smile was stiff and barely curved her cheeks.

Meg looked up and down the hallway. She was still alone. Feeling guilty but doing it anyway, she slipped the photo inside her sweatshirt, left the mess, and speedwalked to the stairway.

Moments later, she shooed a few of those mangy black birds off her windshield and drove back to her grandmother's to get ready for work.

Two in the morning and Meg couldn't sleep. She wandered into the kitchen, poured herself a glass of wine, and went to the living room. She'd left the stolen photo near the stack of letters on the coffee table, and propped it up against a little ceramic swan to keep her company.

Great-Aunt Lorna and Great-Grandma Essie and ten other women watched her as she plucked a letter from the assortment and opened it to read. It was marked Feb. 20th, 1920.

By the end of the second paragraph, the living room and Meg's rumpled clothing and the suffocating black night and all the things that made Meg *Meg*—her life/her time/her very existence—had faded clean away.

Dear Cousin Dell,

She barely speaks to me these days. When I see her at shift change she has a dreamy look on her impish face and a secret smile on her lips. I tried asking her if I had done something wrong. If I had hurt her feelings. She laughed at me, said "Whatever do you mean?" and then she asked if I was feeling alright.

And I'm a hypocrite, aren't I? You are my dearest cousin, and always honest. I can hear your voice now. You'd say, "You can't ask for others' secrets if you're keeping your own." But he asked me not to tell and I won't...

Meg was in a restroom, all white tile and bleach smell, leaning over a toilet. She vomited, tasting old coffee and bile. When she'd finished, she straightened up, flushed, and opened the stall door with shaking hands.

"Honey, I've been telling you; you can't work all night without eating," said a nurse who was waiting by the sink. She had coiffed red hair and redder lipstick. "You'll sick up every time, especially if you fill your empty tank with coffee three times a shift like you do."

Meg read her nametag. N. Wilcox.

Yes. Nurse Bridget Wilcox. Her friend, who worked nightshift alongside her. The only one Lorna had told about her nausea and dizziness.

She splashed her face with cold water at the sink, then blotted with a towel, careful not to smear her makeup. Not that she wore much, but she'd been making an effort, and Roger said mascara made her eyes look bigger.

"You're right," Lorna said, because she was, but also because she didn't want to talk about it anymore. "I'll grab a muffin and some fruit from the cafeteria as soon as shift ends, okay? I promise."

"Good," said Bridget. "You're skinny as a reed, and pale, too. If you're not careful you'll get sick yourself. Don't forget to put your mask on when you're near the White Death, okay? Shoot. Scarlet fever, too."

"I know, I know," Lorna said, smiling. "We did the same courses, remember?"

Bridget rolled her eyes.

"Fine, smarty pants," said Bridget. "Then let's pull 'em on and get back to work."

Lorna fixed her mask on her face and watched Bridget do the same, careful not to smear her lipstick. They left the bathroom and pushed through the lounge door marked *Staff Only*, and were surrounded once again by coughing and crying and the clipped footsteps of those tending the sick and monitoring the dying.

A noise broke into Meg's dream—that's what it had to be. Asleep on the couch again, then, though she found herself sitting up straight, a letter in her hands.

It was Cornflake, yelling for more food.

Meg set her empty wineglass on the table—not spilled, so she drank it—and fed him, muttering "Fatass." Then, because she was up, she helped herself to another glass of wine, and another letter.

She sat down, and the date Jan. 17th, 1920 swam up from the page before the years rolled away like rocks down a hill and Meg was, once again, Lorna.

***

She was in a supply closet, breathing hard through her nose, almost overwhelmed by the smells of ammonia and bleach and camphor. She braced herself against a low shelf, and a man's hand covered her mouth. She sucked on one of his fingers.

He thrust into her from behind, and she could tell by his grunts and the way his other hand squeezed her breast through her uniform that he was almost finished. She wished they could be together somewhere else, like the time they'd stolen a few minutes on the cot in his office, but afterward, he'd said it was too risky—he had to protect his reputation.

With one more hard push, he shuddered and pulled out. He was already zipping up by the time she turned around.

Dr. Danforth. Roger, but only when they were alone. He ran his hand through his hair, smoothed the front of his trousers.

"Wait ten minutes," he said. "And make sure to straighten your uniform."

She leaned forward for a kiss, and he gave her one, long and hard. Then he put a finger on her lips.

"Not a word, now," he said. "You're my delicious little secret, and I want to keep you all to myself."

Then he let her have one of his rare smiles. The one she'd fallen in love with. The one, she told herself, he saved just for her.

He moved the chair he'd wedged beneath the door handle, peeked into the hallway, and slipped out. Lorna put the chair back. It wouldn't do to be discovered there, knickers at her knees, uniform pushed up around her hips.

He never stayed long enough to pleasure her anymore, the way he had at first. It left her distracted, bothered. But she had ten minutes to wait, and her core still pulsed with heat, so she left her knickers down and her skirt up and moved her hand between her legs, first slow and then faster, thinking of Roger.

Meg cried out, hand between her own legs, orgasm rocking her body. She lay on the spare bed in her grandmother's empty house, confused, heart racing. The jogging pants she'd been wearing earlier were in a pile with her underwear on the carpet. She still wore her t-shirt.

She didn't remember moving from the couch to the bedroom. She thought she might be dreaming, and checked—but it was real. The orgasm, anyway. She was still slick with it, and she shuddered with pleasure when she touched herself again.

Ten minutes later, tired and satisfied, she drifted off into a dreamless sleep.

In the morning Meg skipped coffee, called in sick to her cleaning job, and went right to the pile of letters. After her experience the night before, she was eager to read more, to lose herself again. It wasn't weird at all, she told herself; it wasn't obsessive or escapist or creepy.

And she wasn't *really* slipping through time and she wasn't possessed by Lorna or possessing Lorna. Her great-great aunt. Her great-great aunt who she'd never met, never heard her grandmother talk about, because her grandmother barely even talked about her own parents, at least from what Meg remembered.

She was just *immersed*. That was the word. Like with a good television show. Meg was overworked and overtired and lonely and Lorna's life was a channel she couldn't stop watching, and she, Meg, had a vivid imagination, and that was all.

That was all.

She opened another letter, this one marked June 11th, 1920.

Dear Cousin Dell,

That secret I've been keeping has gotten me into trouble. The kind good girls don't get into. I can't tell my parents. I can't even bring myself to tell Essie—what would she think of me? It's Roger's, of course. I haven't told him yet, either. I want to. But he's been asking to see me less and less, and when we are together he's rushed and distracted. I was a fool to think he was falling in love with me, and I was a fool to fall in love with him.

And it gets worse. My friend Bridget worked a double two days ago, filling in for a girl who's sick. She said she saw Dr. Danforth—my Roger— coming out of the supply closet zipping his trousers, looking furtive. She thought it was just a bit of gossip, and was breathless with laughter. I wanted to cry but pretended to laugh, then got away quick, so I could weep in private.

I can't hide my trouble much longer. I've been keeping a loose smock on, telling folks I don't want a TB patient ruining another one of my uniforms. But my ankles are swelling and my belly is growing...

Meg looked down. Her belly bulged beneath a loose cotton smock. Her feet ached. She stood next to an occupied hospital bed, monitoring the oxygen flow going into a patient's tent. Peeking in, she saw that it was Captain Fitzpatrick, laboring to breathe.

He was her favorite patient, and a kind man. Lorna prayed he would recover. He'd contracted tuberculosis on a crowded ship bound for home, and after surviving the war, he deserved an easier life. She pulled down her mask to make a funny face at him, and he made a show of laughing.

When she was satisfied that the oxygen tent was doing its job, she held up her hands to signal "ten minutes" and hurried to the ladies' room in the staff lounge.

Thankfully, it was empty. Lorna shut herself in a stall to relieve her aching bladder, which triggered tears. The tears came with sobs, and the sobs turned into a coughing fit.

This wouldn't do. For better or worse, she had to tell him. If she had to face the music, didn't he deserve to do the same?

She cleared her throat, dried her eyes on toilet tissue, cleaned up, and flushed. Then she splashed her face with cold water at the sink and looked into her own eyes in the mirror, ignoring her pale cheeks and the blotchiness at her throat. "Face the music," she whispered. "For better or worse."

She left the restroom and found Dr. Danforth in the staff lounge, pouring a cup of coffee. He was alone.

Still, he glanced around before saying, "Lorna. How are you? Coffee?"

"No, thank you," she said. "Roger. We need to talk."

His face reddened and he coughed. "Well, Nurse Schaffer, I don't think just now is the time to—"

Lorna untied her smock and lifted it to her chin, showing him the contours of her growing belly. "Isn't it, Dr. Danforth? Then when is the right time? You've been avoiding me for days and—"

"Shit," said Roger, the look on his face one of shock mixed with disgust. Disgust? For *her*? He stared at her stomach until she dropped her smock back into place.

"I don't suppose you want to do the right thing?" she asked, working to keep the tears from her voice. "My coursework wasn't in maternity but I figure I've got about four months left. Maybe three."

"I see," said Roger. His eyes had gone cold. "And I'm to understand that you're pinning your misfortune on me?"

"*Pinning my misfortune?* As if I'm giving myself to every man on the street?"

"Well how can I know?" he asked, his tone the same one he used when lecturing new physicians. "You're a modern woman, aren't you? Single, living alone. And you run around with Nurse Wilcox. We all know what she gets up to."

"Bridget? Leave her out of this! You don't know her at all. And if you're saying these disgusting things, you don't know *me* at all. And I thought I loved you. So I didn't know *you*, either."

Lorna mustered what dignity she could, tied her smock, and walked out. She had rounds to do before she could leave.

***

Meg found herself in the car, driving down a two-lane highway. She gasped and slammed on the brakes, coming to a stop in the middle of the road, breathing hard.

What the fuck? What the fuck was happening?

She looked around. She knew the road. She was on her way to Lychhurst.

She pulled over and turned off the car. Her heart was beating too hard; her mind was spinning with worry. And not just for herself.

For Lorna, too.

What would happen to her? Single mothers didn't keep their jobs in 1920. And forget safe abortions. There was no such thing, and anyway, Lorna was almost in her third trimester.

Almost in her third trimester. Meg was thinking of her in the present, like these events hadn't been carved into history's stone tablet decades ago.

Head still muddled, she turned the car back on and drove the rest of the way to the hospital, finding her grandmother asleep, the head of her bed raised to make breathing less painful.

Meg sat in her usual seat and set her purse in her lap. She was surprised to find it stuffed with letters. Apparently she'd brought them all. Her mind wandered back to Lorna and she pulled the bundle out. If she wanted to know what happened to her great-great aunt, she'd have to keep reading.

Feeling a little bad about using her grandmother's body as a table, she laid the letters down one by one in a grid pattern, changing which one went where until she was sure she had them in order by date. Then she put aside any she'd already read or with dates that came before Lorna's pregnancy. She could read those later.

Only a few remained, some more than one sheet thick.

A tap on the window. Meg looked up. One of those black birds again. Another joined it, and they both tapped, like they were trying to send Meg a message in Morse code.

She ignored them and picked up the letter marked July 6th.

Dell,

Well, dear cousin, I've really done it now. My enemy became so familiar that I ceased to be afraid of it, and now I've contracted tuberculosis.

I meant to write sooner, but I didn't have the heart.

My friend Bridget is carrying out my letters. I sent one to my parents. By the time you're reading this, they'll know, too.

It's all unraveled. My whole life. I'm a patient now, Dell. In my own ward. Third bed from the door, just staring at the grackles as they flock to the windowsill across from me like harbingers of death. And can you guess what else? Essie is my day nurse. I spent so many nights wishing she and I could spend time together. And now we can, to my utter misery.

She is short with me. Impatient. She smiles at me, and calls me her poor, dear sister, but she is not concerned. She is happy. And I know why.

She's the one Roger has been seeing. The man I loved with my little sister, doing to her the things he did to me. I wonder if he's called her his "delicious secret" yet. I bet he has.

I haven't confronted her. What's the point of that now? Bridget caught them in the supply closet. I suppose he forgot to wedge a chair under the doorknob. He threatened to fire Bridget if she told, and she promised she wouldn't, then ran right to me the first chance she got.

Essie hasn't asked me who the father is. That makes me think she already knows…

Meg was lying in a hospital bed. She wore a thin blue gown and was tucked beneath a white sheet. He chest ached, and she shivered though she was bathed in sweat. Her belly was a sad mound beneath the blanket, unloved by anyone but her.

"Lorna, dear?" said a voice, and it was Essie. Lorna could tell she was smiling, even though she wore a mask. She could hear it in her sister's voice: the satisfaction. "Dr. Peterman is here. Do be brave, alright?" She gave Lorna's hand a little squeeze.

Dr. Peterman, the obstetrician Roger had arranged for, stepped closer to the bed. "They're bringing screens for privacy, Miss Schaffer," he said, and Lorna noticed no one called her "Nurse" anymore—the respect had fallen away as soon as she was out of her uniform and into a patient's gown.

The screens were put in place, but Lorna felt the humiliation of the exam, nonetheless—poked and prodded in her most private places by a stranger. When it was done, the doctor pulled a stool closer to the bed, checking to make sure his mask was in place.

"Miss Schaffer," he said. "I'm afraid this will be a difficult conversation for you. But I must tell you, there is a chance, with your illness, that you will lose the baby, even if you pull through. A very good chance."

Lorna nodded slowly. She felt numb. The doctor had gray hair sprouting from his ears and she stared at the left one now, concentrating, counting the strands, so she wouldn't look at his eyes and see the pity she could hear in his voice.

"It may be for the best," he continued. "It's a trying life for unwed mothers, as you no doubt know. You couldn't keep your job, of course. And with no father to support you…" He trailed off. "But if you miscarry, you can start over somewhere else. I'll speak with Dr. Danforth and make sure you receive a glowing recommendation from Lychhurst."

He sounded pleased with his own generosity, like Lorna was a child and he'd just offered her a treat. Her stomach flipped with contempt for him, and for Roger, who walked the ward smug as ever, secure in his power over her and Bridget and Essie, too, though she likely fancied herself in love, as Lorna once had.

She didn't respond, and Dr. Peterman left, taking his privacy screens with him.

Lorna slept.

The phone rang, shrill, again and again. Meg was lying on the living room floor, gasping for breath. She spent only a second or two wondering how she'd gotten there—how many hours had passed, if she'd missed work.

Then she got up and ran to the kitchen to answer the phone. It was her mom.

"Meg?" He mom's voice through static.

"Meg, the nur— tried to —ch you," her mom said. Her voice was strained—Meg could tell even with the spotty connection, the sound going in and out. "They got an emerg—y call through to —e. It's Grandma, —ney. She lost con—ness last night, and she has— woken —p. They don't think —e will. I wi— I could be there —ith her."

Meg listened, fighting off grief and disorientation, keeping it together for her mom, who was sobbing now, stuck a thousand miles away. Meg wanted to cry, too, because she loved her grandma, and also because she'd just been dreaming of, or imagining, *immersed* in, Lorna's pain, and because her own waking life was cutting in and out like her mother's voice.

But if she cried, her mom would want to comfort her. So Meg held her breath, and she listened, and she said, "I'm sorry," over and over, until her mother was calm.

"Can you f— me her laven—r pantsuit, —se?" she asked Meg, calm again. "I'll —der the stone. We'll bury —r next to her mother. I —d around and found her —rents' graves. The cemetery's —bout three —rs aw—. We'll do a —all graves— service. Okay?"

By now, Meg could fill in the gaps: Lavender pantsuit. Graveside service. Bury her next to her mother. "Okay, Mom."

"Or should it be the navy —suit?"

"The lavender's pretty. She liked that one. Let's stick with it."

"Okay. I'll be on tom—ow's transport. I l— you," said her mom.

Meg said the same and hung up, then retreated to the spare bedroom for a few hours of fitful sleep. When she got up, she brewed a pot of coffee and then took a shower. Her grandma might be asleep—*asleep* sounded so much better than *unconscious*—but Meg would go in to see her anyway.

Later, at her bedside, holding her grandmother's hand, Meg read the next letter. It was three sheets thick, and dated August 21st, 1920.

Dell,

She's gone. I feel so weak and the fever is burning me from the inside out but I have to send this to you. You have to keep it safe.

She came too early. Two days ago. She was so small. There was a lot of blood. I delivered her here—I wouldn't be allowed at any other hospital. Not with my illness.

She fit in my two hands, Dell. Dark hair and dark eyes. So small. So very small. But she was warm and her heart beat. I felt it. She was alive and I held her.

They took her away. Essie did. She said they had to help her breathe. And I knew she was right but I wept and wept. They gave me a sedative and I slept. More than twenty-four hours, I slept. And Essie was there waiting for me when I woke up.

She told me my baby was dead. And she handed me this wisp of hair— I've sent it to you, Dell, to keep it safe. I wanted to send her birth certificate, too, but there wasn't time. You see, Essie had told me to fill it out. I told Essie her name. Anna Lee. Isn't that pretty, Dell? But she said I still had to sign it. On the line for the father, they'd already written "Unknown." It was in Roger's handwriting and I wanted to scream, but I was too weak.

The fever still had me and the pen felt so heavy in my hand, but I was her mother and I would love her forever and I signed my name.

Meg waited to slip under. To go back to Lorna's body and life and time. But it didn't happen. Disappointment fell on her like rain. She wanted to know what it was like to hold that baby. Her baby, Lorna's baby. To feel everything else but not that—even the pain and the loss would have been worth it—left Meg with a sense of emptiness. Like she'd been cheated.

But the letter continued, so she read on, wiping away the tears that fell down her cheeks:

Essie said she'd be back soon. She said it needed to be filed—that without the birth certificate, there could be no death certificate. I had only moments, and I couldn't go far, could I? Practically a prisoner, and still bleeding. But there was a gap, between the wood paneling and the wall behind my bed. Barely a gap, but enough to drop in a piece of paper.

Fever and grief drove my logic. I thought, if there is no birth certificate, there can be no death certificate—that's what Essie told me. When she came back to get it, I pretended to be unconscious. She looked for it and then swore, and then Dr. Danforth was there, and they were whispering, and I heard her say she'd just sign for me, so you see my plan didn't work at all.

Anna Lee's birth and death have been filed and she will be cremated and my silly trick didn't do any good because my baby is gone forever.

Now all I have is that lock of hair and my own broken body to prove I ever had her at all. And soon Bridget will fold it up in this letter and then I will have nothing.

I don't think I will see you again, Dell, and with how poorly I'm feeling, this may well be my last letter to you.

So farewell, and thank you.

Your cousin,

Lorna

And then it happened, finally, like sinking below the surface of a warm bath. Meg was once again Lorna, and she was lying in her hospital bed, wasted away to barely anything at all.

Someone was lifting her wrist. It was Essie, and she had a syringe.

"To help you sleep, dear sister," she said.

She was crying, and she wore no mask. Where was her fox-in-the-henhouse smile? She pushed the needle into Lorna's flesh and pushed the plunger. She was gentle; Lorna barely felt it. *Her little sister made a fine nurse after all*, she thought, and in that moment, despite everything, Lorna felt proud of her.

She watched while Essie wheeled over an oxygen tent, fitted it over Lorna's head and upper torso with practiced movements. Still, she cried.

Lorna wanted to ask her why. Why was she so sad? It was Lorna's baby who died. It was Lorna who got thrown aside by a callous man. Lorna who lay in a hospital bed she might not get out of. But she was too tired to speak, and the sedative was already clouding her thoughts.

She continued to watch Essie through the plastic tenting. The air inside grew hot and stale. Lorna's labored breath created condensation that made it harder to see Essie. Why wasn't she turning on the oxygen? It should have been flowing already, filling the tent with cool, merciful air.

Essie looked in and cried silent tears. Lorna watched her, begging with her eyes—eyes that got heavier by the second. *Turn the dial! Turn the dial!* But Essie didn't. After another moment, she reached for Lorna's hand and held it. Lorna tried to squeeze it, to signal her distress, and then realized Essie was saying goodbye.

Lorna tried, one last time, to breathe. Then she closed her eyes.

A frantic beeping brought her back to her grandmother's bedside, to herself, to 1991 again. She'd been crying and her face was bathed in sweat; she sat up.

A doctor rushed in. The beeping was a machine hooked up to Grandma Leeanne, telling Meg and everyone else that her grandmother's heart had stopped beating.

Meg yelled "Help! Help her!" though she knew they couldn't, not anymore, and a nurse—not the mean one with the puffy sleeves, and Meg was grateful for that—was pulling her away from her grandma, saying "Let them do their work, honey," and by then she was howling.

"She's gone," the nurse was saying. "Let go honey, she's gone."

"I know," cried Meg. "I know."

She watched from the hallway as they removed her grandmother's body, only turning toward the staircase when the elevator doors had closed on the gurney and the somber attendants pushing it.

On the third step, she paused, her hand on the railing.

With that first violent storm of grief over, her head was clearing. Memories came back.

Behind the wooden paneling. Lorna's lost treasure—her daughter's birth certificate.

She ran back to the ward, then stopped in the doorway, trying to remember. She looked down the long room. Only a few beds were filled, curtains pulled to offer the patients privacy. Visiting hours were over, but a nurse could come by any minute, doing their rounds. Meg had to hurry.

Third bed from the doorway. That's what Lorna said in her letter. But which side? Meg closed her eyes, picturing the room as it had been, the way it looked when she had lain—no, when *Lorna* had lain—in that awful bed, wasting away.

The grackles.

Those black-rainbow birds. They were grackles, and Lorna had seen them at the window. So her bed was across from it. The paneling was still there, a pattern of large squares framed by trim, though painted many times over.

Meg went to the right square, and praying it wouldn't bring security, hauled her foot back and kicked with everything she had.

It took two more kicks to break through, and by then, Meg heard footsteps in the hallway. She reached into the hole she'd made, feeling around until—*yes*, that was paper! She grabbed it, noticing only vaguely that her wrist bled and her ankle throbbed.

She limped for the door, and almost made it.

The scowling woman stood there, blocking Meg's escape.

"I should have known it was you," she said, and grabbed Meg's wrist with ice-cold fingers. "Making a racket. Up to no good."

This close, the woman smelled like mothballs and rot, and there was something wrong with her eyes. Meg tried to hold her breath as the woman dragged her down the hallway and pushed her toward the staircase, growling, "Get out!"

Meg stumbled down the first few steps but managed to grab the railing. When she looked back, the woman was gone, and Meg didn't need anyone else to tell her to go.

She ran, as fast as her sore ankle would allow.

Back at her grandmother's, she rifled through the master bedroom closet to find what she knew was there: Grandma Leeanne's birth certificate.

Then she took it back to the living room with shaking hands and laid it on the coffee table, right next to the yellowed piece of paper she'd found in the hospital's wall.

Her suspicion was right. The cruelty of it all was like a kick to the stomach.

Leeanne Marie Fitzpatrick. Born August 19th, 1920, 4:10 p.m. Female. Five pounds three ounces. Mother (Maiden Name): Esther Marie Schaffer. Father: Captain Ronald James Fitzpatrick. Signed: Dr. Roger Danforth, Lychhurst Hospital, State of West Virginia

The other:

Anna Lee Schaffer. Born August 19th, 1920, 4:10 p.m. Female. Five pounds three ounces. Mother (Maiden Name): Lorna Lee Schaffer. Father: Unknown. Signed: Dr. Roger Danforth, Lychhurst Hospital, State of West Virginia

Meg would have thought she'd have no more tears to cry, but there they were, dripping onto the birth certificates—one real, one forged.

Essie Schaffer killed her sister to steal her baby.

Essie wasn't Grandma's mother.

Grandma's real name was Anna Lee.

There were details Meg couldn't know—not from Lorna's letters or from the time-slips she'd experienced. How did Essie get Dr. Danforth to go along with it? Did she threaten him with exposure? Did he do it to buy her silence? Who else at the hospital was in on it? Surely not Bridget. Maybe Dr. Peterman?

And Captain Fitzpatrick. He must have pulled through after all, and lived to raise Lorna's baby as his own. Did he exchange his cooperation for a pretty young wife?

Did Essie love him, then or eventually? Did they both love their stolen baby?

And did Grandma Leeanne—Anna Lee—did she ever sense something was wrong? Was that why she never talked about her parents? On some level, did she *know*?

Her mother's first plane was already in the air, so Meg would have to wait to tell her the truth about who Grandma's mother and aunt really were— that it was the other way around, and that they couldn't bury Grandma next to her kidnapper with a fake name. That they had to find Lorna's grave, and bury Grandma next to her.

She remembered the lock of hair and went to the garage, then took it with her back to her grandmother's closet, to find that lavender pantsuit she loved. It had a breast pocket, and Meg tucked the lock of hair inside.

She couldn't give it back to Lorna herself, but she could send it with her daughter.

Meg hoped they were together now. That after more than seven decades, Lorna could finally hold her baby again.

Burn Unit
1954

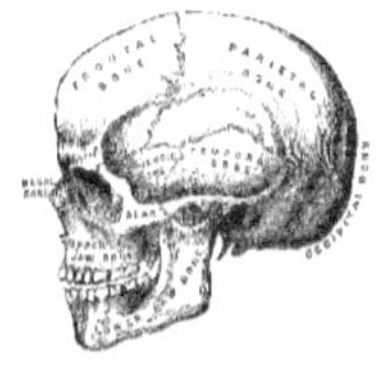

The Custodian
Jason Daughrity

Frankie hated the ghosts.

The double doors to Lychhurst's Burn Unit were cracked open a little bit, so he took the opportunity to slide in without any of the ghosts at the far end of the ward noticing him.

Which was perfectly-fine-thank-you-very-much, in his opinion. Damn ghosts freaked him out. He could go all goddamn day about his work, cleaning the floors and making the beds and whatnot and be fine without them noticing he was there. Suited him right down to the ground, that it did.

Frankie padded into the burn unit with soundless steps, making a mental list of what he had to do in the ward that day. First would be to gather up the trash at each end of the unit, then sweep and mop the floor.

He'd probably end up shining some of the railings on the beds, and maybe make sure the white-painted steel bed pans in the back were all lined up shipshape and bristol fashion.

But as he was walking along, he looked over to where the damn shitbrained workers had left the wood dust and debris from where they were installing the fancy new oxygen lines. Putting them in the walls to "help make everyone breathe easier."

At least, that's what ole' Nurse Gladys said when she had told the hospital cleaning staff about it. Right fine to look at, Gladys was. She and the other nurses seemed to really like old Frankie. Chatted every evening, shared a cuppa Joe from time to time.

He'd entertain them with stories about growing up near Lychhurst. The odd ghost story and all that. He'd tell them about how sometimes you heard someone behind you, pushing a rusted and creaking gurney, one wheel spinning around crazy and you could hear it in push of the whole thing....and you'd turn around and there'd be no one there.

They just called him crazy and tell him they loved him to death! Especially that prim and proper Nurse Gladys.

She was real proper about it, too. The double rows of buttons down her stark white nurse's smock always gleamed bright, and her auburn hair was always done up with the winged look that was all the rage, her crisp nurse's hat perched on top just right. Pretty eyes and a no-nonsense attitude rounded her out.

She was a damn fine put together woman, Gladys was. Wouldn't mind a night with her in the burn ward, when no one was lookin', he thought to himself.

Frankie ran a leathery hand through his thinning and short-cropped grey hair and pushed his horn-rimmed glasses back up on his nose. He liked to joke with the fellas at the bar on an occasional evenin' that his favorite haircut was "only four dollars, and that's a dollar for each corner!" That'd always get a laugh from the boys.

He wore nondescript grey workman's coveralls and smelled like Vitalis if you got up close, which he didn't really like people to do. Liked to keep himself to himself, he did, mostly.

His brown leather work shoes were as worn and creased as his hands, and he kept them that way, cleaned with saddle soap and supple with mink oil.

One of his favorite things to do was sit down every Sunday afternoon on his porch and work on those boots till supper time. He liked the smell, too.

The dull-brown-but-glossy shine of his shoes reflected the lights overhead as he moved around the unit. Frankie had his keys in his right pants pocket, and in his shirt pocket a pack of Lucky Strikes and his matches made a bulge sticking out.

He had the lucky cigarette, the one he always saved till last turned burnside up. His Zippo lighter was there right beside it. A slight smell of cigarette smoke mixed with the aftershave and alcohol smell of his Vitalis.

He walked over to the corner of the burn ward to the left of the double doors and looked over his dustmop, mop, and bucket. The dustmop's handle leaned against the small portion of wall allotted to the cleaning gear, the bucket's wheels straddling over it and the slightly dingy beige of his mop with its head up and in a clip, carefully hung over the small drain and raised bricks in a square that he would dump the dirty water into.

There was a shelf overhead with some cleaning chemicals in bottles, and a few rags hanging from pegs.

There was also a spigot and small hose, along with a scrub brush he could switch out from a long handle to a short one. As usual, everything was in its proper place, and everything proper in its place.

Frankie was nothing if not meticulous about his gear. *A man should know his place in life and take care of the things in it,* he thought to himself.

He glanced down at the ghosts. They still hadn't noticed that he had come in, and like they always did, they were gathered around one or two of the beds looking at the burned patients.

The ward had two burnies, not counting Bed 5. The ghosts were around Beds 8 and 10, looking at the poor souls lying in them, burned all to hell. Crispy critters, his old pa would have said.

"Tragic, really…" Frankie whispered to himself.

He knew that one of them—Bed 8—was just a kid, maybe fourteen or so. Her hair was all burned off and she had bandages wrapped around her scalp and left eye, with red and black flesh burned down to the bone underneath the gauze. Her chest and left arm, stomach and left leg were also similarly clad in bandages.

He'd heard from Nurse Gladys that the girl had been skipping class and went down to her school basement. She wanted to try smoking a cigarette she lifted off her old man, but when she lit the match, a gas leak the school had been neglecting to fix-due-to-this-years-budget-cuts lit up and blew her and Room 11 above her all to hell.

Apparently, the explosion had sent her through that floor above her and her whole left side was a just a ruined mess.

Nurse Gladys was sad about it; she had told the other nurses on the ward that the girl probably wasn't going to make it long since she got a full blast in the face, and it swelled up her throat somethin' fierce. *That'll getcha,* Frankie thought to himself.

Can't breathe right when there's nothing to breathe through.

He had heard that burning was a bad way to go, hurt more'n anything, and he felt a little bit bad for the kid. *But thems the breaks*, he guessed.

But it wasn't gonna stop him none later on tonight when the ghosts left.

In Bed 10, there was an old woman in her sixties or seventies that had burned away most of her right arm and leg in a car accident caused by her drunk son. 'Parently he had a few too many at bowling with his buddies and went to pick up his mother from bingo. They were arguing about his drinking and when his head was turned, yelling at his ma, had ran straight into the back of a paper delivery truck.

Luckily the idiot son had died on impact with a face fulla metal and glass, but his sweet old mother had been trapped in the debris for a while. And when they used a circular saw to try to cut her out, the sparks ignited the gas from the car, and she burned and burned until they were able to pull her out from underneath.

It was a damn shame, really.

The ghosts didn't make any sounds as they surrounded the beds. The damn apparitions just stood there, looking down at each of the burn victims. Sometimes they moved around and Frankie would look up from time to time from whatever it was he was doing, noticing that there would be a few more or a few less around each bed.

There weren't none around Bed 5, which was fine too.

He didn't look at Bed 5.

Frankie finished running the dust mop over the floor of the ward, shook it out in the corner and used a small brush and dustpan to pick up all the dirt and debris there was under the oxygen lines.

He saw there were some dark marks on the wall for some reason, right next to the oxygen lines, but it looked like someone had already tried to clean them off. Hmph. Burn marks. In the burn unit. Why didn't Nurse Gladys say something to him about them before?

He had talked to her at the nurse's station, right?

He went over to his cleaning corner and got a rag, and some vinegar mixed with Castille soap and water in a spray bottle, and came back to the oxygen lines to work on the wall a little bit. He got some of the dark mark off but not all the way. He put some more elbow grease into it and got most of it off.

Hmph. Good for now.

Frankie went back to his cleaning alcove and put the rags in the corner and the bottle of spray on the shelf up above. He got his trusty grey metal mop bucket with some suds and water already in it, dumped it out and refilled it with hot water and fresh suds, then dipped in the head of the mop on its long, pale handle.

Frankie used that as a steering rod and wheeled it out into the middle of the ward.

The wheels on the mop bucket protested and squealed, one spinning just like that damn ghost gurney you heard behind you but never saw, but turned and propelled the bucket on with its soapy water. He pulled it out then re-dipped his mop in, wrung it out, and started swabbing the deck, as his old pa used to say.

"Put some elbow grease into it!" was one of his pa's favorite things to say to a younger Frankie and his sister, back at their little two-bedroom house way back on Fornica Street, about thirty-five minutes or so away from Lychhurst as the crow flies.

Yeah, Frankie was a local and proud of it, and damn the drifters and people moving down from New York or Boston that had swelled the ranks of the town over the last few years.

Frankie liked it nice and quiet where people wouldn't put their noses into things and kept to themselves, mostly. Suited him just fine.

While mulling over the fact that his hometown had gone to shit with all the dregs that had slubbed in, Frankie had been moving closer to the ghosts as he mopped from side to side with his trusty swab and took careful steps backwards.

Reach out far to the left, reach out far to the right, match up with swipes that had gone before, repeat the process, and every six swipes or so, re-dip the mop head in the bucket and wring it out.

Step by step, getting the lines even. He was walking carefully backward so that he wouldn't step on the mopped floor he had already cleaned.

No use in mopping if you're just going to fuck it up with your footprints, he thought to himself.

As he inched his way through the ward, he would look behind him to check on the ghosts. They were just… shapes, he guessed. No real noticeable features; some were tall, some short, but all seemed to have their attentions focused on the burned in front of them.

Guess if they were going to keep to themselves, he would too.

Frankie looked back down to the mopping he was doing, and then as he was passing the newly installed oxygen lines, he glanced over at where he had just swept up the sawdust and debris from where the workers had been installing the oxygen line.

And stopped to stare, his mouth agape, mop forgotten in his hands.

The sawdust, wood and paint chips were back right where they were before he had swept them up, like he had never done it at all.

"Jeezum fucking crow," Frankie said under his breath. He had *just* swept those up, hadn't he? Surely he wasn't getting addled in the head in his old age.

Frankie looked at the wall and sure enough, that was where he had been just a few minutes ago, right next to the oxygen lines. There were the black marks on the wall that he had just cleaned up.

But then he noticed, they didn't look like they had been touched either. He looked back toward the front of the ward toward his cleaning alcove and saw his dustmop was right where it was supposed to be, next to the mop bucket and mop.

Wait.

Next to the mop bucket and mop???

Frankie looked down. There was no mop in his hands and no streaks of drying wetness where he had just fucking mopped. *What the unconstitutional irrational FUCK was going on?*

He walked back over to where the mop and bucket were and saw that the mop was dry and the mop bucket had no water or suds in it. It was dry as a bone. The dustmop looked like it had been there for a while, and the rags were no longer down in the corner but back up on the shelf, also dry.

Frankie's face paled as all the blood rushed to the back of his head.

He quickly looked back around him, turning with his hands out in claws and slightly crouching. His breath was coming in and out in large gulps, and he started sweating on his forehead and in his underarms. What the hell was happening?

He knew that he had just cleaned up the ward, he had just spent the last half hour doing so, so why was this happening to him? What in Lucifer's quivering butthole WAS GOING ON???

Frankie looked down at the ghosts. Did those fuckers have something to do with this? Was someone playing a trick on him? He didn't deserve this. He'd always done right by people and there was no reason to be playing such a mindfuck of a prank on him.

Of course, there was the stuff he did at night to some of the patients, like the burned girl in Bed 8, when they couldn't move or fight back and he knew that they were going to die anyways... but that was in the dark and he wasn't really himself when he did that so it didn't count, right? Sure as hell not!

Frankie got angry. Turned red, mad as hell.

He turned away from the alcove and started walking back to the middle of the ward, eyes never leaving site of those hellish figures. He felt heat flushing his face, felt his pulse quicken and his breath, deep gulps of air, go through wire-thin lips below widened eyes.

As he turned, the end of one of his shoes kicked the dustmop end, just enough to dislodge the handle from where it was leaning against the wall, and it fell down with a clatter of hard wood striking linoleum.

The echoes of the wood striking floor seemed to reach the end of the ward. He didn't give it a second glance.

Frankie moved down the middle of the burn unit, intense glare withering out of his bloodshot eyes toward where the ghosts stood. As he got close to Bed 8, they became more distinct but no more human-looking. Just still-fuzzy-around-the-edges shapes looking down at the beds. Frankie reached out to the closest one as he came around the end of Bed 6.

Right before his hands reached the apparition, they struck something solid and invisible, stopping him in his tracks. He stumbled to a halt and struck his head against the unseen barrier.

What the fuck is this now??? He reached up with both hands and felt in front of him, right next to the spirit. An invisible *something*, solid and unyielding underneath his fingers.

Frankie paled further and stepped back.

He couldn't touch the ghost.

Frankie gulped, then turned and looked at the rest of the ghosts. He went around Bed 8 and tried to do the same thing to the apparition on the other side of the bed but met the same stony resistance.

He tried to touch all the ghosts around the bed, more and more frantic with each crablike movement around them. He then moved over to Bed 10 to see if he could do anything to the ghosts there, but met the same, solid resistance whenever his hands came within a few inches of the ghosts.

It was as if each one had a… a shield of some sort around their bodies that he couldn't get through.

He pounded on the invisible wall surrounding the ghost closest to him, yelling and screaming to get its attention, to no avail. He couldn't touch them and they couldn't hear him. H

Kathy and Martin, both with eyes red and puffed up from a few days spent crying, looked down at their oldest child.

Kathy reached a hand down to the burned girl's face bandages and pulled them a little further down on to her daughter's cheeks. A sniffle from the other side of the bed from Sophia's little sister caught Kathy's attention and she looked at her other two children. Her son was holding hands with the only sister he would have left, after Sophia passed. He was trying to be brave and all, for his little sister's sake, but his eyes were the most wet and lips were quivering. She could hear the occasional sobs in the quiet ward, with only two other patients in beds in the spacious room. This was where her baby would die.

The old doctor had told them that was for the best, that even with the very best care for Sophia, their precious Sophia… That no matter what they did she was going to die because of the swelling and damage that they couldn't do goddamn anything about.

And she was goddamned pissed about it. The frilly old man was professional and all, sure. Very doctor-y, but she'd be damned if he wouldn't meet her tear-filled eyes as he shuffled out of the ward. Kathy wailed and fell to her knees and beat her fists against the bed next to Sophia.

Martin put a hand on her shoulder and looked down. In his right fist, he had a pack of Chesterfields smashed together. It was his last pack. He tossed it over into the trashcan next to the hospital bed.

"My baby girl. My sweet baby girl… why? *WHY*???" sobbed Kathy. The tears bounced off her cheeks and on to the starched white cloth of the sheets her daughter lay on. Reddish and black stains had formed on the pillow underneath her head.

Kathy looked down her daughter's ruined body, and saw something that she hadn't noticed before. Down on the sheets, right in between Sophia's undamaged leg and her burned one, she noticed some stains that had dried to the color of rust. It wasn't near one of her burns, but right in between her little girl's legs, by the crotch.

Her breath caught in her throat.

Just then, there was a loud clatter of wood striking the linoleum floor. Martin, Kathy, and the kids all jumped in the quiet ward as the dustmop handle, that had been leaning against the wall at the custodian's alcove toward the front of the ward, fell over and struck the floor, bouncing a few times before coming to a halt. The sound echoed down the big room they were in.

Martin was the first to turn around and look at his family.

"Just a dustmop, guys. Probably just vibrations of people moving around the hallways and hospital or whatever," he said.

Martin grinned a half-hearted smile he didn't feel and looked back down at Sophia. She hadn't moved a muscle, and her breathing was still the same, steady in and out of her bloodless lips, pumped in by the tube in her throat and the bellowing accordion of the breathing machine the hospital was so proud of getting the previous year.

Martin reached up and caressed his daughter's hair and adjusted the pillowcase on the pillow she had her head on. His eyes welled up with tears again.

Kathy stepped over and put her hand on Martin's shoulder. "I hope she's not in any pain right now. They gave her all kinds of painkillers, so that she could sleep and maybe heal," she said. The red spots on the sheets between Sophia's legs forgotten for the moment.

God, but she didn't know if she could do this. Kathy knew how bad the burns actually were, and that she had to face the sad reality that her baby girl was going to die.

Martin looked up at Kathy. "Yeah, you're right. They gave her a lot. Not as much as they gave to that guy over there, but enough to knock out a horse anyways." Martin waved a hand toward the burned figure in Bed 5 and Kathy looked over to where he pointed.

She saw the sad figure, and was intrigued by all the cards and flowers that were on the shelf over the figure's head. She had seen the man in the bed two days after her daughter was brought in to Lychhurst's burn unit, and apparently the guy was injured right here in the burn unit the night before that.

He had been the custodian in this wing and had been cleaning the ward where workers had just installed oxygen lines. And apparently there was an oxygen leak.

So when the guy went to smoke a cigarette, as soon as he lit the match, a huge fireball had surrounded him and even scorched the wall and the two beds he was standing in between.

The damage to the ward wasn't bad, but the second and third degree burns the man had sustained were very serious.

He was put into Bed 5, and the nurses came a lot to check on their coworker and friend. You could tell that they were going to do their very best to keep him alive, but it seemed like he was in a coma due to the amount of pain he was in.

They bustled in every now and again to check on him or add some medicine to the IV bottles hooked up to his scorched arms.

Damn shame, really. Seemed like a nice guy, the few times he had been in the unit cleaning while they were there, attending Sophia. He had mentioned his condolences the day before the incident, his eyes lingering on Sophia as he moved away from the bed while sweeping.

Wait. Kathy thought about that for a second.

In her grief, she hadn't noticed or put any thought into why the man was looking at Sophia for so much longer. Long enough that she had noticed.

Kathy gasped and looked quickly back to the bed, to the rust-colored spots on the sheets underneath Sophia. *No....it couldn't be. No. No. No. NONONONO!!!!*

Frankie backed away from Bed 10 and ran down to go out the doors of the burn unit. When he reached the double doors that were cracked slightly open when he came through earlier, he saw that they were closed completely. He had never heard them close.

He heard the squeaky, slow and creaky push of a gurney just outside the doors.

He put a trembling hand on the right door and pushed, wanting to get out of this damnable ward and whatever the hell was going on, prank or not. It didn't move an inch.

Frankie cried out, a guttural sound coming from deep in his chest and involuntarily leaving his lips, along with some spittle. His eyes were wide He tried the left door, to no avail. He made his hands into fists and hit both doors as hard as he could, but nothing happened.

Frankie turned around quickly and put his back against the doors, his eyes wild and his horn-rimmed glasses askew on his pale face. Nothing had changed, except that the handle of the dustmop was now on the floor. He stayed there for a few minutes, looking around, expecting something to come at him from the back of the ward or maybe the ghosts to come flying at him.

But… nothing happened.

He looked down once more at the ghosts and Beds 8 and 10, and as he was looking along the rows of beds, his wide and bloodshot eyes focused on Bed 5, and the unmoving figure in it.

He slowly moved away from the double doors of the ward and crept quickly and quietly toward Bed 5. Frankie's eyes quickly darted left and right and his pulse sounded loud in his ears. He got to the edge of the bed and looked down at Bed 5, something which he wasn't supposed to do.

He saw himself.

Frankie stopped, feeling like his heart was going to beat out of chest and through his pressed coveralls and spill blood and fluids on to his polished shoes.

He saw himself, his own damn actual self, lying in the bed, covered in bandages and barely breathing through oxygen tubes running into his mouth.

There was an IV stand next to the bed, and some tubes ran from it down to the man on the bed, going through catheters into his very own withered arms. The sickly burned-pork smell of fire-damaged flesh met Frankie's nostrils, and he recoiled. His already wide eyes got even wider.

"WHAT THE HELL IS HAPPENING?" he yelled, looking over at the ghosts close by. "What the actual fuck and bejeezus shit is going on here, you sick fucks!"

Frankie looked back down at the image of himself lying in the burn unit bed, barely breathing, obviously burned to a crisp.

A damn crispy critter. Him.

He saw then that the bed had several cards and flower arrangements around the head of the bed on the shelf overhead, so he moved closer to inspect those, loathe to pull his eyes away from the burned creature under the swathes of bandages but his curiosity was too great.

He looked at one card and saw that it said *Get Well Soon!* in flowery script and was from Nurse Gladys.

A glance at some of the other cards also had names of some of the other nurses and hospital workers in the ward and other wings of the hospital.

The flowers were drooping and dying, with a few withered petals on the shelf, and some had fallen down on to the pillow that his doppelganger's head was resting on.

There was a half-drunk glass of water on the nightstand and some crumbs on a napkin. The napkin had red lipstick like what Gladys would wear smudged in a stain where she had wiped her lips after her lunch.

Frankie collapsed down to a sitting position, his knees creaking from the strain. He looked down back up at his… the *other* Frankie's body, and saw just how badly burned it was.

Must have been painful as hell, and that body was somehow still alive. The IV bags looked like some of the best work the nurses had ever done, he was completely clean on clean sheets and all his bandages looked fresh, despite the wounds looking old already.

He could tell the nurses and doctors, his coworkers, were taking very, very good care of their friend Frankie the janitor.

Minutes passed while Frankie sat there, thinking furiously and trembling. He looked up frequently at the ghosts and at his body on the bed, and he shivered uncontrollably.

There was a dampness in his crotch and he thought he had to take a shit, but the bathroom was not in the ward.

Finally, he got to his feet and went out to the middle area between the beds and over to his cleaning alcove. Frankie reached down, numb with shock, to pick up the handle of the dust mop and put it back against the wall.

His fingers passed right through the handle, and Frankie's heart stopped.

He retched and heaved as his stomach churned in his belly, but found that nothing came out but bile and nothing. Pain suffused his chest and head.

Frankie went back to the middle of the ward, looking around at all the ghosts, his burned body on the bed, and at the things he couldn't touch and the doors he couldn't get out of.

He was stuck here. He didn't know how, or why. But he was fucking stuck here. He couldn't touch anything and the ghosts couldn't feel or hear him. But he was goddamn stuck in the burn unit.

Frankie screamed and screamed and screamed.

Below, far below in the lonely echoes of the tunnels under Lychhurst, something smiled in its slumber. This something was dark, inky blackness making up its body like a living shadow.

And it was growing.

While hunting in its dark hallways, when it felt the old man do the bad things, it had waited until he took a smoke break to reach out with its mind and sever an oxygen line. Part of its body was made up of some of that.

It didn't know what it did, while it dreamed of rending flesh and growing big, its scalpel-sharp nails tearing and clawing at rats and other prey.

It knew that it had expended some power when it felt evil above its head. What that evil energy did, the dark thing craved.

The thing reveled on in its slumber, pleased that it had more dark energy to siphon off from the Burn Unit up above.

Cardiac Ward
2008

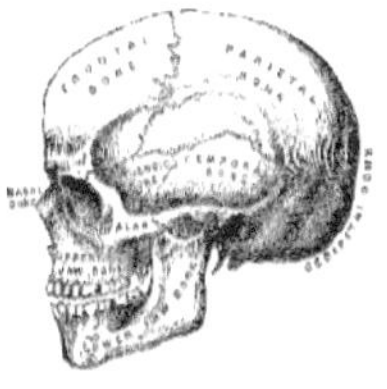

Blood is Thicker
Lexx Christian

1

"Where are we going?"

Billy looked across the cab of Fish Barnett's beat-up Ranger. His old buddy looked a little nervous tonight. His eyes darted here and there and he was leaned just a little too far over the steering wheel, peering out of the windshield into the country dark.

"I told you, I found us a great still site."

Fish reached behind him and slid open the back window.

The sharp, sour smell of the corn mash hit Billy in the face immediately. He turned and looked over his shoulder into the bed of the truck where an old, torn-up tarp had been flung over two large buckets of crushed up corn, sugar, water, and yeast.

Billy always thought that if he could take a mash barrel with him into an AA meeting, one look at that frothy yellow mess and those drunks would be cured for life.

Just below the wail of the wind and the growl of Fish's tires on the rough road, Billy could hear the scraping, metallic sound of the still bumping against the sides of the truck bed.

"Are you out of your mind?" Billy sighed, flopping back into the seat. "We can't be drivin' all over Hell's half-acre with a copper still pot in the back of the truck!"

"How'd you think we was gon' get it out to the site? Levitation?"

Billy rolled his eyes. "No, but we probably shoulda waited till late. Now we got all these cars on the road. The law could be anywhere." He looked back again. "And you coulda done a better job with that tarp."

"Don't be such a candy ass," Fish huffed. "I'm doin' you a favor cuttin' you in on this sweet deal. Trust me. When we get this 'shine run, you'll thank me."

"Have you ever done this before?"

"No. But you ain't either."

"How do you know it's gon' work?"

"I tol' you. I'm usin' my great-great-great-granddaddy's recipe. I followed the directions exactly. And Ennis Railey says that still rig he let me borrow is foolproof."

Billy shook his head, but he didn't ask any more questions.

Probably for the best. That way he wouldn't have to testify at their inevitable trial. He closed his eyes and tried to relax. He hadn't slept a full night in several days and didn't feel like doing this. But he didn't have much choice at this point.

The thought of Fish using his four-time great-granddaddy's moonshine recipe didn't exactly reassure Billy. Hezekiah Barnett had a reputation in his day for being the meanest man in Tucker County.

Some said he saw some scary shit in the Revolution that had made him like that. Other, more reliable sources said he was just born bad. Stories of massacring whole battalions of English were legend. He'd kill a man just for lookin' at him.

His wife, Fish's four-time great-grandmother, ran off shortly after his return from Richmond. But rumor had it, he'd beat her to death with an axe handle and throwed her down the well out behind the old Barnett house. Of course, Old Man Barnett was also the richest man in Tucker County, so there wasn't much of an investigation to speak of. Any moonshine recipe that had been written by Old Zeke Barnett was likely one part corn mash to three parts rat poison.

It only took a mile or so out of town before they were in what the old folks called 'country dark.' That impenetrable night where you couldn't see your hand in front of your face if you was to wander off without your flashlight.

"Fish, I'm starting to get the impression that you're takin' me out to kill me," Billy said.

"Nah, I'm just goin' in the back way. We have to park the truck around back."

"Where exactly are we going?"

It wasn't until that moment that Billy noticed Fish was wearing a uniform: black polyester pants and a green button-down shirt with the Maco Security logo on the pocket.

"Oh hell no… no no no…" Billy scooted toward the passenger door like he was going to jump out.

"What?" Fish asked, feigning ignorance.

"I ain't goin' to Lychhurst. Forget it. Let me out now." He was dead serious. He'd had nightmares about that place since he was a kid and wasn't too keen on bein' within a hundred miles of it.

"Why?"

"One, it's private property and I don't need to catch a charge for trespassin'. Two, that place is freaky as fuck. And three—I ain't goin'."

"Oh, don't be such a little bitch, Billy. We ain't gonna get charged for trespassin'." Fish dangled his ID badge between them. "Remember, I'm the night watchman."

"But I'm not!"

"Look, nobody's gonna see us. That's why the place is perfect for a still site. Nobody ever goes up there anymore, especially at night, 'ceptin' me. Trust me, I been there three weeks and I ain't seen so much as a squirrel nosin' around."

"That's because the last people that went up there at night got themselves killed," Billy said, sliding lower in his seat.

"It was Doug French and Vinnie Kriesel and you know those two ain't got the sense God gave a busted oven. They walked into an abandoned building with no flashlight and fell through the floor. End of story."

Billy shook his head. "That ain't what I heard. I heard Vinnie went crazy and pushed Doug down that old elevator shaft. Only he lost his balance and went down with him. And what's worse—they didn't find 'em till three weeks later, with gray skin peelin' away from their skulls and maggots crawlin' out their eye sockets."

"Why would Vinnie Kriesel kill his best friend?"

Billy shrugged. "Maybe something told him to."

"Something? Like what?"

"Like somethin' I don't want to be messin' with."

"Look, Billy. I been sittin' in that office for three weeks with cameras goin' in every room of that place and I ain't seen nothin' strange but a couple of rats fuckin' in an old medicine cabinet. Trust me. Lychhurst is the perfect place for the still site. We can back the truck up at the old loading dock, put all the stuff on the old freight elevator—"

"The one Doug and Vinnie took a header in…"

Fish ignored him. "—carry it up and run this mash. The old cardiac ward still has running water and I hooked up an old generator. By mornin', we'll have a couple thousand bucks in pure White Lightnin'! Wooo-hooo!" He crowed in excitement and beeped the horn a few times to accentuate his point, and Billy couldn't help laughing.

Fish could always make him laugh. Billy had been a shy kid when they moved to town to live with his aunt after his mom left. But Fish had sort of adopted him from that first day in Miss Muckenfuss's fifth grade class and they'd been together ever since.

Fish wasn't too bright, but he was hilarious and completely unruly. They all said it was on account of the fact that his daddy had drunk a bottle of rotgut whiskey and fell down a ravine in Nelson's Holler. Or maybe it was because his momma and daddy were second cousins. After all, they called him Fish because his eyes were on either side of his head.

The truck bounced off the pavement and on to the winding gravel and dirt road that would lead them to Lychhurst Hospital. The hospital sat on a hill looming over the town of Oleander. You could see its tall spires from just about every point in town.

At one time, it had been a state-of-the-art facility offering the latest treatments. Now, it was just this hulking, gray building with shattered windows that hung from the panes like broken teeth. A building that wore the ghosts of its past like a spring debutante in a brand new ball gown.

The walls were overgrown with ivy and the trees around it wore cauls of cobwebs and twisty vines. Lychhurst didn't look just run-down, it looked insane. The passage of time and evil deeds had stained it like a pristine white linen tablecloth at a Fourth of July picnic.

Fish took a hairpin curve at twenty miles per hour, throwing Billy against his side.

"Damnit, Fish! Take it easy."

"Sorry. The turns kind of sneak up on you."

When Billy was seated upright again, he looked out the window where he could just barely see the road from the glow of the Ranger's headlights. The tires were dangerously close to the edge of the road that dropped off to a ravine below. He pressed himself against the back of the seat and closed his eyes. "Lord Jesus, I don't want to die here."

Fish snorted. "You ain' gon' die, Billy-boy. At least not yet."

"That's comforting."

After a few more near-death experiences on the road, they pulled up outside of the hospital. Fish drove the truck around the back to a dark area where the sodium glow was almost swallowed by the shadows that seemed to surround Lychhurst.

Billy pushed open the passenger-side door and heaved himself out of the truck. He tried to be as quiet as possible when closing the door, but Fish obviously didn't care. He swung the door shut with enough force to shake the whole truck.

"Damn, Fish. Now everybody's going to know we're here."

"Relax. There ain't nobody out here to hear us." He reached through the window and grabbed his hat.

"Then why did you make a big thing out of parking at the back?"

"That's where the loading dock is. And on the off chance that somebody drives by, they won't see the truck." Fish pulled a mangled bag of circus peanuts out of his pocket and plucked one out. He squished it between his fingers in a way that made Billy slightly uncomfortable and then popped it in his mouth.

"Come on. I gotta do my first walkaround before we get started."

2

The campus of Lychhurst Hospital was massive. In front was a cracked asphalt parking lot that the elements had nearly reclaimed. A single street light illuminated the tufts of weeds, broken pavement, and assortment of beer cans and other detritus that littered the lot.

It looked like some kind of post-apocalyptic battleground. At some point, someone must have tried to make the place look a little less depressing as there were a couple of overgrown flowerbeds that had run wild with ragged weeds on either side of the steps leading to the main entrance.

Billy followed Fish into the old employee entrance on the other side of the building. The door looked like it was about to fall out of the frame, but there was a sensor pad and when Fish passed his ID badge over it, there was a loud *ding* and Billy could hear the cogs of the locking mechanism shift so that they could get inside.

Fish held the door and let Billy go first. When the door closed behind them, that mechanism could be heard again, locking the two of them inside. A shudder ran over Billy, but he shook it off and pulled his jacket tighter around his shoulders.

They started down a short corridor. From the street lamp shining through the small window behind them, Billy could just barely make out the linoleum floor beneath their feet. A sick green checkerboard with suspicious-looking cracks. Their shadows along the wall were long and strange, almost monstrous in the yellow light.

"Why can't we just bring the still and stuff in now? I don't like all that copper just laying there unattended."

"Because. I have to do my first check-in before 9:15 and I'm already five minutes late because you couldn't haul your slow ass out to the car on time."

"Yeah, yeah. Whatever." Billy pulled a pack of Pall Mall cigarettes and a lighter out of his front shirt pocket and shook one out. "You ain't never been on time a day in your life, Fish."

He lit the cigarette and took a long drag. The smoke had a pungent, almost sour smell that added to the dank, moldy smell of the hospital.

"Don't smoke that shit in here," Fish said, coughing. He pointed to the No Smoking sign by the door of the makeshift office. "You know I got allergies."

"You didn't tell me I was going to have to go outside every time I wanted to smoke."

"You'll be okay, Puddin' Pop. Exercise is good for you." Fish winked at Billy as he turned the key on the timeclock that was strapped around his waist. "C'mon. It's gettin' late."

Billy heaved an exasperated sigh and threw his backpack down by the desk before following Fish out the door. It slammed behind them with a low boom that made Billy wince. "We better be able to get back in there, Fish."

"Relax. The place is just old. And that door is a heavy steel door. At least a foot thick. It's gonna make noise when it closes." He clicked on his flashlight and headed down the corridor.

As they came back to the main corridor, the smell of mold and decay was stronger. Billy could feel the tentacles of the allergens already sliding into his sinuses. Before the end of the night, he'd be hacking and wheezing like a kitten with distemper.

The floor under their feet looked bone-white under the glow of Fish's flashlight. There were cracks and stains in the linoleum that strangle-y vines had started to come through.

In the darkness, the vines and weeds appeared to move with the phosphenes one might see in the dark. It made Billy think of nasty, Lovecraftian things bursting through the floor and walls, then tangling around their ankles to pull them down into the Hellmouth. Billy could feel the goose flesh popping up along the back of his neck but he shrugged it off.

The endless hallway was so dark and so silent. He wanted to say something, but was almost afraid of what his voice might sound like. Would it be his own, or perhaps the voice of some long dead patient, locked in the psycho ward?

As they turned the corner, Billy gasped. Something moved past a window in one of the old rooms. A gray figure with the gentle curve of the feminine form. An apron so white it hurt his eyes. And when she turned, she stared straight at him and brought a finger to her lips.

Then, she mouthed something that he couldn't quite make out.

"So what's up with these steel doors, Fish?" Billy asked, swallowing the lump of dread that threatened to boil up in the back of his throat. "You said the one at your office was a foot thick. That seems like overkill."

"Well, they didn't used to have those until the forties. My boss told me that there was an incident where some lady in the psycho ward killed an orderly and a doctor and then burned half the damn hospital down."

"I don't think I want to hear the whole story," Billy said.

Fish's eyes had a mischievous gleam as he completely ignored Billy's unease.

"Some society bitch got sent here by her husband to get cured of her irrational tendencies. Course everybody knew that she wasn't crazy, she was just in the way of a new piece of ass. Anyway, she wasn't crazy when she got here, but a little bit of electro-shock did the job real nice."

"Jesus…"

"Anyway, she kills the hell out of some orderly with an axe, then turns on one of the doctors. When she sees what she done, she just burned the place down and never looked back. Fish shrugged. "That's what my boss told me, anyway."

Fish paused as they came to one of the steel doors. With a shove of his shoulder, he pushed it open and shined his flashlight around the walls. When he was satisfied that there was no one there, he took the key hanging by the door and plugged it into the timer on his belt. There was a snap as the time clock recorded the key stamp.

"Anyway, this place is full of stories like that. Probably none of 'em are true." Fish pulled another one of those circus peanuts out of his pocket and popped it in his mouth.

"Yeah. Probably." Billy could feel his dinner of Slim Jims and V8 juice boiling in his belly. "What did that have to do with the steel doors?"

"When they rebuilt the burned-up wing, they put those steel doors in so that if a patient went nuts, they had some place to lock themselves in until the police got there. All the wards have one and then the offices each have one. Plus it would keep the whole damn place from burning down again."

"I guess they didn't care if the patients were slaughtered as long as they could contain them on the floor."

Fish shrugged and started off down the corridor. "This place was a state mental hospital at the time. People dropped their crazy family members off here to forget about 'em."

Billy tried to mask a shudder by reaching for a cigarette. Then he remembered he couldn't smoke and ended up standing there awkwardly, trying to figure out what to do with his hands. "So did they ever find out why the woman killed the orderly and the doctor? I mean, other than the fact that she went nuts."

"That's the weird part. One of the survivors said that while the chick was crazy as fuck that she hadn't ever been violent. In fact, she had been practically catatonic most of the time she'd been there."

They came to another room and Fish shoved the door open. "The only clue they had was a note, written in the doctor's blood—Until the fire."

"What the hell does that mean?"

"Beats the hell outta me," Fish said, shoving the key into his watch clock.

The pair continued down the main hall. Billy wondered how someone as hyperactive as Fish could stand such a tedious occupation. Room after room they went inside, shining the flashlight around the room, finding the key, and closing the doors behind them.

"Damn. How many more areas? I mean, we don't have to go into every single patient room, do we?"

"Nah." Fish ushered Billy up the rickety stairs to the next floor. He was about to ask why they couldn't take the elevator until he saw the elevator. Time and disuse had certainly taken its toll. The call buttons were gone, leaving bare wires sticking out of the wall. The area around the doors that were barely hanging on and halfway open showed signs of rust and mildew that crawled around the edges like greasy tentacles. At best, the damn thing would fall to the basement, leaving them a couple of pancakes on the floor of the shaft.

At worst… well, Billy didn't like to think about worst.

"Come on. Let's get up to the Cardiac Ward. It's the last place I have to check."

They emerged from the stairwell into what used to be a large lobby. A bank of windows stretched from one end of the room to the other. Some still had glass stained with dirt and grime, others were just black maws that opened out into the dark West Virginia night. At some point, someone had covered a few of them with large sheets of plastic that blew and crackled as a chilly breeze blew through.

"Damn!" Fish exclaimed. "It's cold as witch's tit in a brass brassiere up in here."

"It'll warm up soon enough once we get the still in here. Yet another reason for you to move your ass."

"You're like a sore-tailed cat, Billy. Relax. We got time."

"Yeah, well. I don't want to be in here any longer than we have to."

Fish chortled. It was a breathy, hooting sound that echoed off the walls. "Why? You scared?"

"Hell no, I ain't scared. I'm just in a hurry. I need that money by Friday. That means we got to get this 'shine done and find a buyer and collect the money in three days."

"You know," Fish said. "You never really told me why you need this money so bad. You in some kind of trouble?"

"Never mind."

"No really, man…"

"I said never mind!" Billy shouted. His voice boomed off the empty walls and the reverb brought him to his senses. "Look. Do your thing. I'm gonna go down to the truck, smoke a cig, and start unloading those barrels."

"Just wait, now. I don't want you to get lost."

"I ain't gon' get lost. I know my way down well enough."

"But I got the flashlight."

Billy held up his phone and turned the flashlight on. "I got one too."

Before Fish could protest, Billy turned and went back to the staircase. He had to get away for a few minutes.

For one thing, he needed a cigarette. It was a nasty vice, but Billy had been smoking since junior high and it was pretty apparent that he was what you might call 'addicted.' If he was going to have to spend an entire night with Fish, he'd need something to take the edge off.

And for another thing, Lychhurst was starting to creep him out. The air was too close. Too warm. It was almost charged. Like, his reptilian brain was tickling, trying to tell him that something was about to happen. Billy didn't like it.

He had to get out of there, if only for long enough to smoke a cigarette and drag those mash barrels out of the bed of Fish's truck.

Billy tried to stay close to the wall as he descended the stairs. One at a time, his slow footfalls echoed in the empty well. That suffocating feeling was worse here. The dust and mold seemed to be collecting in his lungs, making every breath a struggle.

And he could taste it. The ancient madness and the blood of everyone who had died here had cast a bitter film over his tongue. He wasn't sure if Fish was having the same experience. Likely not if he could find the will to come here every night. They'd been here less than an hour and Billy was ready to bolt. How in the hell was he going to make it through a whole night?

The light from Billy's cell phone was just a little better than a match. He felt along the wall, hoping that there was something to hold on to if he stumbled. He shined the light on the floor in front of him, watching where his feet were going.

If he fell, he wasn't sure that Fish would be able to get to him before he bled out from a gaping head wound. He shivered as the image of his brains leaking out of a crack in the crown of his head flashed behind his eyes.

"Stop it," he scolded himself. "It's just an old building. And you ain't been afraid of the dark since you were ten years old."

One of the steps was uneven and Billy pitched forward. His foot came down on the next step hard and he managed to catch himself on the remnant of the rail. His heart sank as he heard his cell phone hit the ground and bounce down a couple of steps.

"Fuck," he gasped. His heart pounded and he clutched his chest as he leaned against the concrete bricks behind him. His cell phone glowed, and after a little pep talk with himself, Billy continued down the steps and bent down to get it.

Something skittered in the dark and Billy froze. Out of the corner of his eye, he swore he saw the lady in the old-timey white apron move across the landing and disappear into the wall. He squinched his eyes closed and said the Lord's Prayer in his head. When he opened them, there was nothing there.

"God, I need a cigarette," he said.

He picked up his phone and continued down the stairs. By the time he made it to the doors, his hands were shaking so bad that he had to try the knob three times before finally shoving it open.

The cool air that slapped Billy in the face was a welcome companion as he shoved a stray cinder block against the heavy door.

He nearly tripped over his feet trying to get free of the old hospital building. When he reached Fish's truck, every molecule in his skinny body was screaming for him to get inside and drive away as fast as he could, best friend be damned.

But dumb as he was, Fish had enough sense to always keep the keys.

Billy leaned on the bed of the truck and took a deep drag on his cigarette.

"It's just a few hours," he said to the darkness. "Just a few hours and we'll get this 'shine run and I don't ever have to see this godforsaken place ever again."

The truth of the matter was, Billy didn't have a choice but to go through with the plan.

It seemed like everyone in this part of West Virginia had a problem with addiction. Billy's addiction was gambling. It started out innocent enough. Just a couple of scratch-off tickets from the gas station down the street from his apartment. It was just a few dollars, right?

He even won a few times— ten bucks here, twenty there. But once he had tasted the sickly-sweet flavor of *somethin' for nothin'*, he just couldn't stop. He could blow a whole paycheck in an hour. Over and over, week after week, until finally he started borrowing money to feed the monster in his head.

First from places with names like *Daddy's Money Cash Advance*, then from guys who conducted their business in the corners of pool halls.

It was one such upstanding gentleman who had come by the paper plant last week and told Billy that he could either pay what he owed by the end of the month or he was going to break his legs.

To start.

Billy had always figured that was just something that happened in the movies, but joke's on him, right? So he'd gone to his good friend Fish and they had cooked up a couple of barrels of mash.

Fish had assured him that if they could successfully run a batch of Zeke Barnett's Corn Squeezins, they could get at least $120 a gallon from a friend of his over in Bluefield which would be enough to pay off his debt and have a little left over.

Of course, he'd neglected to tell Fish why he was in so much trouble. Better not to complicate things.

A cracking noise from the woods startled Billy out of his thoughts and he nearly lost his cigarette. He looked out toward the edge of the decayed parking lot.

The puddles of yellow light from the streetlamps spilled out toward the trees, but there was nothing to see.

"Probably just a limb falling," he said, but noticed that the end of his cigarette was trembling as he brought it to his mouth.

"Blood is thicker, boy."

Billy gasped. The voice was so close he could feel the heat of her breath.

"Who's there?"

He whipped around, straining to see anyone who might be hiding around corners or in the trees.

"Somebody out there fuckin' with me?"

"You know who I am, boy."

Billy rubbed his eyes and stretched. "I must be too tired for this shit," he said. It wouldn't be far from the truth. He hadn't gotten much sleep since that last visit from his "creditors." It must be catching up.

"I been waitin' for you, boy."

"Waiting for me? For what?"

"Vengeance. This land is ours."

The wind picked up and Billy shivered. Why was it so cold? It shouldn't be this cold. "Look, I don't know who you are… or why you're messin' with us, but… I don't believe in…"

He couldn't get the word out. There was no such thing.

"Ghosts."

The voice laughed and it was a horrible sound. Hollow and jagged like nails on a chalkboard. He covered his ears to block it out.

"You best start believin' boy. The Barnetts got debts to pay. Past due."

"I'm not listening to this anymore…" Billy whined, pressing his hands against his ears and squeezing his eyes shut.

"Remember yourself, boy."

There were footsteps all around and the sound of branches snapping in the trees. He whispered the Lord's Prayer again, this time mouthing the words.

"Please God, let it go away."

He turned away from the woods, not wanting to see what might be coming out of the shadows. The cracking came again, this time accompanied by the steady crunch of footsteps in the leaves. He cupped his hands around his face to block his view. "Don't look. Don't look. Don't…"

"Don't what?"

Billy whipped around when Fish put a hand on his shoulder from behind.

"Jesus!"

"Not at all. What the hell is wrong with you?"

Billy opened his eyes and looked toward the tree line again.

Nothing.

"I just… Nothing."

"Well, come on. I finished my rounds. Let's get this shit upstairs."

3

Fish hadn't been kidding when he said that they would warm up as soon as they got the still set up. Once they lit the propane torch underneath, the room became an oven that was slowly cooking them like a Thanksgiving turkey.

Billy supposed it could be the fact that he'd transferred a hundred gallons of mash from their barrel into the copper still all by himself while Fish sat on the other side of the room eating circus peanuts and reading a moldy porno mag.

"Don't let me bother you or anything," Billy said, wiping the sweat from his forehead on the tail of his shirt. He rubbed his chest. A nagging ache had settled there. Just a throb, a slight pressure, but it was there.

"No worries, man," Fish said. "You're doing a great job."

"Yeah. How about you come over and stir for a little while?"

To his surprise, Fish came over and took the stick from him.

"You're thinkin' too hard about this thing, man." As he said this, he tossed the stirring stick aside. "I know guys who flunked out of kiddie-garten that can make liquor. All we gotta do now is wait."

Fish produced a flask from inside his jacket and took a swig before passing it to Billy.

"No thanks, man. I'm good."

"Oh, come on. Just a little somethin' to take the edge off." Fish took another swig and shoved the flask down the back of his pants where it hovered inexplicably in his waistband.

"You really need to calm down, man," he said as he wandered to where an old, rusted-out wheelchair sat in the corner. "You been uptight as long as I've known you." He flopped down in the chair and rolled it toward the still.

"Well, some of us can't afford to be screw-ups," Billy said. He bit down on his lip and rubbed his chest again. That ache had grown to a sharp stab and he leaned against the warm still.

"What's that supposed to mean?"

"Nothin'," Billy said. "I'm just tired. Ignore me."

"Sure, dude," Fish said, going back to his magazine.

Billy stared at his friend from across the room. In the dim light from the propane stove, he looked like a Halloween pumpkin sitting there with the shadows falling into the lines of his face and the folds of his beer gut. He had this dumb smile as he turned the magazine sideways to examine the naked centerfold.

"Is that even your magazine?" Billy asked. He couldn't help noticing how crinkled the pages were. Like they'd been left out in the rain for a while. The pages stuck together and even the noise they made as Fish flipped them sounded phlegmy.

"Nah. I found it in one of the old patient rooms a couple of weeks ago." His eyes got wide and he whistled through his teeth. "Yeah, Mama." He turned the book to Billy. There was a woman spread-eagled with her 1980s lady garden on full display.

When Billy's eyes focused, the woman in the photograph smiled. He tried not to make any expression as he watched the photo morph and change until it wasn't the barely legal centerfold, but a gnarled crone. Her hair twisted into a frizzy halo. Breasts that a moment ago had been full and inviting were now deflated and hung at her sides like bags of marbles.

"I guess the carpet matches the drapes, eh?"

Billy shook his head, trying to shake the vision. "What?"

"I mean, look at that puuuussssaaaayyy." Fish laughed, almost barking like a seal, and flicked his tongue obscenely between two fingers.

They had been friends forever, but sometimes Billy hated Fish. He had been a lazy, disgusting fuck-up as long as they'd known each other.

Old Man Barnett had been the meanest man in Tucker County, but also the richest. When he came back from the war, he bought up every farm in the county and rented out plots to the ruined planters, making money hand over fist off the misery of his neighbors.

Nearly every building in Oleander had the Barnett name on it somewhere. His family had been coasting off their name ever since, being slum lords and selling off properties, inch by inch.

Fish's mom would get him a job, he'd work for a while until he screwed up, and then she'd pay his way until she found him another job. The world was a hustle for guys like Fish and whenever Billy thought about it, he could feel that bubble of hateful resentment rising.

Meanwhile, Billy was dodging his landlord and making moonshine to make sure his legs didn't get broken.

"Hey, Fish. Didn't this land used to be in your family?"

Before Fish could answer, the wheelchair he was in made a weird noise and lurched forward, throwing Fish to the linoleum floor. "Goddamn!"

"Are you alright?" Billy rushed over and helped him to his feet. "What happened?"

"I don't know. The damn thing just threw me out."

"It's an old wheelchair. You probably hit the brakes or something…"

Fish shook his head. "No, man. I was just sitting there."

"I get it," Billy sighed. "You're just trying to freak me out."

"I swear, man," Fish laughed, flopping back into the chair.

Billy rolled his eyes and grabbed the small bowl full of flour paste he'd prepared. Taking a bit of the sticky dough, he started to press it into the seams along the joints of the copper pipe. Anything to make this happen faster.

He didn't like to admit it, but this place *was* starting to spook him. He glanced over at where Fish had already gone back to his magazine. And Fish was pissing him off. He just sat over there like a perverted toad while Billy did all the work.

"Are you going to do anything to help?" Billy asked finally.

"Hey, I got the still site, didn't I? And it's *my* great-great grandaddy's recipe, so…"

"So?"

"So, I have fulfilled my end of the bargain."

Billy started to say more, but thought better of it. If he started in on Fish now, he might say too much.

"Whatever," he grumbled.

The hours passed in relative quiet. Fish left for another round of walk-throughs just before midnight. The still had started to drip slowly into the first jar. That quiet staccato of the drops hitting the glass bottom was enough to put a man to sleep.

Between that and the heat, Billy could barely keep his eyes open as he sat there watching. The room was so hot that his shirt was sticking to him and he was damn near blind from the sweat droplets that dripped continuously from the ends of his hair. But that gnawing, burning ache in his chest was growing harder to ignore. His heart would flutter and slow, an irregular rhythm the longer he sat there staring at the drip of moonshine.

"You know he'll cheat you."

The voice was so close and so clear that Billy nearly fell out of his chair.

"Who's there?"

Of course there was no one there. Just another trick of the wind slipping through the cracks in the walls or the shards of broken windows. Or maybe just his brain playing tricks again. Ever since they got here tonight, he'd been sure that they were being watched.

Lychhurst had always been a nightmare setting for Billy. When he was little, just after they moved here, his mother told him that they were coming home.

In fact, just down the road in Nelson's Holler used to be his old family homestead. His people had lived in these hills surrounding

Oleander for generations, and his mother insisted that moving away from the fold was where her troubles began.

"Granny Selah warned me," she always said. "These mountains is fickle."

"He'll cheat you. You know it, Billy. Them Barnetts ain' nothin' but thieves and murderers."

"Who are you?" Billy jerked around again, this time jumping to his feet, fists raised. He squinted into the darkness, hoping to catch a glimpse of the person who was obviously playing with them.

"Come out and show yourself!" he called.

"He'll use you to do all the grunt work, but when it comes time to pay up your share, he'll disappear."

"No, no… Fish's my best friend," Billy stammered. "He wouldn't do nothin' to mess this up. He gave me his—aaah… God..." The ache in his chest exploded and Billy lurched forward a bit, but the pain subsided. "He gave me his word

The words came, but he wasn't so sure he believed them. As many times as Fish had offered his help, he very rarely delivered. His faith this time was more based on desperation than friendship.

"Piss on his word."

The voice was like the whispering of autumn leaves blowing down the asphalt. A rasping, sharp whisper that Billy could feel tickling the back of his neck. When he looked around, there wasn't a soul in the room. Nor was there any place to hide. But it had to be Fish. Somehow Fish was doing this for a laugh.

"Fuck you, man! I don't got time for games!"

The voice laughed; a long, gravelly hiss that iced Billy's blood. His skin prickled despite the warmth of the liquor still.

"Barnett will keep the money for himself. And where will that leave you?"

"Fish is my friend!"

"Aww, buddy. I didn't know you cared so much." Fish clapped him on the shoulder as he came back into the room.

When he passed, Billy could smell the whiskey smell all over him. Evidently, he'd finished the bottle on his rounds. He went over and stuck a grimy, meaty finger in the slow stream of liquor coming out of the worm. He brought the finger to his mouth and made a big show of sucking the liquid from the tip.

"God damn!" Fish exclaimed. "That shit is hot as the devil's ass crack."

"Them's the heads," Billy said. "You ain't supposed to drink it."

"Aw, hell. That's an old wives' tale." As if to illustrate the point, Fish reached down and picked up the jar, turning it up. "That... " he said, panting, "that'll get you where you need to be."

"Damnit, you're spillin' it everywhere," Billy said, snatching the jar and putting it back in place.

"Jeezuz creezuz," Fish said, laughing. "You on the rag or somethin'?"

"No, I just don't want to fuck it up."

Fish seemed to accept this and sat back down in the old wheelchair. He pulled out his phone and started flipping through it. Billy tried to ignore the random outbursts of laughter.

Then he tried to tune out when Fish started watching videos at earsplitting volumes. It wasn't until he started using his foot to push the wheelchair back and forth and causing a rhythmic squeaking that echoed that irregular beat of Billy's heart.

"Hey Fish, you know what this place was before the hospital was here?"

"Oh hell yeah," Fish replied. "You know this was my great-great-grandaddy's place back in the day."

"Really?"

"It was. The old Barnett House was a big old mansion that used to sit not far from where our asses are sweatin'. When he come back from the war—of 1812— he found out his daddy had died of pneumonia the winter before and left him a little bit of money. So he come out here to these woods and built the house."

"Thief. Murderer."

Billy nodded. "You know, stories about Old Zeke are legendary."

"I know, right? I 'spect they're only partly true, right?"

"My granny used to tell us stories about him, too." Billy squatted down and replaced the first jar with another, real quick like, ignoring the stab of pain

"Remember. Roots run deep as this valley, boy."

"Oh yeah?"

"Yup. You know, my family is actually from Nelson's Holler." He held out the jar full of cool shine to Fish.

"You know, I never put the two together. Your last name is Nelson and Nelson's Holler…" He chuckled and took a long swig.

"Weird."

"These hills used to all be part of Nelson's Holler. For generations my people lived down here, before there was even an America. So says my granny anyway."

Fish snorted and took another horn of the 'shine and squinted with the afterburn. "No shit, man. Maybe we was cousins back down the line. You know, e'er-body in Oleander's related some kinda way."

Billy nodded. "In fact, the way I heard it, the place where we're sittin' used to be where the Granny Witch lived."

"The Granny Witch? Did you drink some of them heads, Billy?"

"See, Nelson's Holler used to be a place that was forgotten. A place so deep in the woods that most folks didn't even know it was there. Not even the Indian tribes would settle down in this place with the ground full of granite and no light to speak of.

"But there was a community. The Nelsons lived down here in their own little world and Granny Sadie was God. Nobody knew how old she was or where she came from, only that she'd always been down the holler. She was wise, stern, and had a power that they didn't understand."

Fish hiccupped and let out a long, disinterested belch.

"What kind of power was that?"

"She knew about the Old Magic—roots and spells. She could heal the sick. Make the crops grow, or find water in a fallow field. Some people said she could put a hex on anybody who crossed her."

"Bullshit…"

"She always said that it came from the good Lord Hisself, but personally, I don't think Jesus would approve of such dark and treacherous power. The bottom line was, nobody crossed Granny."

"Vengeance is a hard lesson."

"That is, until old Zeke Barnett came back from the war. He came in here and started buyin' up people's places. He'd give 'em a couple dollars here and there, buyin' up homesteads. When he came to Granny Sadie's place, she told him where he could take his money in no uncertain terms."

"Well that was damn stupid, wasn't it?"

"Every day for weeks he'd come down the Holler and beg Granny Sadie to sell him her homestead. I think maybe he knew that the land itself had power and he was so greedy for it. But no matter what Old Zeke offered her, she turned him down cold. Finally, he got tired of askin' nice.

"One night, he hid in the shadows to wait. All night he watched and waited and plotted. He was about to give up when right about midnight, here she come in her white nightgown with her silver hair hangin' 'round her face and her gnarled old beech cane clutched in her hand. She come down the hill and went to the outhouse."

Billy stood up and grabbed the old stir stick. He hoisted it up on his shoulder like a baseball bat, gripping it tight. "Three guesses as to what happened."

Fish's eyes were wide as he stared up at Billy. He held the jar in his hand, paused to take a sip, but he didn't. He just held it.

"I… uh… I dunno, Billy."

"He followed her inside, blocked the door. And he grabbed her. He said—"

"You shoulda taken my offer, you spooky old bitch." Sadie's voice in Billy's head lingered on the words, hissing an echo as he said them.

"And then he beat the old woman with her cane." Wielding the stir stick like a bat, he slammed it down on the old chair.

"He hit her over and over and over!" he shouted. "Until she was dead."

"Jesus, Billy," Fish said, trying to get out of the old wheelchair, but it rolled backward, dumping him into the floor. The jar fell and shattered around them. "What the hell is wrong with you?"

"See now, old Zeke Barnett thought he'd won," Billy said, taking a step toward Fish. "When he stumbled out of that outhouse with Granny Sadie's blood all over him, he was already plannin' where his new venture—this bloody hospital—was gonna be. He was laughin' and shoutin' his victory to the trees. But nobody crossed Granny. She crawled out of that place, barely alive, and she laid a curse on this ground."

"Curse? What curse, man? There ain't no such thing as curses."

"This ground will sour, no bricks will stand." Billy's voice sounded foreign to him as he repeated Sadie's words. He could feel her cool touch just behind him and her whispered words on his ear. *"No Barnett will have a second's peace as long as these mountains stand."*

"And then what?" Fish croaked.

Billy relaxed and looked down at his friend. "She died. But this land—and Lychhurst on it—has been cursed with trouble ever since."

When he said the name, the generator coughed and the lights flickered and died, dropping a blanket of darkness over the room. The only illumination was the blue glow of the propane stove under the still.

"Well shit," Fish sighed, hoisting his drunken body up from the floor. "That generator ain't worth two cents." He felt around his belt, looking for the flashlight.

"What do we do?"

"It should kick back on in a few minutes. It does this every now and then. I uh… better go down to the basement and restart it."

Billy smiled. The pain in his chest throbbed, but it was a welcome friend. He took a step toward Fish, gripping the stirring paddle tight.

Fish took a step back, staring at Billy as if he could see something in his friend's eyes that he'd never seen before.

"Good."

He knew what he had to do.

"I should go down and check the generator."

Billy shook his head. "It's fine."

"The security system… if the power cuts out… you know, somebody may come up here and catch us."

"Ain't nobody around," Billy said, taking another step toward Fish. "Ain't that what you said? Nobody around to see us."

Fish bumped into the wheelchair and stumbled. "What's wrong with you, man?"

"Nothin'," Billy said. "I'm right as rain."

Billy lunged at Fish with the paddle, bringing it down hard against the side of his head. Fish tried to duck away, but the alcohol had made him sloppy. The first blow didn't knock him out, but it knocked him down. He barely had time to throw up his hands before Billy swung again, this time breaking his nose and fracturing his skull.

Over and over Billy slammed the stir stick down until old Fish was nothin' but a bloody mess at his feet. He tossed the paddle to the side.

Something warm dripped down his cheek. He reached up to touch it and his fingers came away wet. He brought the fingers to his mouth and tasted it. The sharp metallic flavor confirmed the blood. Sadie's blood. His family's birthright. He painted his lips with it.

"Blood is thicker, boy," Sadie's voice whispered. *"Roots go deep."*

As her voice faded, the pain in Billy's chest exploded. He fell to the floor, the life draining from his body as sure as the moonshine that drained into the jar beside him.

"Blood is thicker, Granny."

Emergency Room
1981

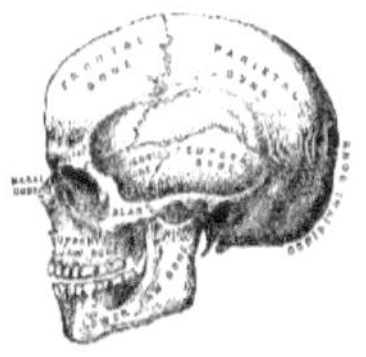

Stronger Connections
Joe DeRouen

What the fuck is going on? shouted Kenny, watching from above as Marvin Bixby, his boyfriend of almost three years, stormed into the Lychhurst Hospital emergency room.

"Is he going to be okay?" asked Marvin, hovering near the door. "They won't tell me anything out there."

Kenny's body lay stretched out on an examination table, not moving, as a doctor and two nurses scurried around him.

Was he… dead?

This couldn't be happening. Kenny had thus far managed to avoid the mysterious sickness that had been going around his circle of friends, though he'd been almost certain he would catch it eventually.

Had he suffered a heart attack instead? He remembered something about his heart, something bad, but couldn't quite put the pieces together.

"What's he doing in here?" asked the doctor, staring at Marvin. "Out!"

"What's wrong with him?" asked Marvin, eyes wide.

I'm up here, screamed Kenny at the top of his lungs, but no words came out. He tried to move toward Marvin, almost swimming through the air, but every time he got close, he found himself snapping back like a rubber band, hovering over his body again.

"Sir," said one of the nurses, a petite young woman with red hair, moving to block Marvin's view, "you need to leave. We're doing everything we can for your friend. I'll come get you the moment we know something more."

The doctor was doing CPR on his body now, as the other nurse wheeled over a machine. The doctor took two paddles from the machine, attached them to his chest, and took a step back.

"Clear!" he yelled, and the other nurse, the one with jet black hair, did something to the machine.

Kenny's body arched and almost seemed to rise from the table.

"What are you doing to him?" yelled Marvin, pushing past the first nurse.

"Sir!" the redheaded nurse yelled, grabbing him by the shoulders. "What we're doing is trying to save his life. You need to leave so we can do our job. I promise I'll come get you the moment we know something."

"But—"

"Clear!"

Kenny hovered above the room, his eyes (or whatever served as eyes in this incorporeal form he was now in) flitting back and forth between Marvin and the empty shell that had once been his body.

"Okay, I'm going," Marvin said, his cheeks wet with tears, "But please... please... let me know the moment you've... fixed him."

"We will, sir," said the nurse. "I promise."

"We need to start locking that door," said the doctor the moment Marvin had left the room, stepping away from Kenny's body. "I'm tired of having to put on these performances."

Performances? What was he talking about?

"Sorry, Dr. Albright, but it looks better if we keep it open."

"I know, I know."

The nurse with the black hair turned off the machine.

Don't give up on me! shouted Kenny, waving his arms at the doctor.

"Sarah, get that... thing out of here," said Dr. Albright, looking directly at Kenny.

The doctor could see him?

Please save me! I'm not ready to die!

"It doesn't really matter if you're ready to die or not, now does it?" asked the doctor, winking at Kenny. "But if it's any consolation, you weren't having a heart attack. It was probably a panic attack, just like your *boyfriend* thought."

He remembered now. They'd been driving through West Virginia, and Kenny's heart had started racing and he thought for sure he was having a heart attack.

"Though it all comes to the same result, doesn't it?" said Sarah, the redheaded nurse, smiling up at Kenny before turning to face the other nurse. "Rachel, can you grab the box?"

Rachel walked up to Sarah and Dr. Albright with a small, very old-looking black wooden chest.

"Time to say bye-bye," said Rachel as she opened the chest.

What's happening? Kenny tried to yell, as he was inextricably pulled downward. *Help me!*

"That's exactly what we're doing," Dr. Albright said, a smirk on his face. "With your abhorrent… lifestyle, you'll be better off dead, so someone else can take your place and lead a better life."

Take his place? What the hell was the doctor talking about?

He tried asking, then tried screaming, but the words would no longer come out. He felt himself getting smaller, smaller, and then the box was closing over him, somehow, and then –

Marvin sat in the little waiting area outside the emergency room, half-heartedly chewing on a Snickers bar he'd grabbed from the hospital's gift shop, feeling like he was going to throw up. He knew Kenny had anxiety problems, but never in a million years had he imagined his heart might stop.

They'd been traveling from Charlottesville, where they had met and fallen in love while both attending the University of Virginia, through West Virginia on their way to a small town in Ohio, to visit one of Kenny's sisters, and gotten lost. They'd had an argument about Kenny's mother yesterday (she didn't "approve" of Kenny's relationship with Marvin) and had left for the trip late, so by the time they hit West Virginia from Charlottesville, it was dark.

Two or three more wrong turns later, and they were deep in the hills of West Virginia.

Kenny, who already seemed agitated, began to complain about his chest hurting. *It's just a panic attack*, Marvin thought but didn't say as much. He knew from experience that would only make things worse.

Instead, he turned on the radio, searching for but failing to find a station that played jazz (Kenny's favorite) to help calm him down, and instead had been inundated with country music. That didn't help anything.

As he took another listless bite from the candy bar, something caught his eye. Movement on the wrapper, something slowly sliding towards his hand, like the "S" in the word "Snickers" had turned into a snake. Startled, he threw the Snickers bar to the ground.

He blinked, staring at the chocolate bar. The "S" was no longer moving. It had probably never moved in the first place. Of course it had never moved. His boyfriend was dying, and his mind was playing tricks on him. That had to be it. Still, he let the Snickers bar lie on the waiting room floor, not able to bring himself to touch it. Someone else could clean it up. He had more important things to worry about.

"Mr. Bixby?" said a voice, startling him. It was one of the nurses, the redhead, from the emergency room. Her name tag read *Sarah*.

Marvin shot up from the chair and darted toward her, all thoughts of the chocolate bar forgotten.

"I'm here. How is he? Is he going to be okay?"

"I'm so sorry, Mr. Bixby," Sarah whispered, eyes downcast, "but we lost him."

"What… what do you mean, 'lost him'? Where did he go?"

He pictured Kenny waking up and somehow wandering out of the hospital without anyone seeing him. He said a silent prayer to whoever might be listening that that was exactly what had happened, because at least then Marvin would have a chance of finding him. He couldn't even comprehend the alternative.

The nurse's hand reached out to take his shoulder, gently squeezing it, and that's when he knew.

"He didn't make it, Mr. Bixby. I'm so sorry. He's dead."

"No!" Marvin yelled, backing away from the nurse. "This can't be happening. It just can't. It was a panic attack, just like all the other panic attacks he's had."

"It was heart failure," the nurse said. "If you'd only gotten him here a few minutes earlier, I think maybe we could have saved him."

Marvin crumpled in on himself. He'd lost the love of his life, and it was his own fault. If only he'd gotten Kenny to the hospital even a minute or two earlier. If only he'd believed Kenny and hadn't insisted it was just a panic attack.

If only, if only, if only.

What a fool he'd been, and his foolishness had cost the man he loved his life.

"Would you like to see him one last time?" asked the nurse, her hand once again squeezing his shoulder.

He couldn't even speak, just nodded his head. If he didn't see Kenny, he'd never believe he was gone, and so he followed the nurse back into the emergency room, past other doctors and nurses, where she knocked on the door leading into the room in which they'd been working on Kenny.

The door slowly opened, and Marvin held his breath, everything in him urging him to run, run far away from this awful place of death. He steeled himself and stepped through the door.

A giant sob escaped Marvin's throat as he saw his beautiful boyfriend lying lifeless on the exam table, and he felt his knees start to buckle. Sarah grabbed his arm, and her grip was the only thing that kept him from collapsing to the floor.

"I know it's hard, Mr. Bixby," she whispered, "but it really will be okay. You'll always hold him in your heart."

He tried to say something, anything, to thank her for her help, for her compassion, but the words wouldn't come.

Instead he knelt and gently kissed Kenny on the lips, whispered how sorry he was, and then, his heart beating staccato in his chest, turned and bolted from the room, thinking of nothing but ending his own life so he could be with Kenny, wherever he was.

Kenny found himself swirling in a soup of darkness, and if he'd still had his stomach he probably would have thrown up.

His head, or whatever now served as his head, was throbbing, and he had absolutely no clue where he was.

It's okay, son, said a voice that sounded close to him.

Who are you? asked Kenny. *Where am I?*

The first question is easier to answer than the second. My name's Frank Godwin. As to where we are… I've been told we're trapped in a cave beneath the hospital, but I don't know that for certain. I don't really know anything for certain.

How long have you been here?

Who knows? said Frank. *All I know is that it was December 2, 1972, when those monsters ripped me from my body and put me in that damned chest.*

Kenny heard himself gasp, though he still couldn't see anything. *That was almost ten years ago,* he managed to get out, still staring into the nothingness surrounding him.

I figured it had been a while. What's your name?

Kenny Green. I thought I was having a heart attack, but then they… they killed me.

I got into a car accident. Broken leg, but they killed me, too.

How could any of this be happening? It felt like Kenny's heart was racing, though that seemed impossible if he were dead. Was it possible to have panic attacks in the afterlife? His first instinct was to run, but instead he bit down on his (imaginary?) lip and stood his ground.

Close your eyes, Kenny, the old man whispered, perhaps sensing his distress, *or at least imagine your eyes closing, whatever works. There you go. Wait thirty seconds or so, take a deep breath, and open them.*

Kenny forced himself to do what the man said, though he wasn't sure he could tell the difference between his eyes being closed and the pure blackness surrounding him.

He opened his eyes.

It was still dark, but it was no longer black. An old man with deep blue eyes wearing a white beard stood before him, dressed in blue jeans, a pair of cowboy boots, and a shirt tie-dyed in all the colors of the rainbow.

Kenny slowly blinked, surveying the area. It really did look like they were in a huge cave of sorts. The floor, walls, and ceiling surrounding him were made of rough stone. Dozens of people, perhaps hundreds, stood around them, staring at him. A man in a long dress wearing a blonde wig waved at him, and a short woman standing beside him smiled.

"How did I get here?" he asked, almost jumping back at the echo of his own voice.

"It takes some getting used to," the short woman said, walking up to them. "At first, it's pitch black, and voices seem to reverberate in your head, and then, wham, it's almost like you're alive again. But you're definitely not alive, and you'll never be alive again, so you may as well get used to it."

"Please be kind," Frank said, staring at the woman.

"Sorry. I'm just being realistic. I'm Emmy, by the way. Been here since 1965, when I came in for a cough. I've always been curious what disease they told Veronica—that was my partner—I died from."

"Hi, Emmy," said Kenny, moving his eyes back and forth to stare at all the others in the cave.

"I'm Jackie," said the man in drag. "They got me in 1969."

"I'm Casper," said a tall, brown-haired man. "1933. I'm gay, too, just like most everyone else here, though I never admitted it in my lifetime. But someone found out, and I was admitted to Lychhurst when it was a psychiatric hospital. Next thing I know, I'm dead."

"Betsy here," said a tall, dark-haired woman standing beside Casper. "1979, so just two years ago. I should never have gone to the hospital when I broke my arm. That Dr. Smalley instantly gave me the heebie-jeebies. He—"

"Wait a minute," Kenny said, interrupting her. "Who's Dr. Smalley? The doctor who murdered me was named Albright."

"Mine was Dr. Montgomery," said Casper.

"And mine was Dr. Goldberg," someone else said, from behind Casper.

"This has been going on a lot longer than you might think," said a man with a British accent from deeper within the cave. "There have been many doctors and nurses at Lychhurst Hospital involved with these murders over the years. Your Dr. Albright is only the latest, I'd imagine."

The man stepped out of the shadows. He was dressed in an old-fashioned gray suit with a black tie and wore a bowler hat. He looked like someone from one of those ancient silent movies.

"Who are you and how do you know that?" asked Kenny, staring at the man.

"My name is Walter Grimes, and I know what happened because I'm the one responsible for all of this."

Kenny stared at him. "If you did all this, why are you here?"

Grimes explained to him that he'd been a member of something called the Society of the Great Exodus, a group of people who'd tasked themselves with bringing about the end of the world.

In the year 1920, Grimes had been ordered to travel to West Virginia to help acquire Lychhurst Hospital so it could transition from being a hospital for tuberculosis victims to a psychiatric hospital. He was never told why, and never asked.

The new owners of the hospital were a subset of the Society, but eventually broke off and formed their own cult of sorts. Anyone who wasn't Christian, white, and straight were their enemies. The Society had loaned them an ancient chest that supposedly once belonged to Merlin the magician, and they began to murder the patients who didn't meet their standards.

Using the magical artifact to transfer their souls to a mystical cave located beneath the hospital, they would then sell the soulless bodies they stole to rich patients who were dying to further grow their fledgling empire.

In 1931, Grimes had once again been sent to West Virginia, this time to investigate this offshoot of the Society, but had been murdered. What happened after that, he had no idea.

"Why were they given the chest in the first place?" asked Kenny, after Grimes had finished talking.

Grimes shrugged his shoulders. "I honestly don't know. It was beyond my purview. In the society, you didn't ask questions."

"Well, maybe you should have," Kenny said.

"In hindsight, I'd have to agree with you."

"All of this is moot anyway," said Jackie. We're stuck here, for eternity."

"Just like I said earlier," interjected Emmy. "Better get used to it, because it's not changing any time soon."

Marvin sat in the parking lot of the Lychhurst Hospital, in his 1979 powder-blue Ford Mustang, contemplating suicide. He wasn't sure how long he'd been wallowing in the car, trying to figure out the best way to take his own life, but it had gotten dark out. Just like his and Kenny's future.

One moment they'd had the whole world in front of them, and the next… it was all gone, like a candle snuffed out in an ocean of darkness.

If he didn't follow through on killing himself, he didn't know what to do next. He knew he should call Kenny's sisters and parents, to tell them Kenny was gone forever, but after that, then what?

He supposed they'd bury Kenny in Kentucky, where he'd been born twenty-four years ago, and where his parents and one of his sister's still lived. Should he kill himself before or after the funeral? And if he waited, would living without Kenny get any easier? The thought shamed him. He couldn't imagine life ever being easy again.

They'd both graduated from Virginia State University earlier this year; Marvin with a master's degree in psychology and Kenny with a master's degree in mathematics. They'd been planning to hold a marriage ceremony early next year with their closest friends in attendance. Just because the world wouldn't recognize their union didn't mean they couldn't live together as a married couple, all the bigots in the world be damned.

They had been eager to take on the world together. And now? Marvin's world had been shattered, because Kenny was gone.

He started his car, knowing suddenly what he needed to do. This part of West Virginia was filled with hills and mountains. Surely it wouldn't be too difficult to find one large enough to drive over. That'd be the end of it.

A giant grackle flew over the windshield just then, catching Marvin's eye. He watched as the bird circled above his car and then flew away. The land surrounding the hospital seemed almost infested with grackles, much more so than the area outside the hospital. He wondered what drew them here, and a part of him realized that he'd probably never know. He shrugged to himself and started to put the car in reverse.

Someone knocked on the car window, and Marvin, heart in his throat, jumped out of his seat, smashing his head on the low ceiling. Rubbing his head, he stared out the window to see one of the nurses from the emergency room, Sarah, staring at him. She was holding a large, metal cannister of some sort in her hands.

Putting the car back in park, he rolled down the window with shaking hands but didn't say anything.

"I'm so glad you're still here. I need to give you this."

"Give me what?" asked Marvin, staring at her, watching as smaller grackle circled the sky about ten feet above her head.

"This," she said, pushing the metal urn through the window and into his hands. "Kenny's remains."

He stared at her in shock, all thoughts of birds leaving his head. Kenny's remains? "You *cremated* him? Why would you do that?"

"Because that's what he wanted," she said, smiling.

He stared at the urn in his hands.

This wasn't right, this wasn't right at all.

"That's not true. How would you know what he wanted?"

"He told us when you brought him in. He said if he didn't make it, he wanted his body cremated. You didn't know this?"

"He wouldn't say that!"

"Well, he did," she said, already backing away from the car. "Maybe you didn't know him as well as you thought you did. Besides, what's done is done. Try to have a nice life, Mr. Bixby. At least as nice as someone like you can have. Now you really need to get out of here before we have to have you arrested for loitering. Have a nice day!"

He watched in confusion as the nurse turned around and walked back into the hospital.

What in the hell was happening? Kenny suffered—*had* suffered, he corrected himself—from pyrophobia. In other words, he was deathly afraid of fire. There was no way on earth he would have chosen to have himself cremated, and he couldn't imagine him having been in a calm enough state to make such a declaration to begin with.

Something very strange was going on, and he couldn't even think about ending his own life before he got some answers. Putting his car in drive, he peeled out of the Lychhurst Hospital parking lot, headed for a cheap, run-down motel he remembered seeing on their way into town.

He desperately needed to get some sleep, to clear his head at least a little, if that were even possible. But tomorrow morning, come hell or high water, he was going to figure out what was going on… or die trying.

There was nothing to do in this cave. Kenny had walked the perimeter of the area over and over, and Emmy was right: there was no escape. They were stuck here forever.

"Don't be so sure," Grimes said, when Kenny repeated his thoughts out loud. "I've been thinking. We are trapped in here, that's for certain, but sometimes the walls seem to grow thinner, and I've been able to make… well, connections. Most recently, with my great grandson. I can feel him sometimes. I can't communicate with him, per se, but I can feel his existence. There's something out there that carries my thoughts to him, I'm almost sure of it, and his to me. But that's as far as it goes. You, however, are new down here. You probably have stronger connections. Do you have a brother or a sister, perhaps?"

"I have two sisters. One lives in Kentucky, where we were going to visit, and one lives in Ohio," Kenny said.

"How about that man you mentioned, the one you were courting?"

"My boyfriend, Marvin," Kenny said, giving a half-smile. "We were very close, and I loved him with all of my heart. I know he's probably going through hell right now."

"If I show you how, maybe… just maybe, you could communicate with him. He needs to destroy the chest. If the chest is gone, I think we might be freed. To go where, I'm not certain, but anywhere must be better than here."

Kenny had to admit Grimes had a point. He couldn't imagine spending even a week in this cave, let alone eternity. However, he refused to put Marvin's life in danger.

"If I could tell him anything, it would be to get as far away from Lychhurst Hospital as fast as he can. After all, he's gay, too. I might be dead, but I want him to have a long, happy life. Even if it has to be without me."

"There's certainly merit in that," agreed Grimes, smiling.

"Okay, tell me what I need to do to connect."

"Just close your eyes and think about him. Imagine you're right there, next to him, and reach out…"

Marvin awoke, and for a moment thought everything had been a bad dream. He rolled over to kiss Kenny, but of course he wasn't there. He was lying in a shitty twin-sized bed in an even shittier motel, and Kenny was still dead.

A thought flitted through his head, like a gossamer thread. Something he'd dreamed last night about driving back to Virginia and something else about Kenny's chest, oddly enough. Or maybe it was a treasure chest of some sort. The thread was slippery and elusive, however, and he couldn't manage to grab hold of it. It seemed important somehow, but try as he might, he couldn't catch hold of that thread.

He heard a strange sound. It was a grackle, perched just outside his hotel room window. The bird almost seemed to make eye contact with him, let out a loud caw, and fluttered off into the morning.

Shaking his head, Marvin looked at the clock on the nightstand: it was just past seven in the morning. He needed answers, but he wasn't going to get them lying in a crappy motel bed trying to remember his dreams. The only way he might get them, in fact, was from Dr. Albright in the emergency room of Lychhurst Hospital.

Marvin rolled out of bed, quickly dressed, and walked out of the dingy hotel room, slamming the door behind him.

Halfway to the hospital, his heart skipped a beat when he saw Kenny. What the hell? Kenny was walking out of a gas station, car keys in one hand and a can of Coca-Cola in the other, heading toward a brand new-looking black Cadillac. Marvin slammed on the brakes, nearly causing a station wagon behind him to ram into the back of the Mustang.

"Asshole!" yelled the man driving the station wagon as it pulled around his car, his window down and looking pissed.

Marvin didn't care. He ignored the man and pulled into the gas station, blocking the Cadillac from exiting. Kenny glanced his way as Marvin got out of the car, but inexplicably, didn't seem to recognize him.

"Kenny?" he asked, feeling like the concrete driveway beneath his feet would fall away at any second.

"Who the hell are you?" Kenny sneered. "You need to get out of my way, now."

Kenny was wearing different clothes than he had on the night before: a gray pair of slacks and a black blazer, along with a fancy pair of shoes that likely cost more than Marvin's entire wardrobe. Clothing that Kenny would probably never wear, but it was definitely Kenny. It had to be him. But how?

"Didn't you hear me?" asked Kenny. "Get out of my way before I call the police."

"You're... dead. I saw your body. You weren't breathing. How are you alive?"

Kenny's face turned white. "Now settle down, mister. I don't want any trouble, but I think you have the wrong person."

Marvin stared at Kenny's face, at the little scar just above his left eye. He'd fallen down a flight of stairs as a very young child. Miraculously, he hadn't been hurt, other than suffering a gash over his left eye. Kenny had told him the story behind the scar when they'd first met.

This was definitely Kenny.

"You don't remember me?"

How could Kenny not know who he was? How could he be alive and healthy, standing less than a foot away from him?

Marvin reached out for the face of the man he loved, but Kenny jerked his head back, his eyes darting back and forth as if looking for a means of escape.

"I think I better get going," Kenny said, starting to walk around the side of the car, toward the driver's side.

"You *are* Kenny, aren't you?" said Marvin, curling a hand around Kenny's wrist. "But somehow, you're not. What did that asshole doctor do to you?"

"I can prove to you I'm not this Kenny person," Kenny said, pulling his arm away. "Just hold on, I'm going to get my driver's license."

It happened in one smooth motion. Kenny opened the car door, dropped his car keys and the can of Coca-Cola onto the passenger seat, reached into the glove compartment, and pulled out a small handgun.

"Now get away from me," Kenny growled, pointing the weapon at Marvin, "because if you don't, I will kill you. I've waited too long and paid way too much for this to let you or anyone else take it away from me."

Marvin raised his hands in the air, slowly walking backward. This wasn't Kenny. This couldn't be Kenny. Kenny hated guns. He'd always swore he'd never own one. This Kenny had a gun, but the Kenny he knew would never even touch such a weapon.

And yet, he was certain beyond a shadow of a doubt that this was Kenny.

He still didn't understand what was going on, but Kenny—no, scratch that, whoever had somehow stolen Kenny's body—clearly had no issue threatening him with a gun in front of a gas station. The whole thing made him feel like he was going insane.

"Hey, I'm going to call the police if you two don't get out of… oh, shit, you have a gun!" said a voice a few feet away from them.

Kenny turned to look at the startled employee, and that's when Marvin punched his lover hard in the face, sending him stumbling into the side of the Cadillac. The gun went flying, skittering halfway between the Cadillac and Marvin's Mustang, as Kenny slid down the side of the car, out like a light.

"Jesus Christ," said the gas station employee, his hands shaking. "Are you okay?"

"I'm fine," said Marvin, thinking quickly. "I'm Marvin… um, Stanley. Marvin Stanley, FBI. I've been tracking this criminal down and you just saved my life, Mister…?"

"Johnny Milligan," he said, eyes wide. "Are you really with the FBI?"

He knew it was a bullshit story, but he had to prevent the man from calling the cops, at least until he could figure out what was going on. He pulled his wallet from his pocket, quickly flashed his old college ID at Milligan, and hoped he'd be too nervous to ask for a second look.

"Yes, I'm really with the FBI. The local police already know I'm here. I need to take this man into custody and then I'll call them. This is a crime scene now. They'll probably close down your store for at least a week or two, and I know your boss wouldn't like that, so maybe I'll just say I apprehended him somewhere else."

"Yeah, okay, the boss would be really upset if we had to close down," Milligan said, slowly backing away. "I didn't see nothing."

"Good man." He couldn't believe that bullshit story had worked. "I can't drive two cars, so I'm going to have to leave his car here. I'll send someone to get it soon. In the meantime, you're welcome to move it around back so it's out of the way of anyone trying to get gas. Or, hell, you can keep it for all I care."

"Keep it?" Milligan said, his eyes going wide. "Is that legal? I don't want to get in trouble."

"I'm with the FBI," Marvin said, "so of course it's legal. Now help me get this asshole into my Mustang so I can take him into custody."

Marvin parked his car behind a copse of huge oak trees just a mile or so from the hospital. After the gas station attendant helped him haul Kenny into the backseat, he'd bound Kenny's hands behind his back with some old rope he'd found in the trunk.

Kenny was awake now, struggling against his bonds as Marvin pressed the barrel of the gun into his chin.

"Talk," Marvin demanded. "At this point, I have nothing left to lose if I kill you."

That wasn't true, of course. He could never kill Kenny, no matter who or what was inhabiting his body. But whatever this thing was that had stolen

Kenny's life had no way of knowing that… at least, that's what Marvin hoped.

"I already told you I have no idea what you're talking about or who this 'Kenny' person is."

Marvin smacked him in the side of the head with the butt of the pistol.

"Ouch! What the hell, man? You'd better let me go, or there will be consequences."

"Like what? Will Dr. Albright steal my body as well?"

He could see by the look in Kenny's eyes that he'd hit upon something.

"Look, how about this? I will pay you $1,000,000, and you can find a new boyfriend. No questions, no repercussions. Okay?"

Marvin pulled back the hammer of the gun. "I don't want your money, so here's a different proposal. How about you tell me what the fuck is going on, or I'll kill you right now."

"All right. All right! Just don't shoot me, okay?"

"Start talking," demanded Marvin, pushing the barrel of the gun into the side of Kenny's face.

"My name is Sebastian Cole. I died from cancer late last year, at the age of 79, and Dr. Albright saved my life."

Marvin's mind was reeling. "If you died, how did he save your life? Explain. Now."

"I'm trying to explain, okay? They came to me when I was in the Mayo Clinic, dying from lung cancer, but I already knew all about them. They said if I paid them $50,000,000, they'd bring me back to life, in a new, healthy body. I had to put the money in a trust that would be released to them after they brought me back to life, when I told the bank a secret code that only I knew. I figured, what did I have to lose?"

"Did you know you'd be stealing a body from someone else?"

Kenny—no, Sebastian Cole—looked away, and that told Marvin all he needed to know about this man currently residing in Kenny's body. He had known someone would have to lose their life so he could regain his, and he didn't care.

"Where were you… your soul, whatever… while you waited? You said you died last year."

"They kept me in a little glass vial," Cole said. "It was awful."

"And they put you into this body today?"

"Last night, actually. I spent the night at the hospital, and tonight I'm supposed to fly back home, to California."

"You know that's not going to happen, don't you?"

"Listen… $10,000,000. Let me go and I'll pay you $10,000,000, and you'll never have to see me again."

Marvin stared at the man. "Jesus Christ, man, how much money do you have?"

"I was… I am a very rich man. My company, the company my grandfather started, Cole Enterprises, is in the Fortune 500. I grew up rich, and I died rich, and I was reborn rich. Look, I'll pay you $60,000,000. Ten million more than I paid to Albright and his crew. Just imagine all you could do with that much money."

"Let me think for a minute, okay?" Marvin had no intention of taking Cole's offer, but Cole didn't need to know that.

"I can go to the bank and wire you the money right now. Farmington Bank and Trust. It's all set up for this body, this identity. I entered the codes first thing this morning."

"Okay, we have a deal. But first… I want you to call Dr. Albright, and then go with me to the hospital."

"But… why?" Cole asked.

"I want you to pay that $60,000,000 you offered me to him," Marvin lied. "If I can't have my boyfriend, at least I can have immortality. I want to make the same deal with him that you did."

It was almost three by the time they arrived at Lychhurst Hospital. Marvin shoved his hand holding the weapon into his jacket and followed Cole, who he'd finally untied in the parking lot, into the emergency room entrance.

It didn't seem very busy today. Good. For what he needed to do, he wanted as few witnesses as possible.

"Can I help you?" asked the old, gray-haired woman at the desk.

"I'm here to see Dr. Albright. He knows I'm coming," said Cole, through Kenny's mouth. "Sebastian Cole…I mean, Kenneth Green."

"He said you'd be coming," said the woman, smiling, "and that you'd be bringing a friend. Xavier Jackson, right?"

The story Marvin had concocted was that Cole had another rich friend, Xavier, who had just learned he was dying from a rare form of non-Hodgkin's Lymphoma and was interested in obtaining Albright's services. The doctor hadn't been very happy about it—Cole had been sworn to secrecy, after all—but had finally relented when the billionaire revealed that his friend would be willing to pay even more than he had paid to switch bodies as soon as possible.

"I'm Mr. Jackson, yes," said Marvin, staring down at the old woman, "and we haven't got all day, so let's get on with this."

"Just go through those doors there," she said, gesturing to the doors that led into the emergency room.

They stepped into the emergency room. Albright and the dark-haired nurse from last night were waiting for them.

"You!" said Albright, looking at him, shifting his gaze to Cole. "What is the meaning of this?"

"I'm sorry," said Cole, from inside Kenny's body. "He made me do it."

Marvin pushed Cole into the doctor, and then pulled the gun out of his jacket. "You stole Kenny from me, and I want him back."

Albright laughed. "I'm afraid it doesn't work that way. Your lifestyle… is an abomination. He gave up any right to his life when he decided to love you."

"You lied to me," screamed Cole. "I won't give up this body. I refuse."

"Then you'll die, along with them. It's that simple."

"I'll die anyway!"

"Settle down, Mr. Bixby," said the nurse, stepping between them. "You don't want to do this."

"We love who we love," Marvin said, ignoring the nurse, staring at Albright. "How is that any of your business?"

"It's God's business!" yelled Albright. "When a man lays with another man, you essentially spit in God's face."

"So you're doing God's work, are you? And the money you received from this jackass had nothing to do with it, right?"

"God rewards his followers," Albright said, smiling, "and we need funding to continue to do His work. It's as simple as that."

"What's simple," Marvin said, pointing the gun at the doctor's face, "is that if you don't give Kenny back to me, I'll kill you."

It was all Marvin could do not to pull the trigger, to put this monster who had more than likely taken countless lives from innocent people into the ground. But if he did that, he'd never get Kenny back. He took a deep breath and steadied himself, his eyes flitting between Albright, the nurse, and Sebastian Cole.

"Mr. Bixby!" yelled the nurse. "Would you really disgrace the Lord this way? Show some dignity."

"You're almost as bad as he is," said Marvin. "You and that other nurse. You help him murder people. Where's *your* dignity?"

He felt a sharp stab on the side of his neck, and immediately felt weak. He spun on his heels, coming face to face with Sarah, the redheaded nurse, the one who'd brought him Kenny's supposed remains last night.

"You… you…" he stuttered, his hands going limp, dropping the gun to the floor. "Where did you come from? What did you do to me?"

She held up a needle, and then everything went black.

Kenny thought he'd managed to connect to Marvin's consciousness a few minutes ago, had told him about the chest and the cave and pleaded for him to run far away from Lychhurst Hospital, but he wasn't sure he'd been able to get through.

He wasn't even sure it had been a few minutes ago. It could have been hours, days, months, or even years. As Emmy explained to him, time seemed to move almost randomly down here.

None of them deserved to be trapped in this cave, not even Grimes. They'd all had their lives taken from them because they were different, because they refused to remake themselves to fit society's norms. It wasn't fair, but then again, what was?

Kenny grabbed his head, a sudden, searing pain throbbing between where his ears used to be. It felt oddly like the connection he may or may not have established with Marvin, but a thousand times stronger.

"Are you alright?" asked Frank, running over to him from the other side of the cave.

"I… don't know," Kenny said, his palm pressed hard against his forehead.

"You screamed," said Emmy, standing beside Frank. "Screamed 'Please, no, not Marvin.'"

"He… Oh God, they're going to kill him. He didn't run, he came back to the hospital, to save me, but they drugged him, put him to sleep, and now they're going to kill him."

He didn't know how he knew this, but he knew without a shadow of a doubt that it was true. Even now, Dr. Albright had Marvin in the emergency room, preparing to end his existence.

He'd get to see the love of his life soon, but as much as he longed to hold Marvin in his arms once again, he didn't want it like this. He never wanted it like this.

"Can you feel him now?" asked Grimes, looking over Emmy's shoulder.

Kenny closed his eyes and pictured Marvin, lying atop the same exam table they'd put him on before they killed him. Albright was there, along with the nurses, and someone else as well.

It was Kenny, or at least his body, inhabited by God-only-knew who.

He told the other spirits what he saw, and Frank reached out to take his hand. Emmy took his other hand, Jackie took Emmy's free hand, Grimes took Jackie's, and Casper took Frank's. Within seconds, they were all connected, every spirit in the cave, pouring whatever strength they had into Kenny.

"We can do this," said Frank. "You're our conduit, Kenny. Everything we are, everything we have, is yours. Now let's wake up Marvin."

Marvin's thoughts were reeling, and nothing made sense anymore. Everything was dark, and it felt like his life was draining away from him, and then…

He felt Kenny's hand in his, somehow. Not the fake Kenny, but *his* Kenny, the man he'd fallen in love with when they'd first met at a party three years ago. The man who had the most beautiful green eyes and wavy black hair, the man he desperately wanted to spend the rest of his life with.

Wake up, whispered Kenny's voice in his ear, so that's exactly what he did.

"…the chest, doctor. I'm ready when you are," said a woman's voice.

"I still don't see why I need to be a part of this," said Cole's voice.

"Because you need to see the result of your carelessness," Albright said. "If Sarah hadn't come in when she did, we might all be dead. As it is, we're wasting this man's body when we could have given it to someone in need."

"Don't you mean sold it?" asked Cole, a sneer in his voice.

"We could always take your body back, Mr. Cole. Don't forget that."

Marvin blinked, the world swimming before him. Albright stood over him, holding a defibrillator. The dark-haired nurse held a little black chest, while the other nurse, the one who had drugged him, stood beside Albright and Cole.

"Oh, shit," said the nurse, their eyes meeting. "He's awake."

"What?" Sarah said. "That's impossible."

Marvin sat up, staring straight into the nurse's startled face. The chest. That little black chest was the key to everything. He wasn't sure how he knew this, but he knew it to be true.

He lashed out with his leg, kicking the chest from her hands. They all watched as the container flew into the air, Sarah and Albright running into each other trying to catch it.

It landed in Cole's hands, but upside down. He watched as Cole's triumphant smile turned to horror as the lid flopped open, and a cacophony of angry screams emerged from the depths of the ancient artifact.

Shadows, hundreds of them, poured from the chest, circling around the room, darting this way and that. One ran through Sarah's body, and then another through the other nurse, whose name he somehow now knew was Rachel, each pushing out another shadow on the other side.

"Someone close that damn chest!" yelled Albright. "If it's opened without the proper protocol, they can—"

Albright's eyes grew wide as a shadow dived into his chest, and another shadow exited from his back. Albright smiled, no longer Albright anymore.

"This feels so good," one of the nurses said, "to be real again."

The other nurse smiled, and Kenny knew they weren't who they'd been just a moment before.

Cole dropped the chest and bolted for the door, but Marvin was on his feet, running for all he was worth, grabbing his shoulder just before he reached the exit.

"Let me go!" demanded Cole. "I'll give you all my money, just let me go!"

"Fuck your money," Martin said, as he turned Cole around and pushed him into the middle of the room, just as another shadow dived straight into his chest.

Martin watched Kenny's body thrash around the room, as if in combat with itself, until finally another shadow exited from his back.

Whoever had taken control of the doctor's body walked over to the chest and smashed his heel down hard on the little wooden monstrosity, shattering it into pieces.

Almost all the shadows filling the room vanished in an instant. A few, however, managed to stay around for another moment, then slowly faded until Marvin could no longer see them. Had they managed to stay in this realm?

The man who used to be Dr. Albright smiled at Martin and mouthed *thank you* before turning to Kenny and saying, "Go be with the man you love, son."

"Kenny?" Marvin asked, staring at him, hoping and praying with all his heart that his lover had come back to him, and he nodded. It was Kenny, back in his own body again.

Trembling, Martin reached out his hand, and Kenny took it, pulling him into his arms, and in that moment they both knew they'd never again let each other go.

Somewhere in the distance a grackle cawed, its work done, at least for now…

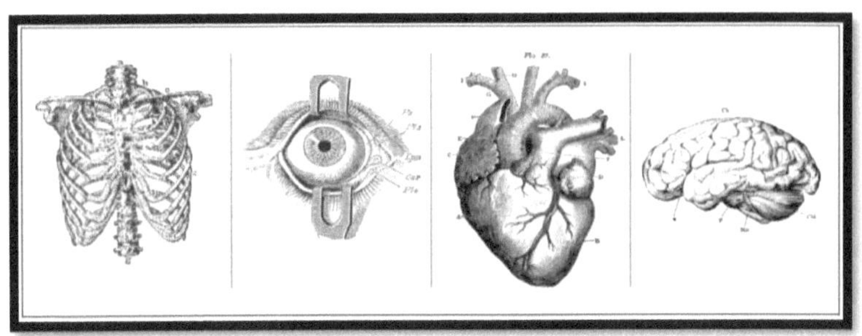

Triage Level: Black

Ah! You're back. What's that? A cave? Of course not! There are no caves at Lychhurst.

I think perhaps you've just been standing for too long. Have a seat.

You're leaning a bit. Are you feeling alright?

Yes, I am definitely worried about you now. Perhaps after we finish the tour, we should check you in. Get you one of those lovely little bracelets. Whatever is wrong with you, Lychhurst will fix it. I guarantee it.

For now, I'm afraid to say that we're about to see the…less desirable parts of the hospital. But you're strong enough, aren't you? Yes, still annoyingly strong.

What? Why did you say *ow*? What's wrong?

No, of course nothing just pricked your neck.

Of course I'm sure. I'm standing right here behind you, aren't I?

I think I'd have seen it if someone walked up and did anything…unsavory…toward you, wouldn't I?

Now, I must swear you to secrecy before we go any further. You're about to see parts of Lychhurst that few people see…and live to tell about.

But I can trust you, I know it.

You're not going to be telling anyone anything, not anytime soon, not ever.

Lots of secret little goodies down here, in the basements.

I know it's not much to look at these days, but in its heyday Lychhurst was on the leading edge of technical advancements and medical research. So what if the things that went on in the Secret Testing Lab weren't always on the up-and-up? We must all make sacrifices for the greater good.

Even you.

What? Hmm? Oh, nothing.

The Isolation Ward is a beautiful place, such crisp white walls and absolute, utter, mind-shattering silence. Don't mind the marks on the wall. Or the sounds. I know…someone slamming their head into the wall over and over *would* sound just like that, but it's just the pipes.

Yes, really. I promise.

Our Records Room is a bit unkempt at the moment—seems like there's always someone rifling around in there, finding things they're not meant to find, things best left hidden.

Locked away.

Buried.

I trust you won't unearth anything too disturbing there, right?

Of course, no hospital tour would be complete without a visit to the Morgue. You're not bothered by dead bodies, are you?

What about undead ones?

Sorry. Just a little joke.

Well, *I* thought it was funny.

Careful in the Tunnels. They were once used to transport corpses and undesirables to the dark, secret cages…er…places where they belonged. They're not used much these days, though there's been a lot of noise down there lately. Banging. Clanking. Slurping.

Just…try to stay in the light.

Once you're finished there, meet me at the Nurses Station. That's my favorite haunt.

Hmm? Spot. My favorite spot.

Now, off with you. Careful, you're still stumbling a bit.

Isolation Ward
2000

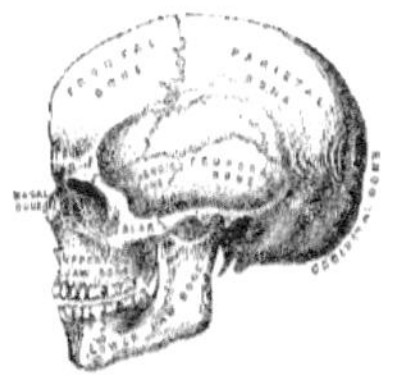

A Bleached White Forever
Gage Greenwood

When Jameson was twelve, he overheard a pseudo-philosophical conversation between his dad and older brother Kinsey in the garage. Jameson sat in the driveway, back leaning against the front of the family's Honda Civic, watching them prep for yard work.

His dad poured gasoline into the push mower and said, "Let's get the yard done by five o'clock so we can clean up before dinner. That means take the stones out of your boots and move it."

Kinsey sat on a wooden table beside a vice grip, spinning the handle, when he absently said, "Time is a manmade invention, Dad."

Pops wasn't the type of guy to take a comment like that without forcing his son to think deeper about his wise remarks.

"We gave numbers to hours, seconds, and minutes, but we didn't invent time, Kins. The days turn whether we name them or not. Beginnings, middles, and ends. They happen. Don't need Webster to define that for me."

Kinsey smirked and gave the vice grip's handle one last big whirl.

"There's no beginning."

Wiping a slick stream of sweat from his forehead, their father said, "Course there is. The universe had to start somewhere."

Kinsey jumped off the table and grabbed a set of hedge shears. "And what existed before that? Before the universes formed, what was there?"

Pops shrugged and lugged the mower out into the driveway. He gave a gentle kick to Jameson's foot and nodded his head toward the yard. "Come on, kiddo."

Then he turned his head back to Kinsey. "Nothing existed before the universe. Nothing."

Kinsey snipped imaginary weeds with the trimmers. "A-ha. Exactly. But when did the nothingness begin? Was it just one big black hole? And if so, where and how did that start? There can never be a beginning to time. There's always something before the next thing."

Twenty years later, Jameson blurred his eyes and stared at the brightest white he'd ever seen on a wall. That conversation haunted him now as it did then. It wasn't the vastness of the universe, or the ridiculously minute role humanity played in it, although those facts didn't help.

More than anything, Jameson hated our limitations, that we could never figure out an answer to Kinsey's questions. What happened before? How could there be a beginning to time?

Jesus. It terrified him.

Grackles chirped outside Lychhurst Hospital, and while the Isolation Room in which Jameson sat had no windows, he could hear those obnoxious birds clearly. It probably helped that all the doors had been stripped from the building, and part of the room's ceiling and upper wall had crumbled down long ago, leaving one hunk of gaping hole in the hospital's skeleton.

Through the cavity, he could see the bones of what was once a cafeteria from the missing roof portion, and a swath of trees through the portion of missing wall.

Even in the somewhat claustrophobic Isolation Room, Jameson could taste the sweet summer dew and hear the fluttering wings of the many bird species hovering around the long-abandoned building.

Despite the cheesy, sci-fi laser-beam sounding chirps from the grackles, Jameson kept his focus on the white walls, trying hard to block out the distractions.

How could the walls stay so bleached white for all these years?

Every other room and hall of the hospital had molded yellow or rotted out entirely or greened with lichen. But the isolation room stayed crisp white, and still carried the disinfectant hospital smell.

He tucked his feet under his legs in a *sukhasana* yoga pose. It hurt, but he forced it anyway, remembering how easily Rosalina did it at their weekly class, and how she picked on him during the drives home for never getting that basic sitting pose down, despite his otherwise athletic disposition.

The corners of the room doubled and moved away from each other as he intentionally focused his vision beyond the wall, bringing back all of the skills he'd developed from finding the hidden images within those Magic Eye pictures in the Sunday comic section years ago.

No three-dimensional image came forward this time. He sighed.

The walls weren't even pocked or dented. They were as smooth as glass.

He imagined the men and women who woke up in this room back when it was a psych hospital, knowing they'd be trapped in there day in and day out until their time ticked its last tick. He pictured the folks trapped in here when it was a normal hospital, coughing up blood and battling incurable viruses, knowing the four uncanny white abysses surrounding them would be the last they'd ever see.

His Nokia phone buzzed, and he took it out of his pocket, glancing at the name.

Rosalina.

Why did he even have to check? Who else called him?

"Hello," he said.

"Where the hell are you? A concert?"

"Huh?"

"Why is it so loud?" she asked.

"I'm alone. I don't know what you're talking about."

After a few seconds of silence, she said loudly, as if talking in a speeding convertible, "I can't take it. Sorry. It's like a thousand people talking at once. Maybe the phone is picking something else up. I'll call you back in a few."

He hung up and put the phone down on the floor in front of him but kept the screen upright so he could see when she called back. He never stopped missing her voice.

Blurring his eyes again, the wall remained just a wall. He wished he could find some imperfection within its surface, something to focus away from. The sleek, smooth nature of the walls, and the stark whiteness, almost made them appear metallic, alien. Like he sat in a UFO.

The Nokia vibrated against the cold, white-tiled floor. Although eager to pick it up, he watched it dance for a second first. It gave life to the otherwise empty hospital.

"Hello," he said again.

"What the fuck? You honestly don't hear that?"

He frowned. "I don't hear anything but some birds."

"Where are you?"

"Lychhurst."

Silence. Then a nervous chuckle. "What?"

"Yeah. Long story." He hoped she'd pry. He *wanted* her to ask questions.

"Okay, listen, that background noise is driving me insane. I'll call you later, but please pick up. The real estate lady wants you to take your stuff out before she starts showing the house. She can't have boxes lying all over the place."

"Okay," he said and hung up, wishing he could run straight into the white wall and disappear. Become one with it. He almost thought he could.

Some leaves rustled out in the hallway, and Jameson shifted to face the door. No wind coursed through the old bones of the hospital, so he worried someone else wandered the halls. A vagrant. Punk kids. After holding his breath and keeping silent for a moment, he risked getting up and peeking out the door.

No one was there, but a few leaves swirled around each other and cycled by the Isolation Room. Just a small draft.

"This place'll get to you like that."

Jameson's heart shot up to his skull and he spun around. An older gentleman stood in the corner. He had a black walrus mustache, and big fuzzy eyebrows. His beige button-down shirt sat under the straps of his brown corduroy overalls.

Jameson put his arms in front of him, ready to protect himself if needed. "Where'd you come from?"

The man's head listed like a ship. "Oh, come on. Let's not play any games. You know the answer to that."

"What are you talking about?"

That funky mustache arched up as the man smirked. He put his hands on each side of his head and shook them while he said, "Booooooooooooooooooooooooo."

"What the fuck?"

That stopped the man in his tracks. He snapped his finger loudly. It echoed through the room. "None of that. You can be as scared as you want, but watch the language, pal. Respect the dead."

As terrified as Jameson was of this crazy intruder, he didn't run; in fact, he moved away from the door, placing his back against the wall and sliding toward the opposite corner of the creepy old man. "This isn't happening."

"It is."

Jameson tried to convince himself he dealt with a crazy person, but the man had simply appeared in the room when Jameson was at the only entrance. Sure, it was possible for the man to have jumped through the opening in the ceiling and wall, but unlikely.

The hole wasn't that wide, so this intruder would have had to struggle his way in, and Jameson would have heard it. And wouldn't the man have gotten himself disheveled and caked with whatever detritus clung to the opening?

But that wasn't the biggest evidence to suggest this man was no man at all. He looked a lot like Jameson's uncle. Not exactly, but close. Jameson had seen photos of

Uncle Duke at two different points in the man's life: before he went to Lychhurst, and two weeks before he died within its walls. These walls.

In the former, his uncle had the same mustache and bushy eyebrows, but less wrinkles, and his dark wavy hair showed no signs of the speckled snowstorm this intruder had. He also weighed a bit more, a bit plump around the waist area.

In the latter, Duke's mustache had turned into a full-grown beard, wild and matted. His hair had turned all grey, almost white. His eyes were sunken, body rail-thin with ribs sticking out of his tight t-shirt.

The fellow across the room fit somewhere in between, but his eyes lacked the stark blue color Jameson noticed in all of Duke's photos.

"Who are you?" Jameson asked.

The man chuckled. "Now, that's what I'd like to know. Don't get me wrong, I'm dead, but I ain't senile. I *know* who I am, but what I don't know is who am I to you?"

Jameson clenched his fists, but he didn't know why. "You're nothing to me. You interrupted me. Not the other way around."

Those bushy eyebrows rose high. "You wanna think that through there, son? I've been here a lot longer than you. A lot longer."

The man pushed himself out of the corner, stepping slowly forward. "There's a lot of spirits around here who come out of the woodwork just to fuck with people." He paused and sighed. "See, now you got me doing it, too. I'm sorry for the vulgarity."

Jameson bit his lip. "I just want to go home."

The old man ignored him. "Anyway, the spirits around here are restless. They do things to occupy themselves. Sometimes good things. Sometimes downright horrific. Me? I keep to myself. In fact, I ain't seen a living soul in many moons. Frankly, I don't enjoy revisiting this room. Do you catch my drift, there, son?"

Eyeing the door, and regretting each step he'd taken away from it, Jameson said, "Not really."

"My point is, I don't ever choose to come out. I come when it's demanded of me. And something demanded I reveal myself to you. And that just don't happen unless there's a good reason. You need me. I don't know why, but I know it's true."

Of course, Jameson knew the answer. This *was* his uncle, matching eye color or not. But that meant one of two things. Jameson had officially cracked, or he talked to an actual ghost. He was in no position to mentally deal with either of those scenarios.

He booked it, running straight for the door. When he reached the threshold, his face smashed into nothing. He fell back, landing on his ass. His nose hurt the most, but his left cheekbone took some damage too.

His eyes watered as he covered his face, yelling, "OW! OW!"

"I just want to make it clear I had nothing to do with that. Something don't want you leaving this room." The old man laughed hard. "Some things never change, I suppose. My face met that door a million times, I'd guess. A place this evil can't be shut down. Sure, you can lock the doors, and fire the staff, but ruthlessness echoes like my laugh just did."

Jameson sat up, wiping the tears from his face. "What just happened?"

"Your face met a barrier. Might not of been something diabolical. See, this place has spirits, some good, some awful, but the building itself has its own temperament. If it don't want you to leave yet, it's cause you got something to accomplish first. Course, maybe it ain't the building." He hammed it up with a shiver. "But let's just hope that isn't the case."

Jameson got to his feet. Was the room smaller? It felt smaller. He couldn't breathe.

Slower this time, he went to the door and put his hand out toward the hall. It stopped at the threshold.

"What the fuck?"

Then he remembered the ceiling. "Listen, I know you're a part of my mental breakdown, but I have no choice but to lean into it. Hoist me up to that hole."

For the first time, the old man lost his smile. "Aw, come on. An invisible wall just smacked you in the face, and you think that hole is gonna magically follow logical rules? I'm a ghost, but it'll still hurt my back trying to lift you, and for what?"

They stared at each other for a few seconds before the man sighed. "Dammit. This is getting tedious already. Can't you just roll with it?"

He stood under the hole, bent low, and cupped his hands. "Let's get this over with, so we can figure out what you really need to get out of here, and I can catch some Zs."

Jameson shrunk. "It's not going to work, is it?"

The old man shook his head.

"Sorry, I have to try anyway." Jameson stepped on the man's hands and jumped up, slapping toward the hole, and finding the same resistance he found at the door. When he dropped back down, he grunted in frustration.

The old man put his hand on Jameson's shoulder. Unlike ghosts in movies, his hand did not pass through, but touched Jameson, sending a wave of tingles down his arm. Probably a combination of supernatural effects and the unfamiliarity of a kind touch.

"If it makes you feel any better, I can't really catch those Zs. We don't sleep. Ghosts. But we still feel tired. All the time. Imagine that? Yearning for sleep but never getting it. Death is a continuous slap in the face with cold water. At least, for those of us in here it is. Can't really blame the sour ones, can ya?"

Jameson stretched his hand across his forehead and pressed his thumb and middle finger into his temples. "Well, what the hell am I supposed to do? How do I get out of here?" He clenched his jaw. "It feels hot."

"Just take it easy. Let's talk a bit and see what we come up with. Remember, you ain't the only one stuck here. Something brought me into this room too. Usually, I kind of float around in the dead space. But I'm here because of you, and I won't be able to leave until I figure out the purpose of that."

Jameson inhaled deeply. "Okay, you mentioned you're here for me for a reason. Is your name Duke?"

One bushy eyebrow went up. "Yes?"

"You're my uncle. Well, great-uncle. I came here to talk to you."

Duke laughed. "All this time? You came here to talk to me and then did everything to get out of it as soon as you had the chance?"

"I meant it metaphorically. I just wanted to get stuff off my chest to an empty room, and I thought the place where you died might be a good spot for it."

"Why?"

"Because I'm alone."

He yelled the words. They shot out of him like fire from a dragon.

Softening his tone, he followed it up with, "And I thought I'd come to the place my long-lost relative had to live alone for years in a much more intense way than I do."

Duke scrunched his face and pointed toward Jameson's hand. "I don't want to be insensitive. Did your wife pass away?"

"What?" Jameson looked where the man pointed, and he realized it was at his wedding ring. "Oh. No. We're getting divorced."

With an eyeroll, Duke said, "So this is just about lost love? You'll be fine, kid. There's a lot of women out there."

"It's not about that. That's just the tip of the iceberg."

Duke moved toward the wall Jameson had stared at earlier. He rubbed his hands on it as if searching for a secret button. "You have family, right? My family. Tell me about them. Is your mom Cecilia's daughter? What was her name again?"

Jameson shook his head. "My dad is Cecilia's son. Charles. And we don't talk anymore. I don't talk to him, my brother, my mom. None of them."

Duke continued his search for whatever he looked for. "What caused that?"

"Politics."

The old man turned away from the wall and back to Jameson. "Politics? Jeez. Must of been some fundamental differences in morality for it go south so badly."

Jameson moved toward the wall, squinting. He thought he saw something he hadn't noticed before. "It wasn't even that. Although that's not untrue. I could have ignored the differences. Politics isn't like it was back when you were around. There are people who care about the issues and there are people who care about the politics.

"The issues people are constantly fighting and arguing and working toward something. Even when I don't agree with them, I can accept it, because they're just trying to make the world better the way they see it.

"But the politics people. My God. They never shut the fuck up, drape themselves in symbolism and logos. And they don't give a shit about anything. They're just desperate for an identity. And it never stops.

"They make enemies out of anyone who doesn't agree with them one hundred percent of the time, looking for patterns to make it all some conspiracy. Ironically, because they're so obsessed with being better than the other guy, they end up letting that other guy determine who they are.

"If one side says they hate farts, the other side will start drinking farts out of bottles."

Duke stared at Jameson intently. "Doesn't sound much different than in my day, kiddo. Hate to break it to you. That shit never changes." Then, "What are you seeing?"

Jameson ran his hand down the wall. "I don't know. It's not there anymore. I thought I saw a triangle."

Duke smiled. "I think I understand how I'm supposed to help you now."

He nudged his way in front of Jameson and ran his finger down the wall. "Tell me when to stop at about the place you saw the triangle."

Jameson stopped him about halfway down. Duke stepped back. "Yup. That's about where it shows up. Maybe you'll be the one."

"What one?"

"Don't worry about that yet. In fact, don't think about the wall at all. Tell me exactly what happened with your family. I get it. Politics. But what was the last straw?"

Jameson shifted away from the man. "No, I want to know more about the wall thing. You have no idea how much I could use a genuine conversation right now in my life, but I also need to get the fu—" He cleared his throat. "Get the heck out of this room, so help me make sense of that first."

Duke's eyes sharpened, and he stepped in front of Jameson, leaning in too close. With a whisper, he said, "Listen, and listen carefully. The only way this hospital is going to let you leave is if you figure out the wall. I spent years on that son of a gun, and we're going to have to get you through in minutes. I have no idea how yet, but we have to."

Something jingled far away, rattling against the hospital walls in a far-off room, echoing through all of it like an alarm bell. They both turned toward the source. Jameson glanced at Duke. The man's eyes were bulging out of his head.

"What was that?" Jameson whispered.

Duke turned back to him and gripped a fist around Jameson's shirt. "I don't know, and I promise you we don't want to find out. We're running out of time, so hear me well. Figuring out the wall requires concentration, but here's the problem. If you focus on it, they'll notice."

"Who?"

Duke pushed him backward.

"All of them. Doesn't matter who. If they figure out you can work the wall, they'll all want a piece. And they'll do anything to reach you. You got that? So, look at the fucking wall, and yes, I'm cursing now too, and don't look away, but *think* about anything else. That'll help you anyway. You gotta see the patterns but place your mind anywhere else."

Jameson pushed the man off him. "I don't get it. You're not making sense."

"Well, you better figure—" Duke caught himself getting loud.

He leaned in again and whispered, "You better figure it out. If they get in here, we're both dead. And dead for me means a different kind of dead than it does for you, but it won't be pleasant for either of us.

"So, look at the God-damned wall, and tell me about your family. Tell me all your damned sad stories. Get personal and emotional and cry. Do not think about the wall. Do not think about the wall. Do you need me to keep repeating it, or do you understand?"

Jameson shivered. "You can't tell me not to do something and expect it to happen." He pulled at his hair. "How do I not think about it?"

The jingling grew louder. Something moaned.

Duke slapped him hard. Jameson jolted back, clutching his red-hot cheek. "What the fuck?"

"Tell me about your family. Why did you stop talking to them? The last straw."

Jameson rubbed his eyes and looked at the floor. "Okay. Alright. Ah, Dinner at my parents' house."

Duke gripped Jameson's chin and lifted his head. "But look at the wall."

Jameson nodded. His fingers trembled. Everything was so insane. Invisible walls, ghosts, the whole lot, but he'd allowed himself to play in this blip of insanity, pretending it was real. He wanted it over now.

But the look of horror scarring Duke's face forced Jameson to plant his feet firmly in this new, ethereal reality.

And that terrified the fuck out of him.

He looked at the wall, seeing nothing but sleek white. "So, I'd had all the arguments with my father and brother. My mom agreed with them, went along with it all anyway, but she didn't say much like the other two did. She was more of a head nodder.

"Anyway, I finally told them they had to stop talking to me about it. And they didn't. It wasn't just conversations, either. They'd send me chain emails, and links. All the fucking time. It was always some bullshit."

"What's a chain email?"

Jameson clenched with anger.

"It's nonsense people pass around to each other with a bunch of simple thoughts in it, but it all sounds nice, so people take to it. It's basically how adults who are too dumb to understand politics feel like they can get it. I don't mean that to knock them, but the political chain emails are always obtuse and intentionally misleading.

"Even the ones that coincide with my thinking. It's like, 'Yeah, I like where you landed, but not how you got there.'"

The triangle reappeared on the wall, popping out just like those old Magic Eye pictures, but as soon as Jameson saw it his heart skipped a beat, and it vanished again.

"Fuck. It was there and then it was gone."

Duke put his hand on Jameson's arm. "It came because you weren't thinking about it. You were angry. That was nice. Keep getting angry and when it reappears, don't lose your concentration on what you're talking about."

Jameson stood up straight and thought about his family. Immediately the anger rushed back.

"I told them over and over to respect my decision to not discuss it in front of me, and they ignored me. Sometimes they'd chill for a little bit, but they'd always come back with some quip about this and that ruining the country, and how could I support it. Of course they did. They had no other identity. Nothing else to talk about. Their only hobbies and interests anymore became watching the fucking news twenty-four seven and getting more and more hateful."

The triangle reappeared. Jameson noticed it, but kept his thoughts on his father, allowing the anger to grow within him. He found it draining, to hold onto it, to use it as a weapon.

"And finally, one night at dinner, we were having a nice conversation about my wife, and how she won a prestigious award from her architecture firm, and my father said, 'She musta graduated back when schools still taught kids how to read and write, before they turned those places into clown shows,' or some other bullshit. I don't even remember his exact words now."

The triangle glowed. At the same time, someone coughed far away in the distance. Jameson hoped it was another person, someone who could snap him out of this madness, but he didn't want to risk shifting his focus.

Duke caught his distraction. "That's Linda. She's far away, but she's coming. Keep talking. It's working. You're doing great."

Jameson blurred his vision around the triangle, wondering if he could create another shape from it. A Magic Eye within a Magic Eye.

"And I'm not some 'two wings of the same bird' type. I have a political side, and I'm passionate about the issues, too, but I prefer to place those feelings where they're most productive.

"It's definitely not at the fucking dinner table. Yes, I disagreed with my family, but I could have forgiven them if they were truly passionate about the things they claimed to be passionate about."

The glowing triangle split apart, and the two pieces morphed into individual circles, each one spinning hypnotically.

Above him, a grackle chirped its obnoxious song. The sound was so close, Jameson had to imagine the bird sat at the hole in the wall.

"They weren't at the town hall meetings, or the school committee meetings, or the midterms or the special elections. They showed up every four years to make a rage-fueled push of a button and then spent the rest of their time ranting in Dunkin' Donuts or on forums online or to me. Bitching.

"Constantly bitching and accusing anyone who thought slightly different of being a pedophile or a Nazi or some other horrific claim."

The circles spun, but nothing else had changed on the wall. The grackle flew around the room now, cawing and chirping anxiously. Down the hall, the coughing grew louder, closer. And there were other noises, too. Footsteps. Jingling. Moaning.

Duke swatted at the bird, "Keep going. Don't let it distract you. Eyes peeled on the wall and tell me about something else now. Your marriage."

"Fuck. I don't even know what happened there. It was perfect one moment, and then I blinked, and it hadn't been good in years. We loved each other. Maybe still do. But we stopped being friends a long time ago, stopped talking or just spending time together for the sake of it.

"I think I took a lot of my anger and hurt from my family and pushed it on her, not toward her, I was never mean or argumentative with her, but I complained to her about everything. I made myself miserable.

"My job. The prices at the market in town. The traffic. Movies. Music. Whatever. I bitched and bitched all the time, never looking at the positive on anything. I was basically the same thing as my family, but instead of making it about politics, I made it about everything else.

"I was unhappy and I made her unhappy. Who wants to be around that? A constant sad sack is a poison on everyone around them. When you're constantly throwing punches at thin air, you don't see the harm, but someone around you is always taking the hit."

The grackle fluttered around Jameson's head. A wing batted against his neck. Duke shooed it away. Linda coughed louder. A hard, powerful, phlegmy thing.

The moaning came closer, too. And Jameson heard screaming now. Lots of it. All different voices.

Duke said, "Okay, I hate to put the pressure on, but they're getting close. Linda will be here any minute, so you need to focus hard and get this done. Keep your focus and tell me about your friends or your work. You must have people you talk to there."

The two circles pulsed, and the white of the walls cracked as light poured forth.

"I work third shift as a security guard. I lost contact with all of my friends years ago." None of this made him angry, just miserable, but it still appeared to work, because the cracks grew wider, and the center of the circles opened its mouth.

"God. The other night I was at work and a baby fox came into the parking lot. I snuck outside, carefully got my camera out of my glove box, and snapped a picture of it as it sat there licking its back paw. I went inside all happy. The happiest I'd been in a while, and then I stared at the camera and thought, 'What's the point?'

"I had no one to share the picture with. And I remembered all those mornings, sitting at the breakfast table with Rosalina, and all the conversations I could have had with her, and how I wished at that moment I could develop the film and show her the fox picture so I could speak with her about it one morning. She would have loved it. She was a huge animal lover."

His voice cracked. "And fuck, I miss her. I miss talking to someone. Even when I do chat with someone, like, in line at the bank or whatever, I can see the boredom in their eyes. No one wants to hear me. I just want someone to hear me."

The grackle chirped and flew out of the room. Through his peripheral, Jameson saw bodies entering the room. The moaning and coughing and jingling all came in at once. Flanking him.

Duke kept his voice even, but the fear in his eyes told a different tale. "I'm hearing you kid. I been hearing you this whole time. You got someone listening."

The fissures in the wall expanded, and the entire wall burst open into a glowing, throbbing other-world. Somewhere else. Within it, voices rang out. Chattering, laughing, happy voices. The clatter of lives busily lived.

Jameson smiled.

Duke said, "I tried to do what you just did for years. Years, kid. I died trying. You did it in less than an hour. Let's get the fuck out of here."

They ran to the gaping hole, but so did the figures on his side, which he still hadn't gotten a good look at. He risked a quick head turn as he dove toward the opening, unsure what the hell he was diving toward, but knowing he needed to get there, needed anything outside of what he knew.

Linda had blood dribbling down her chin, and she coughed even as she charged toward… him? The hole? He wasn't sure, but she was damn close. He could smell the rot on her.

The rest of the figures were less discernable. One was just a shadow, like the wall's opposite, just a thick dark splat. Another was the figure of a man, but his body smoldered and grey smoke tendrilled off him. There were others, but Jameson couldn't get a good glance.

His head went through the wall's opening and for a flash, he saw a cafeteria full of people, sitting, eating, talking, laughing, and they all turned to him, this intruder penetrating the folds of reality and collapsing into their space. But they didn't look distressed, only interested in the phenomenon.

People. Jesus. People. He had so much to share with them.

But before he could land, something ripped him back, tossing him out of the opening and back into the room. He slid across the white tiled floor, skinning his arm and stomach where his shirt rode up.

"No," he shouted and reached out as Linda and the smoking figure dove into the hole. He jumped up and ran back to it, grabbing at the shadow man to stop him, but the spirit was strong, and it pulled Jameson's fingers back. Something snapped and Jameson doubled over in pain, screaming.

As soon as he let out his pained yell, a chorus of screaming came from every direction in the hospital. He stood up, preparing to leap back in, but Duke grabbed his shirt. "Don't. It's theirs now." The old man pointed to the opening.

More screams. This time from within the portal.

"What's happening?" Jameson asked.

"They stole it." And as Duke said the words, the hole closed up, slammed shut with a thunderous clap.

Jameson ran to the wall, pounding on it. "No. Let me in. Damn it. Let me in."

The screaming disappeared, not just from the hole but from the hospital, and the din of bird songs came back just outside the hole. He felt a gentle draft.

Something squeaked behind him. Jameson turned to see a nurse at the doorway. She smiled in a taunting, gleeful way, as if she enjoyed Jameson's defeat. They stared at each other for a moment, before the nurse grabbed a gurney in front of her and walked away with it. Its squeaks were as taunting as the nurse's smile.

"Can I leave now?" He asked. But Duke didn't respond. He turned to find the room empty. Duke gone.

"Duke? Don't fucking do this to me. Where are you?"

The grackle taunted him from atop the edge of the opening in the corner. Jameson ran to the door and reached out only to be met with resistance. "No. Fuck. No."

He ran around the room punching and kicking walls. "Let me out. Help! Let me out."

The last slivers of daylight slipped away from the hole and the room turned dark.

It never changed to light again.

The darkness suffocated him, always there. He had no idea how long he resided in the isolation room. Days, weeks, months, or years.

Without any light, he couldn't know, had nothing to count away from or toward. He couldn't sleep or eat or drink. He had nothing to do but wait for something to change. For a new beginning.

One that could never come, because time is a manmade construct. There can be no beginning. "Oh, dear God," Jameson said as he slammed his head into the white wall, hoping to shatter it open.

"There can be no beginning."

There can be no beginning.

Slam.

Secret Testing Lab
1990

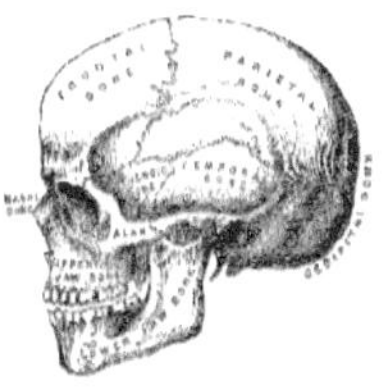

Subliminal Measures
Caleb Jones

The elevator dinged, signifying its absolute zero descent. There was no lower the trio could sink. Doctor, physician's assistant, and patient, well within the deepest depths of the hospital.

As the assistant wheeled the gurney forward with the patient, she felt a cool chill. It was like the old building had swallowed them up, and the three of them were lost in its guts. Destined to wander these bleak halls forever like some indigestible object.

If some of the stories she'd heard were true, that might just be the case for the patient. His name was Haze. He stared blankly at the faded paint on the wall as they inched closer to the operating room.

They passed the morgue, and the attending mortician stood at the door, picking at the dirt under his nails. He stood up straight and looked toward them, like an animal waiting to be fed. The business of death must've been slow that evening.

When he saw the doctor, the mortician's shoulders fell. No food tonight, at least not yet. He gave the P.A. a lascivious smirk that fell everywhere over her, just below the chin. Then he gave the doctor a knowing smile. A *see ya 'round* sort of smile. Last, his eyes drifted to the patient, and the mortician's grin shifted into a grimace.

Caleb Jones

They passed the mortician without a word. There were deeper, darker corners of this lower place to be reached.

The assistant hadn't spoken much since signing the patient out of the geriatric ward. She knew she'd been tapped for something unusual. Lychhurst had a long history of the unusual, dating back to the 1800s.

Some of it was a matter of shameful record. But in these more modern times, it became necessary to hide the hospital's dark underbelly. This was in full evidence as the dim lights reflected off of a sign at the far end of an otherwise unoccupied corridor.

Black setting with red text, it read *Do Not Enter*. The group *would* indeed be entering, and the assistant felt her heart pick up tempo.

"It's a small number;" the doctor said, "those who have been permitted to enter this room."

He placed his hand on hers, signaling for her to stop pushing the gurney. When his hand fell away, she looked toward his gray eyes, which were so hard to hold contact with. She forced herself to look straight into them, refused to look away. She even smiled and nodded.

"Yes, doctor. I know."

"Do you understand why?"

She nodded again. "Discretion, sir."

"That is correct," the doctor said, then indicated they should continue forward. As they walked, he pulled a key on a chain from beneath his shirt. "This is a room that, even in Lychhurst's long, storied history, is not even mentioned in whispers up above, by staff or visitor."

He chuckled. "If such things existed, I doubt the rumored ghosts in this building would have much to say about this room. And that is all because of discretion."

They stopped in front of the door while he put the key in the lock, turned it, then pulled the key free and tucked it back into his shirt in one fluid motion. He placed his hand on the handle and paused to look back at her.

"Do you understand what I am telling you?"

She locked eyes with him again and said, "Yes."

She left the real answer, what he wanted to hear, unsaid. *Keep your mouth shut.*

He pushed the door open, reached into the darkness within, and flipped a switch. The lights flickered in the room as the doctor opened the door wide enough for the gurney to pass through.

The assistant felt her breath catch in her throat as she pushed forward. Despite the doctor's expectations that nobody spoke of this room, it was actually highly speculated upon by the staff.

Not openly, but in hushed conversations. Usually ones that took place far, far away from the hospital itself, and after enough post-shift drinks had been consumed to loosen up the right person's conspiratorial lips.

Rumors left expectations, visions of strange contraptions, medical experiments, the skeletal remains of guinea pig test subjects, still chained to the wall by ankle and wrist.

Then there was the actual room. She could now confirm that deep within the bowels of Lychhurst, there was a secret room, what you might call an *experimental medicine* ward.

The phrase conjured so many images that the mundanity of the room once she finally stood within its four perfectly serene and white walls was a letdown. Nothing but a standard operating table in the middle of the room. Typical wash station in the corner, a table of instruments.

There was an anesthesia set up, and of course, the main reason she'd been summoned by the doctor.

An EEG machine.

She jumped at the low chuckle that came from the doctor's throat, sounding like a frog had been let loose in the hospital's basement.

"Not what you expected, huh?" he asked.

"No, not exactly."

"I can assure you, whatever horrendous image you have in your mind, there is a history in this room to paint it as accurate. But it's damn near the twenty-first century. Those barbaric times are past us."

The assistant nodded as she approached the EEG machine. She thought, if that were true, why were they so far underground at that very moment? Why not perform this test upstairs where all the normal hospital functions took place?

She held her tongue, and tried to ignore the queasy feeling in her stomach when she glanced down at the patient.

Caleb Jones

"Are you feeling bad for him?" the doctor asked.

"It's hard not to," she said. "I mean, for anyone going through what he is."

"I know you are new to practicing medicine, so I will give you a quick word of advice. Leave those feelings at the door. They will cloud your judgment."

She'd heard such things before, and heartily disagreed. But this was not the place for such disagreements.

"He has not felt or thought much of anything in five years. Yes, he will die this evening, but I can assure you, it will not make much difference to him. He's hardly been on this plane of existence for a long time now. It has also been arranged that his family will be more than well compensated for their willingness to donate him to our cause."

Slobber dribbled from the side of the patient's lip. Instinct from her earlier nursing days kicked in, and she grabbed a rag and dabbed at it. When she pulled the cloth away, she thought, for a millisecond, that she saw the man's lips turn up into a grin.

But she blinked and the same lifeless sag was there. No definition in his lips. Just the weight of decades of life and gravity pulling everything in his body down. That's what always got to her about these old patients.

When it got this late, when the brain was no longer firing on all cylinders and they weren't much more than a vegetable, did it discount those years of memories? So much so that, like in this patient's case, his family was so willing to give him up?

"Let's begin," the doctor said. "We will start with intake procedure. Name?"

The assistant snapped out of her stupor and frantically moved to the foot of the bed where the clipboard and all of the patient's paperwork was.

"Daryll Haze," the nurse answered, regaining some composure.

"Daryll Haze."

He heard his name and he blinked. He had no idea how long he was staring up, staring at nothing. He had no idea who'd said his name.

For all he knew it was a whisper from the rusty-looking walls. He never really understood where he was.

The old building he'd arrived at, maybe a week ago, maybe a year ago, felt more permanent than the one with all the other old folks who could barely remember their own name.

My name. Daryll Haze. Lucky I've come this far without that name plastered over headlines.

Now, what the hell did that mean?

"Age?"

He felt his heart thrum at the sound of a voice. He damn near forgot that it was a voice that had got his motor running. He hoped the voice would keep him awake. Everything got so much more vivid when he slept these days.

The dreams and the memories. Those mistakes that he'd loved making in a younger body. He wondered if the family, whose faces he couldn't picture at that moment, knew about those "mistakes," and that was why they didn't come around.

"Eighty-three."

Daryll looked down toward his feet. A middle-aged man towered over the bottom of the bed, looking down at him. The owner of the voice, Daryll realized as the doctor said, "It's astounding the age that can be added by a bed-ridden status. I'd have guessed no less than ninety-five."

"Yes, sir."

This voice came from overhead, and Daryll's eyes fluttered north. He felt his heart tremor in a different way than before. A sympathetic shudder, the gentle rock of a caring mother's arms.

The woman that stood there was beautiful and young. Something familiar in the tone of her cheek or the furrow of her brow. Daryll could perhaps even smell the lingering perfume of a date the night before. All of these things dug at a memory too far submerged to reach.

Too far. The thought brought on the fear of sleep once more. Nothing was too far, he'd realized, for the awakening of the subconscious. Sub becomes super, and a mostly buried life begins to breathe again.

Daryll started to take in his stark surroundings, trying to remember just when he'd ended up in a hospital. He remembered the old folks' home, staring at the pale green walls for hours. Watching reruns every day of game shows. Drooling, practically brain-dead.

These were specific memories, just rote, like a child reading a passage from a book so many times that he can recite it word-for-word. But the transfer from that place to this room was a blur with no definition.

Empty time, lights with no shape. The realization made his stomach clench and he tried to sit up on the bed.

"No, no, Mr. Haze."

He looked up to find the woman's hand on his chest, applying the perfect amount of pressure to steer him back down, but also to comfort. It was like a caring parent preparing a child for a shot. He smiled and nodded at her then slowly returned to his prone position.

"That's right," she said. "We're almost done here."

"Almost done?" the doctor said. "We're barely started."

"Well, I guess he's almost done. We are at least done with the intake information, I believe." She looked down at her clipboard to confirm and nodded. "Yes, no more info needed."

"Right. More formality, anyhow," the doctor said. "Nobody will ever have reason to look for it. His family practically sold him to us."

The nurse narrowed her eyes at the doctor. "Perhaps, sir, it would be best to speak on those matters after he is asleep."

The doctor leaned down into Daryll Haze's face and said, "This man will know more once he's asleep than he could ever possibly know right now. That's why we're here."

Daryl had no way of articulating it. He'd gone non-verbal some time ago. He knew the doctor was right, though. And it horrified him.

Standing back upright, the doctor said, "Let's begin."

Daryll was hit with a sudden urge to flee. To get up, somehow, despite his decrepit old body, and run for the room's only door, into the dark unknown beyond.

Before he made any move, though, that firm hand was on his chest again. The smell of her perfume faded, then the mask went over her face. The smell was nothing, and he was fading fast.

Daryll's eyes fluttered open. The world around him had taken on a blue haze, like the light outside on a spring day following a brief but violent rain shower. He felt a shudder wrench his body. This was sleep. He'd been here before. In the years since his mind had truly left him, this was where he'd been most lucid.

"We're getting some activity, definitely."

He was in the corner of the room, leaning against the wash station, looking at his own body on the gurney. He'd barely noticed the other two. Could hardly even remember them from when he'd first fallen asleep, maybe minutes, or hours, ago.

"Yes," the doctor agreed. "Like we've monitored before. This is why we chose him."

Monitored before?

Daryll had no memory of this. Surely he'd remember.

His body looked so foreign there. Those cables branching off of his head, like deep-digging roots of some science-fiction plant. He was the fruit, his brain the pit that was planted, his brain activity the nutrients that the doctor was seeking.

Daryll took a step forward, but when his arm came away from the wash station, the sleeve of his hospital gown snagged the faucet lever, and pulled ever so slightly.

He heard the *dab-dab-dab* of fat drops of water plopping from the spout, down into the deep well of the sink, and turned around. Scared he would be found outside of himself, he reached back and yanked the lever back to the fully shut position.

"What was that?" the woman asked. Her voice had changed, though. Something familiar, something out of his past. She sounded scared. When Daryll turned back to face her, she was staring at him.

It was no longer the nurse, at least for a moment.

The woman's face was streaked with grime. The smell of dirt filled the room. It was much like the last time he'd seen her.

Eva, this one was called. An early one. A lifetime ago, when his body and mind were still able. He could still see the scratch that he'd left, streaking from the right brow down to the left side of her chin like a meteor shower disrupting a perfect night sky.

When she opened her eyes, though, there was nothing there of the hazel he remembered from those decades ago. The empty white that glared into the corner, searching for the source of the sound, burned like the core of the sun.

"Old building," the doctor said. "Probably just some rusty water got knocked loose from some of the pipes."

Daryll looked toward the doctor. His eyes were blank, too. Only, instead of the white fire that burned in the assistant's eyes, there was a blackness; two consuming, hungry black holes.

Daryll flinched away at the sight, but when he blinked his own eyes and refocused, the two were turned away again. Both focused heavily on the body on the table before them.

His body.

"It has long been my theory," the doctor said, whilst looking at the readings emitted from the EEG machine, "that the declining mind is most active when the body is at rest."

"The readings on Mr. Haze support that claim," the assistant said. "I can already see that."

"Of course. I've been able to prove this with various patients for years now. The question is, what to do with it?"

The assistant cleared her throat. "That is why we're down here."

"A reboot of sorts. It's hard to submit such an idea to any sort of proper organization on paper and expect them to go along with it. Lychhurst has at least noticed the validity to my claims and provided me space to try. And why wouldn't they?"

"If you are able to prove your final theory, it will revolutionize elder care."

The doctor stroked his chin, thoughtfully, then nodded. "Yes. My *final* theory. The last, hard reset. Like a computer."

Daryll didn't like the emphasis the doctor chose, but had little time to react before the doctor spoke again.

"How are his vitals?"

"All check out normal for now," the assistant said with a casual glance toward the Holter monitor. "He's in good condition for us to continue."

Her voice still sounded so like Eva.

The darkness of that memory, in the woods out back of her home, where he'd taken her after, crept from the corners of that barren hospital room, like a film spliced from a former life into that moment. His memories wanted to take over and live in his now. Memories of a life dealing death that was never uncovered.

Daryll rubbed at his eyes as if it would cause the memory to vanish, just go away. Still, he drifted back to that moment for a second. Eva's eyes staring up from that shallow hole, no longer hazel or balls of light. Just dead.

"Psst," a voice hissed. It came from a corner of the room that was barely visible in the darkness trying to shutter Daryll's world. "Hey, I think I know you."

Another familiar voice.

Daryll squinted, walking toward the corner of the room he thought the voice came from. The doctor and his assistant drifted off into his memory. Eva was still floating there in the periphery, echoes of her voice. Somewhere deep down, her screams choked off by shovelfuls of dirt.

Then this one, speaking from the corner. Something pulled up from the deep. Familiar, but cloudy.

He was practically standing in the corner and couldn't see a face. He could just barely see the outline of somebody. It was a little somebody. They looked to barely come to Daryll's shriveled, old belly.

"Yes," the voice said. Daryll could see the kid's shoulders shimmy with a small giggle. "Oh, I remember you."

A small hand reached from the dark and rubbed the stubble on Daryll's cheek.

"Who are you?" he asked.

Eyes opened, much like the assistant's, white stars in the black sky corner of the operating room. A face leaned forward out of the dark and out of his past.

A little girl, no more than ten.

Daryll did indeed remember and he thought he might puke. He did retch, and the body on the gurney behind him made something of a labored cough. The heart monitor raced.

The doctor and the assistant spoke urgently for a moment, but Daryll's focus never left the little girl whose eyes had been replaced with light.

"Katrina," he whispered. It came out hoarse and cracked.

The ghost nodded her head. She opened her mouth to speak and that same smell of dirt poured forth, mixed with something else. A smell that left a tinny grime on his tongue.

Blood.

He flinched away and tripped, slamming into a set of cabinets that lined the wall. One of the cabinet doors opened under the imprinted force of the man who wasn't really there. It made no more sound than a gust of wind against a shutter. Still, it was enough to get the assistant's attention.

She locked eyes with Daryll. The once-fiery stars inside her skull were dimming. Off-white now. He could see the quick rise and fall of her chest.

"What was that?"

"I told you," the doctor responded, starting to sound annoyed, "this building is old. The kind of place that is always creaking and moaning."

"We all creak and moan," the little girl whispered, crouched down behind Daryll. "Somewhere in the back of your mind, we all creak and moan, waiting for you to remember."

He could feel the cold breath from her dead lips on the back of his neck. A complete inverse of the last position he'd seen her in when she was still alive. How he'd stood behind her.

Katrina was the first one he'd gone so far with, and he knew he couldn't hide it. Couldn't hide her. And the results left an eternal musk of dirt and blood on her name and memory.

"I'm sorry," he whispered.

It wasn't exactly true. Like a child being punished, he was sorry he was finally being caught, some forty years later. The words came out as shaky tremors, tectonic movements in his black soul.

He turned to face the girl. "I had no con—"

The girl, Katrina, had stood, and was fading back into the corner. Her eyes were the only thing visible. Unblinking white windows in the dark.

She stared at him for a long time. He could picture her lifeless body on a basement floor, staring at him with—he dug through his clouded memory—blue eyes. Yes, blue eyes but dead, staring up at him from a basement floor, with a halo of blood expanding around her head.

He was going to say he'd had no control, and in a way that seemed right. No control over his entire life, but in those moments, with a blunt object, and her head turned away, was the moment he took control of something in the way only the most pathetic men can do.

Death rows were filled with such men. He should have been alongside such men years ago. But he'd been careful and methodical. Nobody ever knew but him, and the ones who'd been gone too long to matter.

But don't we matter?

This was a question that flowed through every crack and crevice, spewed from every nook and cranny of the room. Maybe they would all step out from the shadows. Crawl out from the cabinets, calling out from the echoey pipes of the wash station. Emerging from a place where they still resided and still mattered.

His memory could release a dozen or more souls that would converge on the one decrepit old man that tied them all together.

Daryll, the one on the floor, curled up into the fetal position and begged his sleeping body to wake.

"It has been," the doctor said suddenly, pausing to get the number right, "one hour and thirty-seven minutes. The majority of the time has been in deep sleep, accompanied by rapid eye movement. Plenty of EEG readings." He looked to the assistant. "I believe we have the data we need to move onto the next step."

Daryll had been on the floor, but now stood over the physician's assistant's shoulder, unsure of how or when he had moved. He wasn't even sure how he'd been asleep for so long. It felt no longer than five minutes.

The assistant nodded her head but made no verbal reply.

"I need you to confirm that you will proceed with the next step," the doctor said.

"Yes, doctor. We will proceed."

"The solution is measured out on your instrument table. I know you have nurse's training, part of the reason I chose you for this study. You simply need to administer through the patient's IV. Then we will move on to the final step."

The doctor pulled another instrument closer to the table. A defibrillator.

Daryll felt his heart rate increase, and all three in the room noticed the spike on the Holter monitor. The nurse looked from the monitor to the doctor with a grimace.

The doctor smiled and said, "It's like he knows."

Daryll felt the chill that ran through the assistant's blood.

She didn't react, though. Simply took the prefilled syringe and walked over to the IV labeled *Haze*. She rechecked the measurement before attaching it to the IV's intake, then slowly plunged.

As she did, Daryll lunged from behind the woman, a motion that he'd committed numerous times throughout his life. Only, his hands didn't wrap around her throat or bring a blunt object down on the back of her head.

He went for her hand that so deftly worked the IV. But he couldn't touch her.

Still, she shivered as his hand passed through hers. She stopped for a moment with another milliliter left in the syringe. She turned and locked eyes with Daryll.

For a moment, the white fire he'd seen before burned in her sockets and Daryll believed she could see him. Then something simple and strange happened, so subtle that Daryll barely clocked it.

The white heat of her eyes dimmed. Not as black as he'd seen in the doctor's eyes, but certainly a shade darker than her eyes had been the first time he'd seen them. She turned back toward the body on the gurney and plunged the last of the solution into his veins.

"Wait for it," the doctor said, looking at his watch, then over at the heart monitor. "Okay, now."

The heart monitor started to pick up steam. Daryll looked down at his body and could even see the pounding of his laboring heart, causing his hospital gown to flutter with the increased speed.

Daryll, the one standing outside of his own body, reached toward his chest, but felt nothing.

"No, no, no," he whispered.

The assistant reached up to the back of her neck and tried to wipe away the moist gust of air that she felt. A sudden draft with no noticeable source.

"Measurements," the doctor said, a note of irritation clawing into his voice. He was walking over to the defibrillator. Daryll could see the power sign go from red to green. What the hell was happening here?

"Sorry," the assistant said. "He is up to three hundred beats per minute. We are approaching cardiac arrest."

"And the brain activity?"

She turned toward the EEG. "According to the live scans we are getting, there certainly is an increase. It'll be better to focus on the heart for now."

"You know what will happen with the heart," the doctor said. "It's what we're here for. Please remain focused on the brain activity."

The heart rate continued to increase. Daryll watched as whatever that solution was coursed through his veins like snake venom, beelining toward his heart.

The ever increasing *beep-beep-beep* of the machine let him know how perilously close he was coming to a dark end. It was blurring the time between *beeps*, attempting to turn that staccato rhythm into a single, one-note hum. Then, that's exactly what it did.

The nurse hadn't turned from the EEG readings. She said, "Doctor, he's flatlined!"

"I know. Now tell me what his damn readings are!"

Daryll blinked. His perspective changed. He was looking down from some place unknown. Not the top of the room, and he was no fool to think it was from heaven; he'd torn that ticket up decades ago.

But somewhere above, looking down at himself and the others. Not just the doctor, who was finally administering the paddles of the defibrillator. Not just the nurse, who read out a litany of words and numbers as the cords attached to his head read the exploding synapses inside his brain.

There were others, too.

Just as he'd imagined earlier, they pulled themselves from the shadows. They crawled out from beneath the tables and stepped out from curtains. All women, all for the most part young.

They were all also very familiar. A range of fashions and hairstyles that carbon dated his victims anywhere between the late fifties and the seventies.

All of them, converging on the one similar, fatal axis line they'd all ended upon.

Daryll Haze.

They all whispered. The Daryll that floated somewhere up above couldn't be sure what they said over the sound of the monitor that declared his own heart had shut down. He thought it might be their own names, called as softly as a gust of wind on an otherwise calm night.

Occasionally, their white shining eyes cast upward, locking with his own. Their hands gestured to follow. After a while, the doctor shouted that he would use the paddles, but did so without much conviction.

Then the room was filled only with those whispers. All Daryll could be sure of was his own name being called.

Summoned.

Daryll, it's time. Come, now.

He heard it in between the leaf flutter of their names whistling through the air, and then, without any gumption to resist, he was going.

The doctor below was wheeling him out of the room, down toward the black-eyed man that stood before the morgue. There was an exchange of some sort between him and the doctor, then he stepped out of the way as the doctor pushed the gurney through.

And all those women led the way through the door. Led both Darylls, the one above and the one lying dead on the gurney, through the door.

There was no time wasted; the doctor shifted the body onto a conveyor and a door opened at the end of the moving stage. The mortician approached, threw a lever, then Daryll was moving toward a smokeless fire.

"Until the fire," the mortician muttered. "Until the fire."

Daryll's nose was filled with the scent of sulfur, it was all he could think of. His last thought as the final bindings to this world were severed was that there should be no sweet smell awaiting his departure. The white eyes still looking up at him from below whispered their agreement.

The assistant held it together until the doctor had left, then ran over to the wash station and plunged her head in the sink to vomit. She did her best to hold the tears to a minimum, but try as she might to control these physical reactions, an absolute truth sang through the walls of the room.

She'd killed a man. Any justification of it—that he was old, a practical vegetable, that he had nobody caring for him—didn't change the facts.

Head still down, she ran the water to hide the evidence of her sick, and also to wash her mouth out. She spit, then took a handful of water and splashed it on her face before standing up straight.

He was standing over her shoulder. Right there, just as she'd seen him in his hospital gown.

The dark holes of a cigarette burn on paper had replaced his eyes, but there was no mistaking that her most recent patient, Daryll Haze, stood behind her.

She screamed and spun around, a natural reaction for those that have seen the dead.

The room was empty. She was alone.

She was too scared to turn back to the mirror, so she walked toward the center of the room and looked over the EEG readings that had spilled across the floor, mindlessly looking at the place where Daryll Haze's brain activity skyrocketed during the few seconds directly following his confirmed death.

She didn't much care.

All she was thinking was that she hoped that ghost, likely just a figment of her imagination created by stress and guilt, would be held within these walls.

She trembled, because she doubted if that could ever be true.

"Please," she whispered, "don't follow me away from this place."

Records Room
1994

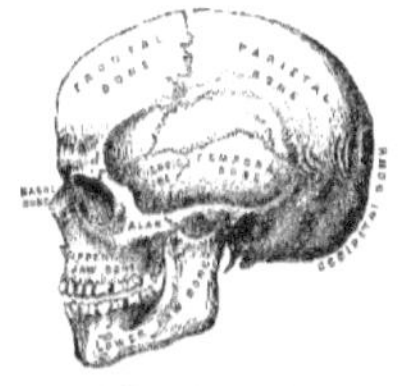

A Crypt of Dust and Paper
Mer Whinery

The old girl hadn't been closed for long. A couple of weeks, maybe.

In his experience, this was the best time to hit it.

The police had come and gone. The remaining staff departed for greener pastures and other opportunities. Not even a single mall cop standing watch.

The chain link fence surrounding the facility, even more imposing in its desolation, looked to have been strung and poled almost as afterthought. Crude. Haphazard. Not really interested in keeping anyone out.

At the time, he had not thought it peculiar. In his experience abandoned places were a little *off* by default. They either attracted thieves or loneliness and were not meant for people any longer. Husks of the past.

He had read about the hospital in a mail order periodical for urban explorers such as himself called *The Shadowland Register*. It being the annual Halloween issue, it contained several extracts on various wrecks and ruins rumored to be inhabited by the unhappy dead.

But he didn't believe in that sort of thing. As with all forsaken constructs, he only concerned himself with the challenge of getting into the place, relishing the delicious secrecy of his trespass, then emerging free and undetected to tell the tale.

It was a seductively short drive from his school to the now shuttered sickhouse. Less than an hour. So he had no reservations in packing up that

Friday evening after his final class and traveling to Lychhurst. He hadn't even bothered to tell anyone where he was going. It never occurred to him, for he had done this more times than he could remember.

And now here he was, knee deep and shivering in a moldering heap of rotting cardboard boxes and dusty journals, in the Records Room of Lychhurst, supposedly empty, wishing he *had* told someone. That he had never subscribed to *The Shadowland Register*. That he had never taken up urban exploring.

The young man knew he was probably never going to get out alive.

He heard the sigh again. Long and drawn out, lazily swelling in volume as if it were thinking about shifting into a scream. Now he realized it was real. He had not imagined it. It sounded closer now. Much closer.

He looked down at his discoveries. It was because of this. All of these things. The documents and the reels of film. This was knowledge not meant for someone like him. Normal people. People who don't want to know things like this. This was why Lychhurst needed to not only be shuttered against the outside world, but razed to the earth with cleansing fire, its bones salted and prayed over.

A battered Trapper Keeper, its plain black plastic casing tattered and decorated with flaking decals of flowers and mushroom, stuffed to bursting. He had found it concealed in a hole in the wall, hidden behind a rusty file cabinet. Within, a single sheet of white construction paper covered with a script of spidery, thin black handwriting. Faded, yet legible. The pockets of the binder filled with various documents. Some mundane. Some so far beyond mundane they passed over into the realm of the horrific.

That first page should have been all of the warning he needed, and now he was going to pay for his arrogance.

Lewis the janitor agrees with me. We have to keep this on the downlow and be quiet about it. It took some convincing on my part, I have to admit. I wanted to go to the news with it, but he talked me out of it. Smart move on his part. Like anyone would believe this. NOBODY would believe it. At least nobody with the power or balls to do anything about it. And what would there be to do about it? There are things in here we found out, even if they are all true, that can't have anything done about them except burn this hexed old castle right down to the dirt that came before it. But I doubt anybody will ever do that. This place will go on and on and on until God himself brings his heel down upon its bricks and beams and crushes it into nothing. Maybe that would get rid of all the bad mojo. Maybe not. Evil never seems to get conquered, just put on hold for a while.

There is no organization to this record, which is what I guess this is, really. Just gathered information and stories. Believe what you want. I am turning in my resignation tomorrow and moving somewhere I can't be found. Not even going to have a phone. It's better that way. I don't know about Lewis. I asked him to come with me, but he has other plans. He didn't tell me what those plans are, and I didn't ask.

I am so glad I don't have a husband and kids. I am so scared by all of this I would probably leave them behind.

The date is 11/1/81. I hope by the time this is found, if it's ever found, this horrible place will be nothing more than a shit stain in history.

(Internal Memo, on standard pale yellow A4 paper. Typed.)
CONFIDENTIAL
Lychhurst Hospital
Date: 11/25/48
TO: Chief of Staff Office
FROM: Otto Klug, Head of Dietary Services
SUBJECT: Stock Supply Overview

It was a good month. Thirteen of them. Well, thirteen and a half if you count the one from Labor and Delivery.

I have to admit, in the beginning I was dubious about this whole enterprise. But now I see so clearly. I see the big picture, and in the end, if we are being frank here, that is all that really matters. SHE only cares about the end result. The goal. To keep this place alive and fruitful so that HER aspirations and designs will continue unabated. It hasn't been easy, but I think we are on the right track. This plan does work so long as everyone involved does their part. You'd be surprised how just a little money goes a long way in that respect.

The fly in the ointment has been figuring out how to dupe the families. Thankfully, most of them are witless bumpkins who can hardly spell their own names, much less decipher the legalese in the paperwork they scribble on. Most of them don't even want to see the corpses, especially the elderly specimens. By that point the families are so exhausted with watching their loved ones wither away they are ready to wash their hands and be done. Yes, take them and take care of it all. Just pour what's left of them in a nice little vase and we will put them on a shelf in the living room with the other tacky bric-a-brac. That will suffice. But every so often a sister, or a husband or a son will become suspicious and want to nose around. A rare occurrence, certainly. But it happens. I have a team assembled now to address this issue. So far I have had no trouble whatsoever. Whatever methods the team is applying to rectify the situation is none of my concern. Again, the big picture.

The patients and most of the staff have absolutely no idea. The chef we hired from down south is a true master of his craft. You'd never know what you were eating unless you had been there, in the kitchen trenches, working beside the man. I was skeptical (apologies for my lack of faith) at first, until I tried a bit for myself. Braised ribs were what he called it, and it tasted just like that. A sweet honey glaze on meat smoked for 24 hours straight. Paired with a side of green beans and dinner rolls. One bite made me want more, and more, and more. An additional perk, something in the food seems to be improving morale among the staff. It seems to have galvanized them. They no longer whine about working that extra two hours a night. Frequent smoke breaks have gone untaken. Absenteeism is at an all-time low. They are always smiling.

If I might be allowed to briefly dip into the disdainful talk of money, we are saving so much budgetarily. Funds which can now be redirected into furthering the work of the church. Her words made flesh grow ever closer to full fruition. We are almost there.

It just presents further evidence as to how SHE works. How SHE works in ways we cannot see or know or understand.

Glory be to HER, as ever. Until the Fire.

(Intercepted letter. Undated. Script is in barely legible pencil, the script smudged with moisture.)

Martin, you have to get me out of this place. I've written you three letters now and you haven't answered me. Why? I have to assume, no, hope, you have not been getting them. You haven't been to see me in three weeks. Why not? You're my husband! You're supposed to be taking care of me. Right? RIGHT? Where are you? You're probably with mom and my brother. All of you make your plans, weaving your little webs. My getting hurt was the best thing that ever happened to you all. I fell right into your little trap.

Something is not right here. This is not a regular hospital. Not a place for sick or hurt people. It's a place that's just pretending to be a place like that. I have seen things here I can't ever hope to explain. I honestly don't know how I could even get started. It all sounds insane. Oh, it looks and acts like a hospital. It's very good at looking like that. I have nurses coming in every couple of hours to take my blood pressure and temperature. Change the dressing on my wounds. They smile and dote. A few of them even joke around and make me, for just a moment, forget the horrible things I have seen and heard. Every day a new doctor comes in to talk with me about my condition. Like the nurses and aides, they are pleasant and formal. Being around them makes me feel calm and like I might be someplace normal. As soon as they leave the bad feelings come back and the noises come back with them and then I start to see those things again. Before you jump to conclusions about my mental state, YES, I have stopped taking my pain meds altogether. At first it was because I was afraid it was the pills making this stuff happen. I've read pain pills can make you hallucinate. But that just seemed to make everything worse. Now I don't dope myself up so I can stay alert. I don't want to be doped up and useless in this place.

Where are you? Goddamn it, Martin. You're my husband and I need you! You have to get me the hell out of here!

Mer Whinery

I have seen the little boy four times now. Same time every night, right after the midnight shift change. He seems to favor this part of the hospital to haunt. I say haunt because he is not alive. He doesn't walk but floats. I would guess he's around six or seven. Not a little bitty kid but not very old either, wearing a hospital gown that looks like it's got blood splashed all over the front. He, or it I guess, hovers a few inches from the floor, his bare toes pointing down like they are stiff and dead. The most awful thing is that he is missing an arm, the poor thing. That makes him more horrible to look at. He holds out that one little arm, outstretched in front of his body like a mummy from one of those black and white scary movies from a long time ago.

He always stops at my door, turns his head, and looks at me. He doesn't try to come into the room. He just floats there, staring at me. His eyes are black and empty, yet somehow, I can see them in the shadows of the room. Like the blackness glows, or something inside whatever passes for his body makes them light up.

He bobs up and down for a little while like a lure in the water waiting for a fish to snag it, then his eyes start to grow bigger and bigger until they're almost the size of dinner plates! His mouth starts to open wide and like his eyes it grows so large it completely blots out his face, like a big empty spot of nothing, and the sound of screaming people and crashing glass and metal comes howling out of it, ending in a horrible gargling noise, like he is choking on dirt or vomit.

He does this for almost a minute, then turns around and glides back in the direction he came from. If I could get up from this bed, in this room you have left me trapped and helpless in, I would follow him.

Very soon, I am afraid he will do more than float and stare. Maybe one night he will stop, turn, and come flying into my room, making that awful racket that just gets louder and louder, and do something horrible to me. Something that will either hurt me, break my mind, or worse. I want to mention it to the nurses, but I have a suspicion they will laugh it off. But I think the laugh will be fake. I know damn well they know about him. Maybe even what happened to him. Maybe they are going to let him get me. Maybe there have been others lying in this very same bed who saw him too. What happened to them, I wonder?

It's not just the dead boy. There are other things too. Sometimes I will hear an awful screaming, usually really early in the morning right before it gets light out. Screaming in a hospital. Big deal, right? No, this is screaming of a different kind. A special kind of screaming. Something like hurt mixed up with being scared so bad, so deep, it digs right down to the bone and spreads through the blood like a poison. A screaming that's contagious. It makes you want to scream until your throat explodes. I have to bite down on hard on the blankets to keep from going into a full-blown freak out. The screaming will go on and on, and I can make out real faint voices in all of the racket. Tones of voices but not words. Then the screaming will stop and turn into something like crying. That's worse than the screaming. It's a lost sound. A hopeless one. I try not to think about what is on the other end of that noise.

Last night was the worst I have had since I've been here. I was so worn out I broke down and took a pain pill so I could get a little bit of shut eye. It was really nice. So nice I didn't care if the dead boy got me, and the screaming sounded like it was coming from a million miles away. I heard something that woke me up. At least I think I heard something. I just remember waking up and things not being right. The feeling in the room, in me, was off. I started to panic and reminded myself to breathe.

Like how my mom would tell me to whenever dad was on one of his benders and would beat the holy hell piss out of us. Breathe in through the nose, deep enough to really eat the air, then blow it out slowly through my mouth. Mom was always right about stuff like that, and she should know better than anyone. She told me the breathing thing made the oxygen in your brain stronger, more powerful or something like that. The oxygen makes you relax and be able to sort your thoughts so you can fight the panic off.

It made me feel better, but the mood in the room didn't change. If anything, it felt more oppressive than ever. Like the way it felt in the crawlspace under the house in the middle of summer. Choking. Disoriented. The thickness in the air just made me feel sleepier and keeping myself alert and awake started to get really hard. The pain pill seemed to really kick in all of a sudden and I started to drift off, my eyelids were heavy like lead weights. It began to feel like something was making me go to sleep. Like a spell being cast on me or something.

Mer Whinery

You're probably laughing at that last part. I know I am hard to live with, with my funny ideas and things I am interested in. You really never loved me, did you? You've always held my weird little habits against me. You're hoping I'll die in this place, and nobody will ever know what happened to me. I have nobody left in this world other than you. I have to hand it to you; this was the perfect plan.

Before I slipped back into unconsciousness, I saw them at last. The ones in charge. Not sure how I knew that. Maybe they wanted me to know. I am part of the hospital now, aren't I? Of course, I am. There were three of them, at least that's all I could make out. It was just before sundown and the room was lit by a little table lamp which was more for comfort than common sense. They were dressed in long red priest robes like Father Morgan back home, but with weird pointy hoods covering their heads. Like what those guys in the KKK wear. In the shadows of my room, I could see their eyes glowing behind the ragged eye holes of their hoods.

The same kind of empty shining I saw in the dead little boy's eyes. So vacant it ate up all of the shadows in the room and just made them look bigger by the second. Bigger. Bigger and filling up the whole room like a stain of black rot spreading over the floor and up the walls and across the ceiling. I opened my mouth to scream, and at the same time all three of them raised their fingers to where their mouths would be on their hoods, as if shushing me.

I tried to do the breathing thing again, but it wasn't working any more. I realized then they had me where they needed me to be. I deserved to be there. A low rumbling filled my ears, getting louder and rougher by the second. The room felt like I was trapped in one of those dollar store snow globes that you wind up and shake the hell out of to trigger a swirl of fake snow in the water. Rumbling and vibrating. Vibrating and trembling and the room swirling like kaleidoscope glass. I soon came to understand the vibrating and trembling was more than just noise and commotion. Much more.

It was not a rumbling, but a growling. This room, the entirety of the hospital, was the needful belly of a monster in a fairy tale. A monster that chewed up and ate stupid little humans like me. Like those bugs that bite their heads off of their mates and gobble them up after they are finished getting knocked up by them.

There were hands on my body. Not hard and mean hands, but gentle and comforting ones. A series of caresses that made parts of my body tingle in ways I don't want to think about, much less tell you. They wanted me to be okay and for this to be as easy and soothing as possible. It got real dark then. True dark. The things I saw in that darkness, Martin, I can't even begin to describe. Not gonna try either. You'll really think I have lost it, and I don't want you to have any ammunition to keep me here after I am better. When I am home again, you'll pay for what you did.

When my eyes opened it was morning. The drapes in my room had been pulled open, revealing a beautiful early summer morning washed in sunshine, the window cracked just wide enough to allow the smell of damp earth into the room.

I've always liked that smell a lot. It smells like a restart. Like things can be better after a long dark night of hardship and hurt.

Oh, my left leg is gone! Well, part of my left leg. Lopped off right below the kneecap. How about that! I have a long row of stitches on my lower back and a really long, ugly black one going right across my belly.

Ain't no amount of shea butter is gonna smooth out the scar that's going to leave behind. I know how particular you are about that sort of thing, dearest one. I hope you aren't too disgusted with me.

They gave me some new pills that work a lot better than the other ones. They are a really pretty bright pink color. Just looking at one right now, turning its smooth little shell over and over between my fingers, I feel calm. Like I don't have a single care or trouble. I have accepted the pill will take care of it. The pill understands. The pill is there because you are not.

When the nurses came in, I didn't ask what was done to me. The doctor either. It doesn't matter. After all, I have the pill to watch over me.

I just want to say it again, I hate you for not being here. You're really one of them, aren't you? That accident I had was your fault. You planned it just to get me here so nobody will ever see me again.

I thought we were happy, Martin.

I thought we mattered.

I will never forgive you for leaving me here. Never.

Mer Whinery

I know that when I walk out of here, if I should walk out of here, I am not going to walk out of here the same person. If that happens my love, my dearest one, I am going to pay you back for all of this.

I'll come after you with black eyes that grow as big as dinner plates and the scream of something dying in steel and fire coming out of my mouth.

I am going to come back for you, and that's a fucking promise.

(Second note stapled to the last page of the original. Typewritten.)
Tagged and ready. Prepare the machine. A lot we can use here. The scraps can feed the kids at the farm. Just the essentials needed. A good haul.
Glory be to HER, as ever. Until the Fire.
 (initialed *JR*)

(Internal Memo, on standard pale blue A4 paper. Typed)
CONFIDENTIAL
Lychhurst Hospital
Date: 7/5/78
TO: Chief of Staff Office
FROM: Reni Ghastmeyer, Head of Media and Public Relations for Lychhurst Hospital.
SUBJECT: Media Project 8 – Summer 1978 - CLASS 6

Members and Partners of Media Project 8,
The shipments from Texas and Oklahoma (henceforth referred to as Class 6) have arrived at last. These specimens have come at a dear cost to us, so handle them with extreme sensitivity until further direction has been provided by our superiors. Place them in barrack **THREE**. I type this in boldface to emphasize the importance of this. I will not have a repeat of the fiasco we endured with Class 2. We only save them for the hog pens at the

very end, obviously. Ensure they are fed and hydrated. Provide any comforts needed if and when asked for. Extra blankets, candy, toys, television, whatever. As you know, this is of extreme importance to the first part of the process. Gain their trust. Make them feel like this is someplace like home and they will be well cared for. Remember where these specimens come from. They would give their lives for just a roof over their heads, a soft and clean place to rest and three hot meals a day. This is the way to properly crush a common person's mind and soul. Nurture them. Tend to them. Smile at them with benevolence. Comfort them when they have bad dreams. This way, when they come to the realization that they are never going to leave this place, at least not in the way they have hoped, they will resign themselves to their fates much more easily. The shock will reduce their will to survive to cinders. They will do as they are told because they won't have a choice. The ones that really behave will be granted the reward of living longer. These will be the ones we can keep going for a while. Our "star performers" if you will.

Next week, probably by Thursday, we can move them into the kennels to start the breakdown activities.

Glory be to HER, as ever. Until the Fire.

CONFIDENTIAL
Lychhurst Hospital
Date: 7/17/78
TO: Chief of Staff Office
FROM: Reni Ghastmeyer, Head of Media and Public Relations for Lychhurst Hospital.
SUBJECT: Media Project 8 – Summer 1978 - CLASS 6

Members and Partners of Media Project 8,

Mer Whinery

Incorporating the specimens of Class 6 has proven more complicated than previous teams. There is a young woman of exceptionally strong will (AKA, a loudmouth) among them, making assimilation procedures incredibly costly and frustrating. This is both a blessing and a curse. The curse being, she's a loudmouth distracting the others from towing the line. The process has been disrupted. She possesses a formidable charisma and can make the others doubt and then, ultimately, disobey. The blessing is, because of these very same undesirable qualities, she will make an excellent focus specimen. One of the star performers I mentioned in my previous missive.

Thankfully last night, praise Her will, this little piggie went to market and is never coming back home again. After my experimental therapy she is now falling apart like an old onion wilting away its rancid layers. Not quite yet a broken husk clinging precariously to the ledge of sanity. Oh, the feistiness is still there alright. But the will to do anything about it has departed. This is exactly what we need from her. She is exactly what our investors are looking for. I don't call them star performers for no good reason.

Truth be told, I actually admire this creature. It makes me wonder what she was like and what her profession was before she fell upon hard times. I'm tempted to keep her around for my own personal amusement.

Glory be to HER, as ever. Until the Fire.

CONFIDENTIAL
Lychhurst Hospital
Date: 8/1/78
TO: Chief of Staff Office
FROM: Reni Ghastmeyer, Head of Media and Public Relations for Lychhurst Hospital.
SUBJECT: Media Project 8 – Summer 1978 Summer 1978 - CLASS 6

Members and Partners of Media Project 8,

The film crew arrived very early this morning, and the consecration sacraments have been performed upon the location for the shoot. I had the dream last night, the portent, as expected, and awoke exactly one hour before dawn to anoint the cast with the designated oils and dyes and administer the elixir. The apothecary, Bertram, had worked through the night to get the blend of charnel thistle and black kettle mushrooms just right. No trivial task. As you might remember, the tiniest miscalculation in dosage for either of these reagents will invoke an incomprehensible torment upon its imbiber. We held communion this morning, donning the hallowed vestments and speaking the words that, when bonded with the elixir, will ignite a spiritual charge within all of us. When this concoction hits the blood, it opens up a hidden passageway in the soul, very much like the hallway of an old house where there are many doors on either side of it. Behind each door a mystery. A surprise. A horror. The Truth.

I feel electrified. Like every nerve inside of my body has been mainlined into a vast engine of atrocity. The suffering today will be phantastic. Fuel for legend.

I depart now for the ceremony. The crew is ready. The camera is ready. The piglets are docile, intoxicated, and ready for the butcher barn.

Glory be to HER, as ever. Until the Fire.

Found within a large lockbox hidden beneath a loose floor tile in Section 13 of the Lychhurst Hospital Records Room. The latch on the lockbox remains firm, reinforced with a sturdy Yale padlock. Opening the box reveals two canisters of 16mm film and a long sheet of yellow legal paper. The script upon the paper is in the same elegant swatches of black Sharpie ink, water stained but quite decipherable. There is a

label on each canister, typewritten, the inscription faded - *Media Project 8 – Summer 1978 - CLASS 6*

This was the straw that broke the camel's back for both Lewis and me. What made us decide it was best we make a record of this before something happened to us. Or if we leave. If we even CAN leave. Somehow, even when we are beyond these beautiful, cursed old walls, rooms, and doors, I feel like it will still be able to see us. The hospital.

The hospital will see us, and it will know. Watching and pinning us under its thumb until our bodies give up and collapse into a pile of bones. I think that's part of the relationship those who work or stay here have to forge with it. You have to give a part of yourself over to whatever horrible thing haunts this hellhole. It requires, no, demands submission. A pact made with something not of this earth that was around before the notion of God was ever considered. Before men and women walked on two legs and could make words with their mouths that made sense.

What is given in return for this devotion, I don't want to think about very much.

The cruelties and perversions dedicated to these two reels of film cannot be described in the way a normal person tells a story to somebody else. Although I have seen these things with my own two eyes, there is still that little part of my brain, the shadowy nook reserved for dissecting things and ideas not of the rational world, which still can't shake off every single bit of disbelief. Maybe that's for the best. Maybe the suspension of disbelief is what's keeping my sanity whole.

I have watched it twice, the second time mostly to convince my mind what I saw the first time actually happened. For weeks after I believed I had dreamed it all, although I really knew better. I just didn't want to know better. That would mean I would have to accept the truth that evil is real, it walks and talks and breathes, and, most certainly, eats. It eats a lot.

Lewis, poor guy, he only made it through one viewing. It was enough for him. He's grown noticeably withdrawn since then. Like what he saw got stuck inside of him, rattled him around like a dog with a squeaky toy in its mouth, and won't turn him loose. Maybe I'm just different. I've been in the military, and I saw a lot of bad stuff there. Bad, but nothing like this. Those things could be explained. Bad things with an explanation are easier to choke down.

You can't really explain things like this because they don't really happen.

The little ones were the worst part of it all. The kids. Watching the things that were done to them. Their crying and struggling and screaming. Oh my God, the screaming! I have never heard anything like that. I've taken care of a lot of scared kids in my day. Usually, a little ice cream or chewing gum and something fun to watch on TV distracts them enough to get the hard parts over with. But this. The look on their faces. The sounds that come out of their mouths.

They don't even sound like something human. It's like they can see the actual face of it. Of the shrouded shape in the closet. The ogre attached to the clawed hand under the bed reaching out for an exposed foot above. The mind of a child is both a marvelous and terrible thing. They are still innocent enough to want to believe in the boogeyman, and it is that very same belief that feeds and fuels whatever devil or God or forgotten thing poisoning this old ramble of brick, wood, and dirt. I wonder if anyone ever bothered to come looking for these little ones?

These cast aside grown-ups down on their luck willing to do anything for a buck or a hot meal or pint of something strong to keep the shakes away. Disposable humans, in spite of their previous troubles, are astonishingly trusting. Any little bit of human kindness is all it takes to hook them in the mouth and reel them in. Even when they can see the fire and the skillet and the fisherman sharpening his blade waiting for them on the shore. Folks who have nothing left to lose... the perfect prey.

The only positive aspect of this filth is that nothing was left behind. Nobody was spared the wrath of this... whatever it was. Not even the ghouls committing it to film.

I tried to get a better look at it the second time around. I almost think I can see it. Or at least something in my brain tries to put a shape to it. A form my pathetic human mind can comprehend. But then it gets all fuzzy, the film seems to swell and groan, my ears start to ring and pound like a church bell in a hurricane, and I have to turn away. I won't look again. The film won't be so kind to me a third time.

Mer Whinery

There is no God. No Heaven. This is too horrible even for Hell to claim ownership to it.

I should burn this. I should burn it. But I can't. I need someone to know these things are real. They exist. We need to know that inconceivable horrors like these are real so they can be defeated.

What good would destroying it be, anyway? It will still be there. It will still exist. Hanging around in whatever dark place it sleeps in waiting to be awoken to perpetrate further perversions. All I know is I will not be here in the morning. I have a bus ticket and I haven't told a single person where I am going. Not even Lewis.

Maybe I'm just being paranoid, but I am not 100% sure I can trust him, or anyone for that matter. It might be out there watching me from any set of eyes. A friend. My mother. It could be there, toying with me. Waiting for the right moment to rip away its mask and show me that face I tried so hard to see on the film.

With that I say goodbye to everyone, including the poor son of a bitch who might have had the misfortune to stumble across this little curiosity. Maybe it will be best if you think this is all just a gag. A bad joke, like plastic vomit.

As they would say. Glory be to HER, as ever. Until the fire.
Fuck them.

Note stapled to the back of the letter. Typewritten. Splotches of something dark stain the paper.

She won't open her mouth again. I made sure of that.

Glory be to HER, as ever. Until the fire.

--LW

Morgue
1845

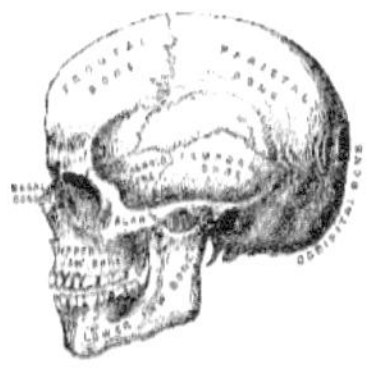

The Dead House
Jeani Rector

He felt perfectly comfortable around dead bodies. He was confident that the dead stayed dead, so when he was offered a position in the new hospital's morgue—morgues were commonly known as Dead Houses—he didn't hesitate to take it.

Lychhurst Hospital had just opened for its wealthy patrons one year before, so it still needed to fill its empty rooms with new doctors and nurses.

On his first day at the hospital, Edmund strolled through the first floor hallway that was lit with gas lamps until he found the stone stairwell leading down. He waved a fly away but it came back to buzz around his head before it finally drifted elsewhere.

Edmund knew that flies were attracted to morgues. Somehow they could find their way even into basements.

He descended the steps and noticed an odd smell. Besides the putrid smell of decay, there was a strangely sweet, pungent scent. It smelled like carbolic acid mixed with alcohol, and he wondered why the Dead House would smell like that.

When he reached the basement, he understood the reason for the smell of decay. Water dripped from the seams of the rock walls and dribbled slowly down to the cobblestone floor. Morgues were always built in basements to keep the bodies cool, but this one felt a bit warmer than it should have been.

Bodies didn't keep so well in warmer temperatures.

He retrieved his key ring and found the lock in the solid, wooden door. He didn't know what to expect when he opened it, and was glad that someone had already lit the gas lamps that were periodically placed along the walls.

He saw forms laid out on black tables, each covered in a white sheet. There were three shrouded bodies on display. He was eager to autopsy them, but a voice from the other side of the room stopped him.

"We have to clean and inspect them," the voice said. "I've prepared the wash buckets for you."

"You'll have to excuse me," Edmund said, "but you are…?"

The man walked into the gaslight. He was revealed to be medium-height with dark hair and dark eyes.

"I'm Charles. I presume you are Doctor Bosworth? I'm your assistant."

"To assist me with autopsies?"

"The 1832 Anatomy Act means we need the consent of the patients' relatives to conduct an autopsy. No permissions were given for these three."

Edmund demanded, "What exactly are your qualifications to be here?" He could see the man flush at the question.

"I'm not a doctor like you," Charles admitted, "but I've worked in hospital Dead Houses for many years. I got this job because of my experience."

"I'm glad you recognize that there is only one doctor here, and it's not you. I am certified, and my ancestors derive from noble England. I'm not Italian like you."

Charles continued to flush. "I'm not Italian. I hail from France, along the northern border near Burgundy."

Edmund was satisfied that he had put Charles in his place. He figured that the assistant would now be more manageable. He needed the other man to be meek in order to proceed with his plans. He wanted to establish a hierarchy, and he had done just that.

He decided to probe a bit. "I'm really interested in anatomy," he said. "It's a shame that the universities have such a shortage of bodies for dissection. Without bodies, there could be no doctors. I feel it's unselfish for patients to give themselves for the benefits of science."

"These patients come from wealthy families," Charles said. "They're not likely to consent to turn their loved ones over to any university. These people have family burial plots that go back a century. Besides, William Burke was hanged two years ago for body snatching in England, so laws have tightened since then about how universities acquire dead bodies, even here in the States."

"Let's see who we are talking about, shall we?" Edmund said, and he knew his annoyance showed. Damn this insolent French man!

He moved to the first shroud. Charles placed scissors in his hand and Edmund cut the material, pulling it away from the face.

Edmund thought he was prepared, but this was the face of a woman ripe with decomposition. It was an assault on his senses. Her face was bone-white with hints of green where mold was taking hold. Her skin was stretched tight over her cheekbones, and her nose appeared beak-like. The lips were drying from decomposition and that made them pull away from the mouth, showing her teeth in an unnatural fashion, like she was gnashing them. There was dried bloody mucus at the corners of her mouth, and he wondered what had killed her.

He continued to pull the shroud away from the body. The woman was dressed in hospital clothes but nothing could contain the smell. She smelled of feces mixed with rotting meat, and there were fruity undertones.

Now Edmund understood why the bodies needed to be stripped and cleaned. It would never do to turn this woman over to her wealthy relatives in this condition… or to turn some of these bodies over to universities in this condition either if he wanted to get the best price, which was his eventual goal.

"You wash, and I'll supervise," Edmund instructed.

"That's fine," Charles consented, and he began to unbutton the woman's clothing. "There, there," he murmured, "it will be fine, Bessie. I'll take good care of you."

"Who is Bessie?" Edmund asked.

"That's the name on this woman's tag."

"Oh for God's sake, don't be daft; this dead woman cannot hear you."

Charles went mute.

Edmund observed that the bloat of the body made the woman appear soft and rounded, as though overweight. There was no sign of rigor mortis, so he knew the death had to have occurred over twenty-four hours ago, because rigor reversed by then.

He saw some squirming, white fly maggots moving in and out of a cut between her breasts and he queried, "Just how long ago did this woman die?"

"Lychhurst is more competent than most hospitals," Charles answered. "It is certainly more competent than the insane asylums. But there is just no way to keep a body fresh, so we have to do our best. I believe this woman died three days ago."

"She should have been dealt with yesterday, or even before," Edmund fumed.

"You weren't here yesterday," Charles said. "But now that you *are* here, I'm sure that you will greatly add to the competency of this hospital."

Edmund didn't allow himself to be mollified. "Enough with the chit-chat. Get to work."

Despite his offer of supervision, Edmund decided to take a stroll around the Dead House to familiarize himself with it. Once again, he noticed that the temperature was too high. No wonder this woman had decomposed so quickly.

There was no need for a public viewing station, because no unidentified bodies wound up in this hospital. Instead, this was a private hospital where the only bodies down here were known patients.

He continued his leisurely stroll. The Dead House was damp and dreary with no embellishments or ornamentations. The walls were stained with soot from the gas lamps. He decided he would make his assistant clean the place, and that cleaning would begin by washing the walls.

He smelled carbolic acid again. Edmund turned around to see that Charles was spraying something from an atomizer over the dead woman's body.

He stepped over. "Just what do you think you are doing?"

Charles immediately froze, then said, "This is a new technique out of London. Your country. Joseph Lister is a scientist over there and he says—"

"Are you mad?" Edmund blustered. "You can't disinfect miasmas! If you were a doctor like me, you'd know that disease is caused by bad air.

Only leeches could have cured her. Once this woman died, the disease died with her. There is nothing to disinfect."

"I'm sorry," Charles said. "Of course you are quite correct."

"Then get the bucket and wash her. Get rid of the damn maggots. Earn your keep and know your place."

Edmund was irritable because he knew he could not do what he came to do until his assistant left for the day. Having an assistant did not change his plans; it only changed how he would carry out those plans.

He would wait until dark.

It was late, very late, on that May night. By the position of the moon, Edmund judged the time to be about two in the morning. He took a deep breath when he walked, sniffing the air. It smelled of soot and chimney smoke, but there was no scent of rain.

The sky was incredibly clear, and the moon was a tiny crescent. Millions of stars sparkled and shimmered, and the sounds were fascinating as the night people went about their business. Edmund took another deep breath of the air, and felt how wonderful it was to be alive in such a world of opportunity.

Silently he traveled through the dark streets of the city until he reached his destination. In this part of town, there were so many possibilities, but he would take the easiest opportunity.

This was the part of town where the desperate people congregated. They would be easy prey for his purposes. Feeling like the predator he was, he moved stealthily and observed everything.

He passed a few ladies of the night, but each one appeared to be too healthy. Like the lions in Africa, he was seeking a victim that was easier prey; one that was damaged either by ill health or intoxication.

And then his eye caught someone moving erratically. The woman was practically dressed in rags and she staggered along the boulevard. He discreetly followed behind her for a while, carefully observing her movements until he felt confident he could overpower her.

As a doctor, he had access to medical supplies. He took a rag out of one pocket and a bottle of ether out of his other pocket. He drenched the rag and then moved quickly to catch up to the intoxicated woman.

He grabbed her shoulder with one hand, and then before she could cry out, his other hand covered her nose and mouth with the rag and she went limp.

He started to drag the woman away when a voice called out to him, "Hey there! What are you doing?"

Edmund answered, "My girlfriend is drunk. I'm taking her home so she doesn't hurt herself."

The man seemed satisfied, because he didn't respond. There were no heroes in this part of town.

After he strangled her, Edmund brought the newly dead woman to the hospital.

The night nurse in the lobby raised a curious eyebrow in his direction.

"Good evening, Doctor Bosworth," she said.

He froze, then put on his most charming smile. "Good evening, Nurse…?"

"Morrow," she supplied. "Eleanor Morrow." Her mouth quirked up in a mischievous, conspiratorial grin as she glanced from Edmund to the bundle he carried. She looked pointedly down at the papers spread before her on the desk. She did not look back up.

Edmund took this as some twisted sign of diving providence and hurried on toward the stairwell.

He paused at the bottom of the basement stairs to take out his key ring. Once inside the Dead House, he dragged the woman over to one of the black tables and strained himself to lift her upon it.

He was unhappy to realize that "Bessie" was still on an adjacent table. She was naked, and Edmund was angry. His assistant was useless!

He took a step closer and looked her over carefully. She appeared to have been washed and the maggots between her breasts were no longer there. He regretted that he had not asked Charles what the complete process was to handle these bodies. Perhaps the assistant's duty was merely to wash them and someone else would handle it from there. He hoped that "someone else" was not him.

He turned his back on Bessie and focused on his new victim. He removed her clothes and dressed her in a hospital gown. He removed a shroud from a drawer and stuffed the dead woman into it and then positioned her as though a hospital attendant had put her on the table.

He scribbled a false name on his victim's card.

Satisfied, he turned to leave the basement.

When morning arrived, he reentered the Dead House to find Charles already there.

"Good morning!" Charles greeted cheerfully. "I see we have a new person to be cleaned."

Edmund didn't respond, but he silently wondered why the hospital felt it needed a doctor for the morgue if the only duties down here were to clean the bodies. When would he finally get to autopsy one?

He knew he was obsessed with autopsies, but he felt the new medical procedure was vital for all doctors in order for them to continue to learn. He wanted to be part of this groundbreaking exploration. It was his right.

"Why is Bessie still here?" He was blunt and to the point.

"Oh, that…" Charles said. "We are having trouble finding her family."

"I thought you said that no permission was given for her autopsy?"

"That's correct. We need to find her family to obtain permission."

"I'm going to autopsy her today. Before she spoils completely."

"But the 1832 Anatomy Act—"

"To hell with that," Edmund said. "If you can't find this Bessie woman's family, then there is no one to complain. And about this new dead body… wash her and get her ready for transport. I have already talked to her family," he lied, "and I will take responsibility for the new body."

"That is not how it works…"

"Who is the boss here? Well, who?"

"You are."

"Then stop being insolent or I will report you to the hospital authorities."

"Yes, sir."

He would wait until dark, then take the new woman to the back door of the closest university. He had a contact there that would pay good money for fresh, clean bodies; no questions asked.

He felt that William Burke had been careless about body snatching and that was why he was caught. Edmund knew that he had an above-average amount of intelligence and that meant he was too clever to need to worry about the police.

In the meantime, he would finally get to autopsy a body.

He stepped over to the woman named Bessie. He stood quietly for a moment, examining her with his eyes and nose. Even though she had been washed and cleaned, her smell was still dreadful.

This was Bessie's fourth day of decomposition. He saw that fluids were leaking from her orifices. She was beginning to liquify, so he hoped he was not too late. Studying the skeleton was a last resort if the rest of her body was ruined, but even that information was valuable if that was all he could get from this dead woman.

He saw a crumbly, white, waxy substance forming on the cheeks, stomach, and thighs; all parts of the body that contained fat.

He recognized the substance as adipocere, the "grave wax," which was some sort of chemical reaction when the dead were exposed to air. He scraped some of the grave wax into an envelope to later be studied under a microscope.

He retrieved his scalpel and positioned it to cut the body, beginning at the sternum. He was surprised that his scalpel did not break the skin. He pushed with more force upon it and the skin dented but held firm.

"Charles!" he bellowed. "This scalpel is defective!"

"I'll get you another," Charles said.

The new scalpel still did not break the skin. Edmund cursed and then commanded, "Get me a knife."

When a knife was placed in his hand, Edmund attempted to cut into her chest once again, but still the skin did not break. He leaned into the knife and pressed with all his might. Sweat from his forehead dripped onto the body.

"I don't know what is happening," Charles said. "This woman is so decomposed that her skin should almost fall off of her body. I've never seen anything like this."

"To hell with it," Edmund said. "I didn't sleep well last night, so I am in no mood for this nonsense. I'm going home. Do whatever you want with this body."

And he punched Bessie's face before he turned around to leave.

It was midnight when Edmund returned to the Dead House. When he opened the morgue door, he was dismayed to discover that Charles had turned off the oil lamps on the walls.

There was a table at the morgue entrance that contained matches. Edmund grabbed a few and entered the Dead House. He lit two lamps inside near the door.

The two lamps barely lit the room at all. Instead, what they did was to produce an eerie effect by creating dancing shadows on the walls. It could seem scary, but again Edmund reminded himself that he was not superstitious. Once a person was dead, they stayed dead. Ghosts did not exist.

He lit two more lamps, and now there was enough light to see further into the room. He glanced at the table that held his victim, and was pleased to see that she had been washed and was ready for delivery to the university.

He would tell his assistant that her family had come in the night to take her.

His eyes moved to the table that once held Bessie. That table was empty, and Edmund felt satisfied that Charles had done whatever one did with a washed body. He suddenly remembered that he had never gotten around to asking his assistant what the complete process entailed. But he felt relieved that whatever that process was, it obviously did not fall to his duties.

He hesitated a moment, wondering if he should light more lamps, but then decided that the fewer lamps he lit meant fewer lamps he had to put out. He could work in the dim morgue, because he only had to grab the dead woman and then get out with her. It would be quick work.

He walked to his victim, then stopped. He thought he heard a sound.

"Charles?" he inquired.

Nothing but silence.

He felt apprehensive. The hairs on his arms prickled and he had an odd feeling like he was being watched. He could feel the sweat on his forehead gather at the hairline. He was shaky and his stomach felt sour.

He surprised himself by recognizing an unfamiliar feeling: fear. He experienced a wave of superstition that overwhelmed him and he suddenly imagined that perhaps the Dead House was not so dead after all.

He became disgusted with himself. "Stop it," he said out loud. But his voice sounded strained in the dark basement, and that unnerved him even more. Maybe he should climb back up the morgue stairs and leave. He couldn't seem to suppress the adrenaline that heightened his fight or flight response.

He would leave, all right, but not without the dead woman on the table.

"Let's proceed, shall we?" he said out loud again. He wanted to console himself, and speaking out loud was like whistling in the dark. He reached his arms out to the murdered victim on the table.

He froze when he heard another noise behind him. This time, it definitely sounded like another person was in the room. He heard a soft rubbing sound, as though someone were brushing up against a wall, stealthily and slowly moving in his direction.

"Who's there?" he called out. "Identify yourself!"

Again there was no response. But this time, Edmund was certain he was not alone. He went to the drawer that held the scalpels and retrieved one.

He turned back around to see movement in the shadows and his stomach turned to ice. He couldn't catch his breath for a moment, and he could hear his heart pounding in his ears.

"I have a weapon!" he announced, unhappy that his voice sounded fearful instead of menacing.

He thought he heard a sighing sound; a soft, wheezing exhale. It had to be Charles; it had to be!

"Charles, I will fire you for this prank!" he tried to shout, but his throat was constricted with tension and only a croak was emitted.

And then the other person in the room stepped into the light.

She was naked and deep into putrefaction. In the dim light, he could see that she had a greenish hue, and once again was infested with maggots that burrowed into the corpse to consume it. Whereas once he could not get a scalpel to penetrate the skin, now the chest and stomach areas had burst open, a result of the build-up of internal gasses. There was an overwhelming smell of rotting eggs.

She no longer looked human; she looked like a hideous monster. Her body appeared marbled with a creamy consistency, and fluid freely leaked from where her chest and stomach had burst open.

This woman was clearly dead, had been dead for some time, yet she moved as though she were alive.

This could not be happening!

He forced himself into action. He ran for the door, completely forgetting about the murdered victim still on the table. He ran in a blind panic; his hands stretched before him on arms that flailed about wildly. He stumbled and looked down at the floor but recovered quickly and looked back up to see the corpse had changed position.

He was stunned by how quickly Bessie moved to block his pathway for escape. She was dead! She could not move! Yet she moved.

Fully terrorized now, Edmund fell to his knees. "You can't blame me for your death!" he cried. "I don't even know who you are!'

A cool breeze blew over him, chilling him. He shivered badly and he didn't know if it was from fright or from the cold. He heard someone sobbing and was surprised to realize it was him crying. He put his arms over his head, trying to shield himself from whatever was to come.

A voice penetrated his fear, and it sounded unearthly—warbling like the voice of a really old woman on her deathbed.

"Say my name."

He wasn't sure if he heard it correctly, or if he even heard it at all.

"Say my name!" The dead woman's voice was suddenly strong.

"Bessie," Edmund sobbed. "Please, Bessie… I didn't kill you. It's not me you should be angry at! Let me go and I promise not to come back here ever again! Please, just let me go and I will change my ways. I promise!"

He closed his eyes but opened them when he heard the dead woman move once again. He was horrified to see that she was closer now; right above where he knelt. He tried to make himself smaller, but in his gut, he knew he was doomed.

He saw her reach a rotted hand out to him and when she touched his shoulder, he felt an electric shock course through him. He felt his heart lurch, and his throat closed so that no breath could travel through it.

He had visions of spectral phantoms moving through the basement, and he understood that he had been very wrong about the afterlife and its powers. The shimmering ghosts seem to swirl for a few moments and then gathered in a single spot. He recognized his assistant in the center of the spirits; they rotated around him as though he were the eye of a hurricane.

He felt a desperate hope that he could have a sort of kinship with the only other living person in the room. He silently begged his assistant to help him; to ward off the dead woman that had once been Bessie.

Maybe there was still time… maybe he could still be saved from a horrible fate!

And then Charles finally spoke. "You never had an assistant. The hospital never hired me, because I am not of the mortal world. I am the protector of this morgue, the defender of the helpless. I too am dead, just as you now are. You will be doomed to spend eternity here, just as I am. Together we will haunt this hospital in an eternal fight of good against evil."

And Edmund was allowed to rise to a standing position as he saw his own body lying motionless on the stone floor beneath him.

Tunnels
1986

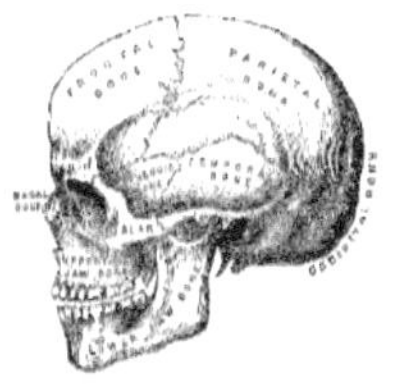

Residue
Simon Bleaken

In the last dwindling decades of its active operational life, Lychhurst Hospital, a place that had seen more than its fair share of births over its long and troubled history, gave one final and unexpected existence to the world.

Although constructed as a sanctuary of healing, scandals and tragedy had clustered around Lychhurst since its founding in 1844. Most who came through its doors felt a shiver, as if aware on some deeply subconscious level that something was terribly wrong with the place, even if they couldn't say why.

All hospitals were haunted, of course, being transitional portals where souls entered and left the world each day, and where grief and trauma, joy and hope, were focused within a single structure like nowhere else. But still, few hospitals felt like Lychhurst.

The scent of death lingered in every breath taken by the living, and visitors and patients alike reported feeling watched constantly. Voices could be heard drifting faintly through the vents from within empty rooms, or down the long gloomy stairwells. Locked doors had a frequent habit of swinging open.

People dressed in clothing styles decades out of date were frequently seen getting into elevators only to never exit on any of the floors. Objects and equipment rarely remained where they had been left, sometimes even disappearing entirely. And hollow echoes of disembodied souls whispered along the dark hallways each night, or were glimpsed as curious shadow figures caught by the flicker of the lights as they flitted through the wards.

The hospital had been an abnormal thing from its very beginning. Set out in a basic cross-shaped floor plan, it should have been easy to navigate, but somehow, once inside those doors everything seemed to shift and warp, becoming a confusing warren of rooms and hallways, as if the internal structure existed in open defiance of any outward plan.

It soon acquired a sinister reputation among those living nearby.

But few could have suspected what lay within the miles of tunnels that ran like a dense warren beneath it all.

In that gloomy maze, far from the bright lights and sterile rooms where the miracle of birth (and the release of death) occurred so often, another secret miracle had taken place, albeit a darkly twisted one.

It was a newborn, of sorts; not actually a life, nor created in the darkness of the womb, but something conscious that was born out of the shadows beneath the ground.

It was the only thing the hospital had truly given to the world.

It began as a residue, gathering for decades down in the darkness. There had been no midwife to oversee the arrival of this new entity; its soul was stillborn. It had floated aimlessly for decades. Not a physical thing, but a festering accumulation of dark emotion, lost and confused, rats and roaches scuttling in terror as it traveled the tunnels.

It had no former life to recall, nor any true understanding of the feelings and thoughts flowing through it. The lessons and experiences of childhood, and those learned through interactions with others, were utterly alien to this entity. It operated solely on instinct.

It gathered and rested in the cracks between the bricks, lurked behind the boards, and coiled greasily about the cables that riddled its hidden domain, though it spent most of its time around the old death chute that had once ferried bodies down to hearses in times gone by.

It took the energy it needed from its environment, absorbing everything that came close to it, even pulling the heat from the air and drawing power from the cables and emergency lights, often burning them out.

It didn't grow, not exactly, but it used the energy to become stronger and to manipulate the world around it in lieu of a physical body.

Eventually, almost imperceptibly, it became aware of itself, consciousness awakening like a smoldering ember gradually being stoked into a flame.

It spoke with the wheezing cough of the tuberculosis victim, and chuckled with the wild, throaty gurgle of a restrained lunatic. It stretched out, reaching through the tiny spaces and forgotten gaps of the tunnels.

Brooding in shadow, it began to think and then finally to hunger for more.

Here it had gathered, stitched, and sutured into itself all the broken and diseased fragments of spiritual energy filtering down into this neglected recess deep below the hospital.

Like some Frankenstein's monster, cobbled together from the energies of dozens of different beings, it had slowly formed an amalgamated whole. Not a true gestalt, it had only one consciousness, and like an infant, it had taken time to grow, learn, and absorb knowledge of the world and its place within it.

Gradually, as it explored its subterranean domain, it learned to better interact with the physical environment around it, discovering how to move and collect objects, drawing them around itself like armor. Within months it had crafted a crude physical shell to hide within, a nightmare conglomeration scraped together from the discarded pieces it encountered.

As with any infant, its first steps were slow, clumsy and faltering.

But it soon learned to master this new form, and reveled in it.

Its hypodermic fingers scratched the walls as it patrolled, and its mouth bristled with discarded scalpel-blade teeth. It lumbered on constructs of old crutches, broken wheelchairs, and twisted fragments of rusting beds.

It could abandon this artificial body at will if it needed to be quick or silent, or wanted to hide, but it liked the feel and weight of the metal limbs as they scraped and clanked and dragged.

It also used them to crush the rats that weren't fast enough.

It didn't eat them, of course. It felt no physical hunger; that impulse belonged to the realm of the living. But it understood the need for energy. So, instead, it absorbed something from the rats, some sort of life essence that gave it renewed vitality. It was different from the power it stole from the lights and the cables. It was… *delicious,* and far more satisfying.

The rats soon grew wise and became cautious, but it was patient.

It had learned to wait, to listen.

It knew all of the tunnels in its network, every corner and alcove, every crevice and hiding space. But it never left this area for the strange, clean lights above. Its empire ended at the long narrow staircases that stretched up toward an alien world of muffled sounds and constant activity.

That was unknown territory and filled with uncertain dangers.

Down here, hidden alone in the dark or wrapped in its armor of discarded junk, it was safe.

Or so it thought, until a stranger entered its world.

It had been the pale spirit of a small boy, lost and lonely, dressed in a hospital gown of a style from several decades past. In one hand, the boy clutched a yellow ball. His other arm was gone, lost to injury and amputation.

This ghostly child had just wandered quietly into the tunnels one evening as if exploring, the echoing patter of his bare feet announcing his presence seconds before his willowy frame turned the corner near the top of the death chute.

It had screamed at the sight of him—recoiled in startled terror from this tiny specter, shedding its accumulated armor across the tunnel floor like leaves in a fall breeze as it fled down the hallway in panic.

"Hello?"

The boy had followed, his hollow eyes filled with curiosity.

"Do you live down here?" the child whispered, finally finding it curled in the darkness, trying to hide. "Don't be scared. I won't hurt you."

It had quivered, curling itself up tighter into a dense pool of shadow.

"My name's Tom," the boy announced as he sat next to it, watching with hopeful interest. "I got so bored up there. I've been waiting for ages for someone to talk to. I've been here so long, but nobody ever talks to me."

Slowly it began to relax, to listen and uncoil.

"So, what *are* you?" the boy asked gently.

The darkness spread itself out a little more.

"Do you want to be my friend? Nobody upstairs does. Well, none of the good ones, I mean. Some of them are scary and bad. I stay away from them."

The boy's energy was weak and shimmered like sunlight through water, smelling of residual life, an echo of existence.

"Can you talk?"

It extended a slender black arm, spread inky talons wide, and cocked its head, appraising this curious being that was smiling so innocently at it.

"Do you have a name?"

It wondered how this one would taste.

It pounced, drawing the terrified and screaming child into itself, absorbing the boy's energy just as it fed on the rats and the power cables.

But, if it had hoped for some marvelous new source of sustenance, it was sorely disappointed. The boy's energy was weak, as insubstantial as the child itself had been, an echo of life rather than something that held any vitality.

It let the rest of the essence dissipate into the environment, unsatisfied, and went back to drawing on the energy from the rats and cables.

It retained one valuable thing from the encounter, though. It took the boy's name and kept it for itself. It practiced saying it over and over for months, a rasping wheeze in the darkness.

Over the following decades, several more spirits found their way down into the tunnels. Tom had stalked and hunted them, observing them with interest before drawing them in too, hoping they would provide better nourishment than the boy had.

But again, it felt hollow and unsatisfied by the weak residual energy they provided, and vowed to leave any other spirits well alone in future.

Even so, there were many voices crowding inside it now, but Tom learned to strangle them into silence, to shape and funnel the chaos of its creation into a single thought, a single mind crafted from half-remembered impulses and shards of stolen memory.

Tom had grown so much over the years, and had expanded through the darkness of the tunnels. But that wasn't enough to satiate it. It always wanted more.

It lay in the dark listening to the noises from the world above, feeling the life and death energies that rippled through the hospital, some ebbing, some growing, and it wondered what was up there, though was too afraid to explore.

From time to time, different invaders entered its realm. These were physical creatures, clad in hard hats and dirty clothing. They smelled of sweat and life and substance. Tom came to learn these were *people*, sent down from the unknown above to check on the pipes and wiring.

For a long time, Tom hid whenever these strangers appeared, studying them from the cracks and nooks, but just as with the dead child so many years earlier, it gradually grew bolder and curious about these fleshy beings.

It began to wonder what these new entities would taste like. They seemed far more vibrant than the specters infesting the hospital, closer in nature to the rats on which it fed as often as it could; only these creatures were far larger.

Curiosity finally beating its fear, Tom decided the next time these humans entered the tunnels, it would find out.

That day came several weeks later.

"It's a real maze down here," a voice echoed through the darkness, followed by the sweeping beam of a flashlight and the sound of approaching footfalls.

"Watch your step, Nick. Not all these lights work."

Intrigued by the new voices in its domain, Tom stirred and moved closer, readying claws of inky blackness lest it need to defend itself. It thought about donning its armor, but decided stealth was better than force to assess these new arrivals.

"Thanks for the warning, Steve. This'd be a hell of a place to get lost in."

"Always carry spare batteries or a backup flashlight, that's my motto."

Nick swallowed nervously as he shone his beam down the seemingly endless stretches of tunnel. "Jeez, yeah, can you imagine being down here in the dark?"

"Don't even joke about that," Steve cautioned. "These tunnels go quite a way."

Nick tapped a dead light bulb set on the wall. "Isn't this something we should be fixing? Isn't it dangerous having so many of these out?"

"With our budget? You're kidding, right? Look, we replace them as often as we can. Damn things just keep burning out. There's a limit to what we can spend on these non-essential areas."

"Seems pretty essential right now."

"Hey, don't let this place get to you," Steve chuckled, sweeping his flashlight across the old walls. "Sure, it's creepy, but that's all. I've never once seen anything odd down here. That's more than I can say for the hospital."

"What do you mean?"

Steve stared at him in surprise. "You don't know Lychhurst's reputation?"

"What reputation?"

"Ah, I forgot. You're new in town. Well, let's just say that stuff goes on up there you wouldn't believe."

"Like what?"

Steve shrugged, feigning nonchalance, but kept a careful eye on his colleague to gauge the reaction to his words.

"Oh, you know, strange noises, stuff moving around by itself, you name it. There are some really messed up stories connected to this place; some odd deaths, too."

"Seriously?"

"Give it a few months. You'll have plenty of stories of your own. Everyone does."

"Yeah, but have you ever actually *seen* a ghost?"

Steve sighed. "Tell you what, you free later? We'll grab a beer after work and talk then. But not down here, okay?"

"Why, do you… think something's *listening*?"

Steve laughed uneasily. "No. Jeez, at least I hope not. Look, it's bad enough having to come down here in the first place. I don't want us getting spooked and distracted, because then I have to come back again to fix your mistakes. And I hate coming down here."

"I'm already spooked—how can you *not* be? I mean, *look* at this place."

"Don't go doing a half-assed job," Steve warned. "I'll send you down here all the time if you do."

Tom approached the men, invisible in the gloom, needle-fingers clicking in anticipation and a thin wheeze echoing from its throat.

Nick tensed and glanced around. "Did you hear that?"

"Aw, see, that's what I'm talking about. Don't let your imagination get the better of you, kid. We've still got half a dozen cables to check and I want to be done by five."

"Yeah, but I…"

"Tell you what, you go take the east tunnel and I'll check south."

"You'd better be kidding me."

"You wanna get this done faster? We need to find the faults quickly."

"Yeah, but… splitting up is always a bad idea."

"I knew I shouldn't have told you about the ghost stories. Go on, you'll be fine. There's never been anything down here."

"You sure? I swear I just heard…"

"Probably just rats, we get them down here. Don't worry; they're more scared of you. Just watch yourself, okay? The lights are real bad down there."

"Wait, are you giving me the short straw?"

Steve nodded. "You're the newbie. It's the rules."

Nick moved off down the tunnel, muttering under his breath, the flashlight beam sweeping quickly left to right as he went. The light played across the walls and danced through forests of old pipes, sometimes plunging into the hearts of abandoned storerooms and forgotten spaces filled with sinister hulks of broken equipment and furniture.

Thick black-grey veils of ancient cobwebs hung from the wires overhead like soiled bunting, tickling his hair as he passed. The floor beneath his feet was heavy with grime that had accumulated over the years. In places, broken glass crunched underfoot, and there was a foul rankness to the stale air.

"Can't believe they can't even get the fucking lights working," he grumbled, turning off down a side passage and past a thick cluster of dusty pipes that loomed out of the blackness.

Tom followed him curiously, noting the way the man's smell grew stronger—he was perspiring, nervous. His breathing was faster too.

Tom waited until the man had gone far enough down the tunnel to be suitably separated from his colleague before drawing closer. The lights here were broken, the shadows deep enough to conceal its inky manifestation. It was interested to see how this one would behave, how it might react.

In places, parts of the walls had crumbled slightly, and it seized a small fragment of stone and threw it along the passageway.

The man tensed, the torch snapping around as the debris skittered past his foot.

"*Steve?*" His voice sounded choked as he stared down the empty tunnel. "That you messing around?"

The sweat stench grew stronger. Tom smiled. It enjoyed toying with the rats. They tasted better when they were scared, and gave off more energy too. It hoped this human would be the same. Playfully, it edged closer and whispered its name in a drawn-out guttural wheeze.

"*Toooooooommmmm…*"

"Steve, I swear to God, if that's you…"

The man glanced around anxiously, light flicking across walls, the floor, momentarily passing over a darker shadow that seemed to be clinging to the pipes, a shadow that the light didn't banish. The flashlight beam snapped back on the spot, but the shadow had already moved, not ready to give the game away just yet.

"No," the man said firmly, though his voice was unsteady, "it's just those stupid ghost stories. Get a grip. There's nothing here."

Tom held back, watching as the man carried on, his pace a little faster, the flashlight beam moving quicker too, as if he were trying to light every part of the corridor simultaneously.

Then Tom rushed past him, going deeper into the tunnels.

It was time to don the armor.

The first Nick knew of this was a heavy clanging from up ahead, as if a dozen metal bed frames were being beaten against the ground like oversized drumsticks. It was a sound that drew rapidly closer and sent a cold shudder of alarm through him.

"Steve?"

He took an unsteady step backward, tripped over a pile of old bricks, and landed heavily on his backside, eyes wide and a thin, whimpering wail escaping his lips.

His flashlight rattled as it rolled on the stone floor, the light glinting on something metallic for a second before darkness took it again, leaving him with the impression that there was some kind of twisted metal skeleton looming in the blackness ahead.

"Ste—" was all that left his lips.

Tom lurched out of the darkness and into the beam of the flashlight, clanking clumsily forward, needles and blades glinting as they swept through the air, excitement and hunger for living energy stripping away decades of careful control.

Nick sprang to his feet and tried to bolt down the hallway. The metal shape lashed out with its arm and swept his legs from under him.

Nick landed heavily, knees and nose cracking against the stone floor. As the shape lumbered nearer, Nick forced himself upward with a thin, warbling shriek, his lower face a mask of blood. He staggered down the passage, confused and shocked, plunging into half-darkness where lights flickered and fizzed.

The impossible conglomeration of broken parts crashed after him, gaining speed as it went. Its heavy bed-post foot struck the flashlight as it gave chase, sending it spinning in a circular motion, turning the stretch of hallway into a wild dance of light and shadow and further enhancing the disorienting, nightmare quality of the moment.

This was better than hunting rats, Tom decided.

It channeled the effort with which it maintained its physical armor into increasing its speed, causing parts of its shell of rusting debris to fall away as it bore down upon the fleeing man, scattering twisted pieces of metal, glass, and equipment behind it in a clattering riot of sound.

Nick stumbled through the darkness, aiming for the distant glow of the lights up ahead that still worked. His lungs burned and his broken nose was a white-hot mass of pain, but he barely felt any of it in the adrenaline-fueled race for survival.

The clanging of the monstrosity behind him rang in his ears above the frantic pounding of his own pulse, but he didn't dare look back. He didn't even waste time screaming, pushing every ounce of energy into moving as fast as possible.

He knew the stairs were nearby—but where? There were no discernible landmarks to guide him, and he could only guess at how many branching tunnels he'd blundered past already.

He turned to the left and found himself emerging into a well-lit section of tunnel, hesitating for a moment at an intersection. It took far longer than it should have to spot the sign on the wall, ancient and dirty, but just still legible. The nearest stairs were off to the right.

He could still hear the entity pursuing him, a hellish scraping and clattering, the pained squeal of metal grinding against metal and dragging against stone. It seemed so loud in the enclosed space, Nick wondered why the entire hospital hadn't come pouring down here to see what all the noise was—but then he remembered how thick the tunnel walls were, and how deep.

He had never felt so isolated before.

Up ahead, a beam of light flashed down the hallway. Steve came hurrying into view, red-faced and out of breath.

"Nick, what the *hell*?" Steve gasped. "What's all the noi…"

His voice trailed off, his eyes widening at the sight of the impossible mass of accumulated items moving like a living body as it thundered along the hallway.

"*Run*!" Nick barreled past him without slowing.

But Steve didn't move. He just stared, slack-jawed and frozen, flashlight locked in a trembling grip.

That was when Tom shed the rest of its armor, the mass of objects tumbling away in a clamorous crash as icy shadows seeped like black fog from around those collapsing artificial limbs.

It kept a hold on the scalpel blades, though.

It would need claws for what was to come.

Steve's eyes were wide, and a squeezing pressure was spreading painfully across his shoulder and neck, clenching like a clamp across his upper belly. He didn't realize it was his heart giving out.

He gave a gasping wheeze, and then that inky mass descended upon him like a dark wave, sweeping him into oblivion before the heart attack could finish the job.

Metal savagely parted flesh and cloth in frenzied and violent strokes as Tom ripped into the man's physical form with its scalpel blades and burrowed inside those bleeding lacerations. It coiled within that still-warm shell, drinking deeply.

This was what Tom had been craving for so long: living energy. It swallowed it all like a rich and nourishing elixir, a burst of pure energy far more satisfying than anything ever leached from the cables and pipes and rats—energy filled with the glorious vibrancy of life.

It took what it needed, leaving behind the desiccated and torn remnants of anything that was of no use to it.

Then, sloughing off the rest of that shredded meat, Tom turned its attention to the other man. It could still hear him, crashing and lumbering through its domain, lost in the semi-dark maze of flickering lights.

*

Nick staggered down the passageway, aware on some distant level that Steve hadn't followed, but too terrified to look back. Everything down here felt endless, as if every path to the world above had simply vanished.

Then, up ahead, he saw the door to a stairwell.

A glimmer of hope flared in his heart, and he forced himself onward, heels stinging as he coaxed more speed out of his legs than he ever had before.

His body, more accustomed to delivery pizzas and Blockbuster rentals than running, protested painfully, and he blinked sweat from his eyes as he gasped for air in the suffocating confines of the tunnel that now seemed chokingly hot and narrow. His racing pulse flooded his ears, blocking out all other sounds.

He almost cried out as his fingers closed around the cold handle of the door. He tugged it open and raced through, a faint smile forming on his bloody face.

He could see the exit door high above, the one that opened into the staff corridor, where the storerooms, post room, and Facilities offices were housed. With another uncharacteristic burst of speed, he started up the steps.

That was when the door behind him crashed open.

Something black and icy slammed into him, driving him against the wall and slugging the air from his lungs. He gave a gasping, reedy shriek as a jagged shard of rusted metal pierced his shoulder like a knife blade.

Then he slipped, tumbling down the stairs to land in a heap at the bottom.

Painfully, groggily, Nick lifted his head. Over the frantic pulse of his heart and the coppery taint of blood where he had bitten his tongue, he could feel a coldness spreading through his limbs and torso.

His shoulder was a mass of hot agony more painful than his broken nose. The fall had plunged the shard more deeply into his flesh, and blood was trickling down his chest. In a panic, he touched the end of the metal with shaking fingers, trying to decide if he should pull it out or not.

Then, too late, he remembered the inky shape that had pursued him.

He turned and it was upon him.

Tom pressed its cold, ethereal claws against Nick's skull. The man trembled as he tried to scream, but Tom didn't allow him to waste any of that energy. It plunged down his throat, seeping through his nose and ears, flowing inside his warm, living body.

Nick clawed weakly at the bottom step as the alien presence suffused him.

He wanted to cry out, to scream, but something was blocking his throat, cutting off his air. He felt weak and giddy, and the world around him was getting darker. At first, he thought the few remaining lights were going out, but somewhere deep in his spinning, confused consciousness came the shocking realization that *he* was the one that was going out.

Inside its victim, Tom explored every inch of this incredible feast, feeling the fast pulse of the human's heart, the warm rush of blood, and the sparking impulses that danced along nerves and flickered in the brain. Why had it waited so long before hunting these creatures? This was ecstasy.

Tom closed its eyes, bathing in the rich sensations… and then, it drank deeply.

The body bucked and thrashed, muscles twitching and limbs trembling, fists and feet beating a final drumbeat against the stone.

But Tom kept a tight rein on his prize. Nothing must be wasted.

Within moments, it was all over.

Nick lay dead and cold on the floor, all life and heat absorbed by the spectral shadows now pouring from his mouth and nose like some ghostly death veil.

Tom stretched and smiled as it left the body, its hunger sated. Then, it quickly dragged both of the bodies away and hid them down in the deepest part of its domain. It knew that these creatures would be missed, that other people would come looking for them, and it didn't want to give itself away.

But Tom knew all the best hiding places.

After carefully disposing of the remains, Tom crept back to the stairwell, drawn by an insatiable curiosity to that distant door so far above. This was entirely new territory, further than it had ever dared go before, closer to the lowest level of the hospital.

It listened, and marveled at the sounds from up there.

There was a new world just waiting for it to explore at the top of that staircase; a rich cornucopia of energy to be savored.

There would likely be even more delicious humans to feed upon, and who knew what else.

Curiously, hungrily, it studied those stairs.

And cautiously, growing braver, Tom began to creep upward.

Nurses Station
1844

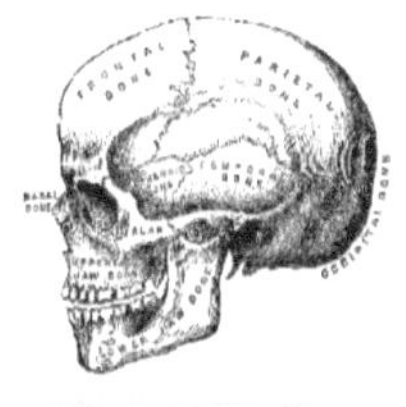

A Dark House
Heather Daughrity

"A dark house is always an unhealthy house, always an ill-aired house, always a dirty house. … People lose their health in a dark house, and if they get ill, they cannot get well again in it."
{Florence Nightingale - *Notes on Nursing: What It Is, and What It Is Not*}

It would be less awful, perhaps, to say that Nurse Morrow came to Lychhurst sweet and unspoiled, an innocent caught up in the evil that dwelt, even in the beginning, in the darkness of Lychhurst's long corridors and lightless tunnels.

It would be understandable, preferable even, to look upon her with a sympathetic gaze, to view her as only an instrument through which the hospital enacted its ghastly nighttime deeds.

But that would be dishonest, for Eleanor Morrow came to Lychhurst carrying a darkness of her own.

Most bright-eyed young women entered the field of nursing with a strong desire to help, to comfort, and to heal, compelled by that maternal instinct that resides within most members of the female sex.

Eleanor Morrow entered that same field with a different kind of desire and compulsion. Behind her lovely eyes, behind that perfectly curved orbital socket that housed them, lived a brain full of brilliant yet bloody ideas. Within her heated bosom beat a heart that yearned to conquer and control, to exercise power over life and death.

Lychhurst was the perfect place to achieve her most menacing and malignant fantasies.

Eleanor was hired on at Lychhurst in the spring of 1844 and was in attendance when the building first opened to the wealthy throngs that would serve as both patrons and patients for the first two decades of its existence.

She watched as the affluent of the area poured through the front doors, the hallways and high-ceilinged rooms lit with warm and friendly flames housed in hundreds of elaborate sconces along the walls.

In her mind, she repeated the words each nurse had been required to learn:

Hello! My name is Nurse Eleanor Morrow, and I will be taking care of you during your time here at Lychhurst. If there is anything I can do to make your stay more comfortable, please let me know.

She caught the eye of many a well-dressed gentleman as she stood among the other nurses, her own eyes demurely downcast and the smile that played at her lips both deliciously sinister and deceptively soft.

Eleanor was used to the attentions of men—a pretty face and supple body had ensured no shortage of looks and leers and unwanted advances over the years—but only one man held *her* attention.

Zeke Barnett.

The Barnett family owned Lychhurst, though the story of that ownership was one fraught with bloody rumors. Zeke had returned home from his time fighting the British in the War of 1812 and had taken it upon himself to use his father's money to buy up every last acre of hill and hollow in and around his hometown of Oleander.

Most of the poor mountain folk had been willing enough to give up their homesteads for a price, except for Sadie Nelson, who had lived on that particular patch of mountain for longer than anyone could remember, her numerous descendants spreading outward like spokes on a wheel from the hub that was Granny Sadie's cabin.

Sadie had put up a years-long fight against Zeke, years in which Zeke's patience in waiting for the old hag to die had worn thin. Finally, he had taken that particular passing into his own hands, and with Sadie gone—with a curse upon her lips as she went, so the rumors said—Zeke was able to buy up the land on which Lychhurst now sat.

Eleanor often lay in her bed in the small, spare attic room afforded to her as a resident nurse at Lychhurst, musing with malicious glee over whether or not Zeke had the slightest idea what he had done when he chose this particular hillock on which to build his new hospital.

She felt almost certain that he had no idea what the name of the place— stolen from Granny Sadie—even meant.

Lychhurst. Corpse Hill.

The Nelson family's burying grounds for gods-only-knew how long.

He had murdered Sadie and then built his house of healing upon her ancestors' graves.

A bad omen, even for someone as uncaring as Zeke Barnett.

At least thirty years her senior, ugly and ornery as they came, still Mr. Barnett held a strange attraction for young Ellie. For what Ellie desired more than anything was power, and Zeke had that thing that would help her attain it: money.

As the spring turned to summer and Lychhurst's rooms filled with spoiled, rich patrons come to relax and convalesce among the shady paths and cooling ponds that surrounded the estate, Nurse Morrow went about her tasks dutifully, offering pampering and coddling more than actual medical care.

Day after day, she presented the lovely smile that hid the truth dwelling within her and welcomed new patients with the well-practiced words:

Hello. My name is Nurse Eleanor Morrow, and I will be taking care of you during your time here at Lychhurst. If there is anything I can do to make your stay more comfortable, please let me know.

In her hours off-shift, she made friends with a special duo of young boys.

Charles and Thomas Morrow, Zeke's sons from a wife years in her grave—dead from the bearing of that younger son—were often given the run of the place, racing and shouting down the halls, much to the amusement of the patrons and the chagrin of the nurses.

Ten-year-old Charles was loud and boisterous, always laughing, always up to one trick or another. Eight-year-old Thomas was quiet, reserved, often found curled up in a corner somewhere with a book or playing quietly among the trees with his favorite yellow ball.

As summer turned to autumn, Eleanor ingratiated herself to the boys and their father, flashing mischievous smiles and funny faces toward the former and shyly suggestive pouts and wanton glances in the direction of the latter.

By the first early snows of December, even a man as clueless as Zeke Barnett had caught on to Ellie's interest, and the hard lines of his face had begun to soften whenever she entered the room, skirts swishing around her, showing just a hint of shapely ankle, her smile reserved but inviting, her body doubly so.

For Christmas, the boys each received a new set of ice skates, razor sharp and ready for racing across the pond in back of the hospital.

That same evening, Mr. Barnett invited Nurse Morrow into his private rooms well after dark, and his long-neglected needs flamed to life, a groan escaping from his lips as Ellie undid his trousers, dropping to her knees on the plush carpet before him, speaking those familiar words given sly new meaning:

Hello. My name is Nurse Eleanor Morrow, and I will be taking care of you during your time here at Lychhurst. If there is anything I can do to make your stay more comfortable, please let me know.

This scenario would be repeated nightly for the next week.

It would not be long now, she was certain, until she had all the power she desired gripped as firmly in her hands as Mr. Barnett's desperately throbbing manhood.

On New Year's Day, Eleanor looked up, startled, when an ear-splitting scream reverberated through the hospital, up each stairway and along every corridor until it reached her where she worked, organizing the medical supply cabinet in back of the Nurses Station on the second floor.

Heart pounding, she rushed toward the sound and the gathering crowd in the lobby. Already the doctors and her fellow nurses were pushing back the group of gawking patrons, clearing a space around the bloody spectacle in the middle of the great room.

The massive front doors stood open, and along the floor a trail of crimson stains was already freezing in the chill wind that blew flurries of snow in upon them all. The trail stopped where Mr. Barnett knelt on the marble, young Thomas's body in his arms, shouting for help with a voice strangled and desperate.

Eleanor assessed the situation quickly with her highly-trained nurse's eyes. Thomas's left arm hung useless at his side, great gashes nearly severing it from the shoulder, the dull glint of bloody bone showing through the lacerated skin.

The boy's head hung backward over the crook of his father's elbow, eyes glazed in a combination of shock and pain.

Ellie looked around, her head cool in the midst of the rising panic that filled the space. In one of the adjoining corridors, she spied a gurney. She commandeered it and pushed her way through the crowd, the gurney's wheels screeching sharply, adding to the cacophony and the chaos.

Dr. Ward, an older man, knelt next to Mr. Barnett, trying to make sense of the story of what happened—a babbling, barely coherent story of the frozen pond, a fall, a tangle of limbs, Charlie's ice skates.

A trembling thrill passed through Eleanor's body at the thought of those razor-sharp blades and the ease with which they would slice through skin and tendon, muscle and bone and nerves.

"Here, Dr. Ward." She spoke quietly but firmly. "We must get him to surgery immediately."

Mr. Barnett was helped to his feet, the boy still clutched in his arms. He lay Thomas down carefully on the gurney, nothing but a small moan escaping the child's lips as he was moved.

Eleanor laid a hand on Mr. Barnett's arm, a gesture that appeared comforting yet hid within it a secret triumph—if she could see him through this tragedy, she felt sure that her place at his side would be secured.

He shrugged her hand off without glancing at her, pushing her away with the rest of the onlookers as he followed Dr. Wade and the gurney with the screeching wheel to the state-of-the-art elevator lift, shouting for the men who manned the pulleys to be at the ready. The surgery theater waited at the top of Lychhurst's central tower.

Eleanor stood silent, ignored, staring after them as the crowd dispersed. Her lips were set into a thin line of disbelief and rage, and in her eyes a new fire, baleful and cold, flamed to life.

That night, when the gas lamps were turned to their lowest flickering glow and only a skeleton crew of nighttime attendants kept watch, Nurse Morrow walked the shadowy halls of Lychhurst Hospital, silent and invisible as a ghost.

She stopped first at the Nurses Station on the second floor, slipping unseen into the same supply closet that she had been organizing earlier that day when the scream had drawn her away from her work. When she left the room, the right-hand pocket of her apron bulged in a way it had not moments before.

She crept quietly down the hall, past the soaring surgical theater with its glass roof, pale moonlight reflecting on the wooden risers that lined its walls. Near the end of the hall, she paused, glancing about her.

She was alone.

The room was dim when she entered it. Thomas's body looked impossibly small in the adult-sized bed. His right arm rested at his side, his small hand atop the blankets that bunched around his hips.

His left arm was gone.

A lump of bloody bandages was held in place against his shoulder with countless layers of gauze that wrapped around his thin chest beneath a pale hospital gown.

Eleanor stood over him for a few moments, watching him in the dark. His chest rose and fell in painfully fragile breaths, and his head turned back and forth against pillows damp with sweat as his mind fought its way away from the pain.

Ellie sat beside Tom on the bed and brushed a shock of hair away from his face. His eyelids fluttered and his mouth opened and closed—a fish gasping for air.

"Shh," Ellie whispered, leaning down close to the boy's face. "Quiet now, Tom. It's only me."

Tom's eyebrows furrowed in confusion. He did not recognize her through the haze of medication.

Ellie's breath brushed against his cheek as she whispered:

Hello. My name is Nurse Eleanor Morrow, and I will be taking care of you during your time here at Lychhurst. If there is anything I can do to make your stay more comfortable, please let me know.

From her apron pocket, Ellie pulled a cloth and a small brown bottle. She hummed a tune as she poured the contents of the bottle onto the cloth, and the humming grew louder as she placed the cloth over Tom's mouth and nose.

He struggled for a brief moment before his body fell limp once more, the ether doing its blessed work.

Ellie took a moment to simply sit and look at the boy's delicate features, the slightest pang of mercy thrumming through her—perhaps some small moment of maternal instinct after all.

Then she picked up one of the extra pillows that adorned the bed and placed it over Tom's face, pressing down firmly but gently. In her head she performed a slow, steady count from one to one thousand.

The hospital breathed its quiet, slumbering breath around them as the life left Tom's body. In still rooms and quiet corners, shadows shimmered with a slow but building energy as Lychhurst soaked up the small boy's final moments of life and first glorious moments of death.

The thrill that coursed through Ellie's body rivaled the hospital's own ecstasy.

She placed the pillow back carefully and smoothed the sheets as she stood. She tucked the bottle of ether and the cloth away in her pocket, giving the room one final glance before she slipped back through the door and into the hallway beyond, creeping quietly up the back stairs to her own room, where she slept more soundly than she had slept in many months.

The hospital was draped in black for the remainder of the winter. Mr. Barnett appeared less and less, content to spend his days alone in mourning with his one living son at their family estate, well away from the place where little Tom had passed away, his young body clearly unable to hold up under the stress and strain—not to mention blood loss—of his injury.

Eleanor found that she did not miss him. Her goal of marriage and the resources that would accompany it had disappeared, her mind and body now focused on a constant search for that thrill that she had felt at Tom's bedside that fateful January night.

A thrill that the following years would afford her many opportunities to savor.

She found that she liked the night shifts best, and the other nurses were happy to leave her to them.

She held court each evening at the Nurses Station, ensuring that all patients were sleeping soundly in their beds and all staff were busy at whatever tasks passed the torturously slow minutes of their shifts.

During the long hours of darkness, Eleanor explored and discovered all the secrets Lychhurst had to offer. The walls sighed beneath her caresses; the dancing flames of the gaslights whispered sweet, sighing words as she passed. The tunnels echoed back her own footsteps to her, the reverberations thrumming through her body in pleasure no man could replicate.

And sometimes, in the small hours of the morning, as she sat at a patient's bedside, her hand reached into her right apron pocket and pulled out a small brown bottle and a cloth. In those stolen moments her soul vibrated with a euphoric trembling as the living, breathing body before her released its grip on the spirit within it.

It was no great sorrow to Nurse Eleanor Morrow when she realized that her own body was failing her. Too much time around ailing patients or too much time wandering the damp tunnels below the hospital—whatever the reason, the cause, the source, Eleanor grew weak and ill.

For two decades, she had haunted the nighttime halls of Lychhurst Hospital, dispensing merciful death as she saw fit, and when it came her own time to die, she had no desire to leave those hallowed halls behind.

She visited the Nurses Station one final time, that night when she knew her time was as short as her breaths. She ran her eyes and fingers over the sleek wooden surfaces, stacked a few loose papers, and straightened the boxes upon the shelves.

Then down into the tunnels she went. In her apron's right-hand pocket, a carefully capped syringe rested, the blessed instrument of her own destruction, filled with a clear liquid drawn from a bottle marked with a skull and crossbones.

The needle entered her arm with all the sweet tenderness of a lover, and the drug coursed through her veins in a ringing, stinging river of rapturous release.

Eleanor's lips moved in soundless speech as the poison did its work, forming words that tethered her there, binding her soul to that place where she had known her happiest, darkest, most gloriously secret hours.

Hello. My name is Nurse Eleanor Morrow, and I will be taking care of you during your time here at Lychhurst. If there is anything I can do to make your stay more comfortable, please let me know.

Farewell

Ah, yes! You did make it back. I'm so glad.

Though I must say, you're looking even worse now than when you first arrived. Perhaps I've put you through a little too much.

Not to worry. Here, let's just lay you down on this lovely little gurney right here, waiting, prepped and ready for you.

It's my favorite gurney—such a funny word, gurney, isn't it?—though it does squeak a bit. That's alright. It means people know when I'm coming.

Yes, yes, lie down. Close your eyes. Rest.

I'm just going to fasten this little strap here.

And here.

And here.

And there.

And…done.

That's nice, isn't it? All comfy and cozy?

Oops! I almost forgot. Have to make things correct and proper, now that you're officially checking in. Let me see if I remember my little speech—it's been so long since I got to give it.

Hello! My name is Nurse Eleanor Morrow, and I will be taking care of you during your time here at Lychhurst. If there is anything I can do to make your stay more comfortable, please let me know.

Now, hold still. I just need to grab something. I know it's in this drawer somewhere.

Ah! Here it is! My trusty bottle of ether. And this nifty little mask.

No, no, don't struggle.
Just breathe.
Never fear.
Lychhurst is happy to have you.
I'm happy to have you.
We're going to have such fun together.
Forever.

About the Authors

Christy Aldridge

Christy Aldridge is the crowned Southern Belle of horror, conjuring spine-tingling tales from moonlit porches and Spanish moss-draped oaks. With four feline phantoms, a faithful hound, a quacking duo, and Lily, her emotional support chicken, she orchestrates her own eerie menagerie.

Anthologized in chilling collections such as *25 Gates of Hell* and *These Lingering Shadows*, Christy's craft lies in creepy twists and dark tales. Her latest novel, *The Breaking of Mona Hill*, invites you to a world where the line between Southern charm and unsettling fear blurs with every turn of the page.

Simon Bleaken

Simon Bleaken lives in Wiltshire, England. His work has appeared in magazines, ezines and podcasts including *Lovecraft's Disciples; Tales of the Talisman; Dark Dossier; Strange Sorcery; Lovecraftiana; The Horror Zine; Schlock Webzine; Night Land; Weird Fiction Quarterly, Eternal Haunted Summer* and on *The NoSleep Podcast* and *HorrorBabble Originals*.

He has also appeared in the anthologies: *Eldritch Horrors: Dark Tales* (2008); *Eldritch Embraces: Putting the Love Back in Lovecraft* (2016); *Kepler's Cowboys* (2017); *Twilight Madhouse Vol. 2* (2017*); The Shadow Over Doggerland* (2022); *The Horror Zine Magazine Summer 2022* (2022); *HellBound Books' Anthology of Science Fiction Vol.1* (2023); *From Beyond The Threshold* (2023); *Eldritch Investigations* (2023); *House of Haunts* (2023); *The Horror Zine's Book of Monster Stories* (2024); *Witchcraft and Black Magic in the United States* (2024); *When Shadows Creep* (2024); and in the forthcoming *The Whisperer in Valhalla* (2024).

His first collection of short stories, *A Touch of Silence & Other Tales* was released in 2017, followed by *The Basement of Dreams & Other Tales* in 2019 and *Within the Flames & Other Stories* in 2021.

Bridget D. Brave

Bridget D. Brave hails from the dead center of the US of A. A lawyer by day, Bridget spends her remaining waking hours writing weird horror in short, long, and game formats and playtesting tabletop RPGs with the Wandering Monster Cast. Find more writing and weird anywhere online at beedeebrave, especially at beedeebrave.com.

Brooklyn Ann Butler

Formerly an auto-mechanic, Brooklyn Ann Butler writes supernatural horror and contributes to the HWA's mental health initiative. She is also the author of the B Mine series, horror romances that follow 80s horror movie plots, but with a Final Couple instead of a Final Girl, as well as urban fantasy and paranormal series under the pen name Brooklyn Ann.

She lives in Coeur d'Alene, Idaho with her family, a few project cars, an extensive book collection, and miscellaneous horror memorabilia. She can be found online at https://brooklynannauthor.com as well as on most social sites.

Alexandra Christian

Alexandra Christian is an award-winning author of both paranormal and contemporary romance with forays into horror and urban fantasy as Lexx Christian. Her love of Stephen King and sweet tea has flavored her fiction with a Southern Gothic sensibility that reeks of magnolia blossoms, steamy nights, and deep-fried eccentricity.

Lexx is a native South Carolinian who lives in a creepy small town with the love of her life and an overexcited goldendoodle named George Bailey. Comments, complaints, and photos of pets (she ALWAYS wants to see pictures of your pets) can be sent through her website at www.alexandrachristian.com.

Rebecca Cuthbert

Rebecca Cuthbert writes dark fiction and poetry. Her books include *In Memory of Exoskeletons* (poetry, Alien Buddha Press, 2024 Imadjinn Award winner); *Creep This Way: How to Become a Horror Writer with 24 Tips to Get You Ghouling* (nonfiction, Seamus & Nunzio Productions, 2024 Golden Scoop Award nominee); and *Self-Made Monsters* (fiction and poetry, 2024, Alien Buddha Press). For publications, awards, reviews, and more, visit rebeccacuthbert.com.

Blaine Daigle

Having lived his entire life deep in the gut of Louisiana, Blaine Daigle grew up surrounded by ghost stories of haunted plantations and cursed woodlands. He still lives in Louisiana with his wife and two children and can't wait to pass on the nightmares to his kids when they are old enough.

During the day he teaches high school English. At night, he enjoys diving deep into the fears that shape and mold the world around him.

Heather Daughrity

Heather Daughrity loves all things macabre, dark, autumnal, supernatural, and horrific.

She lives in Oklahoma with her husband, author and publisher Joshua Loyd Fox, where together they spend their days reading, writing, and being blissfully bookish.

Heather writes horror—the quiet, creeping, psychological kind, full of moaning wind, shifting shadows, and psychological pain.

She is the author of *Knock Knock, Tales My Grandmother Told Me,* and *Echoes of the Dead,* and her short stories have been featured in various anthologies. When she's not writing, she works as a freelance editor, helping authors make their stories the best they can be.

Heather loves digging in the dirt, hiking in the woods, whipping up delicious desserts in the kitchen, and generally soaking up all the weird and wild beauty of the world.

Jason Daughrity

"Doc" Jason Daughrity is a former US Navy Hospital Corpsman of Marines and an Iraqi War veteran, working in Florida as an Industrial Construction Safety Trainer for the largest solar company in the US.

Besides stints as a paramedic, state health inspector, night club manager, and casino security, Doc Jason goes all over the country teaching First Aid and other classes to construction workers.

He is the brother of author Joshua Loyd Fox, and brother-in-law to Heather Daughrity.

At home he has a beautiful fiancée and five dogs as well as a cat or two.

He loves fantasy novels and sci-fi movies, and writing has always been an aspiration. *Hospital of Haunts* is his first publishing credit.

Joe DeRouen

Joe DeRouen (joederouen.com) is a best-selling author of contemporary fantasy and horror novels. His most recent release, the *Small Things Trilogy Omnibus*, has enjoyed strong reviews and currently has a five-star rating on Amazon. His other works include stand-alone novels Leap Year and *Memories of a Ghost*, as well as *Odds and Endings*, his collection of short stories and novellas.

Joe was born in Carthage, Illinois and currently lives in Rogers, Arkansas with his wife Andee, their son Fletcher, and their cats Archer, Biscuit, Frosty, Weiss, Grilled Cheese, and Eclipse.

Joe is a freelance writer, editor, and web designer. In addition to writing, he enjoys listening to music, collecting Mego action figures, and playing video games. When he's not crafting words, you can usually find Joe playing *City of Heroes: Homecoming* on his PC or *Stardew Valley* on his phone.

John Durgin

John Durgin is a proud active HWA member and lifelong horror fan. Growing up in New Hampshire, he discovered Stephen King much younger than most probably should have, reading *IT* before he reached high school - and knew from that moment on he wanted to write horror.

He had his first story accepted in the summer of 2021 in the *Beach Bodies* anthology through DarkLit Press.

His debut novel, *The Cursed Among Us* was released June 3, 2022, and went on to become an Amazon bestseller.

Next up, his sophomore novel, titled *Inside The Devil's Nest*, released in January of 2023, followed by his debut collection, *Sleeping In The Fire* in June of 2023.

In 2024 he is set to release two more novels, starting with *Kosa* and followed by *Consumed by Evil* through Crystal Lake Publishing in the fall.

Stephanie Ellis

Stephanie Ellis writes dark speculative prose and poetry and is based in Wrexham, UK. Her novels include *The Five Turns of the Wheel, Reborn, The Woodcutter*, and *The Barricade* as well as the novellas *Bottled* and *Paused.*

Her short stories appear in the collections *The Reckoning* and *Devil Kin.*

She is a Rhysling and Elgin Award nominated poet and has written the collection *Foundlings* (with Cindy O'Quinn), *Lilith Rising* (with Shane Douglas Keene) and *Metallurgy*, as well as appearing in the HWA Poetry Showcase.

She can be found at https://stephanieellis.org as well as supporting indie authors at HorrorTree.com via the weekly Indie Bookshelf Releases.

Joshua Loyd Fox

Joshua Loyd Fox is the author of several novels including the non-fiction *I Won't Be Shaken*, and the ArchAngel Missions fantasy series that includes: *Had I Not Chosen, Amongst You, To Build a Tower, One Becomes a Thousand, Unto This Mountain,* and the upcoming *Least of These.*

He is also the author of the upcoming *I Don't Write Poetry: A Collection*, his first book of poems.

His short stories, *The Book of the Tower and the Traitor,* a companion series to The ArchAngel Missions, can be found on Amazon Vella.

Joshua Loyd Fox has been a soldier, Master aircraft mechanic, line cook, amateur MMA fighter, engineer, technical writer, and most recently works a day job as an IT consultant to the US government.

He is also the owner and publisher at Watertower Hill Publishing (www.watertowerhill.com) and now works to make other authors' dreams come true.

He and his wife, author and editor, Heather Daughrity, live in NE Oklahoma where he can be found with a fine cigar, an even better whiskey, and feet up next to a wood fire on most evenings.

Jennifer Anne Gordon

Jennifer Anne Gordon is an award-winning author and podcast host. Her debut novel *Beautiful, Frightening and Silent* won the Kindle Book Award for Best Horror/Suspense for 2020, as well as the Best Horror Novel of the Year from Authors on the Air and was a finalist for American Book Fest's Best Book Award- Horror, 2020.

Her novel *Pretty/Ugly* won the Helicon Award for Best Horror for 2022 and the Kindle Book Award for Best Novel of the Year (Reader's Choice). Her collection *The Japanese Box: And Other Stories* was an instant Amazon Bestseller and her story "The Japanese Box" won the Lit Nastie Award for 2023 for Best Short Story.

Her personal essays have been featured on *Horror Tree, Nerd Daily, Ladies of Horror Fiction, Writers After Dark*, and *Quail Bell Magazine*, and are featured in *Such a Loss and Letting Grief Speak: Writing Portals for Life After Loss.*

Jennifer is the creator and co-host of the popular comedic literary podcast *Vox Vomitus*, as well as a co-host of *House of Mystery* on NBC Radio. For benevolent stalking please visit www.JenniferAnneGordon.com.

Gage Greenwood

Gage Greenwood is the best-selling author of the Winter's Myths Saga and *Bunker Dogs*.

He's a proud member of the Horror Writers Association and Science Fiction and Fantasy Writers association. He's been an actor, comedian, podcaster, and even the Vice President of an escape room company.

Since childhood, he's been a big fan of comic books, horror movies, and depressing music that fills him with existential dread.

He lives in New England with his girlfriend and son, and he spends his time writing, hiking, and decorating for various holidays. Find out more at www.gagegreenwood.com.

Caleb Jones

Caleb Jones can be found in his own secret laboratory in Norfolk, Virginia. He experiments in the wee hours of morning with stories of the macabre and sinister.

His lab assistants include his wife, Courtney, daughter Lorraine, and hound dog, Edgar Allan Pup.

Marie Lanza

Marie Lanza writes fast-paced horror and thrillers. She is the author of post-apocalyptic series *Fractured* and *The Colony*, along with other short stories part of larger anthologies. She also writes in various genres as a ghostwriter bringing others' visions to life.

Marie is always creating, whether it's for a new book series, feature film, or television. She currently resides in Los Angeles, California with her husband and two daughters.

To learn about upcoming book releases and projects for Marie Lanza, visit her website, www.MarieLanza.com.

Stephen Mark Rainey

Stephen Mark Rainey is the author of numerous novels, including *Balak, The Lebo Coven, Dark Shadows: Dreams of the Dark* (with

Elizabeth Massie), *Blue Devil Island*, the upcoming *House at Black Tooth Pond*, and others, including several in Elizabeth Massie's Ameri-Scares series for young readers.

In addition, Mark's work includes six short story collections; over 200 published works of short fiction; and the scripts for several *Dark Shadows* audio productions, which feature members of the original ABC-TV series cast.

For ten years, he edited the award-winning *Deathrealm* magazine and, most recently, the best-selling anthology, *Deathrealm: Spirits* (Shortwave Publishing).

He has also edited anthologies for Delirium Press, Chaosium, and Arkham House.

Mark lives in Martinsville, VA, with his wife, Kimberly, and a passel of precocious house cats. He is an active member of the Horror Writers Association.

Jeani Rector

While most people go to Disneyland while in Southern California, Jeani Rector went to the Fangoria Weekend of Horror there instead.

She grew up watching the Bob Wilkins Creature Feature on television and lived in a house that had the walls covered with framed Universal Monsters posters. It is all in good fun and actually, most people who know Jeani personally are of the opinion that she is a very normal person. She just writes abnormal stories.

She is the founder and editor of *The Horror Zine*, and has had her stories featured in magazines such as *Aphelion, Schlock!, Strange Weird and Wonderful, Black Petals, Bewildering Stories*, and many others.

Susan H. Roddey

S.H. Roddey writes dark speculative fiction and works as a book formatter, cover designer, and developmental editor. She is also the Art Director at Watertower Hill Publishing.

She is a voracious reader, wanna-be chef, and amateur gamer, who lives in the Piedmont area of South Carolina with a house full of humans, cats, books, and yarn, and spends entirely too much time yelling at her sewing machine.

Cat Scully

Cat Scully is a spooky southerner from Atlanta who now lives outside of Salem, MA.

She is the author of the upcoming horror novel *Below the Grand Hotel* and the author-illustrator of YA horror series, *Jennifer Strange* (2020).

As an illustrator, she's best known for her world maps in the Brooklyn Brujas series by Zoraida Cordova and *Give the Dark My Love* by Beth Revis. Her first picture book, *The Mayor of Halloween is Missing* (2021), was written by Emily S. Sullivan.

When she's not writing and illustrating books, Cat works in video game development and is an artist-in-residence at Porter Mill Studios where she designs clothing, accessories, and home decor for her shop Haints and Hollows.

Westley Smith

Westley Smith is the author of two horror novels, *Along Came the Tricksters* and *All Hallows Eve*, as well as the crime thrillers *Some Kind of Truth* and *In The Pale Light*.

His short fiction has been published in various magazines and websites.

Wes lives with his wife and two dogs in the beautiful woodlands of southern Pennsylvania--the perfect place to hide a body.

Mer Whinery

Mer Whinery resides in an old house filled with ominous creaks and random spectral shenanigans along with his wife Annie and their two sons, Kameron and Harper. Several critters roam freely about the house, looking for trouble. Sometimes it feels like there is someone watching you from around the corner, or walking so close behind you in the upstairs hallway that you can almost feel them breathing on the back of your neck. This is just fine with the Whinery family. They are a strange bunch.

Mer affectionately refers to his genre as rural macabre and is the author of three collections of short fiction, *The Little Dixie Horror Show*, *Phantasmagoria Blues*, and *Obscene Folklore*.

Also on his resume are the weird western *Trade Your Coffin for a Gun* and the coming-of-age terror novel, *The Country Girl's Guide to Hags, Hexes, and Haints*.